Consummatum Est
(It Is Finished)

By
Nicholas Di Bello

Booklocker.com, Inc.
2004

"Father, my heart is heavy and my body weary because of a grievous sin I committed against you when I was a foolish young seminarian. That sin became my cross to bear. I stand at the base of this ridge where my son is trapped. He is the product of that sin, but he is an innocent boy. If you find it in your heart and you feel that my cause is just, then let me be victorious over my enemy. Father, do not judge me on that sin alone, but judge me on my priesthood where every day I accepted you as my Lord and Savior, at the same time lifting your cross up high so that people could understand the pain and suffering you went through on the cross to die for our sins. Those people whose lives I touched accepted you as their Lord and Savior. Tonight, Father, I lay down your cross and take up mine."

Acknowledgements

This story has been in my mind and heart for more than 20 years.

Thanks to Jennette De Moura who began the initial draft of this book years ago, and to Steve Oskie for his help in the reconstruction of various chapters.

Special thanks to Stephanie Elliot for her tireless efforts in the writing, editing and organization of the final draft. She helped tell the story the way I imagined it to be.

Finally, tremendous love and gratitude for my dear Joan, who offered much support and patience as this dream of mine became a reality.

In my beginning is my end. – T.S. Eliot

Chapter One
1928

Five-year-old Jimmy Gabriel stood in awe as he watched his father perform his world famous act. The gathering crowd held their breath as Gordon the Great readied himself to throw a large knife at the spinning wheel that was ten feet away from where he stood. The scariest thing about it was that there was a real live person on that big wheel, and not just any person, but *Mommy*. He watched her spin 'round and 'round as the sequins on her bright red leotard glistened in the early morning sun. He knew just what Daddy was going to do next; he had seen him do it hundreds of times.

Jimmy stood just outside the crowd and imitated his father's throwing style. He wound up by bringing one small hand back towards his ear and lunged forward while pretending to release a throwing knife in a full forward motion.

All at once the crowd gasped in a combination of horror and amazement as the knife flew from his father's hand and raced through the air like a hawk honing in on its prey. Jimmy closed his eyes tightly. He never watched this part if the target was his mother. The sound of the knife striking the wooden wheel was deafening. The crowd cheered loudly, for the auburn haired beauty was still alive and spinning on the large wheel. The knife had landed just two inches from her left ear – his father's trademark throw.

Five more knives were thrown in this fashion before the show was over. Jimmy ran up to the great spinning wheel and said, "Don't worry Mommy, the men are going to get you down now."

Two large men appeared and quickly steadied the wheel. He did not notice how wet his mother's cheeks were from the tears. Jimmy smiled as Kate was released and freed from the contraption. She muttered to herself as she rubbed her sore wrists.

Jimmy waited for her to give him a big hug and tell him everything was all right like she always did after the show. He looked at her face more closely and saw that it was wet.

"Why are you crying?" His voice was alarmed. Without answering she wrapped her painted nails around his slender arm and yanked him in the direction of his father.

Gordon was standing on a soapbox waving heroically to the men, women and children who had gathered in the small sideshow tent to see him perform his amazing act. Jimmy was scared. His arm was beginning to hurt from his mother's tight grip; he had never seen her like this.

"Gordon the Great, huh? Your name might be Gordon but if you're Great then I'm the Queen of England." Her voice was dripping with sarcasm. Gordon spun around.

"Not now Katherine, can't you see I'm working?" Jimmy knew his father was angry whenever he called his mother Katherine.

"How about I tell all these people how you almost killed me! I bet you would have time for me then!"

Gordon jumped off the wooden crate and told Jimmy and his mother to follow him. He led them outside the small tent. The air was thick with the scent of animals, hay and dirt. Once they were out of earshot of the crowd Gordon started to yell, "Who in God's name do you think you are making a scene in front of my audience? You should just be glad that you are in my act at all."

Jimmy saw his mother's face grow red. Frightened, he watched as her eyes welled up again with new tears.

"I guess I should be glad that one of your mighty knives was just a hair away from my face?" Her voice was shaky with anger. "I've had it with you. Jimmy and I deserve better than this. You promised me three years ago that we would quit the circus and raise our son like a normal family." She abruptly dropped Jimmy's aching arm as if just realizing she was still holding it and grabbed Gordon's instead. "Can't we leave this all behind us?" she asked hopefully.

"I will never leave. And another thing, if you don't want to be in my act anymore I'm sure that Sheila won't mind taking your spot on a permanent basis. She doesn't moan and cry the way you do anyhow," he mumbled the last of his words.

Sheila was a newer member of the traveling circus. With pale blue eyes and long curly hair the color of spun gold, she was quite breathtaking. She had taken an immediate interest in Gordon, which was no surprise. He was a lady's man with thick hair and eyes that appeared black. Always a charmer, women swooned when Gordon the Great appeared, larger than life, in his famous sideshow act. Sheila started filling in as his assistant a few summers ago when Kate had proclaimed that spinning around on a ridiculous wheel while knives were being thrown at her was wearing thin. Gordon - a little too quickly - recommended that Sheila take Kate's place. Suddenly alarmed, Kate told her handsome husband that maybe she was overreacting and that maybe she was just tired because three-year-old Jimmy was so active. So Sheila filled in for Kate two or three times a week.

Although Sheila *was* beautiful, Kate had her own distinctive features that were every bit as lovely. Her silky auburn hair would catch the sunlight and shimmer radiantly around creamy clear skin. The contrast was truly stunning. Her most alluring feature was her dark green eyes. Cat's eyes, Gordon called them. Jimmy thought they looked more like the beautiful sparkling sequins on some of the costumes she wore and not at all like the nuisance circus cats that hung around.

Kate was tired of hearing Gordon say that Sheila would be a better assistant and sprinted off in the direction of the Big Top. Gordon continued muttering under his breath; Jimmy could not make out what he was saying. Then, suddenly, Gordon became boisterous again as if the scene had never occurred, smiled at Jimmy and said, "Come on son, let's get back to the crowd and sell some tickets for Mr. Robinson."

Mr. Thomas Robinson was someone Jimmy knew by name only, and it was one he had heard often enough around the circus. No ordinary man, he was the owner of the world famous Thomas Robinson's Circus. Jimmy knew he was someone of great importance. He pictured him to be six feet tall with a constant sneer on his face; everyone talked about him as if he was a heartless man. The men and women of the troupe, including his parents, would say things like, "That Tom Robinson is so cheap, he'd have us working night and day while feeding us nothing but water and bread if he could get away with it." Jimmy thought he must be a dreadful man to want to feed them only bread and water. Jimmy loved when the cooks would call out "Flag's up!" That meant it was time for the performers and their families to go to the tent for meals, or "scoffins" as they were called. He loved to sit with his mother and father and hear the chatter of the other circus people during mealtime. But his favorite time of day was evening time, when the day's performances were over and he could sit with his father while he sharpened his knives. Sometimes he would even let him throw one, which was a treat indeed.

This must be my lucky day, thought Jimmy. After he and his father had successfully sold some tickets for the circus, they walked over to a shady spot past the Big Top, called the pasture. It was an exceptionally hot day, even for August. The only relief they could find from the sun's unrelenting rays was beneath a towering chestnut tree. Nearby, some horses were lazily chomping on the long yellow-green blades of grass that grew along the banks of the Delaware River. He took a deep breath and let the fresh air fill his lungs. He had never been to Philadelphia before, and he was enjoying all the new sights and sounds. Except for the river, all the smells were basically the same from city to city as not much changed when traveling with the circus. There was the constant smells Jimmy had begun to rely upon – the stench of dirty animals, manure, sweat, and roasted peanuts. To Jimmy, this was how the entire world smelled for he had never known any other existence.

"Daddy, where's Mommy?"

"Don't know, son."

"Let's go find her."

"Jimmy, you can either sit next to me and keep quiet or you can leave."

Jimmy didn't answer. He had no desire to go anywhere. He simply sat cross-legged with his back propped up against the large tree and stared with his clear blue eyes at his father's knives. Gordon did not look at his son. Instead, he carefully removed the six throwing knives from the protective pouch. At the sight of his beloved knives, he smiled and began humming a tune that Jimmy recognized immediately - "Ol' Man River." He loved being with his father when he sharpened the knives. Sometimes, if he had been an especially good boy, his father would show him how to throw the knives. He must have been good today, because his father suddenly stopped humming and said, "Jimmy, would you like to take a couple of throws?"

Jimmy was so excited it was difficult to uncross his legs so that he could stand up. Once on his feet he exclaimed, "Oh yes, Daddy!"

Gordon handed him a knife. The large leather handle was much too big for his childish hands, but he gripped it as tight as he could.

"Stand like I showed you," Gordon reminded him, "and keep your eyes focused on the center of the target."

The target was a wooden plank propped up against some hay not more than five feet from where Jimmy stood. He took his stance the way he had been shown time and again by his father. Jimmy hesitated for just a second, then let the big knife fly out of his palm and prayed it would hit its mark. It did not. Instead of hitting the bright red circle, it went careening off to the right, almost missing the board completely. At the sound of the knife striking the edge of the board, the nearby horses lifted their heads to see what all of the commotion was about. Jimmy's heart sank. He hated to miss the mark and was usually very good at striking the board dead center. Other than his father, Jimmy was sure he could throw a knife better than any other man in the world.

"Let me try again, Daddy," Jimmy pleaded.

Gordon handed his son another knife. Jimmy got into position, drew his arm behind his curly hair and threw the knife swiftly. A bird squawked and flew from a nearby tree as the knife flew toward its target. One, two, three turns of the handle before it landed squarely in the red circle.

"Yahoo!" Jimmy jumped up and down. "I did it!"

Gordon smiled and said, "I'd better watch out. Someday you'll be a better thrower than your old man."

Jimmy was excited to have hit the target. "When I grow up, I want to be just like you, daddy. We can throw knives together and travel all over the world. Except I don't want to throw knives at mommy, I would be too scared. Maybe I could throw them at Sheila, then I wouldn't be so scared."

Gordon laughed at the possibility. Jimmy laughed with him, and they threw knives and laughed for a long time that night.

Jimmy woke to the sound of crows scouring for leftover circus food. Their high-pitched screeches were not a welcome way to awaken. He shivered under the covers even though it was very warm inside the confined tent. He lay in a tiny metal bunk bed above his mother and father, who bunked below. There was not much more room in the tent for anything else other than their personal belongings. Actually, they were quite fortunate. Because of their tenure with the circus they did not have to share the cramped quarters with anyone else, like most of the other circus members did.

Jimmy squeezed his eyes shut even tighter as he wished that the crow would stop screeching. He hated the pillaging dark crows. When he was younger, he would jump out of his bed and into his parent's bed when he heard the cry of the raven birds attacking each other to get the scraps of food left behind. He was afraid the birds would get into their tent and peck at his face. He shuddered under the covers at the mere thought of his old nightmare. He dared not jump into his parent's bed now, though. Some time ago they had scolded him for such behavior and told him big boys did not run into their parent's bed when they were scared. Jimmy had cried and told them that he didn't care and that he couldn't be alone when he knew the birds were out there. His father had finally threatened Jimmy and said he would not show him how to throw knives anymore unless he stopped acting like a baby. This worked. So, whenever Jimmy became afraid, he tried to imagine a happy thought to cheer him up. He pictured the silly clowns that ran around the Big Top. He imagined their painted faces smiling as they skipped around the center ring with brightly colored streamers in their hands. He always thought of Happy Henry, his favorite clown, jumping through large wire hoops. That always made him laugh.

He was still having a difficult time blocking out the noisy crows. They seemed to be getting closer and closer. He covered large angelic eyes with both hands and wished the mean birds would fly away. After a long while, the crows silenced. Jimmy took a deep breath and pushed back white cotton sheets to uncover his round face. He resembled neither his mother nor his father. His mother always told him that with his blond hair and blue eyes he was going to be a lady-killer when he grew up. He did not know what that meant, but he was sure he had no desire to kill ladies when he got big. Rather, he wanted to be a world famous knife thrower, just like his father.

Jimmy dressed and considered what a lady-killer was, shrugged off his thoughts and went outside to feed the elephants, something he enjoyed almost daily. The grass was moist with morning dew and Jimmy walked quickly and quietly past the small village of tents. It was still early and most of the crew was still sleeping. He made his way to where the humongous gray beasts were locked in ornate wagons. He felt sad that the elephants were like prisoners. He cringed as their strong odor wafted through the still morning air and hit his nostrils. He sneezed as he approached the intricately hand painted wagons harboring the giant dusty elephants. They were his friends, the animals. He would rather spend time with the animals instead of all the men, women and children who toured with the circus. While all the other kids were running about the lot, Jimmy could usually be found hanging around the elephants, lions and horses.

He spoke now to Bloomy, the elephant he had named so because she reminded him of a character in one of the few books he owned. Bloomy was always getting in the way, even though she was one of the smallest elephants, just like the character in the story. Jimmy giggled as she pushed her way through the larger animals and poked her small trunk through the shiny metal bars.

"Come and get some peanuts girl," he called to Bloomy.

Bloomy moved closer to the bars and opened her mouth as Jimmy threw a few peanuts into her large mouth.

"That a girl. How did you sleep? Did those nasty crows scare you? They didn't scare me," Jimmy lied. He always spoke to the small elephant as though she were a person. He stayed with her until the loud clanging bell signaled that it was time for breakfast.

Kate woke to the smell of bacon, eggs and grits. She smiled as she breathed in the aroma. She turned to face her husband, which was not a difficult task. The bed they shared was so small that it was nearly impossible to move during the night. Gordon was still sleeping, and Kate sighed at how good-looking he was. She could hardly believe that they had been married for eight years now and she wondered if he still found her attractive. He never showed her much affection anymore. She saw the way he stared at Sheila and remembered the days when he used to look at her with the same longing in his eyes.

As Kate thought of Gordon's new and younger assistant, she felt a jealousy sweep over her like a cold front intruding on the tranquility of a warm summer's day. Her body grew stiff beneath her thin cotton nightgown as thoughts of Gordon and Sheila rambled through her mind. Gordon seemed to sense something; he grumbled softly in his sleep. Kate hated Sheila. This very fact was upsetting to her, because she hated no one save the devil himself. She prided herself on being a woman of faith, even though attending church was not an option when traveling with the circus. She thought that maybe God had sent Sheila to punish her for not being a good Catholic these past few years. Could He really be that cruel, she wondered? Kate knew that Sheila lusted after her husband, and she had no doubt that Gordon was attracted to Sheila. She prayed for the day when Gordon would take them away from this world and settle down in a nice neighborhood, just like the ones she had heard about from all of the townspeople she had met while traveling with the circus. She just knew she could make him happy then. Besides, she wanted Jimmy to go to school like a normal boy. This was no life for a small child, or a grown one for that matter.

She remembered back before Jimmy was born, when she had loved performing with Gordon. They would practice their act for hours. She would spin like a child's pinwheel while he threw knives at balloons surrounding her costumed body. She was never afraid. Gordon was too good for her to be afraid. After all, he really was the best in the world, she thought. She knew that Gordon had loved to look at her slender body in sparkling sequined costumes that showed all of her womanly curves. She knew he had loved and desired her then. Now she was not so sure.

For Jimmy, the day was passing very slowly. He was excited because tomorrow he would turn six. His father had promised him a very special gift. He had told him that on his birthday he would give him his very own set of knives, just like the ones he threw in his act. Jimmy thought this would be the best gift ever. It was definitely the most frivolous. He customarily received boring gifts for his birthday like clothes and undergarments.

He ran around in a big circle on the dusty unpaved street outside the sideshow tents. He pretended to throw knives as he made himself dizzy from spinning. He would spin and spin and then try to walk a straight line like the tightrope walkers did. He was so involved with his game that Kate had to yell to Jimmy a couple of times before he heard her. He spun around and saw his mother waiting for a response from him.

"Hi mommy! Is it dinner time already?"

"Not just yet. I came to see what my baby boy wanted for dinner tomorrow night. The cook said you can order anything you want."

"I'm not a baby, Mommy. I will be six tomorrow!"

"I can't help it, Jimmy. To me you will always be my little boy. But you're right. You're not a baby anymore."

"I want pasketti and meatballs. With lots of gravy, too."

Kate smiled at her son. She knew that he would ask for spaghetti and meatballs. It had been his favorite meal even before he could ask for it. "Okay, Jimmy, I'll let the kitchen know. Supper is in thirty minutes. Come with me so I can clean you up. You're all dusty," she said.

Jimmy obediently followed his mother to the washtubs, still wobbling slightly from his spinning game. He was so preoccupied with thoughts of his birthday gift that he didn't put up a fuss while his mother scrubbed him clean. He sat in the oversized aluminum tub as his mother poured in pail after pail of lukewarm water. He hated the way the rough bar of soap felt on his sensitive skin as the day's grime was washed away. After he was rubbed dry, his mother handed him a green cotton jumper to put on. She told him he looked very handsome as they walked hand in hand to dinner.

He slept restlessly that night and could hardly wait for morning. He was so excited he was even looking forward to hearing the crows signifying daybreak. That would mean that it was his birthday! He was sure his father would surprise him with a knife set of his own, because whenever he brought it up Gordon acted like he had no idea what his son was talking about. For a split second Jimmy feared that his father had forgotten about his promised gift. With childlike certainty he quickly dismissed the thought. He just *knew* his father had not forgotten.

He finally drifted off into sleep with dreams of standing beside his father while they both threw knives at spinning wheels. He could smell the peanuts and hear the crowd cheering for Gordon the Great and his amazing son Jimmy.

His parents were still asleep when Jimmy inched off the bunk bed early on his birthday. As quietly as he could he jumped to the hard ground below. His tiny feet thumped on the makeshift floor and he stared at his parent's faces with blue eyes shining hopefully. They were still sleeping, and Jimmy knew better than to wake them up. So he silently pulled on brown leather moccasins and tiptoed out of the tent.

He plodded through the soggy grass, until he arrived at the animal cages. "It's my birthday today," he called out to the animals. "Hey, Bloomy, did you hear me? My daddy is going to give me the best present in the whole world today," his voice was filled with excitement.

Unimpressed by Jimmy's senseless commotion, Bloomy waited with her enormous mouth open for peanuts. "Ah, Bloomy, this is important! It's not every day that I turn six," he scolded the baby elephant. "Oh, okay, have some peanuts." Jimmy tossed some into Bloomy's mouth and continued quiet conversations with the animals until he heard the call for breakfast.

He ran into the dining tent and searched the room for his parents. His eyes settled on his mother, who was sitting alone at one of the tables set for four. He ran over to where she sat, knocking over a chair in the process. The smell of bacon was heavy in the air. Jimmy's stomach grumbled loudly as he steadied the chair back on its wooden legs.

"Someone must be hungry. Sit next to me. I didn't even hear you get up this morning."

"How could I think about food now, mommy. Don't you know what today is?"

"How could I forget my baby boy's birthday? Of course I know what today is, but that doesn't mean that you get to skip breakfast."

Jimmy sullenly sank into one of the chairs, his feet dangling way above the ground. He glanced over at the long line of performers waiting to get some food from the buffet tables.

"The line is too long. Can't I open up my present first?" he asked eagerly. "Let's wait for your father." Kate's reply was firm.

Breakfast seemed to last forever. Kate made him finish all of his scrambled eggs and hash browns before excusing him from the table. His father had not joined them for breakfast and Jimmy was in a hurry to find him.

Jimmy spent the next few hours searching for his father. Up and down the street he walked, his head swishing back and forth. He passed the big colorful booth where people could buy tickets to Tom Robinson's circus. He passed the Big Top and stopped momentarily to see what was going on. Nothing unusual, he thought to himself as he watched acrobats and clowns practice for the show later that day. He thought that maybe his father and Sheila were practicing somewhere so Jimmy headed in the direction of Sheila's sleeping tent.

"Sheila," he called. "Sheila, are you in there? It's Jimmy. Jimmy Gabriel." He peered through the coarse green cloth that was the makeshift door. His nose itched as he pushed it into the harsh material to try and see through it. He could see nothing, but he thought he heard something.

"Is anybody in there?" he called. "I'm looking for my daddy." It sounded like someone was jumping on a bed. He could hear the sound of springs creaking. It is way too late for anyone to still be sleeping, thought Jimmy. Surely somebody was jumping on the bed and Jimmy knew that was not allowed. He was guessing it was Sam, the son of two of the acrobats. With scraggly hair the color of a blazing fire, Gordon always said Sam was nothing but trouble. Jimmy wanted to catch Sam in the act of getting in trouble.

He unlatched the hooks of the canvas door but the final hook was much too high for Jimmy to reach. He jumped and tried to swipe at it with outstretched arms. The effort was futile. He was more curious now than ever to see what little kid was behaving so badly. The sound of the jumping was growing louder. Could it be Sam, Jimmy wondered again? Sam was always getting into trouble. Most of the younger children of the troupe feared the ten-year-old frizzy haired boy. Even his freckles looked mean, the way they resembled angry little ants crawling over his pale skin. Many children had gotten punished because of participating in Sam's antics and Jimmy knew that if it was Sam jumping on the bed, the smart thing to do would be just to leave him be. But then he thought that maybe Sam could tell him where Sheila was, and then he would be one step closer to finding his father and his birthday gift.

Jimmy wildly swung both hands at the tiny top metal loop and his fingertips brushed against the cold metal. He tried again and this time the latch came free.

The early afternoon sunlight poured into the gaping hole, eerily mingling with the darkness and dust inside. Jimmy took a feeble step forward. Then, with more confidence, he jumped with both feet into the musty tent.

"Ah ha!" He yelled as his feet landed on the wood paneled floor, causing more swirls of dust and grime to fly around his legs. It is surely Sam, he thought as his eyes adjusted to the dimness. Jimmy tried hard to see the person standing on the bed. It suddenly became very quiet. The springs had stopped rattling and the culprit was stunned into silence at the sight of Jimmy.

"I caught you," Jimmy said in a self-satisfied voice. Now that he could see well enough to make out who the child with the bad behavior was, his mouth fell open. It wasn't Sam at all! It was little Molly Gladstone, the biggest loudmouth in the circus. She *never* did anything wrong but was always telling on other kids and getting them into trouble. None of the kids, including Jimmy, liked her very much. She was quick to run and tell an adult if she thought that someone was not behaving appropriately.

Now she stood silently, so surprised with the intrusion that she didn't even have time to jump down from the bed that proved her guilt. Her hair was separated at the crown into two long, corkscrew ponytails and her arms lay limp at her sides. She stood still, with socks loosely around her skinny ankles, having fallen down her shins from the jumping up and down.

Jimmy didn't know what to say. If it had been Sam, he would have pretended to look strict, like a grownup, and made the little monster beg for him to not tell on him. Then Sam would have owed him a favor, which could always come in handy. But this ruined everything. In his mind, he had already figured out how he would handle Sam when he caught him jumping on the bed. But this situation was different. Molly was liable to start blubbering or something equally unappealing. Jimmy didn't know what to do or what to say.

Before he could say anything, Molly spoke, her voice trembling with fear. "Jimmy, don't tell on me, okay? I wa...was jus...just playing around."

Jimmy wondered why she was acting so afraid. Sure, it was bad to jump on beds, but come on, there were a thousand worse things she could be doing. It was then that he realized why Molly was so nervous. She was holding something in her right hand. Jimmy took a few steps closer to the rumpled bed to make out what it was. It was a handwritten letter. His eyes fell to the floor surrounding the bed and saw a cigar box lying open, overflowing with letters. Molly had been snooping, going through Sheila's personal belongings! That was way worse than jumping on a bed, thought Jimmy.

"Molly, what are you doing? What are all those letters?" he asked, pointing to the box.

She scrambled off the bed, still clutching the piece of paper tightly. "I was looking for my doll, Harriet, and when I looked under the bed I found this box." Molly's large brown eyes were quickly filling up with tears.

Oh no, here we go, thought Jimmy. "What are they?" he asked.

"They're love letters," Molly replied. She realized that if Jimmy were going to yell at her he would have already done so and she wiped away her tears and smiled mischievously. "Do you know how to read?" She looked at him hopefully.

"No," he replied.

"Well, I do. Well, a little bit. I think these words here spell 'I love you,' see?" She smiled triumphantly as she pointed to the bottom of the letter. Jimmy noticed another letter at the end that looked similar to the letter that adorned his father's circus costume. A G for Gordon, he thought, but he was too young to put two and two together. It was obvious the letter had been read over and over. The paper was crumpled and some of the words were blurry, as if tears had stained the words.

"Yuck! Who would want to read icky love letters?" Jimmy could not imagine ever liking a girl so much that he would give her such a thing.

"I think it is sooo romantic," Molly held the letter to her chest. She was only a year older than Jimmy and dreamed of the day when a boy would tell her he loved her. Then she too could hide a box filled with love notes under her bed.

"We have to put these back before you get into trouble," Jimmy announced.

"Does that mean you are not going to tell on me?" Molly was surprised. If she had found someone doing something so naughty as snooping through someone else's belongings, she would have told on him. She was shocked that, instead of telling on her, Jimmy was crouched on the ground trying to reassemble the box's contents. She looked at him gratefully and was about to thank him when a shrill voice behind her made her jump.

"What are you kids doing?" Sheila stood in the doorway of her tent, one hand holding the canvas flap open, the other pressed against her forehead as if her head ached from the sight of them.

Molly began to cry immediately; great heaving sobs shook her tiny frame. Jimmy quickly tried to hide the box behind his back, but Sheila had already spotted the disassembled box of letters.

Sheila darted over to where the children sat on the floor. Her cheeks were the same color of her bright print dress. She snatched the old cigar box from behind Jimmy and looked at Molly, who was still crouched on the floor crying, and then back at Jimmy before she spoke again.

"You rotten little brats," she whispered angrily. "What are you doing snooping through my personal belongings, and why are you in my tent?" She clutched the box possessively, afraid of what the children might have had read.

Jimmy looked at Molly. She was so frightened she could not stop shaking, and her ponytails were swinging back and forth with each shudder and cry. He made up his mind. "It was me, Sheila, not Molly. I was looking for my birthday gift, and I thought that my daddy might have hidden it under your bed. Molly came in when I was trying to put the box back under your bed. I am really sorry. You won't tell on me, will you?"

Sheila stared first at him, then at Molly, her eyes squinty with rage. Jimmy could hear laughter coming from outside the tent. Inside, the air was thick with dust and silence. It seemed like a very long time had passed before Sheila spoke again. "Molly, since you had nothing to do with this, you may leave now." Without looking at Jimmy, Molly jumped to her feet and scrambled out of the tent. Jimmy got to his feet too, expecting to be dismissed as well.

"Hold on, Jimmy. Where do you think you are going? You have some explaining to do. How dare you sneak in my sleeping quarters like a roustabout and go through my personal things." Sheila's tone suddenly changed from anger to fear. "You didn't actually *read* the letters, did you?"

Jimmy wondered why she looked so frightened over some dumb love letters that he wouldn't have wanted to read if he could have read them. "No, I can't read." He was about to confess that Molly had told him that she had read 'I love you' on one of the letters, but then decided that would be a mistake. Instead, he told her again, "I don't know how to read yet."

Sheila's face seemed to relax when she realized that Jimmy was too young to read and her tone lightened up a bit. "There is not much to read anyway," she sighed, "They are just some old letters from a friend."

She sat on the bed, both hands still gripping the box. Jimmy thought it was strange that Sheila said the letters were from a friend while Molly had been adamant that they were love letters, but at this point he did not care who wrote the stupid letters. All he cared about was getting out of this tent and away from the whole mess.

Sheila too, had wanted to finish the conversation. "You can go if you promise me you will never sneak in here again. I'm very disappointed in you, Jimmy. I never would have thought that you would do something like this. You keep quiet about these letters and I won't tell your parents that you were snooping, you hear?"

Jimmy could sense Sheila was anxious to be rid of him. "Yes, Sheila. I won't tell anyone. Please don't tell my parents." If she told on him, he would surely be punished and he probably would not get his birthday gift. He wished he had told Sheila what had really happened. After all, it was Molly's fault. Jimmy really wanted to make sure he got his knife set today, and Sheila was making him very nervous. He looked at her. They were eye to eye, her sitting on the bed and him standing a foot away.

"You keep your end of the bargain, and I'll keep mine," Sheila threatened. "Now go and be a good boy."

She didn't have to tell him twice. He wanted nothing more than to be far, far away from Sheila and that stupid box. He ran out of the tent and was momentarily blinded by the sun's harsh rays. He ran and ran, past the tents and crowds of people. He didn't stop until he was far enough away that he could no longer hear the sound of voices and laughter.

The next morning Jimmy woke early. He could not wait to go to the pasture so he could throw his brand new knives at the makeshift targets. Sheila had kept her end of the deal and hadn't told his parents she found him in her room. His father had given him a strange look at dinner, though, right before handing him his gift. It had come with a warning – he was never to throw his knives without a grownup present. Jimmy thought it was strange that his father had said "a grownup" had to be with him when he threw his knives, as he had never practiced with anyone other than his father. He was about to remind his father of this fact when something about the look in his father's eyes stopped him. Had Sheila told on him? Now he was not certain. Jimmy had accepted the treasured knives in silence and his mother commented that for a boy who had been so desperate to get his birthday present he was awfully quiet. She had told Gordon that he should take Jimmy out to the pasture to try them first thing in the morning. Gordon had nodded vaguely and muttered, "We'll see, we'll see."

That morning, Jimmy had awakened and was looking forward to throwing knives with his father. But, as Jimmy slithered off the top bunk with knife satchel in hand (he had kept them at the foot of his bed), he noticed that his father was not in the tent.

Where could his father be this early in the morning? He thought about finding Sheila to see if her father was with her, then decided to stay as far away from her as possible. He could never look at her in the eyes again. That stupid Molly had gotten Jimmy into so much trouble. Still, he was glad that he had taken the blame for he didn't like to see people unhappy, especially girls, even if it had been blabbermouth Molly. Kate was always telling Jimmy that girls were precious, and Jimmy believed everything his mother said.

Jimmy decided to walk to the sideshow tents to see if he could find his father there. As he stepped down the curb to cross the street, a shiny black automobile flew past him with the intensity of a locomotive.

The driver yelled an obscenity from the window and honked loudly. Startled, Jimmy teetered backwards as swirls of debris lifted off the ground and dirt flew into his face. He tried to stop himself from falling, but failed and hit the sidewalk.

Jimmy inspected himself for any blood and realized his knee was scraped pretty badly. He thought he might cry, and then cautioned himself that six-year-old boys do not cry. He clumsily got to his feet, brushed the dirt off, and looked around to see who might have seen him fall. He had been more embarrassed than hurt and was thankful that no one had witnessed the incident. Since the circus hadn't opened for the day, there was no one around.

He ventured out into the street once more, this time looking carefully before crossing. Once safely on the opposite side of the street, he made his way to the sideshow tents.

"Hi, Bertha!" he called to the eight hundred pound woman. At 28, Bertha was the heaviest woman in the world, but her claim to fame did not make her an unhappy or angry person.

"Hi, sweetie. Where are you off to in such a hurry?" She yelled after him in her thick steady voice.

"I'm looking for my daddy, Gordon the Great – the greatest knife thrower in all of the universe!" Jimmy shouted proudly. "Have you seen him?"

"Nope, sorry!" Bertha waved goodbye and shoved a cookie into her mouth as Jimmy headed on with his search.

The townspeople would line up outside just to get a look at Bertha's vulgar body. She wore a satin bathing suit, and rolls of fat oozed everywhere. Her performance consisted of her shoving large quantities of food into her mouth while she proclaimed how good it all was, how hungry she was and then when she was finished eating everything on the table, she demanded more. People would leave her sideshow, exclaiming that they had never seen anything like that in all their lives, and swear they would never eat again. Upon exiting, another performer would try and sell them tickets to the Big Top show later that afternoon. And so it went, from town to town - sideshows, clowns, performing animals, acrobats and more strange people, presenting their abnormalities to all who wanted to gawk at them.

Once Jimmy had asked Bertha if she cared that people stared at her day after day. Jimmy noted how some of the people could be really mean. They would talk loudly about how grotesque she was, thinking not only was she fat, but she must not care about her own self as well. If people openly ridiculed Bertha, they were escorted out of the tent and refused entry into the circus. Bertha had told Jimmy that this was her way of making a living, and admitted that she could do nothing else. Besides, she had learned to ignore the comments; she knew she was a kind, good person and she truly loved her circus family. And God had made her this way so she was doing her best to get by. Jimmy cried when she told him this, and she held him close to her immense bosom and told him that he was not to cry any tears for her when there were plenty of less fortunate people in the world. "Besides," she told him, "I am happy here. Where else would I fit in?" She was right about that. There were plenty of other curiosities to keep her company.

Jimmy continued his search for his father and he began to really wonder why he kept disappearing? Jimmy next found Old Man Johnson, another sideshow performer. He was only about thirty years old, but had an extraordinarily long white beard, making him appear very old. He pictured him as the "old man" when his father sang Ol' Man River. Sometimes he would practice throwing knives with him and his father. Of course, he was not nearly as good as his father or himself for that matter. But since Jimmy couldn't find his father, and Old Man Johnson was definitely a grownup who could throw knives, he would have to do this morning for lack of better available talent.

Kate was upset. Gordon had acted cooler than usual last night at Jimmy's birthday dinner, and then disappeared shortly thereafter. She woke to find that he had never come to bed at all, and that was disturbing. She looked for him all day, to no avail. Mr. Robinson would surely be outraged that he had not performed today. Gordon never missed a performance. Now it was getting dark and she had this gnawing feeling that he wasn't returning anytime soon. And Sheila was missing too. Maybe the two of them had gone into town for something, maybe to have the knives sharpened professionally. Kate tried hard to find a reasonable explanation. She sat alone on their bed wondering where could he be? Her mind was playing tricks on her, making her conjure up images better left forgotten. It kept wandering to Sheila, standing in her tight, flimsy costume laughing with Gordon as they shared a private joke. The joke better not be on me, she thought, her face growing hot and red. Before she could fully dismiss the ugly image from her mind, she noticed someone outside the canvas door of her tent.

"Who's there?" she called out in a shaky voice, half-angry from her daydreaming, half-fearful at the dark shadow against the fabric walls of the tent.

"Gordon, is that you?" Kate was uncertain. If it was Gordon why didn't he just come in instead of hovering outside like a thief in the night? A woman's voice floated through the thin canvas curtain that was latched onto the siding of the tent.

"I'm sorry if I have frightened you. I'm looking for Katherine Gabriel."

Kate stood from the bed, her robe brushing against the floor. She went to the entrance of her tent and unlatched the catches of the curtain. The flap fell back and there stood a petite young woman with brown hair pulled tightly back in a large bun.

"Kate! It is you!" The woman exclaimed with a slight southern accent. Kate blinked hard to make out the face of the woman. It was very difficult to see, her eyes had not yet adjusted to the bright light posts from outside.

"It's me, you old bitty!" exclaimed the stranger.

Then, all at once Kate recognized the woman standing before her wearing a smart pink blouse and a long tan skirt. There was only one person who called her an old bitty, and as her eyes began to focus, she saw that it was indeed her old friend Anita. Kate grabbed at her friend's shoulders and erupted into genuine laughter.

"Anita! What a surprise! What on earth…"

"Katherine Gabriel, it is so good to see you! When I heard what circus was in town I just had to come down and see if y'all were still performing. How are you? My God, Jimmy must be so big by now. I haven't seen him since he was a baby."

Kate couldn't believe that her friend was here with her now. Anita had been an acrobat with the circus years ago, and they had been the best of friends. Then one day she ran off without a word to anyone, not even to Kate. She had been deeply hurt that Anita had not confided in her, but she was here now and that was enough.

"I can't believe it's really you! Come in and tell me what you've been up to the past few years," Kate motioned for Anita to follow her inside.

"Well," Anita sat on the scratchy green blanket covering the bed, and began to talk. "Do you remember when we were performing in Detroit, and the man that used to bring me a red rose each night after the acrobat show?

Kate slowly nodded her head as she remembered the handsome banker named John. He had such a crush on Anita and would come to the circus just to see her each night.

Anita smiled and told her story. "We spent a lot of time together, we fell in love and I got pregnant. I was too scared and ashamed to tell anyone, even you. I'm truly sorry that I didn't confide in you, but I was just a scared kid. So when John asked me to marry him and stay in Detroit with him, what else could I do?"

Kate nodded her head in agreement as Anita continued.

"I said yes. I did love him, and it was the only way out of the mess. We eloped and were married two days after I skipped out on the circus. I had always wanted a big wedding though," she sighed heavily, "but things never seem to turn out as planned. I had a miscarriage and John was transferred to Philadelphia shortly after. We've been here since then. I have waited for the circus to come to town so I could finally see you and explain my actions." Anita, finished with her story, placed her hands in her lap and waited for Kate to respond.

"I am sorry about your baby, I had no idea. Had I known I might have been able to help somehow. I am really glad you found me now," Kate hugged her old friend. Then Kate began telling Anita of her own unhappiness at the way her own life was unfolding, how she just wanted a safe and secure home for Jimmy and how Gordon had gone missing.

When the two women had finished talking, Kate realized she had been wringing her hands tightly together and they had begun to burn from the force of her own strength. She was concerned that her life was going to take a sudden and unsure new route if Gordon didn't return soon.

Anita placed her own hand over Kate's. "I want you to know that I am still your friend. If you ever need anything you are always welcome in my home. We have shared much more than just a circus friendship and I am so glad that I've found you again."

Kate smiled gratefully and thanked her. Anita wrote down her address and after a long goodbye and many hugs, she left for home, only a few miles from where the circus was.

On the fourth day of Gordon's disappearance, Kate and Jimmy rose from their tent and packed up the few personal belongings they owned. The night before, Kate had explained to Jimmy that she didn't think daddy was coming back for them. She couldn't explain anything more, she had told her weeping son, but she did know that daddy had loved Jimmy greatly, and Kate was sure that for whatever reason he had left, it had nothing to do with Jimmy and that Gordon would never forget his son.

"Come on Jimmy. It's time to go," Kate called to him.

He knew it was time. All the tents had been packed up yesterday. All the animals and circus props were safely tucked away in the traveling wagons that lined the street. Jimmy was looking at his only-known world and tears filled his eyes. His father had been gone now for four days, and the circus was moving to Maryland. His father had known the circus schedule and still chose not to come back to be with his wife and son. Just then Kate appeared with a worried look in her tired eyes. She hugged Jimmy tighter than she ever had.

"I have been looking everywhere for you. We have to go now."

Jimmy still didn't understand why his father had disappeared. "We can't leave without Daddy. We have to wait for him to come back. He'll come back."

"Honey, we can't wait for him. He knows our next stop is Maryland and I'm sure he'll meet up with us there."

In her heart, Kate feared she would never see Gordon again; never see the father to her precious child. Everyone at the circus had been whispering about how Gordon and Sheila had run off together. Kate ignored their whispers and the tiresome gossip, for her sake as well as Jimmy's. All she could do was keep the faith that Gordon would do what was right and meet them in Maryland without Sheila. She was angry, hurt and miserable. All she wanted to do was sit and cry and if it were not for Jimmy she would do just that. She knew she had to be strong for Jimmy so she grasped onto the hope that her husband would come back to them. She could not entertain the notion that he would not, despite what the entire troupe was whispering behind her back. To hell with them, she thought with renewed confidence, they do not know Gordon like I do.

Chapter Two
1934

The school bell rang promptly at three o'clock. The sound of children laughing and shouting to one another echoed down the long narrow hallway of St. Dominic's Elementary School. Children hurried to find coats and lunch pails in coat closets stuffed to maximum capacity.

"You better give me my coat right now, Jimmy Gabriel, or I'll tell Sister Mary." Anna Murphy's pigtails swung back and forth as she tried to grab her thin blue jacket from Jimmy, who was holding it high in the air, taunting Anna.

"Don't give it to her!" Billy yelled.

"Let her jump, Jimmy!" shouted Dante Russo, Jimmy's best friend in the whole world.

The boys and girls of the seventh grade hovered around Jimmy and Anna, shouting words of encouragement to Jimmy. They were all amused at the situation that was unfolding in the back of Sister Mary's classroom. Girls were whispering to each other that Jimmy Gabriel had a crush on Anna, and that was why he was always teasing her.

Jimmy was smiling at Anna, holding her coat out so she could grab at it and then yanking it away from her dainty fingers at the last second. Anna was one of his closest friends and had been extremely kind to him on his first day of school six years prior. He hadn't known anyone, and had started the first grade two weeks late. When Anna noticed that the new student was sitting alone at lunch for the third time that week, she had come over and sat down on the bench with him. Anna and Jimmy had been close friends ever since first grade, and when Dante arrived at St. Dominic's in second grade, Anna and Jimmy fast became friends with him as well. They had been an inseparable trio.

Jimmy hadn't realized that Anna was upset from the teasing. When he glanced at her, he saw her rosy lips were set in a pout and her pretty brown eyes were beginning to tear. He dropped the jacket, realizing he had gone too far with the joke.

"Here, you can have your jacket back. I was just kidding around."

"You are being so cruel, James Gabriel." She only called him James Gabriel when she was furious, and she was definitely furious right now.

Anna spun around on squeaky Mary Janes and held her jacket tightly in both hands. She ran down the corridor, the soles of her shoes clanging against the tiled floor. She pulled open the heavy school door and ran outside into the crisp autumn air. Jimmy yelled goodbye to Dante and raced out the door to catch up with Anna, who was still running.

When Jimmy reached her, he was breathless and holding his side. "Hey Speedy, slow down." He pushed the words out of his tired lungs. "I'll walk you home. Give me your books."

She handed her books to Jimmy and exclaimed, "You were being a real creep back there you know?"

"Aw Anna, you know I was just kidding around with you. I would never do anything to hurt you. After all, you're going to be my wife someday!" He always made jokes about the two of them getting married someday and joining the circus so he could throw knives at her while she spun around and around. And Anna always stated matter-of-factly that there was no way she was going to marry him and let him toss knives at her.

They walked in silence down the tree-lined street and Jimmy commented on the pretty fall leaves. He did a little tap dance around Anna, picked up a pile of leaves and threw them into the air. As the leaves drifted downward, Jimmy joked, "It's snowing!"

"You're crazy, Jimmy!"

"I know, I know." He handed Anna's books back to her and said, "I'm sorry I was teasing you today. It was mean of me, but Dante put me up to it. You know I can never pass up a dare from Dante." He smiled at her the way he could that always made her stop being mad at him.

33

They walked up the steps toward Anna's house just as her father, Officer Murphy, opened the front door. He must have had the day off today, thought Jimmy.

"Hey Jimmy, can you stay for dinner?" Officer Murphy hollered. "Anna's mom is making meatballs and gravy!"

"Can't tonight, Mr. Murphy. Mom wants me to start dinner at home!"

"Some other time then, son." Jimmy cringed at the sound of someone calling him son. He knew Officer Murphy was just being friendly, but oh, how Jimmy had wanted to hear that from his own father. He pushed his sadness aside and waved to them as Anna shouted, "See you in school tomorrow."

As he made his way home, he thought about what he was going to do about the assignment for tomorrow. All the kids were expected to make a speech about their fathers. And what was Jimmy going to say? That his father left him and his mother and took off with another circus performer when he was only six? That would make him the laughing stock of the whole seventh grade class. Why had Sister Mary been so insensitive about this assignment? Even Dante was fatherless, but at least Dante knew where his father was. He had been buried a hero for saving another young man from drowning in a boating accident.

When Gordon had never met up with him and his mother in Baltimore, Kate had remembered Anita's offer for help and sent a letter. Anita immediately insisted Kate and Jimmy come back to Philadelphia to stay with her for as long as they needed. He and his mother had been devastated when the reality set in that they had been abandoned but they set forth to create a new life for themselves.

Jimmy was enrolled in St. Dominic's for first grade and Kate found a job scrubbing floors at the Fox Theatre. There was no chance Jimmy would ever be reunited with his father now since Kate had made an arrangement with Tom Robinson one night, which allowed Kate and Jimmy to leave the circus quietly, and with a portion of their pride left. The circus had only been in Maryland for a week, but Kate felt sure that Gordon was never coming to get them, and she was not really needed any longer since the Great Knife Thrower had left his "target" and her son behind. Tom Robinson was all too ready to offer them a severance pay worth bus tickets back to Philadelphia.

Jimmy didn't want to mention the class assignment to his mother because he knew it would upset her. She had cried a million tears over his father these past six years and he swore that he would do everything in his power to not have her cry over Gordon ever again. Instead of having to tell her about the special dad assignment and Jimmy having to go to school to be laughed at by the other students, he decided he would pretend to be sick so he didn't have to face the other kids. He didn't want to listen about how great all their dads were anyway.

Jimmy smiled at his plan and raced up the old rickety steps to his front door two at a time. He knew his mother worked hard so that she could pay the rent on their row home. He also knew that they could make more money in the circus, with him throwing knives, than his mother could ever make cleaning the movie theater floors. He thought it was such degrading work for his mother, who had been so glamorous performing in red, sequined outfits, wowing the crowds with her beautiful smile. But there would be no returning to the circus. Kate had steady work cleaning the Fox Theatre and swore to Jimmy that she would work as hard as she could so that they could live in a real neighborhood with real schools and a real church, too. She explained that nothing meant more to her than seeing him live the life of a normal boy. That was what she had always dreamed for her son.

And Jimmy repaid his mother by being one of the best students at St. Dominic's. Most of the nuns would comment to Kate that Jimmy was a very talented and kind student. He had to work very hard though, as good grades did not come naturally to him, but since he wanted nothing more than to make his mother proud, he continued to strive and always made the honor roll at school. He had decided long ago that he would never disappoint her like his father had. Oh, how he hated him when he thought of the pain he had bestowed upon his mother.

Jimmy unlocked the front door to their less than modest home, read the instructions on how to start dinner, and began his homework.

His mother would be home in a couple of hours and he always made sure his homework was done so they could spend time together, playing cards or just recapping the day.

"Jimmy, hurry on down here or you'll to be late for school," Kate shouted from the kitchen. "Your breakfast is getting cold and I have to leave for work." Her callused hands gripped the handle of the hot frying pan and she quickly scooped scrambled eggs onto the plate. She never thought much about things anymore, how her life had been so drastically changed when Gordon had deserted them. She had not even known how to cook for herself and Jimmy! She laughed inwardly. All of their meals had been prepared for them in the circus. It was true, she did miss certain aspects of that time and she had sworn that had she ever gotten away from there, she would never look back. But she found herself thinking back to those days quite often, and would remember the glamour of it all. Like wearing makeup and pretty costumes every day, and having people pay her attention because she was so beautiful. These days it was all she could do to drag her tired muscles out of bed in the morning, and she never had the urge to put makeup or pretty clothes on. Who would see her in the dark of the movie theater anyway, hunched over, scrubbing away until the floors sparkled?

She sighed tiredly and pushed her short auburn hair away from her face. She had cut her hair after she had been hired at Fox Theatre for practical reasons. She didn't have time in the mornings to fix it up, and left down it was a nuisance when she was on her hands and knees scrubbing. The movie playing this week was *Bright Eyes*, starring that adorable little girl who was all dimples and ringlets, Shirley Temple. The audiences loved her, and gladly paid their twelve cents to see her smiling face on the big screen. She guessed it made them forget about how hard their own lives were for a couple of hours. Everyone was having tough times these days. The carefree twenties were definitely behind them.

She had grown quietly bitter over the years but kept her feelings to herself for fear that Jimmy would also turn to stone like she had. She had become cynical and she hated Gordon for changing the way she viewed the world and the people around her. She hated him for leaving her without a husband and Jimmy without a father; for the life she was forced to lead to support herself and her twelve-year-old son; and most of all, for the shame he caused her to feel that somehow she *made* him leave them. Maybe if she had been more beautiful, more loving or more attentive, he would not have run into the arms of another woman.

Jimmy came down the stairs slowly, still in his pajamas, and forced himself to cough. "Mom, I don't feel so good," and he coughed again. "I don't think I can go to school today. Should Aunt Anita come over and stay with me?" He thought his performance was pretty good and that his mother would let him miss school for sure.

"James Gabriel, you are to go upstairs and get dressed this instant. You are about as sick as a… as a… well, I don't know what, but you are not sick and you have two minutes to get back upstairs and get dressed," she ordered sternly. Kate could always tell when Jimmy was trying to get out of something and wondered what was his reason for not wanting to go to school.

"Ah, Mom, do I have to?"

"What's the matter? Did you not study for a test?"

Jimmy thought about telling her about today's assignment being about fathers and what they did, but quickly changed his mind. She would just get upset, and he didn't want to do that to her. He had seen her upset too many times before.

"Nothing's the matter. I'll go get dressed." He ran up the creaky stairs and hurriedly put on his uniform, a starched white shirt with blue pants.

The school bell was clanging as he shuffled into classroom amidst his fellow students. He still did not know how he was going to handle this particular assignment.

Sister Mary asked for a volunteer and Anna eagerly agreed to be first. Everyone knew Anna's father and was excited to hear about the latest police news in town. Jimmy loved to hear stories of robbery attempts thwarted by Officer Murphy and even he listened intently as Anna spoke proudly of her father.

Sarah went next, describing in detail how her father, the butcher, would gut and clean a pig. She even had pictures to share with the class. Dante spoke next. Even though his father had died four years earlier, Dante was very proud of the heroism he had displayed and was not at all concerned about speaking of his father.

One by one, students were called up to the front of the class and spoke of their dads – one was a lawyer; there were a couple door-to-door salesmen, one had started his own woodshop and had become very successful in town.

Jimmy quickly surveyed the small room. There were only a few more students that had to speak. Sister Mary looked at him and asked, "Jimmy, would you like to go next?" All eyes were on him as he made his way slowly to the front of the class. No one but Anna and Dante knew the story of Jimmy's father.

"Uh, my dad is, uh… have you heard of…" and that's when Jimmy got the courage and strength to talk proudly of the father that had not existed for more than half his young life. He cleared his throat and continued. "My dad is on the road. He's Gordon the Great, the world's most famous knife thrower. You may have heard of him, or even seen him long ago when the Tom Robinson circus was in Philadelphia."

Billy interrupted excitedly, "Hey, I went to the circus a long time ago and saw some man throwing knives at a really pretty lady who was spinning around and around. He got really close to her face, but never even hit her!"

Jimmy looked at Billy straight in the eye, and felt an unfamiliar feeling. It was a small part of pride to realize that someone else had seen his father and he also felt a harsh sadness to know that his father did, in fact, exist. So many times throughout his life, Jimmy had tried to convince himself that he had no father. "That's my dad," Jimmy said softly.

He went on to say that it was his mother's choice to leave the circus so that Jimmy could attend St. Dominic's and live a normal life, while all the time Jimmy had loved the circus and hadn't wanted to leave. The students were excited to learn more about the workings of a real live circus so the conversation soon turned away from fathers and towards clowns, knife throwing, and flying acrobats.

Later, realizing he had placed the blame on his mother, Jimmy felt a terrible guilt rush over him. How could he have made his mother look like the one who had decided their fate? Jimmy was greatly ashamed at the lie he had told to his classmates and swore he would ask for forgiveness next time he went to confession.

When the bell signaled school was over, Jimmy ran ahead of Anna and Dante who usually walked home with him. Other students yelled out for Jimmy to wait because they wanted to hear more circus stories. They were particularly interested in Jimmy's friendship with the other sideshow performers and wanted to know how fat the fat lady really was.

He pushed open the red school door to freedom. Out of nowhere hot tears squeezed from Jimmy's eyes as he tried to chase memories of his father away. But oh, how he missed him and wished he were there with them. He was certain his life would be so much better, and his mom certainly would be happier with Gordon back home. He couldn't even remember the last time his mother had been happy, really happy, and this caused most of the heartbreak that Jimmy was feeling. And to think that he had openly blamed his mother for the fate of their family, and that his father had nothing to do with him not being here.

Jimmy ran past St. Dominic's Church, which was adjacent to the school, and mentally promised to confess his sin later on. He ran until he reached home and sprinted up the stairs to his bedroom, tripping over one of his shoes. His mother was always reminding him to put his shoes away and now he had wished he listened to her. In his room, he searched his tiny closet for his satchel of throwing knives and panicked when he realized they were not there. He stuck one arm underneath his bed and felt around until he located the pliable leather pouch that held his precious knives. He grabbed it quickly and ran out of the house toward Pennypack Park.

Pennypack Park was one of Philadelphia's hugest parks with over eight thousand acres of untamed land. Jimmy loved the park as he could get lost over and over again throughout the wooded paths and trails, always knowing he was not too far from home. He often pretended he was a mighty war soldier, throwing his knives at the enemy, becoming a hero for saving his country. What a dream! Sometimes he and Dante would sneak to the park after dark and play war soldiers. They both loved the idea of protecting their country and desired to go into the military someday, although for Dante, it would be impossible because when he got older, he would have to be the sole supporter of his family since his father was dead. And since Gordon the Great was more than likely alive and well, Jimmy knew that he could get drafted into the war with no problem. Jimmy often told Dante that they would find a way to go to war together as they both knew it was the admirable thing to do. Besides, the two friends had spent many years planning top-secret ways to save their country in a battle someday.

For as much as the boys loved exploring the park and pretending to be war soldiers together, there was one private spot that Jimmy had found and kept to himself. It was nestled in the outer edges and it was very difficult to find this particular clearing. In fact, Jimmy had found it, and then forgotten where it was only to stumble across the place months later. The pathway to the clearing was heavy with bent tree limbs, fallen branches, twisted vines and tree roots. Jimmy had even gotten poison ivy once from pushing his way through the shrubbery that led to the small clearing. Today, the smell of pine and damp grass was heavy in the air as he crept through to his secret space in Pennypack Park. He pulled a leaf out of his tousled hair and wiped his dirty hands on his pants. Although it was a sunny day, very little light was funneling through the dense roof of leaves. It was cool within the covered clearing and Jimmy shivered, wishing he had his jacket. He walked over to the rotting piece of wood on the edge of the clearing that he used as his target, picked it up and propped it against the oak tree. Whenever he was feeling angry, sad, confused or misguided, he would come to his secret place and practice throwing at the target. It gave him a chance to be alone, think through his problems and do his favorite thing in the whole world – throw his precious knives. This place brought him closer to his father too, as he knew that somewhere in the world, Gordon the Great still performed and was known as the world's best knife thrower.

Jimmy untied the old cord on his satchel and pulled out one of his knives. He stood in position, focused on the red dot on his makeshift target, pulled back his arm steadily and threw ferociously.

The silver blade flew through the air with a mighty force, and the wood reverberated as the knife cut into it with a loud thump. Not yet satisfied, Jimmy threw the other five in the same fashion. He shook his hand to rid it of the cramps he had from gripping the handles too tightly. All six knives had landed within the boundaries of the red circle, and a slow grin began to grow at the edge of his lips. He was not surprised; he expected nothing less. If there was one thing he had learned from his father, it was to not give up on your dreams, even though it made Jimmy angry that his father's dreams hadn't included him and his mother. Every day of Jimmy's life, he wondered how his father could have deserted them in such a cruel way?

Sometimes Jimmy wished his father would find them; that the three would be reunited as a family. Then, other times, he hated his father so much he never wanted to see him again. He hated him for all the grief he had put upon his mother, and for discarding his family as if they had meant nothing to him. Once he had confessed to Father Peter during penance that he hated his father. Father Peter had scolded Jimmy, telling him that hate was such a strong word. He continued to tell Jimmy that what he was feeling was probably more like severe anger and nothing more. Without waiting for Jimmy to respond, Father Peter had dismissed Jimmy, giving him a penance of one "Our Father" and one "Hail Mary." Jimmy had done his penance as instructed but had not felt forgiven, mostly in part because he didn't want to seek forgiveness for what his father had done. Until then, he would always hate his father and confession and a penance would mean nothing. Because of his feelings, he kept his secret sin to himself for many years.

Jimmy was running late. It was his Sunday to serve as altar boy for the seven o'clock Mass at St. Dominic's. As he ran through the cool and foggy street, he prayed that he would not mess anything up like

Christopher Butner had done last week. The whole congregation watched as young Christopher tripped on the hem of his cassock and nearly dropped the chalice. But Jimmy was older and smarter than Christopher and wouldn't get preoccupied during Mass.

Today's Mass was one of great importance so it was extremely necessary that Jimmy not make a mistake. It was November 30, the feast of Saint Andrew the Apostle, and Father Peter would be wearing his red chasuble, stole and maniple to signify the feast of the martyrs.

Jimmy arrived at the church breathless, wheezing from his early morning run. He greeted Father Peter and readied himself for Mass.

"Good morning, James," Father Peter said.

Although Father Peter had scolded him for confessing to hatred, Jimmy respected him more than any other man he knew, even more than Officer Murphy, who was indeed a great man too. But a priest - there was no man more important on earth, except for the Pope, according to his mother. Kate had hinted quite often that Jimmy would make a perfect priest. He was so conscious, so caring and so willing to help others. After all, those are the qualities of a great priest, she would say to Jimmy, time and time again.

And although Jimmy never outwardly admitted it, he was fascinated with the idea of priesthood and loved participating as altar boy. He was fascinated with the prestigious garments Father Peter wore, and how he could command respect from a church filled with people searching for peace, salvation and forgiveness.

Jimmy noticed Father Peter had already dressed and he rushed to put on his own black cassock and white surplice. When he was properly outfitted, he walked out to the sanctuary and lit two candles. While his hands trembled, he reminded himself not to be nervous and if this was to be his calling, he had to get over the fear of being in front of the congregation. He told himself that his father and mother both had been performers and that being in front of an audience should come naturally to him. He placed the missal on the altar, and slowly, so as not to spill, he filled two cruets with the wine and water that would be mixed later to become the Blood of Christ. He inhaled deeply when he completed these pre-service tasks and he stood attentively, waiting for Father Peter. The church smelled of burnt matchsticks and stale air, and a young child was crying. The bells outside began to ring. It was time for Mass to start.

Father Peter nodded his head and Jimmy rang a small bell outside the door from the sacristy to the sanctuary. Jimmy felt a feeling of anxiety mixed with complete humility. He had never felt closer to God than on those days he assisted as altar boy. His mind cleared and his thoughts were only of God and the goodness of the church. He loved feeling this way.

In Latin Father Peter proclaimed, "In nomine Patris, et Filii, et Spiritus Sancti. Amen. Introibo ad altere Dei."

"Ad Deum qui leatificat juventutem meam," Jimmy responded. "I will go unto the altar of God. Unto God, who giveth joy to my youth."

It was now time for Holy Communion and although Jimmy had made it through half of the Mass without a mistake, he began to get nervous, knowing he had to brave the altar steps once more. He had wobbled the first time he descended them so he took careful slow steps up toward Father Peter who was waiting for the cruets of water and wine.

Once Jimmy arrived at his spot next to Father Peter, an unconscious, rather loud sigh escaped his lips. Those in the front pew surely had heard the untimely sigh of relief, and Jimmy, red-faced, looked up to see who was there.

And of course, his mother, front and center, was frowning a bit at his open display of emotion. He could practically read her mind and imagined her telling him that he should be more conscious of his actions. She was always reminding him that what he would do in this life would have a direct affect on others around him. How true in this particular case. But, after a half-frown, mother and son made eye contact and her eyes lit up with pride and Jimmy met her smile with a smile of his own.

The truth was that he loved everything about Mass. He loved the prayers, the songs, the Latin language that enhanced the service, making it all the more holy. And he revered in accepting Holy Communion. There was nothing more sacred than experiencing the Body and Blood of Jesus Christ. He knew that God was giving himself to Jimmy, and Jimmy was humbly accepting God into his own unworthy body.

And Jimmy knew the joy he experienced by participating in Mass could not compare to the elation that his mother felt watching her only son up on the great altar, helping serve his community and openly loving and worshipping God wholly and completely, without reservation.

Jimmy knew that his mother had spent endless hours praying, crying and hoping that her son would be taken care of, that she could make a good life for the two of them. He also knew that nothing in the world would make her more proud than to be able to say, "My son is James Gabriel, Father James Gabriel."

Chapter Three
1941

In May, Jim Gabriel waited at a bus stop with the three most important people in his life. His mother, his girlfriend, Anna Murphy, and his best friend, Dante, were seeing him off to fight the war. It was a scene that was playing itself out all over the United States as the German army threatened its neighbors throughout the European theater. Like all of the other young men at bus and train stations across America at that moment, Jim was leaving behind the life and the loved ones he knew; he was giving up the security of his neighborhood in Holmesburg and proceeding headlong into an unknown destiny. For Jim and so many others, the moment was bittersweet. Proud of his country – and fiercely determined to defend it – he had a strong sense of the rectitude of his decision to enlist; and yet, at the same time, he deeply regretted leaving his mother behind. Ever since his father had abandoned them all of those years before, Jim and Kate had grown closer, and Jim had grown into the role of protecting his mother as she had protected him throughout his infancy and childhood. By the time Jim enlisted at the age of nineteen, they enjoyed a sturdy relationship in which they loved, respected, and looked out for each other; and Jim felt a strong sense of guilt in leaving Kate behind, despite the confidence he had in her as a strong and resilient human being. When Jim had first told Kate of his decision to enlist, she had fallen to the ground, overcome with emotion; but he was surprised at how well she was taking it now. There were tears in her eyes, and Jim could not determine if they were tears of sadness or pride. All he was sure of was that she held onto him for a long time, as though she were reluctant to let him go.

Anna Murphy, of course, represented an entirely different set of feelings. Although they had conducted their courtship in an honorable manner – and had conformed to the teachings of the Catholic Church – Anna had provided Jim with his first real experience of romantic love, and they had developed an attachment that was physical, emotional, and spiritual. Jim loved being with Anna; he loved how she made him feel; and he marveled at the fact that she brought out the best in him. In their kisses and embraces, he had experienced the excitement that brings men and women together, and yet they were equally determined to conduct their relationship appropriately; and in that too they found a common ground. As he held her tightly at the bus stop, the thought of leaving her very nearly sickened him; and now, in their last few minutes together, all they could do was hold on to one another as long as possible and utter the three words that seem so inadequate at times like that: "I love you." And yet those were the only words they had.

In Dante Russo, Jim had found a true friend – loyal, like-minded, and equally determined to defend his country. But Dante's circumstances had prevented him from enlisting. His father had died when Dante was in elementary school, his mother was an invalid, and Dante was forced to stay behind. As the bus came to a halt in front of them, Jim shook Dante's hand vigorously and asked him to watch over his "two women." Dante nodded solemnly, they embraced, and Jim climbed the steps of the bus.

As he made his way to the Pennsylvania Armory at 32nd Street and Lancaster Avenue in West Philadelphia, Jim realized that in a very real way his youth was coming to an end. The enormous event that was World War II was changing his life forever, just as it was changing the lives of the other young men who were converging on induction centers all over the United States. At the time, Jim was only faintly aware that he was about to embark upon the single most important experience of his life, one that would make an indelible impression on him as a young man and remain in his consciousness deep into old age. For the men of his generation, the experience of becoming a husband and father would be the greatest blessing of all; but the bonds they formed with their fellow soldiers would stand apart as something else entirely, and would occupy a special place that eluded the more traditional roles of husband and father. At the time, however, Jim was only vaguely aware of the indelible impression that fighting in the war would make.

The Pennsylvania Armory in West Philadelphia served as the starting point of Jim's Army experience. Together with hundreds of other young men, Jim shed his civilian clothing and lined up for his physical, as naked as the day he was born. No matter how dissimilar these young men might be in temperament or in character, they had come together for a common purpose; and over the course of the next few days, the seeds were sown for the kind of unbreakable bond that soldiers often feel. Later, as their strengths and weaknesses were identified – and as decisions were made on where they would be placed in the vast organization that the United States Army had become – some of their individuality would be returned to them; but for the time being, the routine was the same for every one of those young men: they answered the same questions, they filled out the same paperwork, and they underwent the same brusque treatment from the Army doctors, who barked short, clipped phrases at them, phrases like "Spread 'em!" and "Cough, soldier!", as they searched for hernias, communicable diseases, and any other weakness that could render a man unfit for duty.

For Jim and his fellow soldiers, the next step was another bus ride, this time to Fort Meade, Maryland, where they would be outfitted from head to toe in their Army issue gear. At approximately the same time, the men would have an opportunity to request a specific branch of the Army, including the Signal Corps, Field Artillery, Tank Division, and the Rangers; and those who did not make such a request were assigned to the Infantry and transported to Camp Attaberry, Indiana. Because Jim selected the Rangers, however, he was among the men who left immediately for Fort Benning, Georgia, where he was assigned to the 82nd Airborne Division, which was second only to the Marines in difficulty and in reputation.

It was during basic training at Fort Benning that Jim began to show promise and distinguish himself as a soldier. He qualified as a 1st Class Paratrooper at that juncture, and was selected for the 408th Demolition Detachment; at least in part because of the knife throwing ability he had developed as the son of Gordon the Great. Responding to a directive from the Commander in Chief of the Allied Forces in the European theater, the Army had formed an elite unit of highly skilled individuals and trained them as demolition experts. This eleven-man unit consisted of a Chief Warrant Officer (CWO) who was expert in the use of all military explosives, including C4; two men who were fluent in the German language; two who were specifically trained for underwater demolition; four who were trained in knife throwing and the use of the garrote, a deadly device that could strangle an enemy silently; and two men who had performed on the high wire during their civilian lives. In addition to their demolition training, each member of the unit successfully completed Ranger training, including airborne maneuvers.

By the time Jim and his fellow soldiers completed their training, they were not only combat efficient but fully capable of executing the most dangerous missions behind enemy lines by using their agility, specialized training, and a variety of stealth tactics. Because their missions involved the destruction of bridges, tunnels, ammunition depots, and other facilities that were critical to the success of the enemy, these elite fighting men depended upon the element of surprise, so that they could position themselves for highly specialized, time-sensitive maneuvers without eliciting gunfire from the enemy. Even a single shot could cause missions of that nature to be aborted or to go horribly wrong, and Jim and the others received hazardous pay for the vital work they were doing. Every one of them held the rank of Sergeant or Sergeant First Class, with the exception of the CWO and his top assistant, who held the rank of Master Sergeant.

Within eighteen months of the formation of their unit, the 408th had successfully completed missions in several countries throughout the European theater; earned countless awards, ribbons, and citations for valor; and developed deep and abiding relationships with one another. For Jim, the strongest bond that he had formed was with Thomas Young. Tom had lived in Pennsylvania as well, in a town not too far from Holmesburg. As a fellow knife thrower, the two young men had gravitated toward one another from the start. By the eighteen-month mark, they knew nearly everything there was to know about one another – their family situations, their likes and dislikes, and the girls they had left back home. Because he missed her tremendously, Jim had talked about Anna incessantly – her lean body, her creamy complexion, her blond hair, and the sheer fragrance of her when she and Jim embraced. Jim's habit of doing so might have been too much for Tom to bear if Tom hadn't had a girl of his own. And so, the two of them took turns and shared the time equally as two close friends should do, Jim conveying the many wonders of Anna while Tom talked about Lora, his fiancé who was waiting for him back home. Thankfully, however, there was never any one-upmanship in it; it was simply a diversion for them as they attempted to deal with the anxiety and the nerve-wracking tension of combat.

One day, however, an Army mail carrier tracked Jim down at his latest remote outpost in the European theater, handing him the kind of letter that every soldier dreaded. Jim's mother was fine – as well as could be expected really, with her only son facing the possibility of death on a daily basis – but Anna had important news for him:

My Dearest Jim –

This is the most difficult letter that I have ever had to write. During the years that we were together, I came to love you deeply, and I never dreamed that anything could come between us; and for the longest time, nothing did. But war is a very big thing – as I'm sure you are aware – and loneliness is even bigger. As the days and weeks wore on, I realized how much I had lost when you went away. Having a man in my life – a good and strong and spiritual man like yourself – meant the world to me. You were my rock, my comfort, and my greatest joy. Losing you to the war left an enormous hole in my life. I thought I was strong enough to bear it, but in the end I wasn't.

None of this is your fault, Jim. You are still the fine man that I came to know and cherish – and now that you are serving your country with such distinction, you are even finer. My problem is this: I love you, but you are not here for me to love.

Believe me, I know how painful this must be for you. I won't speak any more of my own pain, and I only bring it up so that you know how anguished I am about what I have done. And if there were any way for me to spare you the additional pain that I am about to bring you, I would certainly protect you from it. But I care for you too deeply and I respect you too much to keep any of this from you any longer. Try and forgive me, Jim, for falling in love with another man; and try if you can to forgive me for my choice of men, knowing that it was the most painful choice of all. Although we did our best to ignore our feelings as they developed, Dante and I cannot ignore our feelings any longer.

I will never be able to express how much I regret this. I imagine you reading it somewhere very difficult – in a dangerous part of the world – and I know that you are losing two of the people that meant the most to you, and that you are losing them at the same time in a single turn of events. And I also know that you still mean a great deal to both Dante and myself, although I am not sure that we have a right to express that sentiment to you any longer. I suspect that it is for you to say.

My only source of comfort now is the strong conviction that you are a survivor, and that your faith will pull you through. When your father left you, you survived your abandonment as a child; and I have no doubt that you will survive this as one of the strongest men I know.

May God bless you, Jim. I will not ask for your forgiveness, but it would mean a great deal to me if I could have it.

With much love and regret,
Anna

From the very first line of her letter, Anna's intent was clear, although it remained for her to furnish the details. As she did so, Jim began to lose his best self. He would regain it eventually - weeks and months down the road - but the pain of the betrayal never entirely left him, and it was at its strongest in the seconds it took him to run his eyes over the sentences that Anna had composed. As in all things, her delicacy was apparent; but now, all of the magnificent qualities that had drawn him to her began to mock him as he read her letter. The hurt he felt was deeper precisely because Anna was as wise, as sensitive, and as lovely as she had ever been. All at once, he felt the sense of loss that Anna had described in the early part of her letter; but he was afflicted with the knowledge that Anna had felt the loss over a period of time and that she had been given a chance to prepare for it simply by knowing that Jim was going off to war. His own sense of loss had come upon him suddenly, without any forewarning whatsoever; and it seemed much crueler to him. Really, he was like all of the soldiers in past centuries who fought so hard to protect their loved ones back home, so that they could be spared the loneliness, the danger, and the deprivation of what the soldiers were experiencing, only to be betrayed by the very loved ones that had personalized their reasons to fight. Forgiving them was out of the question, and despite his Catholic upbringing, he immediately sensed that the love could soon be supplanted by hatred. In his wild state of mind, it was impossible for him to contemplate any of it clearly, much less summon the enormous effort that would be required for him to forgive them in a Catholic manner; and in the days that followed, the only outlet that Jim had was to throw himself into battle with any even greater resolve than he had before. In those first few days and weeks, however, he had lost one of his strongest qualities: the ability to think rationally in the direst of circumstances, with guns firing in the middle distance and bullets flying around his head; but in one of those curious laws of nature, the loss of rationality was counterbalanced by a zeal for combat that was almost unnatural. Since the first days of basic training, Jim had demonstrated uncommon valor and a seeming unconcern for his own well-being; but he had never been reckless in his actions. Now, however, a week or so after receiving Anna's letter, an incident occurred that caused the others in his unit to suspect that Jim had become temporarily unhinged.

At the time, the 408th Demolition Detachment was working in unison with a group of British Commandos in an attempt to recapture a rural French village. The Germans had overrun the village and had seized a key strategic advantage over the allies; and they were threatening to expand their stranglehold over that part of the European theater. For the first time since the 408th had been formed, it appeared as though a mission would have to be aborted. Although the 408th was completely intact, a number of British Commandos had been lost, and now the 408th was coming under heavy fire from a German pillbox. This pillbox was strategically placed on a hill overlooking the village, and to that time it had prevented the Commandos from making any progress in their attempt to reclaim the village for the Allied cause. Just when the CWO was about to give the order to retreat, however, Jim rushed over to him and announced his intention of storming the pillbox himself. All he asked was that the remaining British Commandos and the rest of the demolition detachment provide ample cover for him to sneak to within range of the pillbox. Before the CWO could command Jim to stand down, and to abandon the lunacy that he was contemplating, Jim grabbed a number of hand grenades, attached them to his pistol belt, and hurried away with the sound of German machine guns blasting away in the air above their heads.

As Jim departed from them bearing the weaponry that would either earn an improbable victory or cost him his life, the CWO and the men under his command had no choice but to provide the cover that Jim requested. Zigzagging across the rough terrain, with German bullets biting into the ground at his feet, Jim was able to approach to within fifty yards of the pillbox, pausing behind intermittent rocks on the hillside. His only hope of survival depended upon the unlikely ability to escape the field of vision that the two German machine gunners enjoyed from the side of the pillbox; but none of the others thought that he could do it. Tom Young, the man who was closest to Jim among them, fired his machine gun with tears streaming down his eyes, as though he were already mourning Jim as he provided as much cover as a lone gunner could provide; but even with the cover provided by the score of men next to him, it seemed unlikely that Jim could get close enough to the pillbox and low enough to the ground to take out the Germans – unlikely that is, until the seconds passed and he did exactly that. Reaching down to his pistol belt, Jim hurled a series of grenades into an opening in the pillbox, where they exploded with a sufficient force to send the two German machine gunners into the air, separate them from their limbs, and kill them instantly. Somehow, at that moment, the betrayal he had suffered at the hands of Anna and Dante found its way into his mind, as though it were irrevocably linked with his singular act of heroism; and still numb with the betrayal and the triumph he had the honor of waving his fellow soldiers on, turning Tom's tears into an expression of sheer joy as he realized that Jim had not only survived his own lunacy but paved the way for them to recapture the village a day later.

After being nominated by the Commandos, Jim received a Silver Star; and later, the British government awarded him the Victoria Cross. This was the highest honor available in the British military; and Jim had the extraordinary pleasure of being awarded it as a member of the United States Army. His work with the 408th was far from done, however, and in the end, the medals became an unforeseen burden to him by reminding him of Anna.

As the death and destruction continued during World War II, the German Air Force found an ingenious way to bomb the city of London. Initially, the Germans were frustrated by the strict blackout that the British government had imposed, so that the skies above their most populated city were completely dark and the German pilots had no precise idea where their bombs were falling. By erecting radar stations in two rural villages in occupied France, however – approximately 25 miles apart – the Germans were able to transmit radar signals of a fixed frequency and direct them to a precise spot high above London. In their cockpits, the German pilots had a receiving device that enabled them to lock on to the signal transmitted from the radar station to the North. The receiving device gave off a beeping sound, and this audio signal enabled them to determine if they were flying on the correct course. When the fixed radar beam from the more Southern of the two radar stations crossed the signal from the Northern station, it intensified the audio signal in the cockpit, alerting the pilots to the fact that they were directly over London, at which point they dropped their payload, defeating the blackout, causing billions of dollars in damages, and taking an even higher toll in the loss of human life. This practice went unabated for a period of several weeks, while the Allied forces worked furiously to devise a counter-strategy.

Working closely with the French Underground, the Allies were able to locate the two radar stations, gather sufficient intelligence, and make an informed decision on which of the radar stations to destroy. Both of the radar stations were heavily fortified, well guarded, and seemingly impregnable, since the Germans had overrun the area and could not be attacked by air, land, or sea. The Allies simply could not stand by while one of the greatest cities in Western civilization was obliterated bit by bit, and it became equally important to eliminate one of the radar stations in order to adequately prepare for D-Day in 1944.

Not surprisingly, Jim Gabriel's unit, the 408th Demolition Detachment, was selected for the critical objective of destroying one of the two radar stations and preventing the Germans from pinpointing their bombing targets by following the signals as they converged. At the same time, Allied forces were developing the technology to alter the two signals, impart inaccurate data to the German bombers, and redirect their bombs so that they fell harmlessly into the English Channel; but at that critical juncture when the technology was still weeks away from being ready, it became imperative for the 408th to intercede. In addition to the destruction caused by the increased accuracy of the German bombing, the two radar stations enabled the Germans to detect American and British aircraft as it flew over the English Channel. This additional capability provided the Germans with a reliable method of deploying its anti-aircraft artillery during a period in which the two radar stations searched the skies over the entire area and furnished data to four German battalions, each of which consisted of four batteries. In turn, each battery possessed four anti-aircraft guns that were the finest in the world – 88 millimeter weapons that employed state-of-the-art technology – thereby providing the Germans with a total of 64 anti-aircraft weapons in the region. These advantages enabled the enemy to control the skies over the English Channel and enjoy air supremacy.

By the latter stages of World War II, the 408th had successfully executed approximately 35-40 missions all over Europe. More than ever before, they had shown themselves to be a confident, highly skilled group of demolition experts that could anticipate one another's movements, synchronize their activities down to the millisecond, and overcome nearly impossible logistical impediments to reach their military objectives. Now that Jim's heroism had enabled them to avoid their only mishap in the battle over the German pillbox approximately 18 months before, the harmony that they had achieved as a group of men working together for a single purpose had become almost legendary; but to a man, they each realized that the radar station represented the ultimate test of their daring, their courage, and their proficiency.

The radar station that the 408th selected was located along the English Channel in one of the many rural villages in Southwestern France. The 408th knew that they would be able to fly into the area under the German radar and use their Ranger training to parachute into a field that adjoined a wooded area. They also knew that prior to the hostilities, the French had recognized the strategic importance of an abandoned chemical plant at that location. For that reason, the French Army dug an underground tunnel that extended from a location fifty yards into the woods to the very edge of a sewer that had previously carried non-polluting water from the chemical plant to the English Channel. The Germans were unaware of this tunnel.

Although the various components of the compound were necessarily crude – owing to the deprivations of war and its own remote location – the compound was extremely ingenious, and its various components made it seem as though it were a world unto itself. Bordered by the English Channel on the West, the aforementioned wooded area on the South, and the French countryside on the North and East, the chemical plant had been converted into a barracks, a courtyard, and a radar room that housed the electronic equipment that produced the signals that proved so deadly for the population of London. The radar room was adjoined by 20-foot high walls, which were of the same height as the radar room and the barracks themselves; and two German sentries patrolled the roofs of the radar room and the barracks while two soldiers manning Quad 50 machine guns on adjacent walls fortified the station as well. These four positions were manned around the clock in rotating shifts.

As in so many of their previous missions, the ultimate success of the 408th depended upon its ability to eliminate these soldiers without their firing a shot, because the minute a shot rang out the entire barracks would be emptied of German soldiers, the 408th would be outnumbered, and the mission would be a failure. Therefore, the responsibility to eliminate the guards fell to the two knife throwers, Jim Gabriel and Tom Young.

Before Jim and his partner could accomplish their objective, however, a plan had to be devised for the deployment of the other men. Two of them intended to use pre-fabricated materials to barricade two of the doors of the barracks. Two others were charged with the responsibility of climbing a set of stairs and taking out the Quad 50 machine gunners with garrotes. Still another pair – the CWO and the Master Sergeant - intended to place timed explosives on each door of the radar room, destroy the doors, gain access to the interior, and place explosives on all of cabinets that housed electronic equipment. The remaining three members of the 408th would place explosives in the abandoned sewer. Each of the members of the 11-man detachment had a series of tasks to perform for essentially the same purpose: preventing the Germans from realizing that their radar station was being attacked.

As in most military operations, the mission depended upon the ability of the 408th to identify a lapse in judgment by the enemy; but for the longest time an appropriate strategy eluded them. For days, the leadership of the 408th pored over the information they were receiving from the French Underground, proposing and rejecting one strategy after another as they waited for the one piece of information that would provide a breakthrough for them. While they deliberated, they were pressured by the fact that the City of London was being systematically destroyed by the German bombers who relied so confidently on the radar signal being produced by that crucial facility. Eventually, the break they were waiting for occurred when members of the French Underground discovered that the German Commander in charge of the radar station had an inordinate fondness for roses, and that he maintained a small garden in the courtyard that separated the barracks from the radar room. The potentially fatal mistake that the Germans made lay in the fact that they did not believe that their enemies could gain access to the courtyard through the manhole at the end of the sewer. Over the years, a good deal of corrosion had developed, sealing the manhole cover to the lip of the sewer line. The Germans had been lured into a false sense of security by the corrosion, and by the fact that the manhole lay beneath twelve or thirteen inches of topsoil. Therefore, they reasoned, it would be impossible to open.

Similarly, the Germans were confident that the opposite end of the sewer was impregnable as well, since they had welded a huge iron grate at the precise spot where the sewer emerged from the jagged cliffs overlooking the English Channel. At the time of this critical mission, they had no idea that a highly trained demolition unit was operating in their vicinity, and that their radar station had been targeted for destruction. Nor were they aware that the French Underground had equipped the 408th with blowtorches to remove the layers of rust and with a means of raising the lid of the manhole cover. Thus, the Commander's beloved rose garden led to a fatal lapse in judgment that enabled the 408th to gain access to the radar station.

This operation was deliberately planned so that the German sentries and machine gunners would be at the very end of their shift. In that way, they would be far less alert and more susceptible to errors. By 1:45 a.m. on a March night in 1944, the 408th had successfully parachuted into the area, made their way through the forest, and entered the man-made, underground tunnel, fully aware that the French Underground had already broken the cast concrete of the sewer pipe with sledgehammers, enabling them to make their way through the tunnel, pass through the sewer, climb an iron ladder, and lift the manhole cover from below. Making their way through the manhole and into the Commander's garden, the members of the 408th assumed their positions.

As Jim and Tom removed their knives from the worn leather cases that held them, they reviewed the plan of attack one final time in the privacy of their own thoughts. To that point, everything had gone as planned. But when Jim broke the silence by whistling shrilly to attract the attention of the two German sentries, causing them to turn toward the source of the sound and give the two knife throwers a clear shot at their throats, which in turn would enable them to hurl their knives and kill them before they could utter a sound and alert the Germans sleeping in the barracks below, something unexpected happened. As the sentries turned toward them, Jim hurled his knife and accomplished the first of their objectives, causing his target to succumb to a gaping wound in his throat, a look of horror crossing the man's features in the split second before he died, making only a soft gurgling sound as he perished. At the same time, however, Tom locked onto his own target and discovered to his horror that he was about to kill a young boy. By that late stage of the war, the Germans had suffered enough attrition in their ranks as to force them to turn to 15 and 16 year olds as fighting men; and it was Tom's destiny to be assigned to one of them. "He's just a kid!" Tom thought, hesitating just enough to give the young man a chance to notice the CWO and Master Sergeant approaching the doors of the radar room. Despite all of his training and previous success, Tom was unable to cross the threshold into taking a boy's life, and in less than five seconds, the young sentry unleashed a torrent of bullets and killed the CWO and Master Sergeant, until Jim hurled his knife and ripped open the young sentry's throat. Realizing what had happened – and that Tom was in a state of shock - Jim directed the two men who had barricaded the doors of the barracks to transport the two limp bodies and lead Tom down into the manhole and make their way toward the tunnel. Simultaneously, the two men with garrotes eliminated the German machine gunners.

Now, as the Germans began to stir in their barracks – awakened by the sound of machine gun fire – Jim directed the men with garrotes to take over the Quad 50 machine guns and eliminate the Germans as they exited by the side doors of the barracks. The side doors were not barricaded in the original plan because that would not have been necessary if Tom had eliminated the young sentry and prevented machine gun fire.

Recalling the intelligence provided by the French Underground, Jim knew that there was a trap door on the roof of the radar room that enabled the radar technicians to make repairs on the antennas. In quick succession, he recovered one of the satchels of explosives that had been left behind by the CWO and Master Sergeant, hurried up the stairs to the roof, and destroyed the trap door. Then he set the timer on one of the explosives for ten seconds, returned it to the satchel, and dropped the entire satchel into the radar room, giving himself and the two machine gunners enough time to clear that area. Jim immediately ordered the two machine gunners to climb down steps and run to the manhole while he provided cover for them with the machine gun of the man he had killed with his knife.

With German soldiers pouring onto the roof of the barracks and closing in on Jim, he used his athleticism to leap from the roof of the radar room and land safely on the ground. Recovering the remaining satchel, he set a timer on one of the explosives, returned it to the satchel, and on his way to the manhole threw the entire satchel onto the roof of the barracks, not only to impede the progress of the German soldiers approaching from the back of the barracks but to blow a hole in the roof, hoping that the barracks would catch on fire. As he threw the satchel onto the roof of the barracks, the radar room detonated and all of its equipment was destroyed. Just before Jim reached the manhole, one of the German soldiers fired his weapon, sending a bullet into Jim's left shoulder. Thankfully, this was not the shoulder of his throwing arm and he would maintain the ability to throw knives.

As Jim rejoined the other members of the 408th in the sewer, they began to make their way to the tunnel that led to the woods, blowing up sections of the sewer behind them and preventing the Germans from pursuing them from that direction. Once they left the sewer and entered the tunnel, they destroyed the section of the sewer that led to the English Channel, robbing the Germans of their only other means of pursuit. One by one, the timed detonations exploded, enabling the remaining members of the 408th to safely retreat through the tunnel.

While the other members of the 408th made their way through the tunnel to safety, Jim directed two men from the French Underground to remove the dead bodies of the CWO and Master Sergeant from the tunnel and turn them over to the American authorities. Like the Marines, the elite 408th Demolition Detachment not only removed their wounded from the battlefield, but they also removed their dead.

As planned, the surviving members of the 408th climbed through the tunnel into the dense foliage of the wooded area to the South. After running for a quarter of a mile, they were met by a German personnel carrier that had been provided by the French Underground. Within minutes, this vehicle conveyed them to the nearest farm. Hiding in a barn along with the personnel carrier, they changed into German uniforms and applied bandages to Jim's bleeding shoulder. In donning the German uniforms, they were keenly aware that they were taking one of the ultimate wartime risks and that they could have been executed as spies if they had fallen into enemy hands.

With the two German-speaking members of the 408th doing their talking for them, the men were able to reach a second location fifteen miles away, where they expected to be picked up by an airplane that would fly them back to England. Although they had been able to destroy the radar station and the barracks, they were far less fortunate when they reached the next pickup point, when the plane that was supposed to pick them up failed to do so. The contingency plan was for them to make their way to a small French town 25 miles away, and while they were in route Tom continually expressed regret for what had happened. "He was just a kid, Jim... How can you kill a kid?" And when Jim attempted to comfort him, Tom took on a haunted expression and said, "Ray and Warren are dead. You're shoulder's all shot up. Look what I've done." From that moment on, Jim became concerned with Tom's well-being.

Eventually the men found temporary lodging in a barn operated by French farmers and removed the German uniforms; but despite the fact that he had salvaged a mission that had gone horribly wrong, accomplished his primary objective of destroying the radar station, and led his men to safety, Jim confronted another important challenge. Looking in Tom Young's eyes – a man who had become like a brother to him – it was readily apparent that Tom was distraught over his failure to eliminate the young sentry, and that he was tortured by the fact that the failure had directly led to the deaths of their CWO and Master Sergeant. Fearing the worst, Jim gathered the others around him and said, "Whatever you do, do not let him have a weapon." The implication was clear to all of them - Jim strongly suspected that Tom would attempt to take his own life.

By that point, most of the remaining members of the 408th made their way to the closest town in order to unwind from the harrowing experience of the radar station, and to find whatever means they could to recover from their close encounter with death. Jim, however, was too badly injured to accompany them, and went off in search of a doctor, eager to receive treatment for the bullet that had pierced his shoulder. One of the other men remained at the barn, and Jim took him aside and specifically instructed him to keep an eye on Tom at all times.

The French Underground furnished them with a Jeep that carried them to the town, and while the others found their way to a modest little restaurant, Jim obtained medical treatment from an elderly physician whose methods and equipment were lacking. Still, the man did what he could for Jim and sent him on his way.

When Jim rejoined the others at the restaurant, he was shocked to see the man who was supposed to monitor Tom Young, and Jim immediately tore into him for disobeying his order. The man attempted to defend himself by saying that Tom was "sleeping like a baby," but Jim would have none of it, and he let the soldier know in no uncertain terms that he would deal with him later. After commandeering the Jeep and speeding back to the barn, Jim found his friend hanging from the rafters, his limp body already growing cold. As he stared at the awful sight of Tom's body, all of the emotion that he had been keeping inside him since the mission had first gone astray began to pour out, and he began to sob heavily as he cut the rope and gently cradled his friend in his arms. Pulling himself together, he took off in the Jeep again, located the Mayor of the town, and found his way to the St. Francis of Assisi Church, where he persuaded the Pastor to perform a Requiem Mass and bury Tom's body in the church cemetery. Once the Pastor agreed to do that, Jim made the necessary arrangements with a local undertaker. Somehow, Jim knew that this was the only way that he could live with himself after leaving Tom to obtain treatment for his shoulder.

Now that three of the 11 members of the 408th were dead, the detachment was disbanded and they were flown back to England, where Jim turned over nearly all of Tom's personal possessions to the authorities. The only items he withheld were a packet of letters from

Tom's fiancé, Lora, and a letter that Tom had written to Lora but never mailed. Jim swore that he would return them to her personally.

After several days in England, Jim returned to the United States for additional treatment on his shoulder, and he was eventually awarded a Medal of Honor, the Croix de Guerre, and his third Purple Heart for his heroic effort to deprive the Germans of the radar station. He was a decorated war hero, but the taste of death stayed with him; and for a long time, his sleep was interrupted by images of death on both sides – the friends that he had made and lost, and the enemies that he had killed. In the end, the battle over the radar station had lasted for less than five minutes, but those five minutes had effectively ended Tom's life and altered Jim's forever.

Chapter Four

Even though Jim had returned from war a decorated hero – having received the Medal of Honor, a Silver Star, Purple Heart, Croix de Guerre, and the British Victoria Cross for his bravery – nothing could have prepared him for the pain he had felt when he returned home and saw Anna and Dante together, married, and obviously, very much in love. They stood there, among the crowd, arms intertwined, anxious to welcome him home, for although they had betrayed Jim, they still longed for his forgiveness and friendship.

Jim had not reached a point in his life where he felt he could forgive them, so he greeted them with a hurried hello, and rushed through the crowd to get to his mother. Kate was the one that had kept him focused all through the war, and the pride that had shown brightly in her eyes was enough for him to forget briefly about Dante and Anna.

The years had been difficult for Kate, Jim knew. She had been lonely without him there, and now that he was home, Jim vowed to make her happy. She tried to talk lightly of Anna and Dante, to tell Jim that she was never the right one for him, but that didn't ease the pain he had felt. He had lost his girlfriend and his best friend too. Jim didn't know who was to blame more – her for being weak, or Dante for going after his girl. The betrayal that Jim felt was such that he doubted he would ever be able to speak to them again.

He found solace in attending daily Mass with his mother. After receiving Anna's letter, it was Jim's faith in God that carried him through the war, and that faith had brought him safely home. He felt closer to the Lord now than he ever had, and having lost Anna, he felt that maybe it had been a sign, some sort of calling. Jim spent hours at St. Dominic's attending church, praying, volunteering in any capacity, and had made his decision, one that he was sure would please his mother.

"Mom," he called, closing the front door behind him.

"What is it, dear," Kate emerged from the kitchen, wiping her hands on the front of her apron.

"I need to talk to you about something," he smiled and led her into the living room.

"I hope this is important, dinner's not going to cook itself, you know," she laughed.

"It is, it is," he promised and they sat side by side on the faded sofa.

"Mom, what is the one thing in the world that would make you proud of me?"

"Don't be silly, Jim. I have always been proud of you. You're a war hero and you've sacrificed so much for our country, there is nothing else. That is enough."

"I know, I know. But if I could be anything in the world, what is it you would want me to be?"

"Jim, the potatoes are probably boiling over in there. What is this all about? Don't you know that as long as you're happy, I'm happy?" She sighed at him, exasperated.

"Okay, okay. Well, since you're not playing along, I'll just come out and tell you."

Jim grinned at his mother, still baiting her by pausing again before speaking.

"I have decided to join the seminary."

"Oh, Jim!" she exclaimed. "That's wonderful news! But are you positive this is what you want to do?"

Looking away from her, he said, "Yes, I'm pretty sure. It feels right, I guess. Besides, what girl would marry me?"

"Jim!" Kate looked shocked.

"Just kidding Ma," Jim assured her and hugged her tightly.

"Just when I think I couldn't possibly be any prouder of you, you go ahead and prove me wrong," Kate smiled.

And so, James Gabriel enrolled at St. Charles Seminary, with his mother's blessing, and began his life as a seminarian.

There are two tragedies in life. One is to lose your heart's desire.
The other is to gain it. —George Bernard Shaw

Chapter Five
1949

It was a sweltering Monday July morning as Jennifer Whalen stepped off the rattling steel steps of the large gray bus that had brought her back to the town where she had grown up. It had been a long trip. From the Sisters of Good Works Convent she had taken a train into Holmesburg where she then picked up the bus that would take her to her street. The overpowering stench of diesel exhaust mingled with a heat so thick she could barely breathe as she made her way off the noisy bus. For a moment she thought she might be ill as she placed one foot shakily on the sidewalk. Her body was slender, and a belt around her waist defined its smallness. Knees wobbling, she quickly regained her composure as the wretched bus pulled itself back into oncoming traffic. Little beads of perspiration were forming on her delicate forehead, threatening to roll into deep brown eyes flecked and ringed with gold. She ran her slender fingers through her thick chestnut colored hair, picked up her small floral suitcase and began walking toward home.

Some home, she thought to herself with a small sigh. When her parents had died when she was just twelve years old, her aunt and uncle had taken her in, and while they hadn't been very happy about it, they did the best they could to raise her. And with no children of their own, they had been very content with their lives the way they were before she came to disrupt their egocentric existence, and it hadn't been the happiest of childhoods.

"But I have to see them off to California, I owe them that much," she mumbled as she huffed her way down Frankford Avenue. If only the Mother Superior had not granted me leave from the convent, Jennie thought, I wouldn't have to be here at all. She really would rather be at the convent, helping adoptive parents find children of their own; children they were desperate to have and love. Jennie loved the fact that The Sisters of Good Works Convent had an adoption program, and working with the families always brought her great joy.

When Jennie finally reached the modest white-shingled home of her aunt and uncle, she opened the door, which was always unlocked, and yelled, "Hello, is anybody home? Aunt Madgie, are you here?" She was grateful for the coolness of the old house; she felt sticky and dirty from the trip.

"Jennie? Come in the parlor, I've been waiting for you to get here!" Madge drawled. Jennie immediately knew that her aunt had been drinking and prepared for a confrontation.

"Dearest, where in God's name have you been?" Madge asked.

Jennie cringed. She hated when her aunt was drunk and she especially didn't like the fact that she was taking God's name in vain. Madge ambled down the dimly lit hallway towards her, wiry gray hair sprouting out of her bobbing head, and reached out to Jennie for a hug.

Jennie stiffened as she hugged her aunt back and managed to greet her. "It's good to see you, Aunt Madgie."

"I'm sure it is," her aunt replied snidely.

"Come on now, Aunt Madgie, I'm happy to be here to help with the packing and I really did want to see you and Uncle Hank off to California. It's going to be an exciting venture for the both of you."

Jennie was trying to be strong. Growing up in a household with alcoholic guardians had not been an easy life. Now, at age twenty-four, Jennie was finding her inner strength to overcome feelings of bitterness at a less than memorable childhood.

Suddenly, Aunt Madge slumped against the wall and began to cry. She smelled of alcohol and was in need of a shower. Jennie placed her arms on her aunt's shoulders and attempted a smile.

"I am sorry Aunt Madgie, I didn't mean to upset you. Please stop crying. I thought you wanted to move to California. Think about the palm trees and the ocean. It will be so beautiful. You're going to love it. Please stop crying." Jennie cradled the shaking woman in her arms. From her position she could not see much of the house, yet her dark eyes tried to make out some sign of her uncle.

"Where's Uncle Hank? Shouldn't he be packing?"

"He hurt his back and went into town to see the doctor about getting a prescription," Madge replied.

"Okay, let me help you up and we'll get you cleaned up. Then you can tell me where you'd like me to start. I'm sure there are some things in my old room I could pack up."

Madge rose from the floor and took a few tentative steps forward as if she were not an adult at all, but rather a small child taking her first wobbly steps on unsure ground.

She stuttered as she spoke. "J-Jennie, I am so tired, dear. I have been trying to pack this old house up, and with Uncle Hank's back not right, it's just been really difficult to get much done around here."

Without a word Jennie helped her aunt up the creaky stairs and brought her to her bed. Once she was lying comfortably on the quilt, Jennie hurriedly closed the small bedroom door behind her. She placed her suitcase in her old, dusty bedroom and walked out of the house toward the cemetery. She had something important to do.

The war had turned Jim into a man, seminary school was molding him into a man of God, and summers digging graves at St. Dominic's were making him a sensitive and stronger man. This was his fourth summer working for Neil Shaunessay at the cemetery, and Neil had come to depend on Jim's strength, humor and friendship.

Jim wiped a dirty palm across his dripping forehead. He could not remember a hotter day than this. He stood next to the large hole he had just dug, with one hand resting on the wooden handle of the shovel that had carved out the great empty mass. Although he was covered in dirt and grime, he was a strikingly handsome man of twenty-six. The war had turned his adolescent body into that of a man's, and digging graves at St. Dominic's Cemetery each summer had kept him firm and strong. He had let his hair grow longer than the seminary would have preferred during the summer and the curls captured the sun's light and glistened from sweat. The expression on his face – even though he was dreadfully hot and tired – made him look as though he were smiling. His once white tee shirt was soaked through and filthy; dirty green khakis and work boots completed his outfit.

"Hey, where you guys going?" Jim let the shovel fall to the ground as he called to his friends. "It's not time for a break yet, is it?"

His friend and fellow seminarian, Mike Donaldson, was headed toward the entrance. Mike was grateful to Jim for getting him a job at the cemetery and had spent the last three summers digging graves and mowing grass alongside his buddy.

"We're taking our break now Jim. It's too hot. Come on up with us. We're going to Paul's Pantry for a cold soda," Mike shouted from where he was walking, his small but sturdy frame outlined against the clear backdrop of the sky.

"Nah, you guys go on. I'm almost done with this grave!" Jim hollered as Mike and another cemetery worker continued on. "But bring me back a Pepsi!"

Jim really wanted to get the grave completed, so despite the sweltering sun and his parched throat, he continued digging. Usually he would have a digging partner, but one of the guys had called in sick today so he was on his own. Neil had mentioned that this particular plot would need to be done by tomorrow and Jim had never let Neil down. And he wouldn't do so today, just because he was short some help.

The cemetery was situated directly behind St. Dominic's Church. Of Gothic design, the stately church served as the pinnacle of holiness with its splendid vaults, majestic stained glass dome that connected to two stone flying buttresses flanking either side of regal steeples that seemed to stretch beyond the Heavens. St. Dominic's Elementary School, Rectory and Convent completed the square. Jim knew every part of the compound since he had spent his childhood attending school and church here. This was home to him, and he was comfortable at St. Dominic's. He even hoped to be able to return after he completed seminary school and lead his childhood congregation in worship. This would be another dream come true for his mother. How perfect would it be for Jim to not only become a priest - which was his mother's heart's desire - but to also be able to say Mass and distribute the body and blood of Christ to her each Sunday in the church he had been raised in.

His tired muscles ached as he worked up the energy to lift himself out of the great pit he had been digging. He sat on the edge and told himself to take a break, go meet his friends for a cold drink. The graveyard appeared to be deserted, but as Jim looked out across the tombstones, he noticed he was not actually alone.

There was a woman kneeling at a double gravesite down near the old freight train tracks. Because Jim was behind an immense pile of fresh dirt, there was no way the woman could see him, and she probably thought she was alone. Jim continued to stare at her, and wondered whose grave she was visiting. He often thought about the people he saw at the cemetery—were they visiting relatives, a spouse, a child or a friend. Although a cemetery was a place of great sadness because of the loss of life, Jim always felt a sense of comfort being there, and hoped others felt the same way.

Jim brushed some of the dirt off his pants and decided to go ahead and meet his friends. He headed to the maintenance shed, feeling like an intruder because to get there, he would have to pass the woman, who was clearly grieving privately. When he got closer, he noticed the woman was kneeling and sobbing softly, and that she was perhaps the most beautiful woman he had ever laid eyes on. He didn't feel right just walking past ignoring her, but also didn't know what to say to her. He immediately felt the need to offer some words of comfort.

As he approached, she seemed to sense his presence, cleared her throat and wiped her eyes. She was a slender woman, with silky flowing hair, the color of warm cinnamon. He imagined her hair smelled that way too, and immediately felt guilty for having such a thought about a woman he had just seen from a distance.

She wore a pink cotton dress with satin-covered buttons running from her neck to the hemline. Jim could not yet see her face, as she had turned her head and was trying to pull herself together, having realized company was approaching. When she finally looked up, Jim's mind reeled at how beautiful she really was.

Jim spoke first. "Sorry ma'am. I had to pass by to get to the shed. I'm terribly sorry to interrupt." He could feel his cheeks grow warm and he didn't know if he should continue toward the shed. What he really wanted to do was scoop her up and make things okay for her, which was the craziest thought he ever had, but the urge to comfort her was incredibly strong.

"It's alright," she sniffled. "I think I was done talking to them anyway." She made an attempt to smile, and Jim noticed how white and perfect her teeth were.

"If you don't mind me asking…"

Before Jim could finish, the woman said, "They're my parents."

"You miss them?" Jim wished he could take back the words as soon as he said it. Of course she missed her parents. He was not thinking clearly and quickly decided to move the conversation into another direction.

"I'm sorry, how rude of me. My name is Jim. Jim Gabriel." He stuck out his hand to offer it to her and wondered how her smooth skin would feel enclosed in his hand.

"I'm Jennie Whalen." And she offered her hand to him in a warm and familiar handshake that struck them both. Then Jim realized that his own hand was still covered in dirt. He grinned up at Jennie when he saw that she was in no rush to remove her hand from his, and when he finally broke the contact, he offered his handkerchief so that she could wipe her hand off. She took it and held it to the tears that were still wet on her face.

"Would you like to wash your hands and face? There is a fresh water spring nearby."

Jennie was confused. This handsome stranger had just appeared at her parent's graves, had seen her cry, and now wanted to help her clean up. She knew she should be humiliated, but she was not, and although she had always been warned of strangers, she felt inexplicably drawn to this kind man. He was filthy from head to toe, and still she found she could not turn away from his startlingly blue eyes.

He smiled at her and said, "I've got a break coming anyway. That is, if you could use company for a bit?"

Jennie giggled, a shy, schoolgirl type of laugh, "I really should fix myself up. I must look a horrible mess. This happens every time I come to visit their graves."

Jim and Jennie began walking out of the cemetery and Jim asked, "So, Jennie Whalen, do you live around here?"

"Yes and no. Right now I live in the next town over, but my aunt and uncle live near here."

She didn't know why she didn't say she lived in the convent. She supposed it was because she was lonely and he was friendly, not to mention extremely handsome.

They continued talking as they walked to the far left of the cemetery, where Jim knew of an opening in the brush where they could slide through to the back of Pennypack Park.

"Once we go through these bushes there will be a path that will take us down to the creek," he told her. Sensing some hesitation he quickly added, "If you don't want to go I understand. I just thought you might like to feel some cold water on your face."

"Oh no, it is not that. I never knew there was a way to get through to the park from here," she ducked to keep from hitting her head on the branches of the overgrown shrubs.

"Well, here we are," Jim motioned to the pathway ahead of him. About a dozen birds were lined up on the train trestle overhead. They seemed delighted that they had the best view in the park. The sound of children's laughter wafted through the thick, hot air. Just below the trestle a modest waterfall spilled down into the creek. Honeysuckle, the color of butter, surrounded its opening and seemed to dangle serenely over the edge.

"The water looks so beautiful, the way the sun seems to glisten on the ripples. I had forgotten how pretty this place was," Jennie said.

"Do you smell that?" Jim asked.

Jennie shook her head and inhaled deeply. "It smells like roasted peanuts to me."

"Yep, it smells like peanuts, definitely. Maybe someone is selling them," Jim answered. "Follow me, the spring is not far from here. We just have to follow this path," he spoke quietly, not wanting to disturb the serenity of the park.

They came to the fresh water spring, which rushed out of the side of the hill through a metal pipe. It was cold and clear as ice, and Jim took Jennie's hands in his and showed her how to cup her hands to catch the water in them. When his own rough fingertips touched her tender ones, a shock as strong as a lightning bolt coursed through him. Surprised, his head flew up and he found himself peering into her sparkling brown-gold eyes. Once again, he felt a large knot form in his throat.

Jennie saw the strange look on Jim's face and quickly pulled her hands away. "Is something wrong?"

"Uh, no. Nothing is the matter. I'm sorry. I don't know where my mind is today. Must be the heat. Anyway, go ahead and get some more water," he stammered. He did not know what was wrong with him. These were not normal feelings for a seminarian to have.

Once again, Jennie placed her palms under the pipe. "The water feels so wonderful. I had no idea this was here." Her voice was slightly muffled as she splashed some on her face. "Much better. It's so hot out, that spring is a lifesaver. Thank you for bringing me here, I really appreciate your kindness. I was having a bad day."

She knew she should probably leave now, but she didn't want to. She was drawn to this handsome and kind-hearted man and wanted to know more about him. Jim also wanted to know more about this Jennie Whalen, and about her parents who were buried in the cemetery.

"I don't mean to pry, and you can tell me to mind my own business, but I've never seen you visit the cemetery before." He saw a shadow fall over her delicate features and wished he hadn't said anything. It was something that had obviously upset her.

"Look, I am sorry. Sometimes my mouth just…"

"No, don't be sorry. You just surprised me. It is not often I get to talk about my parents. You seem to be a nice enough man, and maybe it would be nice to share them with someone. When I was younger, we lived not far from here, over on Canal Street. In fact, we used to come to this very park and would have so much fun together. My dad loved baseball. We would bring our mitts and throw a ball for hours while my mother sat and laughed with us under our favorite cherry tree, here in this very park. In the winter, we would come down to the creek with our ice skates. You know how the water gets. It freezes up, smooth as ice, hard as a rock. The three of us would hold each other's hands tightly as we glided by crystal trees that shimmered with icicles. Back then, I would imagine the whole park was an ice castle and I was the ice princess whirling around the creek. Mom was an excellent skater and she taught me how to skate when I was very young. I remember feeling so safe when my parents would snuggle me between them and hold me up until I could do it myself. I was never afraid, because I knew they would never let me fall. I haven't felt that safe since," Jennie stopped suddenly, and looked at Jim, her cheeks growing warm. "I'm sorry to be rambling. Let's talk about something else."

"No, no. Please go on. Your mother and father seemed like wonderful people. I like hearing about them." He was truly interested and couldn't get enough of the sound of her voice. So sweet and lilting, he thought he could listen to her talk for hours.

"When I was twelve we were coming home from a Phillies game, driving on Delaware Avenue. My mom and dad were in the front of our new black Chevy, and I was in the back seat playing with the baseball I had caught at the game. There were very few cars on the road, mostly trucks. A big flatbed truck loaded with neatly layered steel pipe pulled along side of our car. I was just about to ask my father where would they use all those pipes when the truck started to pick up speed and it raced by us. I sat up straight in my seat as it whizzed by, and then it switched lanes so that it was directly in front of our car. The next thing I knew, one of the steel pipes slid from the top of the stack and crashed through the front of our car. I thought the whole world was exploding because there was so much noise. The next thing I remember was waking up in a hospital with a nurse by my side. After my parents died, I was left in my aunt and uncle's care." Jennie sighed heavily, and Jim realized the story had been difficult for Jennie to tell.

"I don't know what to say," Jim lightly touched her hand. "I am really sorry…"

Jennie didn't let him finish. She pulled her hand away from his touch as if he had burned her flesh, and not just touched her gently with concern.

"I have to go now," she said, the tone of her voice suddenly changing, as if she had revealed more than she had wanted to. She stood up to leave.

Awkwardly, Jim rose from the rock as well and said, "It was a pleasure meeting you Jennie. I hope I didn't upset you. There's a short cut out of here that will take you to the street if you don't want to go back through the cemetery."

"Oh, well it really doesn't matter. Which way should I go?" It was obvious she was in a hurry to leave.

"See that large oak over there," he said, and pointed to a towering tree. "Right next to it is a bridal path which will lead you out of here. Not many people know the path," Jim confided. "It was very nice meeting you, Miss Jennifer Whalen. I hope to see you again."

"It was nice meeting you too, Jim." With that, Jennie turned and quickly walked toward the path.

Jim watched her leave, not taking his eyes off her. When he could no longer see her, he turned to walk back through the clearing toward the cemetery. Break time had been over for a while now.

"Geeze, you just getting back *now*? Where have you been?" Mike asked. "We thought you went home for the day. I knew you couldn't handle all this good hard work for long," Mike teased.

"Oh, I just went for a walk in the park," Jim responded cautiously. "I was hot and went to cool off by the spring." He didn't mention meeting Jennie. There was no need for Mike to know of her. After all, Jim was studying to be a priest and what would Mike think of him spending time with a girl down by the spring?

"What have you bums been doing? From the looks of it, not digging much!" Jim pointed at the hole in the ground. "You call that a grave? Go take a look at the one I'm digging for old Mr. Anderson. Now there's a hole, boys." He laughed as he walked away from the men.

For the rest of the afternoon he continued digging the grave for Mr. Anderson's funeral. Mr. Anderson had led a long life, and had died in his sleep. Jim took solace in knowing that Mr. Anderson would finally rest with his wife beside him.

As Jim continued digging, his mind wandered back to his meeting with Jennie. It was not every day that he met a beautiful and captivating woman. He kept repeating her name in his mind, under his breath. By the end of his shift he was wondering if he would ever see her again. His reasoning mind wished he never would, but something deeper inside him had a different and disturbing wish. He was disturbed because he was a seminarian! He should not be having these ridiculous thoughts and pushed them from his mind when he walked home for dinner.

Jim rose for six-thirty Mass Tuesday morning a little more eagerly than usual. He wanted to pray and ask for God to forgive him for his unholy thoughts. If he was ever going to be a truly holy priest he must live by God's will, among which was chastity. He had been fairly certain over the past few years of training that he could live up to all of his duties, now he wanted nothing more than to go to St. Dominic's and hear God's word.

He arrived early and observed the eerie stillness of the great place and remembered what it felt like to help serve Mass as an altar boy. Soon he would be standing up there on that altar, his parish hanging on his every word. It would be wonderful, if only he could rid himself of the doubts that crept uninvited into his head.

Slowly, the church began to fill. Some fellow seminarians arrived, dressed in their religious garb. Mrs. Carlson, who never missed the early Mass, came hobbling in leaning on her cane for support. Mr. Richards, newly widowed, arrived next and sat near an elderly man Jim didn't recognize. All the nuns from St. Dominic's Convent filed in and sat in the right side front pews. Late as usual, Mike slid into the front row pew beside Jim. Jim always teased Mike saying that when he became a priest he would probably be late for his own Mass!

"Hey Jim, how are you?" Mike asked.

"Good, just a little sore from yesterday," Jim rubbed his arm for effect.

"What's the matter? Cemetery work too hard for you?" taunted Mike.

"You're one to talk! Last week you were crying like a baby!"

"I had two graves to back fill that day, with no help from you I might add."

They laughed good-naturedly. Their laughter echoed off the walls portraying the Stations of the Cross, and a few people turned to look in their direction. From the front pew, some of the novices from the local convent glared at them.

Throughout Mass, Jim focused on the word of God and concentrated especially during the Consecration, where the bread and wine were changed into the body and blood of Jesus Christ. Holy Communion would be distributed soon and Jim always looked forward to the closeness he felt to Jesus during the distribution of the body and blood of Christ.

Jim watched the nuns file out of their pews as they went to receive Communion. They lowered their veils as they walked to the front altar rail. When the priest came to distribute the host, each nun would raise her veil, accept the wafer on her tongue, lower her veil, make the sign of the cross and return to their seat.

When Mass was over, Jim felt cleaner, purer, holier somehow. His mind was clear.

Mike tapped his shoe on the floor and said, "Hey Jim, let's go."

"Go ahead without me. I'll see you at work later." Jim was still feeling the closeness of God and remembered why he was taking this vow to become a priest. He wanted to stay in church a while longer.

"All right. See you later." Mike was already making his way out of the pew.

St. Dominic's was almost empty. A few people lingered, kneeling in prayer or lighting a candle near the Blessed Virgin Mary. Jim knelt and prayed to God that he would be filled with the Holy Spirit all of the time and not just sometimes. He knew he would never be a great priest unless this was to occur, however difficult it would be. The Rector at the seminary was always telling them to look into the depths of their very souls to make absolutely sure their calling was true. He often pointed out that not every seminarian had a true vocation, that some would not be ordained into the priesthood. It was through these formative years at the seminary that the seminarians, with the help of the faculty and God, would discover if they were indeed chosen to live their lives in the clergy.

There were times he wondered if this was his calling, as he had seen quite a few seminarians drop out. Some were married now, and some even had children. When he asked them how they *knew* this was not how they were supposed to live their lives, they all gave him similar answers. One of the men who had decided to give up his calling into the priesthood was Joel David. He had told Jim, "My life with the church is extremely important to me, to my very existence. I found myself questioning the vows I would have to take, and found that I was not completely sure that it was how God wanted me to serve Him. Also, I had very strong desires towards the opposite sex, and it saddened me to think I could never be fulfilled in that way – marriage, children, and a family of my own. The more I prayed for an answer, the clearer it became, so I left."

Jim had been appreciative of his friend's candor. He too, had very similar thoughts, but had not yet reached a crucial decision to leave the seminary. He continued to pray in search of the answers God could lead him to.

Jim had been there for a long time, deep in thought, deeper in prayer. His knees were beginning to ache from the hard wooden kneeler – the thin cushion on top was not much help in easing the tension. Jim glanced down at the watch and was surprised to see that almost an hour had passed. He rose from his position, stretched, and smiled as he breathed the stale smell of incense that lingered in the air.

As Jim bent to pick his hat up from the pew, he brushed shoulders with someone who was walking past in the aisle. As he turned to say excuse me, he realized he had just bumped into Jennie Whalen.

"Jennie!" His breath caught in his throat.

"Jim? What are you doing here?" The look on her face was one of equal surprise.

Jim was shocked to see that she was dressed similarly to the nuns that had filed into the front pew earlier for Mass. *She was a nun?* Jim's mind shouted in disbelief. Then he blurted out the question that was scorching his mind.

"Are you in a *convent*?" He slowly took in the large collared white shirt and floor-length black skirt that she was wearing. This outfit was quite different than the pink dress she had worn to the cemetery just yesterday. Why hadn't she told him she was a nun yesterday when they had met, he wondered?

Jennie looked quite surprised herself and blurted out, "You're in the seminary?" She seemed to be having trouble speaking, the look of astonishment on her face mirrored his own.

When Jim noticed that the few people left in church were staring at them, he said, "Let's go outside." He placed his hand gently on her back as they began walking down the aisle to the front doors of the church. His mind was racing.

Once outside, they stood looking at each other awkwardly. "I know I should have told you yesterday that I was in the seminary, but you just seemed so distraught and I was just so busy listening to your story. And, it never even crossed my mind that you might have been in a convent!" Jim said shocked.

"I might say the same about you! When I saw you in church with all of the other seminarians, I about fell over." She smiled shyly. Even though she thought he was attractive yesterday at the cemetery when he was filthy, she couldn't help but notice how nice he looked in his clean shirt today.

"Want to take a walk to the park? I really enjoyed talking with you yesterday," Jim asked hopefully.

"I guess that would be all right. I am sure my Mother Superior would not mind," she giggled nervously. "After all you are going to be a priest."

Jim took in the soft pink color of her cheeks and once again thought how pretty she was. "Let's take the short cut, like yesterday." He began walking and waited for Jennie to follow him but she didn't move.

"Oh, wait," Jennie said suddenly, "I have to get back to the house. Aunt Madgie really needs my help. I guess I didn't mention that I'm visiting them because they are moving to California for my Uncle Hank's job, and this is the last time I'll see them for a while, I suppose. Anyway, Uncle Hank's been having back trouble and is in no shape for packing up their belongings. Guess who got nominated to help them out?" The smile that had graced her face was replaced with a look of dismay.

Jim's face fell as well. "That's too bad. Can I at least walk you back then?"

"Well... Sure, why not." The smile returned as she answered him.

They walked in silence down the street and Jim wondered what she was thinking. She had to be as stunned as he had been. Had she felt the same strange feelings he had yesterday? He felt incredibly guilty and knew it was not right to be so consumed with thoughts of her or of any woman for that matter! The fact that she was training to become a nun made the situation even worse.

"Obviously, you are not from St. Dominic's Convent?" Jim asked in order to break the uncomfortable silence.

"I'm a novice at the Sisters of Good Works and was granted a two-week leave to visit my aunt and uncle and to help them get organized for their move... and, to say goodbye, of course."

"How much longer do you have until you become a nun, if you don't mind me asking?" Jim was afraid he was asking too many questions and that she would think he was terribly nosey. Maybe that was why she had run off after talking about her parents at the creek yesterday.

"I'm actually in my last year. I joined the convent right after high school."

Jim knew that it took seven years to become a nun so he guessed Jennie to be about twenty-four, just two years younger than he was.

Jennie interrupted his thought and asked, "How about you? Are you almost ready to take your vows?" Her eyes widened slightly.

He was suddenly uncomfortable with the subject. He did not feel right talking about his forthcoming vows so he answered quickly, "Six more years."

They continued to walk in silence, both content yet struck at the oddity of the situation.

"So, do you think things around here look different?" Jim asked.

"Actually, yes. I haven't been in St. Dominic's in a long time. It brought back memories from when I attended elementary school there."

Jim stopped in his tracks, dumbfounded at the coincidence. "You went to school at St. Dominic's? So did I!"

"You're kidding!" Jennie exclaimed. "When did you graduate from there?"

"I'm twenty-six now so I guess it was in..." Jim tried to do the math quickly in his head but Jennie interrupted.

"I'm twenty-four so I was two years behind you in school. I guess that's why we didn't know each other," Jennie said.

"Hey, do you remember old Sister Josephine? She was really a strict one, always walking around the classroom banging that ruler of hers?" Jim asked.

"Oh boy, did she scare me!" Jennie suddenly stood taller and started waving an imaginary ruler in the air, "Boys and girls, discipline and good manners are what sets us apart from the rest of God's creatures. You must always listen to and obey your elders." She stopped walking, pointed her imaginary ruler at Jim and began to laugh. Jim laughed too, remembering just how stern Sister Josephine had been and how all of the children were frightened of her.

"Poor Sister Josephine and that drawer full of wooden rulers. She must have broken a million of those. I know she ruined a few on me!" Jim broke into a huge grin and the laughter shook his muscular frame. Jennie was laughing loudly too. They were both enjoying the memory of elementary school.

"So, it obviously was not Sister Josephine who inspired you to become a nun. What did?" He looked at her curiously, waiting for an answer.

She hesitated before responding, "Well, it's a complicated story, one for another time. Besides, that's Aunt Madgie and Uncle Hank's house right up there." Jennie pointed to the house at the end of the street.

He wished she lived further away from the church so they could keep walking. He didn't want to say goodbye yet. He was trying to come up with something to say, something that would make her smile, when she spoke.

"Thanks for walking me home Jim. Maybe I will see you at Mass tomorrow. Bye." She turned and walked quickly up the steps to the house. When she reached the front door, she turned, waved, and vanished inside, shutting the door behind her.

Jim waved in return and stared at the closed door, wishing it would open to let her back out. When it didn't, he slowly turned away and began his own walk home. His heart was pounding in his ears. Why was he feeling this way? He thought about how different she looked in her summer dress than how she looked today, wearing the habit of a novice. Still he found her remarkably beautiful. She was going to be a nun! How ironic. He hummed to himself the rest of the way home, picturing Jennie laughing at the childhood memories they had shared separately.

When Jim arrived home, he greeted his mother, who was weeding the small garden.

"Need some help mom?" he asked. "I don't have to go to the cemetery for a while yet."

"I can always use an extra set of hands, Jimmy," Kate replied. Jim went inside the house to change his clothes. When he came back out, he knelt next to his mother in the garden and the two worked side by side comfortably for a long while, pulling weeds and picking tomatoes. When Jim rose from the ground, his knees were stiff, probably from all that kneeling and praying he had done earlier that morning, he thought to himself. A lot of good that had done him – trying to rid thoughts of Jennie from his mind at church, only to run into her immediately afterwards!

Jim wanted to learn as much as he could about this mysterious Jennie Whalen so he thought he would ask his mother if she knew of the family.

"Mom, have you ever heard of the Whalen's? They live on the other side of town." He tried to sound as if he were just making general conversation.

Kate stopped plucking ripe tomatoes, put one hand on top of her large rimmed straw hat and looked up at her son curiously.

"You know, I think I have heard of them. I believe Mr. Whalen is some sort of a banker, and I had heard a rumor that both he and his wife are heavy drinkers. That's what Mrs. Carson told me anyway, and you know how Mrs. Carson likes to keep up with everything." Kate rolled her eyes.

"I think they raised a niece, now that I think about it. I don't think I know her but heard that her parents had died in some sort of freak accident long ago." Kate paused to remember more of what Mrs. Carson had told her. "I hear she is quite the beauty." She squinted in the sun and asked Jim, "Why are you so curious about them anyway?"

Jim couldn't look his mother in the eye so he turned his gaze to the pile of weeds he had pulled. "No reason. I met her at church today – her name's Jennie and she seems like a very nice young lady."

"Well, if you ask me, the family is pretty dysfunctional and you shouldn't be bothered with the likes of people like that." Kate's tone was unusually abrupt. It was as if she had heard something she didn't approve of in her son's voice. "Besides, what difference should it make to you?" Her voice turned soft and sweet, "You are going to become a priest soon, my darling son. I am so proud of you."

"I know Mom, I know," he forced a smile. "All I want in life is to make you proud. I have to get to the cemetery now but will be home for dinner. Want me to pick anything up for you at the market?"

"No, no. I have dinner all planned out for us tonight. I'm making your favorite - spaghetti and meatballs. I remember when you couldn't even say it right! Pasketti and muttbeels, you would say."

Suddenly Kate dropped the tomato she was holding and brought trembling fingers up to her breast, inhaling sharply.

"Mom!" Jim dropped to his knees beside her. "What's the matter, are you all right?"

She was crouched over, gasping for air. "I, I... I'm okay," she whispered. Her face contorted in pain as she struggled to regain her breath.

Jim felt as if the world was stopping. "Stay here mom, I'll go call Doc Sommers." Jim jumped to his feet, but as he turned toward the house, his mother yelled after him. "No Jim!" Kate's voice was weak but fervent. "I'm okay, don't call the doctor." She raised a slightly shaky hand up to her son. "Help me inside. I just need to lie down Jimmy, really."

Jim looked uncertainly at his mother's hand. Should he help her up and risk making the problem worse by moving her, or should he go call Doc Sommers? He knew he should probably call the doctor, but he also knew his mother. She was a strong-willed woman who never displayed any type of weakness. To need the attention of a doctor was a major circumstance. In the circus, if someone needed a doctor it meant they were either dying or had sustained an injury serious enough to warrant them no longer able to perform. Either scenario was equally appalling. Kate was proud that in her forty-six years she had never needed medical attention. Doc Sommers had come to the house a few times to take care of Jim - once when he had gotten chicken pox and once when he had had a frighteningly high fever.

"Look Mom. I have to call the doctor. You can't even stand up! Doc Sommers can help you. I don't know what to do. Please, please let me call him," Jim pleaded with his mother. He was beginning to feel nauseous.

"No, no. I'm okay. Look, I can stand on my own." Kate pulled her thin frame from the ground with great effort. "See, I even have my breath back," she inhaled triumphantly, as if this proved she was in perfect health and certainly did not need a doctor.

Jim eyed her suspiciously. "Okay, huh? If you're okay, then why are you wobbling right now?"

Kate didn't answer Jim. She simply grabbed his arm and said, "Take me inside. I want to lie down. I'm just a little tired and the sun has been so hot today."

Realizing it would be pointless to argue, Jim took hold of her waist and together they slowly walked to the back door of the house. Once inside, Jim helped Kate up the creaky stairs to her bedroom, pulled down the white English lace bedspread for her and helped her climb in.

"I'll get you some tea, Mom."

Kate smiled weakly and nodded her head. "Tea would be nice."

In the kitchen, Jim wondered what he should do. She seemed to be feeling better now and if he called the doctor she would never forgive him. But Jim was due in to work in half an hour and didn't want to leave his mother home all alone right now.

He picked up the telephone and dialed Neil Shaunessay's number at the cemetery. Jim was certain Neil would understand his situation. He had always been an understanding boss and a good friend as well.

Neil picked up the phone on the third ring. "Neil here." It was his standard way of answering the phone.

"Neil, it's Jim."

"Hey Jimmy boy, what's going on?" Neil asked.

"My mom's not feeling well and I don't think I should leave her here alone right now. Would you mind if I was a little late today? I've already finished Mr. Anderson's grave you know." Jim waited for Neil's reply, which came quickly.

"No problem Jimmy. You take care of that momma of yours and just get in when you can. We've got things pretty well covered here."

"Thanks Neil, I really appreciate it. I'll be in when I'm sure mom is feeling better."

"You take your time, things are slow around here."

Jim thanked Neil and placed the phone back on its receiver, made some hot tea for his mother, and went back upstairs to sit beside her.

By the time he made it to the cemetery, the other men were already scattered about the plots. Today he had to mow the east side of the cemetery, which stretched from the elementary school to just past the convent. As he headed to the shed to get the mower, he spotted Mike and shouted hello.

"Hello there, Jim. Glad you could join us on this fine Tuesday afternoon. Where have you been?" Mike called out and joined his friend near the shed.

Jim, always one for giving Mike an equally hard time, grinned and said, "The Rector called me in to the seminary for a private meeting. He told me they chose *me* to go to Rome, so how about that!"

"Yeah right! You know they are going to send *me*. Why on earth would the Rector choose you to go to Rome to study for ordination into the priesthood when I'm obviously the best man for the job?" Mike laughed good-naturedly. "Besides, you know they pick the top two seminarians at St. Charles so maybe we will both be able to go. Can you imagine the two of us in Rome, studying at the Vatican with Pope Pius XII so close by?" Mike looked at Jim wistfully. It was every seminarians dream to study in Rome.

"Well, don't pack your bags yet my friend. We won't find out who is going until summer's over and were back at the seminary." Jim paused, and then looked directly at Mike. "Besides, how do you know that's what you really want anyway?"

"What are you talking about?" Mike asked incredulously. "You're kidding right? It's all I ever wanted."

Jim didn't know what to say. He hadn't been joking, but he couldn't let Mike know that. For the four years they had known each other, Jim was sure that Mike had never had a single doubt about becoming a priest, and Jim did not want to admit his own doubts to his friend.

"Of course I was kidding. It would be great to go together. Think of all those Italian women." Jim raised his eyebrow and smiled amiably.

Mike laughed out loud and feigned a look of shock. "My friend, whatever do you mean? Priests do not look at women. It is God's will, He has deemed it so." Mike deepened his voice in an attempt to sound like one of their teachers at St. Charles. "Speaking of women, one came looking for you about an hour ago. She was quite the looker too, I might add."

Jim tried to keep the excitement out of his voice but made a weak attempt when he asked who it had been, knowing full well it had to have been Jennie.

"She didn't say, quite mysterious, if you ask me. She had brownish-gold hair and wore a green dress and she asked if you were around. That's all I know. Don't you know who it was? It's not like you have a flurry of beautiful women following you around, my friend." Mike looked at him curiously.

"Oh, yeah, it must have been this novice I met the other day at church," Jim shrugged his shoulders in an attempt to appear indifferent.

"Yeah, right," Mike responded suspiciously.

"Seriously," Jim answered. "She was nobody, just a nice person I spoke to briefly." He would not divulge any more information as it was really none of Mike's business. Besides, nothing was going on between him and Jennie, so what was there *to* tell?

"Hey, I was just kidding around. No need to get all worked up," Mike said defensively. "Anyway, have fun mowing." Mike turned his attention to the tombstone he was tending to and began pulling weeds.

Jim was embarrassed. Mike must have thought he was a fool. What was Jennie doing stopping by to visit him? He felt a strange feeling that he had not felt in a long time, a feeling he had experienced when he was dating Anna. He felt it was inappropriate for a seminarian to feel this way and wished he could just feel normal again, like he did before he had met Jennie.

For the next few hours Jim mowed the grass with such vigor it appeared as though he and his mower had a vendetta against the grass. Beads of perspiration trickled down his face, and he could not clear his mind of thoughts of Jennie Whalen. Why had she come into his life? He felt that he was being given the greatest test of his vocation. He thought of the story of Adam and Eve, the serpent and the forbidden fruit and prayed to God for an answer as to why he was being tested by this beautiful woman.

It had been especially difficult to sit through Father Peter's homily today, knowing that Jennie was just across the aisle. Jim shifted in his seat every few minutes and glanced her way whenever possible. At one point Mike leaned over and asked if everything was all right. Jim nodded and wished for Mass to end. He wanted to talk to Jennie.

When it was finally over, Jim turned to Mike and said, "I think I'll stay for a little longer."

"Stay longer? You were so antsy during the homily, it seemed like you couldn't wait to get out of here," Mike grinned at Jim and jabbed him in the arm.

"Don't be late for work again. You wouldn't want to miss out on any more beautiful women stopping by to say hello." Mike joked.

"Yeah, yeah. Just tell them all to line up and wait for me. I'll see you at the cemetery a little later," Jim replied.

A few minutes later, Jim watched Jennie stand, bless herself and leave the pew without even glancing his way. Jim's heart sank. He continued to pray, and thanked God that his mother seemed to be feeling better. He crossed himself and left the church.

The early morning air felt cool and fresh on his skin. It was a welcome change from the stifling heat of the afternoons. As he walked towards home he thought about how foolish he was acting. He hardly knew this mysterious girl, yet he was obsessing about her day and night and thoughts of her were consuming him. He made a solemn promise to himself that he would put her out of his mind and focus on what was really important – becoming a priest.

Jennie tugged at her straw hat in an attempt to push it back into place. Her scalp was itching but she didn't want to scratch and ruin the bun she had made atop her head. She felt very self-conscious in her blue dress. *The same color blue as his eyes,* she thought. She had mentally memorized every part of him, every image, every word he had spoken to her. She couldn't get him out of her mind, and she wasn't sure that she wanted to.

She couldn't stand being so close to him in church today yet not being able to talk to him, but it was her own fault. Jennie had felt the intensity of his gaze on her during Mass, and had rushed to leave as soon as it was over. It wasn't that she didn't *want* to talk to him. She wanted to talk to him so badly it was frightening. She didn't fully trust herself when in his company - her pulse quickened and her whole body felt warm. She had felt like a fool and wondered what had urged her to go looking for him at the cemetery yesterday? She was relieved to find that he wasn't there because she wasn't sure what she would have said to him, but today, she had it all thought out. This time, she had a legitimate excuse for seeking him out. She would ask him and his friend to help pack up some things for her aunt and uncle. What a perfect excuse for seeing him! And Jennie was sure he would agree to help. What seminarian would have the heart to say no to a woman in need of a strong man's assistance?

Aunt Madgie had been driving her crazy, Uncle Hank was whining about his back pain and Jennie just really needed to get away from the house for a while. Jennie held a brown paper bag that contained some juice, two apples, a wedge of cheddar cheese and a slice of pound cake.

Jennie reached the cemetery gates and stepped carefully onto the dry grass. She was wearing shoes she had only worn once before, and wasn't accustomed to the low heel. She felt pretty in her dress and pumps, a welcome change from her required black and white "uniform."

She scanned the expanse of the cemetery with squinted eyes and began to perspire. She hoped it would not show through her dress. Two men pushed lawnmowers around the tombstones and the noise was deafening. Jennie didn't see Jim anywhere and wondered if he had already taken his break. She took a few steps further out but still couldn't see him. She felt conspicuous among the graves and turned to go, discouraged. That's when she spotted Jim near the cemetery shed, walking toward her, with sharp garden shears in his hand. She stood still and watched as he approached, smiling wildly.

"Hi Jennie!"

"Hello Jim. I uh…" She wanted to say she was coming to visit her parents' graves but didn't feel right telling a fib to him. "I thought you might like a snack. Can you take a break now?" Jennie could not believe how calm she sounded. Inside, she felt like she was a shaking bundle of nerves.

"Sure, I would really like that. Let me just put these shears away and tell my boss, Neil that I'm going on break. Don't go anywhere, I'll be right back," Jim smiled again at her.

Jennie watched as he went back to the work shed, and she liked the way his strong legs crunched over the grass. She abruptly dropped her gaze when Jim turned around and waved. Slightly embarrassed to be caught staring, she lifted her hand quickly and waved back.

Jim tossed the shears into the shed, yelled to Neil that he was taking a break, and headed back to where Jennie was waiting. He noticed a couple of the guys turn their heads and look at Jennie. Jim immediately felt protective over her.

"Where should we go?" Jim asked a little breathlessly.

"Well, I was thinking we could go back to the spring, by the creek and waterfall, like the other day?" Jennie asked.

"Sounds good," Jim smiled. "Oh, Mike said that you came by yesterday."

Jennie blushed, "Oh, I just happened to be in the area and thought I would stop and say hello."

"Yeah," Jim said. "I was sorry that I missed you. And then this morning at church, I wanted to talk but you ran out of there so quickly, I figured you had somewhere to be."

"Actually, Aunt Madge and Uncle Hank needed me home to do more stuff for them. Lately I'm feeling a bit like Cinderella with all the chores. It's a lot of work to get their house packed up and in order for the movers."

They made small talk until they reached the fresh water spring and sat down by the oak tree near the water. "I love this place," Jim remarked. "It's so quiet and calm. I come here a lot to think. Sometimes I feel like the creek is the world and I'm this little insignificant spring, falling helplessly into the creek. It reminds me that no matter how I'm feeling or what I'm doing, my actions are still important to God, and that what I do in this life directly affects those around me." Jim stopped suddenly and looked into Jennie's eyes. "Sounds pretty silly, doesn't it?"

"Not at all. I think it sounds beautiful," Jennie looked back at him. "Besides, that is one of the reasons I went into the convent. After my parents died I felt so alone. I wanted to make a difference and help people. I chose the Sisters of Good Works because we help the Catholic Social Services in town find homes for babies. It's kind of like an adoption agency, really. It is so wonderful to find innocent babies a safe and secure family. I feel as it is my calling and cherish the work that I do there..." Jennie hesitated and then became silent.

"So that's why you want to become a nun?" Jim asked.

"That's part of it. It feels really nice to be a part of something greater than yourself, to be part of a very special family. Aunt Madgie and Hank weren't really the best guardians, and hardly ideal parents. For me, the church and the sisters are the only real family I have had in a very long time," Jennie said as she handed him an apple.

Since they were having such a deep conversation, Jim didn't hesitate to ask, "Have you ever had any doubts about your calling? Have you ever wondered if becoming a nun is not how God intended you to serve Him?" Jim asked as he took a large bite of the juicy fruit.

"That's some question, Mr. War Hero!" Jennie teased.

"How do you know about that?" Jim looked stunned, and realized that she too had been gathering information on him.

"Holmesburg is a small town. I know about all your awards and honors you received. I think it's wonderful, and so brave how you defended our country. Very impressive." She smiled at Jim, who was looking at her sheepishly.

"There's nothing really impressive about war. I did what I had to do, that's all. Plenty of other men would have done the same thing if they had been in my situation," Jim lowered his head modestly.

"Well, now it's my turn to ask a question. With all of your options after coming back from the war, why did you decide to enter the seminary?"

Jim propped his back against the trunk of the oak tree and closed his eyes for a moment, contemplating the question seriously. He sighed and tossed his apple onto the ground. The park was unusually quiet. It was as if God Himself had stopped the world and was waiting to hear Jim's answer.

"It's hard to say exactly why I decided to join the seminary. I have always felt very close to God, and like you, have always wanted to help others. To be honest, I was in love once," he looked up at the sky, hoping he was answering the question correctly, and not revealing too much information about his past to Jennie. "Anna and I dated for a long time. I even thought we would get married, but apparently she thought differently. She began dating my best friend while I was still in the war. I can't believe I'm telling you about this. I have never really told anyone about Anna." Jim stared at the ground.

"You must have really loved her. Do you think that's one of the reasons you went into the seminary, because you came home with a broken heart?" Jennie asked.

"Maybe." Then, trying to lighten the conversation, Jim continued, "Besides, there's not much demand for knife throwers around these parts," Jim smiled.

"What are you talking about?" Jennie asked.

"Hmm… apparently, when you were doing your investigating on my war story, you didn't dig deep enough."

"Okay, you got me. I'm intrigued about this knife throwing stuff. Do tell," Jennie said.

"Knife throwing is what I'm good at; extremely good at," Jim exclaimed.

Jennie looked at him doubtfully.

"You see, when I was young, my family was in the circus," Jim said.

"Really? No way!" Jennie laughed out loud.

"No, no. Seriously. My dad was the famous knife-thrower in the circus, Gordon the Great, and mom was his assistant. My father taught me everything about knives and how to throw them. My talent actually came in quite handy during the war. I guess he did teach me something useful after all," Jim snickered softly.

"I guess you don't have a good relationship with your father," Jennie said.

"Let's just say that we were completely different from one another," Jim said. "He was a liar and a cheat who never cared about anyone but himself," Jim said harshly.

"Is he dead?" Jennie asked softly.

"For all I know. He left us when I was six years old, so I really don't know, or care much for that matter," Jim stated curtly. "All I know is that every single day I pray to God that I don't turn out the way he did."

"From what I can tell, that would be impossible," Jennie moved a little closer to where he was sitting under the tree, "You are the nicest, most sincere person I have ever met. I know this is going to sound ridiculous, but I feel like I've known you forever, like I could tell you anything. I just feel really comfortable being with you and talking like this with you."

"I know what you mean," Jim whispered.

They sat in comfortable silence for a while, both consumed with their own thoughts, both feeling an awkward desire for the other. Jennie looked at Jim and wondered how his hair would feel if she were to run her fingers through the blond curls that lay just below his collar. He reminded her of her father. He had been strong and caring, good and kind. She missed him greatly. He would have never harmed anyone, and he had loved her and her mother so much. She wondered what they would think of her becoming a nun. Would they have been happy for her devotion to God and the church, or would they be sad that their only daughter would never know the love of a man or have her own family to love?

The sound of Jim's voice brought Jennie back to the present and Jennie shook her head slightly, as if clearing the past from her mind.

Jim laughed when he realized she had been daydreaming. "My company is that exciting, huh? Well, lucky for you then because my break is over and I have to get back to work. This was such a nice way to spend my break. Thanks for coming to see me, and I really appreciated the snack. That was some cake!"

"I really enjoyed spending time with you too Jim," Jennie said shyly.

"Will you be at Mass tomorrow?" Jim asked hopefully. He knew he wanted to see her again, sooner than later.

"Yes, but afterward I have to get back to help Madge and Hank with the packing. It's been such a hassle. His back is a mess so he can't do any of the heavy lifting, and she isn't much help either, unless you consider clearing out the liquor cabinet helping," Jennie joked.

"Hey listen, Jennie. Things at the cemetery are pretty slow this week. I'm sure that I can ask Neil for a little time off. I bet Mike could take time off too..."

Jennie looked at Jim confused, not knowing where he was going with this statement.

Jim continued, "Why don't we come by and help out a little bit this week? Heck, we dig graves all day. Helping around the house should be a piece of cake!"

"That sounds really wonderful Jim. You are just too good to be true!" Jennie hugged him timidly and Jim pressed himself against her, relishing her warmth and smelling her hair.

"I have to get back or Mike and the guys are gonna let me have it for sure. Tomorrow then, after church? Is it a date?"

"It's a date," Jennie replied.

"Jimmy, is that you?" Kate called.

"Yeah, mom. I'm home," Jim answered. "How are you feeling?" She had not been her usual bustling self since she had collapsed in the garden, and Jim was concerned.

"Stop asking me that question. I will outlive you, you hear? Now come in the kitchen and help me with this filthy floor," Kate's voice was slightly muffled, and when Jim walked into the kitchen, he saw his mother on all fours scrubbing the not-so-filthy floor diligently.

"Ma, what are you doing? I thought I told you to take it easy," Jim scolded. As he stood in the narrow kitchen doorway he looked down at his mother in dismay. "Why on earth are you scrubbing the floor? Hadn't you scrubbed enough of that old theater floor to last you a lifetime? You've got to take it easy."

"Oh, stop it, Jim. How many times do I have to tell you that I'm fine? The other day was just the result of being out in that hot sun for too long." She continued to scour away at the virtually spotless floor.

"Look mom, the floor is immaculate. We could eat off this floor." He grabbed the wet rag out of his mother's hand.

"Give me that!" she yelled as she tried to yank it out of Jim's hand. Jim held it high above his head and the memory of him in seventh grade holding Anna's coat above her head flashed through his mind. He dropped the rag to the ground and hugged his mother tightly while she began to laugh. She was laughing at how silly she must have appeared, jumping up to reach a filthy rag in which to clean an already sparkling floor.

Jim eyed her as if to say "You're crazy" but then joined in once he saw the absurdity of the situation; him standing over his mother waving a dingy wash rag forbidding her to clean her own house.

He just wanted her to finally be able to relax, after all those years of working so hard. Ironically, he thought the only good thing the war had done was make it possible for her to quit scrubbing floors at the Fox Theatre because she was able to get war work. She had been hired along with several other local women to cut fresh cardboard soles to line shoes that had worn through. It was not glamorous, but it paid better than her old job and was a lot easier on her back, too. Once the war ended, her position had been terminated, as had all of the women's jobs. When Jim came home he didn't want her to go back to her old job of scrubbing floors, so he had asked around town and got her a job taking care of old Mrs. Winters, who lived alone on the east side of town in a large house. Her children never came by, and since she had outlived her husband, there was no one around to help out. She was not well, and since the doctor could not diagnose a specific problem, he chalked it up to old age. She was too frail to walk up and down the stairs, and she often fell asleep while Kate was talking to her. It was Kate's job to keep her company, fix meals, and do some light housekeeping. It was a good job that paid well.

"Mom. How about we go into town and get something to eat at the Mayfair Diner? We haven't been there in forever." Jim said.

"Oh, Jim. I can just as easily make us a nice meal right here, and you said it yourself, this floor is clean enough to eat off!" Kate answered matter-of-factly and smoothed her cotton dress with her splotchy, calloused hands.

"Nope mom, you are not cooking tonight. And that's that. You deserve a night off. Besides, I have a hankering for their beef stroganoff." Jim winked at his mother.

"You are one persistent child, James Gabriel." And taking that as his mother's okay for a night out, Jim grabbed Kate by her tiny waist and spun her around the kitchen as if a waltz were playing right then and there.

Around and around they went, Jim humming along with their movements and Kate laughing and begging Jim to let her go. When Jim finally twirled his mother from his arms, she reached for the countertop to regain her balance, and touched her forehead, pushing a strand of hair from her eyes.

"You're worried about me overdoing it and here you are twirling me all over the place making me dizzy as a drunk!" Kate exclaimed. "You nearly gave me a heart attack. What are you trying to do, get rid of me?" But deep down, Kate was having a wonderful time and was basking in Jimmy's attention.

Smiling at the bemused tone of her voice, Jim responded, "Come now. When was the last time you danced with a handsome seminarian? Now, if it pleases you, I would like to take the most beautiful woman I know out to dinner." Even as Jim said the words aloud, inside he was thinking that Jennie was actually the most beautiful woman in the world, his mom certainly a close second.

"My, you are acting so foolish today. If I didn't know you were so committed to becoming a priest, I would think that you were in love!"

Startled at what seemed to be an accusation, Jim asked, "Why would you say such a thing, mom?"

"It's just, I guess I haven't seen you this happy since you were with Anna."

Jim's face fell at the mention of Anna, the one who had taken his heart and broken it. He thought for sure his vocation into priesthood would be the thing to fix his heart, to help him find true happiness in life, but now he wondered seriously if it were Jennie who would bring him eternal happiness?

Brought back to the present, Jim said, "Go on mom, change your clothes and let's go to the Mayfair Diner." And he gave Kate a gentle shove toward the stairs. As she was leaving the kitchen to go upstairs and get ready, she turned and said, "Thank you for being so good to me, Jimmy. A mother could not have mail-ordered a more perfect son."

It had been a long time since they had gone out to dinner. Jim was usually exhausted from working at the cemetery, and most nights Kate had already prepared a homemade specialty for them to eat. He was looking forward to a night out with his mother, would enjoy having her on his arm, and being able to show her off in town. She was a beautiful woman and Jim never understood why she hadn't shown interest in another man after his father had deserted them. Although her hair was slightly graying at the temples and she had earned a few worldly wrinkles, she still looked as beautiful and graceful as she had when she was hooked up to that spinning circus wheel, smiling brightly, waiting for her husband to hurl daggers at her.

Jim took a glass out of the cabinet and filled it with iced tea. He sat at the kitchen table and watched as the late afternoon sun streamed through the small window above the sink, bounced off the walls, and created a brilliant spectacle of color on the table. He always remembered what his mother had told him when he was little. She had said, "Every rainbow ends in a pot of gold, Jimmy." As he gazed at the muted hues he wondered about his own fortune, his own pot of gold waiting at the end of his rainbow. Was it with the church or was there some other path that was supposed to take him to his own pot of gold? He wished he wasn't still having these persistent doubts of the church and wondered if it was normal for a seminarian to have doubts this strong? He reassured himself that it was. Didn't all priests have doubts about their vocation before they took their vows? Jim feared he was becoming obsessed and disillusioned over his friendship with Jennie. He just felt so close to her. They had so much in common and she was so easy to talk to. She seemed to understand him better than anyone had in a long time. He felt closer to Jennie than he even had with Anna, and he had known Anna practically his whole life while he had just met Jennie days ago. He had no desire to get close to a woman in *that* way ever again, not after what had happened with Anna, and the memories of her deserting him the way she had always left him feeling frustrated and angry. At the time, it had seemed that the only comfort he could find was in the church. Nothing and no one else made him feel so at peace. He thanked God for saving him. He had been in a dark place when he had come home from the war and had it not been for the seminary he did not know where he would be now. Surely, it had been the best decision he could have made. Of course it was, Jim thought with confidence as he stood from the table and went upstairs to shower and shave for dinner.

Jim and Kate walked the half-mile from their house to the diner. It was such a pleasant evening, there was no humidity and Jim knew the cool night air would do his mother good. He turned to face her and smiled.

"Mom, you look really beautiful."

"Oh, stop," she patted his hand lovingly. "You're making me blush!"

Kate did look beautiful though, and was happy that she had chosen to wear a flowing peasant skirt and colorful blouse for dinner. Her hair fell gracefully around her shoulders making her look younger than her years. It had been a good decision to let her hair grow longer after she had cut it short some years ago.

As Jim looked into her eyes he noticed a gleam he had not seen for a very long time. He was glad he had insisted they go out tonight and told himself that they would do this more often. He enjoyed seeing her look so happy.

They strolled down Main Street and greeted people they knew. It was a busy night out in Holmesburg. The ice cream parlor was filled with families laughing and gobbling down sundaes with whipped cream piled sky high. Kate stopped to admire a lace shawl at one of the consignment shops and commented on a pair of shoes she saw. Each time she pointed to an interesting item, Jim would say, "Mom, when I grow up, I'll buy that for you." Then they had laughed at the absurdity of waiting for Jim to grow up.

Both Kate and Jim stopped directly in front of Grant's Jewelry Store where the window housed a beautiful display of sparkling jewels strewn out on red velvet. They were drawn to the magnificence of the jewels and peered at them in awe.

"Jim, do you see how big that diamond ring is?" Kate asked. "It's as big as a marble!" The cuts of the diamond captured the overhead lighting in the display case and flashed tiny bits of sunlit rays that danced across the window.

"It's huge mom. I wonder how much it costs?" Jim tried to see if there was a price tag attached. He turned his head sideways and placed his hand on the cool smooth surface of the glass. He could not see the price, but looked at his mom slyly and said, "When I grow up, I want to buy that one for you!" And the two of them laughed and laughed. But what Jim was really thinking was how beautiful the ring would look on Jennie's finger. He imagined that if he had the money he would have run inside and bought it right now and go find Jennie. He could not think of anyone else who deserved a diamond as beautiful as this.

"Jim! Get your hands off of the glass! You're practically drooling," Kate said, shaking Jim out of his daydream. She continued, caught up in her own memory. "I once had a piece of costume jewelry that looked very similar to that ring. It didn't sparkle like that, though. I used to wear it in the act..." Kate trailed off as a far-away look invaded the brightness of her eyes. It was unusual for her to speak of the circus, and it was even more unusual to hear sentimentality instead of hostility.

Jim was surprised at the tone of her voice, but didn't comment because he didn't want to change the mood of the evening when they were clearly enjoying themselves. Instead, he said, "Come on, we had better get going or we'll be eating dinner at midnight!"

They arrived at the Mayfair Diner and Jim pulled open the front door, motioning for his mother to go in ahead of him. It was a quaint little diner, the place young families could go and where old men could reminisce and drink coffee for hours. There was a counter where customers could sit on vinyl topped stools and little kids could spin around until they got dizzy or their mothers scolded them. The Mayfair Diner smelled of home cooking and hot coffee, no matter what time of the day it was. It had been a long time since either Kate or Jim had been there, but they felt warm, comfortable and welcome immediately. This was a good place. Jim realized he was suddenly starving.

As the hostess led them to their booth, Jim heard a woman laugh and instinctively turned his head in her direction. It was Jennie, and she was sitting with the only obvious people she would be dining with – her aunt and her uncle. Jim was stunned. He didn't know what to do. She hadn't seen him as her back was to him. She was in the middle of a story and was flailing her arms outward in a gesture while her aunt and uncle, who were facing toward Jim, laughed at whatever Jennie was saying.

"Jim, come on, our table's this way," his mother said.

Jim had a choice. He could follow his mother and sit at their table, missing the opportunity to speak with Jennie, or he could simply go up and say hello. After all, he would be meeting the Whalen's tomorrow anyway, when he arrived at their home to help with the packing.

"Hang on a minute mom, there is someone I want you to meet over there." Jim told the hostess they would be over in a second and he pulled his mother in the direction of Jennie and her aunt and uncle. As he neared the table, he swallowed the knot that had risen in his throat and told himself there was nothing to be nervous about. He was just stopping by to say hello to a friend.

Jennie's aunt and uncle moved their gaze from Jennie as she was finishing her story and glanced up when they realized they had company joining them. Jennie turned around to see who was approaching and her brows went up in a surprised look when she saw it was Jim.

"Uh, hi Jennie," Jim greeted her as if he was a schoolboy asking a girl out on a date for the first time.

"Jim! Speak of the devil! No pun intended!" Jennie laughed and turned to her aunt and uncle.

"Aunt Madgie, Uncle Hank, this is the seminarian I was just telling you about who offered his assistance at the house tomorrow. Jim, this is Madge and Hank Whalen."

Hank and Madge perked up when they realized that this was the young man who would be helping them pack. Hank Whalen stood up immediately and held out his hand to Jim.

"Nice to meet you, Jim! Jennie told us she met you down at the cemetery and that you've offered your assistance."

"Good to meet you sir." Then Jim focused on Madge, who was fidgeting in her seat. "Ma'am," Jim nodded at her and smiled. Jim pulled his mother forward who had been hovering behind him. "This is my mom, Kate Gabriel. I thought I'd treat her out to dinner tonight and we haven't been to the Mayfair Diner in a long time…"

Everyone exchanged pleasantries while Jennie continued to stare at Jim with a look that told him she was just as excited to be seeing him as he was to see her.

"… if you could join us?" Hank said.

Jim realized his ears had gone deaf on the conversation and that Hank was inviting his mother and him to join them for dinner. "Really, there's plenty of room in the booth, and since you'll be helping us out at home tomorrow, it might be nice to get to know you a little."

Jim searched his mother's eyes for an answer and she perked up and said, "We'd be delighted to join you. The more the merrier I always say!"

Madge piped in, "I always say that too!" And as Jim squeezed in next to Jennie, and Kate next to Jim, everyone laughed.

Jim had been worried that his mother wouldn't have wanted to sit with them at dinner. After all, she had heard that the Whalen family was a dysfunctional group and big drinkers as well. But as Jim watched his mother talk animatedly with Hank, Jennie and Madge, he realized she was just as happy as he was to be dining with them.

Jennie turned her attention to Kate. "Did Jim tell you we met in the cemetery? He helped me out a bit. I was visiting my parents' grave and was a little upset that day."

Kate perked up, "That's my Jimmy! He's such a good boy, always wanting to help people. That's why he's going to make a great priest!"

"Isn't that the funniest story… neither of us knew about our separate callings. I had no idea he was studying to be a priest and he didn't know I was in the convent until we ran into each other at St.

Dominic's with our religious attire on!" Jennie laughed and the others joined in.

Throughout dinner, Jim stole little glances Jennie's way, watched her eat delicately and was mesmerized at how she was so gracious and pleasant. Even though he had been starving, he only managed to finish half his meal. He was wondering if Jennie had stolen his heart and his appetite as well?

When the check arrived, Mr. Whalen grabbed it and said, "This is my treat folks. It was such a nice time, and we're very thankful that Jim and his buddy will be helping us tomorrow. You've done my back a great favor, son!"

"Thank you sir, that's very kind of you," Jim said respectfully.

As they stood up to leave, Jim brushed against Jennie's cool skin and felt the softness of her arm. It caught them both off guard and they took in each other's expressions, not saying a word, but knowing exactly what the other was thinking. They felt connected, they felt like one, but separated by a calling too strong to ignore – the calling of God.

Jim's mother broke the spell by grabbing his arm and saying, "This was a wonderful evening. Thank you so much for dinner. It was really nice to meet you all." And she looked at Jennie with admiration. "You're such a lovely girl, and how nice of you to spend time with your aunt and uncle before they leave for California."

Jennie thanked Kate and hugged her. Jim shook Hank's hand and said, "I'll be by tomorrow after Mass so make sure there's work for me to do!"

"Would you like a ride home?" Madge asked.

Kate said, "Thanks, but I think we'll walk. It's not often I get to spend time with Jimmy and the walk will do us both good after all that food!"

Jim pushed open the door to the Mayfair Diner, gave the Whalen's a wave, and he and his mother began walking toward home. The evening air was cool, and it felt good to walk after such a big meal.

"What a nice family," Kate commented. "I guess I shouldn't be so quick to judge just by what I hear from others."

Jim agreed and they walked home in comfortable silence.

The next day, all through church, Jim could only stare at Jennie's back. He hadn't listened to Father at all, and if questioned, would not know a thing about the homily. Mike, who had been sitting next to Jim, even had to nudge him to let him know it was time to receive communion. Jim couldn't remember a time when he had paid less attention in church. His mind rolled with thoughts of Jennie.

Neil had given them both time off, with no problems at all. They planned to work at the Whalen's all of today, and tomorrow morning. They would be back in the cemetery Friday afternoon. If needed, Jim and Mike would be around during the weekend to assist the Whalen's as well. According to Jennie, her aunt and uncle had accumulated more than their share of junk, and she warned them that they had their work cut out for them.

After Mass, as Mike and Jim were waiting for Jennie, who was inside talking with another novice, Mike said, "What was up in there today Jim? Your mind was definitely not in the spirit of worship!"

"Just tired I guess," Jim replied.

"Well, from what it sounds like, we've got a lot of work ahead of us in the next few days so you'd better get un-tired, my friend," Mike said. "You know, if I didn't know any better, I'd say that you've got a thing for this girl."

"Oh come on Mike!"

"Seriously, you haven't been yourself since you met her. You're not paying attention in church; you're taking breaks longer than you're supposed to at work. Man, your head is definitely not in the right place these days."

Jim sighed. "I don't know Mike. I just don't know." Jim looked down at his shoe and swiped his toe at an ant crawling on the cement.

"What do you mean? Are you falling in love?"

Jim snapped out of it. "Mike, you kidding me? There's no way I'm going to mess things up and let *you* take my place in Rome. No siree, there's a plane ticket with my name on it already!" The tension was gone now that Jim had made a joke of things and the two friends laughed heartily.

"What's so amusing boys?" Jennie asked as she approached. Jim hadn't seen her walk out of the church.

"Uh, we were just…" Jim said but Mike interrupted him.

"I was telling Jimmy old boy that he's got to get in shape for the task at hand today. Sounds like there's a house full of stuff waiting for us to pack?"

"I think Jim's in fine shape for the job." Jennie exclaimed. She eyed Jim approvingly and this made Jim both excited and nervous.

"Come on, let's get going," Jim said, and the three headed to the Whalen's home.

For four hours, Jim, Mike and Jennie cleaned up clutter, and wrapped and boxed miscellaneous items. Madge was nearby, giving orders on what could be tossed, what needed to be packed, and what was going to be given to charity. They had gone through six closets, and still nowhere near finishing just the upstairs of the house.

Madge did find the time to make a spectacular lunch and Jennie, Mike and Jim took a break and ate chicken salad sandwiches and fruit outside on the front porch.

"You don't know how much I appreciate your help," Jennie said. "I can't believe Aunt Madgie and Hank thought that with my help alone, they'd be able to get this place organized and packed up."

Jim looked at Jennie and said, "It's our pleasure, Miss Jennie Whalen."

The following day, they repeated the same actions. Mike and Jim waited for Jennie after church; they walked to the Whalen's and continued to pack up their belongings while Madge and Hank told them what to do with each item. Hank's back was feeling slightly better so he was able to pitch in a bit. Both Jim and Mike had felt sore from the day before and agreed that helping the Whalen's was almost as hard as digging ten-foot-deep graves. At least at the Whalen's they got homemade chicken salad for lunch and fresh iced tea throughout the day.

After lunch, they worked a bit more then bid farewell as they were needed at the cemetery. "Mr. Whalen, do you think you'll need us tomorrow, sir?" Jim asked.

"Actually, I could use you. There are a couple things in the basement that need to be brought up, and I don't think my back can handle that."

Mike said, "I've got plans for tomorrow sir, so I won't be able to come by."

"That's okay, I'll be around," Jim quickly exclaimed. He was excited to think he could spend some time with Jennie without Mike lurking over his shoulder, even if it was just to clean out the basement. They said their goodbyes and Mike and Jim headed to the cemetery.

Mike went to see if the guys near the tombstones needed some help with the trimming and weeding while Jim headed to get the lawnmower. Neil was inside the shed and Jim greeted him with a friendly hello.

"How's that packing coming along?" Neil asked.

"Good Neil, very good. Thanks so much for giving us some time off to help the Whalen's. They sure do appreciate it."

"Hey Jimmy, no problem. You've been around here four years and you're one of the best guys I've had working here. You know I'd do anything for ya!"

"Thanks Neil."

"Now get back to work!" Neil laughed and Jim headed out to mow the grass.

Jim woke early to the smell of bacon and eggs wafting upstairs. Kate didn't go to Mrs. Winters on Saturdays and Jim could always count on a hearty breakfast. He showered, got dressed and bounded down the stairs.

"My you are a cheery one today," Kate said as Jim touched her cheek with a kiss.

"Just happy to be here ma!" Jim said.

After breakfast, Kate and Jim went to church and when it was over, Kate headed to the market while Jim left for the Whalen's. Jennie hadn't been in church, which seemed unusual. He hoped she was all right.

When he arrived at the house, Jennie opened the door and Jim could tell that she had been crying. He felt an overwhelming urge to protect her and so he reached out and took her in his arms, holding her tighter than he should have, but he wanted to be as close to her as possible, to take in some of the hurt she was feeling.

"Jennie, what's the matter?"

"Oh Jim, Aunt Madgie was drinking last night and she said some terrible things to me."

"What kind of things?" Jim asked.

"She said that I wasn't cut out to be a nun and said I was not worthy of the church."

"Why on earth would she say something so untrue and hurtful to you?" Jim asked.

"This is what she does when she's drinking. Oh Jim, I can't stand it when she's this way. It just hurts me so much. I suppose she doesn't mean it, but it doesn't matter. I wonder if she's right though?"

Jim grabbed Jennie by the shoulders and said, "Jennie Whalen, you look at me. You are a beautiful, beautiful person and the angels in Heaven are surely praising your name that you will take the call of our God and honor Him by serving Him."

Jennie wiped a tear from her eye and attempted a small smile. Jim knew exactly just the right things to say to her. She had never cherished a friend more than Jim.

"Where are Hank and Madge, Jennie?"

"Hank went to the hardware store and Madge is upstairs complaining of a headache."

"Good, grab a snack and let's go for a walk. I'll help Hank when we get back. You could use some fresh air, and there's something I want to show you." Jennie ran into the kitchen, put some apples, crackers and cheese into a bag and went out front to where Jim was waiting. He grabbed her hand and they headed to Pennypack Park.

As they walked through the park, tiny splatters of rain began to fall from the sky. It was not enough to soak them, but it would have been nice to have an umbrella.

"Jim, it's starting to rain, we should go back," Jennie said.

"It's okay, where we're going, we won't get too wet." And so, Jennie followed Jim obediently, trusting that he was taking her somewhere safe, where they could talk and just be together in the quiet morning drizzle.

As droplets of rain continued to fall, Jim led Jennie deeper into the grounds until all there was left to see were massive trees and sprawling shrubbery. He pushed aside an overgrowth of ivy and motioned for Jennie to follow as he crouched and slowly made his way through the underbrush. Jennie began to question what they were doing, but Jim remained silent.

Finally free of scratchy bushes, they stretched themselves back into a standing position. Jim looked at Jennie as she gazed in amazement at this wonderful place. He watched her eyes survey the surroundings with the curiosity of a child – the round clearing where they stood, the endless growth which shaped it but did not actually extend into the empty space, and the strangely out of place lilac bushes which lined one curve of the sphere and sent its sweet fragrance wafting through the damp air. His eyes followed hers as they lifted upward and realized that they were no longer wet, the drizzle could not reach them through the mass of trees that hovered above them, protecting them. Slowly, Jennie turned to face him.

"It feels like we're a thousand miles from home, like we left our world and landed in another, more beautiful one," Jennie whispered.

"This is my favorite place in the world. Here, there is only peace and serenity. This is my sanctuary. I've been coming here ever since I was a little kid. This place sort of heals me when things are going wrong, or when I'm confused or frustrated, tired or worn out. I have never taken anyone here, ever. Well, until now," Jim looked at Jennie. His eyes fell to the ground. He slowly raised them and his gaze rested on hers again. She was so beautiful.

"It is an amazing place Jim. Thank you for taking me here," Jennie smiled.

They stood in silence for a long time. He reached out and touched her hand gently, and she warmly placed hers in his.

"Are you okay now Jennie, I mean, with what happened between you and your aunt last night?"

"Yes, I know she's got a problem, and it's nothing that I've done."

"You know I never want to see you hurt. I care about you," Jim spoke the words in haste. Surprised at his own words, he trailed off into silence.

Jennie seemed oblivious, as if he had said the sky was blue rather than an implication of something far greater. She turned from him and began walking towards a large rock near one of the lilac bushes and inhaled deeply to smell the floral aroma that permeated the damp air.

"What's this?" she asked, and without waiting for an answer she reached behind the round, charcoal colored stone.

"Wait a second, it's too heavy for you to lift by yourself," Jim called as he jogged over to where she stood glancing at the rock.

"What is it?" Jennie asked.

"It's my target board," Jim answered proudly. He leaned the old, round, plywood board against a nearby pine tree. The paint was peeling off the round red dot he had painted long ago in the center of the board, and the entire surface of it was covered with deep nicks from where he had hit his target. This board had served him well over the years, and as he ran his fingers over it, he could still picture himself creating every single mark with clarity. This was his third target board, the first two having split right down the middle after taking a few years of abuse, always in the same place - dead center. This one had taken less of a beating than the others, though. Not from lack of talent, but rather from lack of time. First there was high school, which had taken up a lot of his time, and when he was dating Anna, she had shown no interest in his passion for knife throwing. Then he had left for the war, and had entered the seminary promptly upon his return. That had not left much time for throwing knives, and besides, the war had sucked most of the fun out of knife throwing anyway. Up until then he had thrown just for fun, and well, because he was good at it. The war had shown him that his game could also be a deadly weapon, and things had never been the same since.

Now he eyed his target board with mixed emotions. It had been a while since he had thrown. Jim put the board down, walked over to the rock and reached behind it once more. The ground was damp from the moisture in the air, even though it was not raining directly in the clearing. His long fingers scraped at the dirt as he bent over searching for his satchel of knives. He had not kept them in his bedroom since he was twelve and his mother had found them and thrown the knives in the garbage, enraged that he had them at all. He felt something cool and smooth and yanked the leather pouch out. He was grateful that no one had stumbled upon his treasure hidden there.

"What are those?" Jennie asked.

"These are my knives," Jim smiled. "Go sit down over there on that rock and I will show you what these babies can do."

Jennie sat down and Jim propped the makeshift target up against the pine tree he had rested it on. He strode five paces backward, stretched his muscles and Jennie looked at him oddly. Seeing the questioning look on her face, Jim said, "It's been awhile, so I'm just getting warmed up." He did a few more curious exercises before he was ready.

"Are you ready to see me in action?" Jim smiled at her and she smiled back, flattered that he wanted to share his talent with her. He lunged forward in one graceful movement and released two knives from the same hand. It was a move he had discovered during the war. One after the other they sliced through the muggy air and made a small slapping sound as they ate their way into the center of the target board.

"All right!" Jim whooped and ran over to Jennie swooping her up into his arms and spinning her around.

Laughing, but kicking her feet, Jennie exclaimed, "Put me down you crazy lunatic!"

Jim put her down carefully, and laughed with her as she straightened her skirt. "I'm sorry, I just got carried away. Will the fair lady ever forgive me?" he smiled charmingly.

Still laughing, Jennie answered, "I don't think I have a choice. I have never seen anything like that in all my life! Where on earth did you learn how to do that?"

"I told you my family was in the circus when I was younger, I guess I just picked it up from my father," Jim said.

"Oh, that's right. You told me about him, I forgot. So, you are a man of many talents. What other tricks do you have up those sleeves?" Jennie batted her eyelashes teasingly.

"Well, since you asked… No, I couldn't. It's much too risky," Jim said.

The risk factor excited Jennie and she pleaded with Jim to tell her.

Jim looked at her doubtfully, "How much do you trust me?"

"What are you talking about?" Jennie asked suspiciously.

"Well, I know this great trick, but in order for it to work you have to believe in me with all your heart. Do you?" He looked at her hopefully.

"Without knowing what the trick is, how can I answer you?" Jennie questioned.

"Forget about it, it was a stupid idea anyway." Jim turned away from her.

"No. I don't want to forget about it. Jim, turn around and look at me," she said and looked him directly in the eye. "Maybe I am crazy, but I do. I do trust you, completely, probably more so than anyone else on earth." She touched his hand lightly.

Jim shivered at her honest expression of faith and took her delicate hand in his leading her over to where the target was. Moving it aside, he told her to stand still. She did so without question and with a tingle of excitement for what he was going to show her.

"What did you bring for a snack?" Jim asked.

"You're hungry now?" Jennie asked incredulously.

"No, I need a prop."

"I brought cheese and crackers, and some apples," Jennie replied.

"Perfect!" Jim exclaimed as he picked up the soggy bag and removed one of the shiny red apples.

Without explanation he jogged back to Jennie and placed an apple in her hand. She felt that she should be trembling but she was calm and still. He positioned the apple gently in her hand, and told her to raise her arm out to her side.

"All right Jim, what's going on?" she asked.

"I'm going to stand back there, throw a knife, and cut the apple in two," Jim exclaimed.

"You're going to do what?" Jennie cried. "I don't think so, James Gabriel. Are you crazy?"

Jim laughed. "I might just be, but that is not the question. The question is, how much you trust me, remember? Jennie, I promise I won't miss the mark. I would never put you in danger. I did this hundreds of times in the army. Don't you trust me?"

She still felt as if she should be frightened but she wasn't and whispered, "Yes Jim, I said I trust you completely, and I do, honestly."

Jennie squeezed her eyes shut and held the apple as far out as she could. Jim paced himself away from her, and removed one of the smaller knives from his satchel. He glanced at Jennie and for a brief moment and felt a sliver of doubt himself. What if he missed? She looked so beautiful and innocent standing by the tree. If he missed... He wouldn't, he told himself. He knew he had to throw the knife soon or Jennie would become too scared, so he positioned himself and focused only on the apple.

He held his breath, pulled his arm back and let the knife fly from his hand. He heard Jennie squeal and prayed that she would stay still. The knife zoomed and for a second he thought he might miss. What a horrible idea this was! How could his father have thrown knives at his mother every day in the circus and not have felt terrible? Maybe this was what love really felt like and that's why it had been so easy for his father to throw knives at his mother – because maybe he hadn't loved her? Jim knew he did not want to put Jennie in this position ever again for he felt miserable at the thought of risking her safety for a stupid trick. Then he saw that he had not missed at all. The apple was sliced in two, and the knife was sticking out of the trunk of the pine tree he had positioned Jennie and the apple in front of.

"Jennie! Are you all right?" Jim yelled. She had slid down the base of the tree, and her head hung low against her chest. "Jennie?" Jim cried. Perhaps he had struck her after all! He raced to her side and pulled her into his arms. With fear in his heart he lifted up her head. She wasn't cut, but she wasn't responding. What was wrong with her? "Jennie? Jennie, what's the matter?" He was almost in tears. The remains of the apple, two large chunks, were lying near the base of the tree.

"Oh Jim," Jennie exhaled loudly and blinked her eyes. "Did you do it?" she asked.

Squeezing her tightly into his broad chest, he sighed. "Jennie, did you faint? Thank God you are okay. I don't know what I would do if anything had happened to you." Jim rocked her back and forth gently, and she held onto his strong shoulders.

"Oh Jim, I got so scared right before you threw the knife. But I trusted you, I trusted you," Jennie murmured. "I think I am in love with you," she whispered so softly she might not have said the words at all.

Without hesitation he whispered back, "I love you, Jennie."

The silence that ensued was deafening. It was as if the whole world had been stunned into being quiet. Then, as suddenly as Jennie had professed her love, she tore herself out of Jim's arms and stood up. Jim followed, at a loss for words. He couldn't let the conversation end there and he started, "Jennie…"

"Stop. Don't say anything, please. Let's just forget about it, we don't know what we are saying," Jennie had her back turned towards him and her muffled voice sounded as if she were going to cry.

Jim's throat began to tighten and he felt as though someone had sucker-punched him in the stomach.

"Look, let's just get back to Aunt Madgie's and Hank's house. There is still so much to do," Jennie began inching her way out of the clearing.

Things were quiet as they walked back to the Whalen's, each deep in thought, equally confused by what had occurred at the clearing moments ago. Jim decided to push it from his mind for a while and Jennie did the same. The subject was not brought up again, and finally, when they got closer to the house, they both were able to make small conversation, commenting on a house they had passed, or a puppy walking alongside its owner.

Hank was waiting for them, and put them to work in the basement right away. It was a busy afternoon, and when they were finished, Hank suggested Jim stay for dinner. Jim looked to Jennie to see if she had wanted him there and Jennie spoke, "Yes, Jim, why don't you stay for dinner. That would be nice."

Madge had somehow made it to the kitchen that afternoon, after nursing her hangover, and had prepared a stuffed chicken, mashed potatoes and gravy.

Jim, who was hungry after working so hard all day, ate heartily, and this pleased Madge. "Now that's a man who can eat!" Jim looked up from his plate, sheepishly, and Jennie giggled.

After dinner, Jim cleared the table while Jennie washed the dishes. They worked side by side, laughing at nonsense things. So, this is what it must feel like to be married, Jim thought. He realized he had spent the whole day with Jennie, doing mundane things like clearing out the basement and cleaning up after dinner, and he couldn't have been happier.

"Would you all like to go out for some ice cream?" Jim asked, after the dishes had been washed and put away.

"Oh, you two go on ahead, I've got some reading I've got to catch up on, some stuff required of my new job," answered Hank.

"And I'm going to spend a little time reading up on California. I don't want to get there and seem like a tourist!" Madge added.

"We'll get in touch with you if we need more help with the packing Jim. My back and I thank you greatly for all of your help," said Hank.

Jim thanked the Whalen's for dinner and he and Jennie left for the ice cream parlor. This felt to Jim like an actual date! He remembered taking Anna out for ice cream in the summer, and he was very proud to have such a beautiful woman with him now. Without thinking, Jim asked Jennie, "Do you know how beautiful you are?"

Jennie blushed and pushed him away. "You stop this nonsense, James Gabriel." But secretly, Jennie felt like the luckiest girl in the world at that moment. She reached over to Jim's sundae and hooked her finger into his whipped cream and smeared it on his nose.

The next day, Jim and his mother went to church and then they spent the day gardening and doing chores around the house. Jim had seemed distant to his mother, but Kate figured he was just exhausted from all the work he had been doing for the Whalen's.

Monday, Tuesday and Wednesday came and went, and Jim had not received a call asking for his assistance at the Whalen home. He knew there was still packing to do, but felt strange about calling them up to ask if they needed more help. He spent his days concentrating on digging graves, which he did with gusto. He tried to push Jennie from his mind. He knew this was not the way a priest in training should be thinking, and at night she visited him in his dreams. He awoke thinking that Jennie should be next to him as she had been in his dreams, and was usually miserable when he realized he had just been dreaming of her.

On Thursday, Jim's frustration was growing. How he missed seeing Jennie. It had been four days since they had shared ice cream and he longed to see her, to talk with her, to be close to her. He was afraid of the way he was feeling; was afraid he was being unfaithful to his Lord by having such thoughts of a woman.

Mike worked next to Jim, digging diligently alongside, and he could tell something was not right with Jim. But Jim wasn't talking, and he didn't want to hear Mike tell him to get his head out of the clouds. He was in no mood for Mike's opinion on what was the matter, and so when break time arrived, Jim headed off by himself.

He took his lunch over to the spring and the creek, where he had taken Jennie just over a week ago. He needed some quiet time to think, but instead of thinking, he dozed off next to the big oak tree. He was indeed exhausted, emotionally and physically.

Jim couldn't have been sure if he'd been sleeping for two minutes or two hours, but he was gently nudged awake later. With a start, his eyes flew open, not realizing where he was. When his vision cleared, he saw that Jennie was sitting next to him, and she was smiling.

"Jennie," he said. "I've missed you."

"I'm sorry that I haven't been around, Jim. Uncle Hank tripped and fell on Monday, messing up his back more than it already was. I was playing nurse to him while Aunt Madgie was running around town all week visiting friends." Jennie rolled her eyes. "I swear that woman has no concept of the important things."

Jim asked anxiously, "Well, do they need more help over at the house?"

"I think they are pretty close to being done with everything. You and Mike sure did help out a lot last week."

Before he could stop himself, Jim asked, "But when am I going to get to see you?"

"You're seeing me right now," Jennie replied.

"But I've got to get back to work. What time is it anyway?" he asked. When Jennie told him, he was relieved to know that he had not been sleeping all that long and his break was not quite over yet.

Suddenly, Jim had an idea and blurted out to Jennie, "Would you like to go see a movie tomorrow night?"

"Well, I don't know Jim. What would people think? A novice going out with a seminarian?" She looked at him doubtfully.

"We could go to the Palace Theatre downtown. No one would know us there," Jim gently touched her arm.

Jennie smiled up at him.

"I take it that's a yes?" Jim asked.

"I would be honored to go to the theater with you tomorrow."

"Wonderful! I'll stop by the house tomorrow at seven o'clock," Jim said. "Do you think your aunt and uncle will mind me taking you out?"

"They won't think anything of it. Besides, after Tuesday, they won't even be around anymore."

"And neither will you," Jim whispered and held Jennie in a warm embrace, never wanting to let go.

The lights dimmed in the small, but courtly theater. The audience grew quiet as the long, heavy drapes parted to reveal the screen. It was quite crowded, but that was to be expected on a Friday night. They had agreed to see Casablanca, since neither one had seen it when it had debuted seven years ago. Besides, the other two choices did not interest them - The Third Man starring Orson Welles or Abbott and Costello Meet the Killer, Boris Karloff.

Jim reached across the arm bar separating himself from Jennie and felt for her hand in the darkened room. She gave it to him freely and he couldn't help but think how nice it felt as he linked his fingers comfortably through hers. Neither spoke, as the picture was about to begin.

When the credits rolled and the lights came on, Jim removed his hand from Jennie's and asked, "So, what did you think? I'm so glad we were able to see the movie together. I loved the last line – 'This could be the beginning of a beautiful friendship.' You know, you're a friend, and you're quite beautiful too," Jim said as they walked to the bus stop that would take them back to Holmesburg. Jennie grinned. He was always saying such nice things to her. It was a wonderful feeling to be here with him, and not to have to hide their feelings for one another. Nobody here knew them or knew that they were both planning on committing their lives to God.

"Thank you, Jim. I think that was the most romantic movie I have ever seen," Jennie sighed and looked up at the sky.

Jim followed her gaze and commented, "Isn't it amazing how clear the sky is? The stars seem to be sparkling just a little brighter than usual." He turned to face her, "They're dull compared to the light in your eyes."

Jennie blushed and continued walking. "Look! Here comes the bus! If we hurry, we can make it."

They ran to the corner where a small crowd of people stood waiting for the bus. They were the last to get on, and were breathing heavily as they sank into an empty seat towards the back.

The bus driver spoke in his microphone, "Next stop, Holmesburg."

"Hey, do you know how Holmesburg got its name?" Jim asked Jennie.

"Nope, but please enlighten this curious woman," Jennie answered.

"Thomas Holme was the chief surveyor to William Penn and was responsible for surveying all of the boundaries in the state of Pennsylvania. He was buried in a separate plot near Holme Avenue, so not only did he get a street named after him, a whole town was named after him too!" Jim reported proudly.

"My, what a history lesson!" Jennie was impressed at his knowledge. "Not only are you a mighty war hero, but you're a history buff as well!"

"I've always been interested in history, even back at St. Dominic's Elementary, I was the smartest kid in class," he boasted.

They sat in silence for the rest of the trip home, touching fingers lightly and glancing at each other occasionally. Jim could not remember ever being this happy.

When the bus stopped and they got off, they found themselves across the street from Pennypack Park.

"I know it's getting late, but would you like to go for a walk in the park?" Jim asked.

"Yes, let's take a walk. It is a nice night," she replied.

Jim took her hand and led her down the bridal path. He had never been here this late at night before and everything seemed different. The darkness of the night covered the park like a blanket, transforming all familiar objects into unrecognizable obscurity. It was so quiet this late at night. Jim felt the silence was soothing, interrupted by the occasional cricket or owl.

"Maybe this wasn't such a good idea after all," Jim said slowly, trying to gauge what Jennie was thinking.

"Why?" Jennie sounded surprised. "It's beautiful out. See how the trees blend into the backdrop of the stars? Close your eyes for a minute. Can't you hear the waterfall?" She took a deep breath, "The flowers smell so much stronger at night! Even the air feels fresher," Jennie shivered slightly in her pale yellow dress.

Jim quickly shrugged off the light coat he had been wearing, draped it over her, and then protectively put his arm around her to keep her warm. "Is that better, or are you still chilly?" he asked.

"No, this is much better. Thank you," she said and turned to face him.

They looked into each other's eyes and neither spoke. Silently, Jim leaned forward and gently placed his lips on Jennie's. She responded to his kiss, tentatively, softly, and they savored the moment. His body trembled as he placed his hand on the small of her back. Jennie pressed her lips firmly into his. He could hear nothing except the beating of his own heart, and didn't want the kiss to end.

When Jennie pulled away slowly, they both looked at one another, surprised at what had just happened between them. He was sure the look on Jennie's face mirrored his own, and since he had no idea what to say, how to make light of this intimate moment, he said nothing. Instead, he simply reached down, took her slightly damp hand in his own, and continued walking down the path.

The sounds of the night had been quiet earlier, but now everything seemed intensified. Crickets chirped and frogs croaked noisily. They heard the roar of the waterfall, and it grew stronger as they walked toward it. Soon they were settled near the waterfall and being in a familiar place seemed to put them both at ease.

"Let's sit down for awhile," Jim spoke in a hushed tone. He led Jennie to the overgrowth of honeysuckle, where they could inhale the flowers' sweetness and where they had a clear view of the waterfall cascading down into the creek below. The stars reflected brightly and they were able to see more clearly here by the water.

"Oh, Jim. It's so much more beautiful here at night," Jennie sighed. "If I close my eyes, it feels like we are in another world, with the splashing of the water and the sweet, sweet smell of honeysuckle."

Jim smiled tenderly. "You make everything an adventure, did you know that?"

He touched her cheek and saw the moon reflecting in her eyes. He was mesmerized by her beauty and leaned forward to once again feel the tenderness of her lips.

"Jim, we shouldn't..."

"I know, I know. But just for tonight, let's not think of anyone but each other. I don't want to know if this is right or wrong, tomorrow is so far away and tonight lies right before us," Jim spoke barely above a whisper. He was afraid that if he spoke any louder, they would be woken from a beautiful dream. He didn't want the magic spell to be broken; he didn't want to face reality. A reality he was not ready to confront. She must have felt it too, he thought, because without another word she leaned closer to him, until he could feel her warm breath on his face.

They pressed their lips together, creating an unbreakable bond that they didn't know would last a lifetime. Jim felt dizzy and all of his senses came to life because of Jennie. He searched her eyes, looking longingly into the depths of the windows to her soul. He wanted to smell her until he could breathe no more. He wanted to touch her until his hands ached. He was aching for her in a way he had never ached for a woman.

He hugged her to him and he felt her skin for the first time. She was soft and warm and eager to feel him too. He wanted to feel what he had never felt with a woman before. He touched her shoulder gently, as if asking a silent question. She looked into his eyes, and her eyes said yes.

She buried her face against his strong chest and he moved his body above hers, slowly lowering her onto the grass. He caressed her skin, lovingly, slowly, with care and concern. Oh, how he loved this woman. He knew this was more than just a sexual desire; he desired to know everything about Jennie, to be in her head with her thoughts and dreams, to be one with her in every possible way.

Jim took a deep breath and touched Jennie's hair. He whispered in her ear, "I've never done this before, Jennie." This was a confession he did not expect to make.

"I'm not afraid, Jim. I know you would never hurt me."

As the two moved under the moonlight, and the waterfall continued to flow, everything else in the world ceased to exist. They were alone in their private world, discovering each other; discovering a love that would consume them for an eternity. They moved together, he gave his love to her freely, without reservation, and they became one.

Exhausted and filled with emotion, Jim embraced Jennie's trembling body and lifted his face to meet hers. "I am so in love with you." He nestled his face in her hair and marveled at the love they had just created together.

"I knew I loved you the moment I saw you standing alone in the cemetery, at your parent's grave. I have never felt happier in my entire life. He looked at her inquisitively, was she feeling the same, or was she remorseful for the mortal sin they had just committed? Jim felt nothing except a serene sense of wholeness. He knew this is where he belonged.

Jennie, stunned by the powerful feelings she was experiencing, said thoughtfully, "I have never felt this way before. My love for the church can't even come close to the love I feel for you. I don't feel guilty. Being with you is the most right thing I have ever felt." She clung to Jim and thought she may never let go.

Jim pondered quietly for a moment, touching her shoulder gently. "Do you think that maybe we never really had a vocation? It's completely amazing to think that if we weren't giving our lives to Christ and the church, we never would have met. I think that God planned for us to be together, as strange as it may sound. I don't think God would want us to forsake our love for each other in order to serve Him, do you? God would understand if we didn't follow through with our callings, wouldn't he?" Jim was trying to wrap his mind around the situation, and it wasn't easy. For so long he had been unsure about his destiny with the church, and it all seemed so clear now. He and Jennie belonged together. In his heart, they were now one.

"What are you saying? Are you suggesting that we *leave* the church?" Her tone was extremely uncertain, and this confused Jim. He wanted Jennie to feel the same way he did – he wanted her to want to be with him for the rest of their lives.

"I'm not sure, Jennie," Jim touched her arm, "but would you consider it?"

"I don't know how I feel. What do you think people would say?" Jennie stared at him with eyes wide.

"The only person other than you that I'm concerned about is my mother," Jim said, "and I really don't care what anyone else would think. Jennie, I do know that I love you wholly and completely. Surely God would not have put us in each other's arms if He didn't want us to be together? I have always believed God to be kind and loving."

He gently grasped both of her hands, held them to his chest and said, "Jennie, I think that truly in my heart, I want to be with you for all of eternity. I want to be married to you. I want to live our lives together. I want to wake up every morning in a home we would call our own, with children and pets, and laughter and love. I do believe I want all of that, and I want it all because of you. I have never felt this way before – ever!"

Jennie's mouth dropped open, and for a second it seemed as if she were going to fall backwards, but Jim kept her steady in his arms. Jennie said, "Oh Jim, that sounds like the most beautiful life!"

"Then say it Jennie, say you'll marry me!"

Without hesitation, Jennie hugged Jim tightly and said, "Yes," over and over again.

They continued to embrace as they discussed their plans as the stars and moon winked in approval above. They knew they had to leave the church immediately, and wed as soon as possible. They accepted the fact that they had committed a mortal sin, and knew they must go to confession immediately. They decided not to confess at St. Dominic's because of Jim's relationship with the church. They would go to confession at a nearby parish, and see a priest who didn't know them to avoid the humiliation of their sin. They knew they had sinned, but also knew they deserved forgiveness because the sin was brought upon by their love for one another.

The next day they met at Sacred Heart Church in Frankford, where they expected to receive a hefty penance for their mortal sin. Instead, Father Johaski, who they had never met, offered them absolution but strongly recommended they depart from their plans to serve the Lord in the manner they originally chose to do so. Although still guilt-ridden, Jennie and Jim felt a sort of calm over their decision to withdraw from their callings once they had confessed.

Jennie was scheduled to leave for the convent early the following week, and Jim knew he had to tell his mother soon that he was not returning to St. Charles Seminary. He decided that he would bring Jennie to his house on Monday night, after he had finished his shift in the cemetery. That way, they would be together when Jim told his mother the news. He needed the support of Jennie by his side. He wasn't sure how his mother would take it. Jim knew Kate had been fond of Jennie at the diner when they had met, but was it enough fondness for her to accept that her son was leaving the seminary for this woman? Jim prayed it was so, and then felt oddly hypocritical to be praying to God for the exact same thing that had changed his mind about his calling. It was a surreal situation, but one he hoped to get through.

Jim and Mike were digging a grave together when Neil came over, leaned down and said, "Jim, I need to talk to you for a sec." Mike lowered the ladder so Jim could come up out of the grave.

"Yeah Neil?" Jim asked.

"Jim, I just got a call. Your mother's not feeling well. I think you should get home right away."

The urgency in Neil's voice pushed Jim's mind into overdrive and he raced home to find Doc Sommers there, and his mother in her bed, looking pale and weak.

"Ma? What's going on?" Jim ran to her side and grabbed her hand.

"Oh Jimmy. I had another one of those spells."

"What happened?"

"I don't really know. This pain shot up my arm, and it was difficult to breathe. Next thing you know, here I am being visited by Doc Sommers." Kate tried to grin, but even that seemed to make her uncomfortable.

Doc Sommers explained, "Jim, your mother had a heart attack. It was a mild one, but it's a good thing your neighbor was out mowing his lawn. Seems your mother's been having a little trouble with the old beater. She mentioned a 'spell' last week too?"

Jim nodded, and Doc continued, "Well, this one left her flat on the ground – fainted straight to the ground. I came as quick as I could."

"Oh mom, I'm so sorry. I knew I should have called Doc last week."

Doc suggested plenty of rest and recommended that Kate come into the office for some tests later in the week. Jim walked Doc to the front door and he advised, "You keep an eye out for your momma, ya' hear? Although the heart attack was not severe, another one would certainly do more damage. Don't let her do anything that will put a strain on her heart, and make sure not to upset her. Poor woman has had plenty of stress in her life, and she deserves no more. Keep her happy, keep her comfortable, and we'll get her fixed up." Doc Sommers looked Jim directly in the eye and said, "Got that?"

"Yes sir." And Jim understood perfectly at that moment that his plans with Jennie would have to be put on hold temporarily, until his mother was well enough to accept the news.

Jim returned to his mother's room and sat in the chair beside her bed. He thought she had dozed off and it caught him off guard when she spoke.

"I am so proud of you. You are such a good boy," she whispered, her body suddenly so frail and childlike.

"Shush," Jim held one finger up to his lips. "You don't need to talk. I just came upstairs to sit with you. Just rest a while, okay mom? You're going to be okay."

Kate knew her son well enough to know when he was not being truthful. Something in his eyes gave him away, and for a minute, she felt very tired and afraid. She didn't want Jim to know she was scared, so she smiled widely and took his large hand in her own small one.

"Jimmy, I'm sorry this messed up your plans to have Jennie join us for dinner tonight. I'm sorry I won't get to see her before she goes back to the convent. She's a lovely girl."

"Yeah mom, she is, but you're the priority now. Don't worry about dinner – you just get some rest. I'll call Aunt Anita to come over. You'll probably need some help around here when I go back to the seminary."

"You are too good to me Jimmy. I'm so glad you are going to be a priest and be able to help others. Who knows, maybe that'll be my ticket through the Pearly Gates. Surely a mother of a son of God gets special attention up there."

When Kate was sleeping comfortably, Jim went to see Jennie. He knew he couldn't possibly break the news to his mother tonight, and he had to talk to Jennie about reforming their plan. Besides, she was expecting Jim to pick her up for dinner.

When Jim arrived at Jennie's door, the look on his face clearly told her something was terribly wrong. He suggested a walk and as they headed to the park, Jim explained that they would have to wait until his mother got better before they could be together. He couldn't risk it and cause his mother even more serious illness. He swore to Jennie they would still be married, but they had to wait. Jennie clung to him and cried. She didn't want to go back to the convent. There was nothing there for her now. The only thing she needed was standing before her.

"Jennie, please try to understand. We will be together soon, by Christmas, I promise," Jim pleaded. They were sitting near the creek, and Jennie was leaning into Jim's strong chest, crying uncontrollably. Jim pulled her into his arms and cupped her face in his hands. He tilted her chin up as she wiped her eyes and turned away. She couldn't look him in the eyes, and Jim was relieved because if she did, she would see the anguish on his own face.

"I am trying very hard to understand. December is so far away. I can't bear being away from you for so long," Jennie's voice was filled with despair.

"I know it seems like a long time, but it really isn't. Besides, we have the rest of our lives to spend with each other and we will grow old together," he said firmly.

He gently brushed more tears from her face and wondered if he was doing the right thing by not telling his mother. "Jennie, I've only had two true loves in my life. One of those is the church, and the other is you. I'm willing to forsake my vocation because my love for you is too strong to deny, but please be patient. I know where you are, and you know where I am. I promise I will come to you when I am certain my mother is well enough to hear my truth."

Jennie didn't respond, but wrapped her arms around his waist, hugging him close to her heart. Their beats matched each other as if their hearts were pounding to reach each other, knowing this would be the last time they would embrace for a while. Jim wondered if he had the strength to leave her.

They parted ways at the edge of the bridal path that would lead them out of the park. Jennie insisted he get back home to Kate, and this made Jim feel even more in love with her. For all the pain Jennie was experiencing, she knew that Jim needed to be with his mother.

He wished their future looked clear, but for now it was vague and shadowy. He searched her eyes and felt a stab of pain in his chest. He knew he was hurting Jennie terribly but what could he do? Kate was his mother; she had raised him single-handedly and now it was his turn to take care of her.

Jim felt waves of grief and sorrow, and his eyes mirrored Jennie's tear-filled ones. Jim felt overwhelming guilt for so many reasons. He had let his passion lead him, and in doing so he committed a mortal sin. He had stolen a woman of God and taken her into his own unworthy arms. Jim wondered what God would be most angered by – the fact that he was going to leave the seminary or that he had made Jennie dismiss her vocation as well. The blame was so worthy and great he couldn't begin to address it now for fear that it would eat him whole and he would never recover. He would pray and repent later, but now his heart was breaking and he focused on the greatest love of his life.

"Don't say goodbye, because then it will be real. Just kiss me and tell me you will see me later," Jim murmured quietly, inhaling the scent of her hair deeply, so as not to forget.

"All right then, my love. Think of me by the waterfall. Smell the honeysuckle, hear the water rushing and know that my heart is beating only for you. You are my one true love, and I have waited this long to find you, I can wait an eternity if it means a lifetime with you."

Jim seared the memory of her face into his mind. "We will be together soon, but in the meantime, I will think of the waterfall and how the water continues to flow, as our love does. This love shall sustain us until we can be together again."

Chapter Six

Jennie knelt with clammy hands clasped tightly together. Although it was only mid October, there was already a chill in the air, and it could be felt throughout the small chapel where the postulants, novitiates and nuns congregated to worship through daily Mass.

The coarse polyester blend of her black floor-length skirt was making her knees itchy beneath the thin cushioned kneeler, and the close-fitting collar of her starched white blouse made her feel as though she were suffocating. Funny, the novitiate outfit had never bothered her before, but then a lot of things were bothering her these days.

She had not heard from Jim since she had left Holmesburg, nearly three whole months ago. She was beginning to wonder if he would ever come for her, maybe she had imagined his feelings to be stronger than they actually were. Unconsciously she bit down on her full lower lip and chewed it nervously, a habit she had picked up during the last few months. Lifting her veiled head slightly, she looked around the simple chapel with its twenty or so pews, glass stained windows overlooking the hill on which the convent sat, the altar at the front of the room, and the statues of Mary and Joseph on either side. Her eyes fell now on the statue of Mary, the Mother of God, who had her own porcelain hands pushed together and held up to the Lord in prayer. Jennie knew she should be praying for the grace to take her vows and become a bride of Christ along with the other girls, but she had only one thought on her mind that overpowered all others. A single, solitary thought that grew stronger daily and intruded on her every waking moment as though it were trying to drive her mad. She had to go to him. Had to go *now*. She was to be the bride of James Gabriel, not of Christ.

It was Saturday, and that meant that all thirty of the girls training to become nuns were called to help at the Catholic Social Services that was run by the local pastor and the Sisters of Good Works

Convent. It was only about a mile away from the convent itself, and it housed unwed mothers until they delivered whereupon the babies were placed up for adoption.

They silently boarded the reverted school bus that told the world in bright blue letters painted on either side that it belonged to the Sister of Good Works Convent. The Mother Superior insisted that her girls be respectful and reverent at all times. Although all the girls were friendly towards one another, close friendships between novitiates were prohibited. They were at the convent to pray and explore their souls with the Lord's divine intervention. All the same, some of the girls had made special friendships anyway, whispering secrets like school girls wherever they had the opportunity; usually late at night in their rooms, if they were lucky enough to be sharing one with their friend.

Jennie had found just such a confidant in Martha, and she slid easily into the green bus seat next to her. She smiled at the way her plump friend's blond hair stuck out wildly from beneath her dark veil. Martha was the only one who knew about Jim, and confiding in her had helped to keep Jennie sane. The best thing about Martha was that she didn't judge people; she simply accepted them for who they were. She had been shocked at the story Jennie had told her, but also very compassionate and understanding. She told Jennie that she would hate to see her leave the convent, but that one could serve God in many ways. Jennie admired Martha's strength, and wished she herself had even a fraction of it.

The bus door closed with a bang as the Mother Superior climbed behind the large wheel and revved the engine. It was an older vehicle, and the entire cavity shook as the tired, old engine spurted to life.

"Here we go, girls!" The Mother Superior called out in a loud and forceful voice, her large frame bobbing up and down in the driver's seat as they sped over the bumpy rode leading down the hill.

Jennie glanced over her shoulder to look at the convent. She loved the way the stately brick house stood guard at the top of the mountain overlooking the town of Fort Washington. It was an overcast day, and the cross that adorned the peak of the chapel was silhouetted against the backdrop of the foreboding sky as if it were actually etched into the Heavens. Squirming uncomfortably in her seat, Jennie tore her eyes away from the sight of it and turned instead to Martha.

"I wish we could just stay in our rooms today and study," Jennie whispered.

"Why? You love to talk to the pregnant girls and hold the babies, if there happens to be any that day. Sister Mary told me that they're caring for a newborn until her new adoptive parents finish all the paperwork. See, so it won't be so bad after all." Martha stated matter-of-factly in a hushed tone.

Jennie spoke no more as the loud bus came to a halt at the base of the mountain, directly in front of the Catholic Social Services building. As they all piled into the large center hallway, they were quickly given their duties and disbursed. Jennie and Martha were assigned the task of welcoming new applicants as one of the Sisters walked them through the requirements for adoption.

The couples usually arrived early, they were so excited about the prospect of having a baby, Jennie supposed. So while one couple was behind closed doors discussing the possibility of adoption with Sister Mary, Jennie and Martha welcomed the next couple waiting and offered them coffee or tea, and a comfortable place to wait.

"This day is dragging on forever! What time is it?" Jennie asked Martha as she sank into the plush sofa in the waiting room.

"Why are you acting so strange? Is everything alright?" Martha gave her a concerned look as she fell into the soft cushion beside her.

Jennie sat up and fidgeted with her collar, and answered quickly and defensively. "I just have a lot on my mind."

Martha perked up, her round face gaining a mischievous quality that did not suit it. "What things do you have on your mind? You haven't heard from *him* have you? Oh, I could just kill you if you kept something like that from me!"

Jennie snickered loudly to indicate the absurdity of the accusation. "Don't be ludicrous, Martha. Besides, he's probably gone for good." Her tone softened as she spoke the last words, and a faraway look stole the gleam out of her eyes. She did have a secret to tell her, but now was not the time. She hoped their friendship was as strong as she thought it was, as strong as she needed it to be now.

"Oh, don't talk nonsense…" Martha began to chide, but abruptly closed her mouth as the front door swung open and a middle-aged couple entered the room.

"Hello, we have an appointment to meet with Sister Mary at four o'clock," the woman spoke animatedly, and brushed a lock of her blond and silver hair behind one ear as she stepped into the room holding her husband's hand. "We're a little early."

Jennie liked her immediately, and held out her hand as she introduced herself to the kind looking couple. "My name is Jennie, and this is Martha. You must be the Goddard's?"

"I'm David and this is my wife, Nancy," the man said as he took Jennie's small hand in his own strong one and shook it gently. His broad shoulders filled the coat he wore, and as he shook it off she noticed that he had the build of an athlete. "We're a little nervous today," he said with a chuckle.

"Please, have a seat. I'll see if Sister Mary is ready for you," Jennie motioned to the couch and walked to the closed door on the other side of the room and knocked on it lightly.

The high-pitched voice on the other side of the door was muffled as Sister Mary told Jennie to come inside. "Sister, Mr. and Mrs. Goddard are here. Should I send them in?" Jennie asked.

"Yes, yes, send them right in," Sister Mary said from behind her massive oak desk.

Jennie closed the door and went back into the room where the Goddard's were waiting anxiously. "You may go in now," Jennie's soft voice floated through the room. She smiled as Mrs. Goddard nervously bit her lip and tugged at the belt on her smart wool suit. She watched as her husband stood and lovingly placed his fingers on the small of her back, reassuringly. Something about the way they looked at each other before going into the room warmed her heart.

"They seem like nice people," Jennie sighed.

"Yes, they're very nice," Martha agreed. "You know, they mentioned they were from Holmesburg…"

"Holmesburg!" Jennie exclaimed, "I don't believe it. I wonder if… " She left the rest of the sentence unfinished as her thoughts returned to Jim. I wonder if he knows these people, she thought. Her pulsating heart slowed its rhythm as she realized it didn't really matter. She couldn't come right out and ask them, not here, and besides, Jim probably wasn't thinking of her at all.

She slumped into a nearby chair and felt the anguished arms of dismay envelope her slender frame. She had visited this dark place often throughout the past three months as she lost hope that he would come for her. Even though he had told her they would be together in December and it was still October, she had this nagging feeling that something was wrong. Besides, how could she go to him like this?

"Come back to Earth, Jennie," Martha interrupted Jennie's thoughts. "What is on your mind? You look like you're in another world!" Martha placed her hands on her wide hips and waited for Jennie to answer her.

Gratefully, Jennie did not have to respond because the door to Sister Mary's office opened and the Goddard's stepped into the room silently, their heads hung low. Mrs. Goddard clutched her husband's arm as if without its support she would crumble to the floor. Jennie could see she had been crying and felt immediate sadness for the couple.

"I'm so sorry we can't help you, but you must understand that there are rules we must abide by," Sister Mary's voice was firm and void of emotion as she escorted the heartbroken couple to the front door.

After the door was closed, Jennie turned to Sister Mary. "What happened?"

Sister Mary responded curtly, "They didn't meet all of the requirements so they were not eligible to adopt."

"What do you mean, they didn't meet the requirements?" Jennie was baffled. The couple seemed perfectly fine to her.

Sister Mary answered Jennie as she was collecting her materials from the room since it was time to return to the convent, "Ah, Jennie, why do you take such a personal interest in these matters? The Goddard's were simply too old to adopt a child. Our guidelines indicate prospective parents be thirty-five years old or younger. He was thirty-eight and she was thirty-seven, so they were ineligible."

Clearly finished with the conversation, Sister Mary turned her back on her and began making her way to the door.

Unable to restrain her emotions Jennie cried out, "But that is so unfair! They're only a few years out of the age limit!" Jennie felt Martha's fingernails dig into her arm as her friend tried to silence her. She shouldn't be speaking to Sister Mary in such a disrespectful tone.

Sister Mary spun around in a cloud of blackness which mirrored the foreboding gleam in her squinted eyes, and she said, "It is not for us to decide what is or isn't fair. Such matters are in the hands of the Bishop. Now, if you are quite through, I am returning to the convent. I should say that you do have much work left to do in the area of reverence and obedience. Perhaps you should pray harder for these graces, my dear." With a final turn of her head she walked briskly out the room, letting the door bang shut after her.

"Jennie! What on earth got into you, speaking to the Sister like that? It's so unlike you," Martha's voice was high pitched as she stared at Jennie incredulously.

Surprised at her own outburst, Jennie said, "I really don't know. It just doesn't seem fair that the Goddard's couldn't adopt because they were a little bit older than the rules allowed. It just seems so wrong. Why should a child be denied a loving home because of something so trivial?"

"That's not for us to decide, you heard Sister Mary. Now, why are you acting so strange about all of this?" Martha settled herself into a nearby chair and motioned for Jennie to do the same. "We still have a few minutes before the bus heads back to the convent, so let's talk," Martha spoke decisively, as if Jennie didn't have a choice in the matter at all.

Jennie decided she might as well tell Martha what was on her mind and she sighed heavily as she fell back into the chair. She leaned her head into the cushion, closed her eyes, and rested her hand on her forehead. She spoke softly, as if speaking any louder would make her words more real. "I don't know how to tell you this, I can hardly believe it has happened at all," she moaned as she opened her eyes revealing the extreme guilt and sadness she felt. "Well, you know how I feel about Jim. We spent so much time at the park, near the waterfall…" Jennie wrung her hands nervously as Martha waited patiently.

"Well, I left out one very important detail," Jennie sat on the edge of the chair, and stared straight into Martha's eyes. "We made love – only once, and while I have confessed my sin, I still feel that I have betrayed God in ways that would not be acceptable for a nun. But that's not all," Jennie continued. "I'm pregnant." Jennie tried to read the startled look on Martha's face. Embarrassed and ashamed, Jennie could feel the hot tears sliding down her cheeks as she turned her gaze away from her friend.

Astonished, Martha asked, "Are you sure? How can you be *sure* you are pregnant?"

"I've missed my period for two months now, and I have morning sickness," Jennie whispered hoarsely.

"Oh good Lord in Heaven above," Martha's eyes grew wide with disbelief.

Not knowing what else to say, Jennie covered her face with her quivering hands and the black cloth of her veil draped down either side of her head, sufficiently wrapping her in sorrowful irony.

Jim hung up the phone as if in a dream. There was little privacy in the narrow hallway where he stood numbly in his cassock. Fellow seminarians hurried by on their way to Bible class, mindless of him standing alone in a corner next to the only phone at St. Charles Seminary in Overbrook. Unable to move, it wasn't until he looked up at the sound of his name that he regained some of his composure.

"James, shouldn't you be in class now?" Father Robert asked inquisitively. As Rector of the seminary, he was in charge of all things scholastic and otherwise, and he took this duty very seriously. He was a burly man, and took his appointment to the letter of the law.

"Yes, Father, but I just received an urgent call from Nazareth Hospital saying that my mother has just been admitted with a heart attack. I would need to go to the hospital, if you should approve," Jim bowed his head in respect to Father Robert as he waited for a response.

In an uncharacteristically tender voice, Father Robert replied, "Of course, Jim. You may leave at once. Take as long as you need, just make sure to phone me to let me know how long you will be gone." Not a man of outward displays of emotion, he gave Jim a weak smile and resumed his stroll down the hall, his heavy cassock swaying around his sturdy frame as he turned the corner and was gone from sight.

Not realizing he had been holding his breath, Jim exhaled forcibly and felt relieved that he had been granted leave so easily.

He made it to the hospital in record time. Lucky enough to catch the first bus back to Holmesburg, thirty minutes later he was walking up to the emergency entrance at Nazareth Hospital. His stomach felt like someone had poured Mexican jumping beans into it, the way it was flip-flopping about. He practically ran over to the reception desk, nearly knocking over a nurse dressed in white as he did so. Before he could apologize, he saw his family doctor, Doc Sommers, walking briskly towards him with a stethoscope swinging back and forth around his slender neck.

"Jim! I am glad you are here," he pulled Jim to one side of the large, noisy room and placed a comforting hand on his broad shoulder. "Your Aunt Anita was with her when it happened. Apparently she was washing some dishes and felt a sharp pain in her chest before collapsing. We have her stabilized, but there was serious damage. She is going to have to be closely monitored for a while. Jim, I don't mean to frighten you, but you must know. She is very weak, and it is very difficult for her to speak, to catch her breath."

"But you said she is okay now, right?" Jim asked, confused by his grave tone. "It is not like she is going to die, right?"

Sighing heavily, he lowered his voice and said, "Jim, I really don't know what is going to happen. Her body would not be able to withstand another attack. Do you understand what I am saying?"

Swallowing hard, Jim replied, "Yes, Doc, I think I do. Can I see her now?"

Jim tentatively stepped into the dark room, half wanting to see his mother, the other half wishing he was anywhere but here. He hoped he wouldn't get too upset when he saw her, but the Doc had warned him about her appearance and he was at least somewhat prepared.

She was sleeping. The ghastly pallor of her typically rosy cheeks and the bluish hue of her lips brought tears to his eyes even though he had expected as much. Not wanting to wake her, he quietly slipped into a wooden chair beside the bed. As he looked around the sterile room, he wished he had thought to bring flowers. It was a cheerless room, with stark white walls and sheets, and the only window allowed no light through its drawn shades. She was breathing so heavily, as if every breath was painful. He gently reached for her pale hand on top of her chest, and felt its icy clamminess. As he stroked her fingers in an effort to give them warmth, he realized now that he had been right to not tell her about Jennie yet. This proved that she would not have been able to take the news of their plans to marry. She surely would have had an attack, and it would have no doubt been more devastating than this one. Yes, he had been right in keeping their secret. Besides, it was only October, and he had not promised Jennie that they would be together before December. He would just have to wait until his mother was completely well, surely it would not be more than two months more.

Deep in thought, he did not see Kate's eyelids flutter for an instant before slowly opening to reveal eyes that had lost their spark.

"I am so happy you are here," Kate spoke slowly and softly, breathing heavily.

"Shush. Try not to talk. Doc Sommers says you are doing great," he gushed. "Before you know it, we will be dancing around the kitchen, just like the old days," Jim forced a smile, but his eyes betrayed his sorrow.

"We'll see, we'll see," Kate whispered, pulling her hand away from his and placing it on her heaving chest. "My son, I am so proud of you…"

"Mom, please stop talking."

"No, let me finish. I think you know how important it is for me that you become a priest. It means more to me than anything in the world. I want you to promise me that you will fulfill your vocation and become a priest," Kate spoke slowly and deliberately, each word an obvious struggle.

"Mom! Why are you talking like you are not going to be around?" Jim demanded.

"Just promise me," Kate said.

His head was whirling. What could he say? Now was not the time to tell her about Jennie, but how could he tell her that he would become a priest when he did not think he would be able to fulfill his vows? He couldn't lie to his mother. He was about to tell her about his plans when suddenly her breathing became very shallow, and her face contorted as if in excruciating pain.

"Mom! What is wrong?" Jim cried.

When there was no response, he ran out of the room and down the hall, searching for a doctor.

When he got back to the room, he was horrified to see that his mother was gasping for breath and her skin looked more like the color of ashes. Running over to her side, he grasped her shaky hand as the doctor's tried to appease her suffering. He peered into her eyes with his own anguished ones, searching for some hope. What he saw there terrified him, and he found he was speechless at the sight of her beautiful eyes becoming cloudier and cloudier, shadows dancing across her pupils.

"Jim!" Kate exclaimed with a sudden burst of energy, "Promise me you will become a priest." With the last breath of life running through her, she gazed at Jim with imploring eyes.

"Yes, mom. I promise you," he choked out the words through his tears, praying this was not the end.

The nurses pushed Jim out of the way, and told him to stay outside the room while they helped his mother.

An hour later Doc Sommers emerged from the closed door and from the look on his face, Jim knew his mother had not survived. He fell into the arms of the sympathetic physician and sobbed uncontrollably.

Katherine Gabriel was buried later that same week in St. Dominic's Cemetery. Jim had to borrow money to buy the handsome marble gravestone, the words 'Loving Mother' carved carefully into its surface.

Jim returned to the seminary to try and sort out the mess in his head and decide what his plan of action would be. As if God Himself were listening, he had not so much as stepped into the stately building when Father Robert and the cardinal approached him.

"Jim, you remember Cardinal Donohue, don't you?" Father Robert asked.

"Yes, Father, of course. Cardinal Donohue... " Jim leaned over and kissed the cardinal's ring with respect.

"I would like to discuss a matter of utmost importance with you," Cardinal Donohue motioned for Jim to follow him as he started down the corridor towards the main office of the seminary.

Bewildered and a little frightened, he had never actually spoken directly to the cardinal, he tagged along after the magnificent man bestowed in his holy vestments.

"Take a seat," Cardinal Donohue motioned to a chair while he sat behind an impressive mahogany desk. "James, Jim, I have come today to speak with you about the possibility of sending you to study at our seminary in Rome." He paused and looked directly into Jim's eyes before continuing. "We would like you to study at the Pontifical North American College in Rome. As you know, only two students are selected to go, and they left last month, in September. However, your files have been reviewed upon the recommendations of several of your professors here. Based upon your outstanding scholastic record and because you are a Medal of Honor recipient, it has been decided that you be allowed to join the other men in Rome." Obviously pleased with himself for bestowing this honor on Jim, Cardinal Donohue leaned back in his oversized chair and folded his lean arms over his chest, waiting for an undoubtedly excited response from Jim.

Taken aback by the proposal, he said in a guarded tone, "I am very honored that you would consider me worthy of such distinction. If I were to accept, when would I have to leave for Rome?"

Surprised at his lack of enthusiasm, Cardinal Donohue replied, "Well, immediately. Is there a problem, James?"

Not wanting to seem disrespectful as this was the dream of every seminarian usually resulted in a high appointment within the Catholic clergy hierarchy, Jim stammered, "No, no problem your holiness. However, if it would please the committee, may I have a few days to think about it?"

Cardinal Donohue looked dumbfounded and spoke slowly, "Yes, of course you may. I'll need an answer by the end of the week."

Jim spent the next few days praying. He hoped that if he sat in the cozy chapel at the seminary long enough surely divine intervention would be granted. If ever he needed his prayers to be answered, this was the time. Kneeling on the cold, hard wooden kneeler, gazing up into the sorrowful eyes of Jesus Christ as he hung from a cross high above the marble altar, he thought he finally knew how alone his Savior must have felt that day. At the same time that he felt this connection with the Lord, he also realized that he had never before felt so far away from Him and the church as he did right at that moment. The harder he prayed the more complex his dilemma seemed. He knew he should feel very honored at having been asked to go to study in Rome. It was the pinnacle of the seminarian experience that only the chosen few ever experienced. He had made a promise to his mother - the last one he would ever make to her - that he would fulfill her dream of becoming a priest. He knew she had meant no harm with her demand as she had truly thought that it was his dream as well.

The summer and its incredulous events were becoming a shadowy memory in his head and some days he had to remind himself that it hadn't been a dream. Jennie. Just the thought of her creamy complexion and silky hair brought on a wave of intense emotions. What if she had forgotten about him? What if she regretted everything and hoped to never see him again? And if not, was he really ready to forsake the church for a woman and break his promise to his mother? He had many questions and no answers. The longer he sat in the chapel the angrier he became at God for not gracing him with any answers. This was the God he was going to devote his life to? Where was He in Jim's hour of need?

Exhausted and emotionally drained, Jim decided that the best thing for him to do was to go to his confessor and talk things through with him. With newfound hope, he scheduled an appointment to meet with Father Phillip, who had been his assigned confessor when he joined the seminary. All new students were expected to meet with their confessors throughout seminary life and their confessors acted as a mentor and advisor of sorts, leading them through problems or questions that would arise during seminary life. Father Phillip had met with Jim almost every week for four years and knew everything of Jim's life. He knew about him being deserted by his father and his mother's struggle to care for a son on her own. Father knew of the pain Jim had felt to have fought and killed in the war, and the pain from losing his sweetheart Anna to his best friend, Dante. And throughout Jim's years in the seminary, he had trusted Father Phillip and knew that he would shed some light on his dismal situation.

Jim met with Father Phillip face to face as all students did when meeting with their confessors. Jim knew he had to look him in the eye and tell him of his troubles. No one else would be able to help him.

"Father Phillip, I have a very important decision to make. This decision could alter my future within the church." Jim told Father Phillip how he had fallen in love with Jennie and that he desired to go to her but he had promised his mother on her deathbed that he would become a priest in order to honor her last dying wish. In spite of Jim's wish to be completely honest with Father Phillip, he could not bring himself to confess that he and Jennie had committed a mortal sin by making love.

After hearing Jim's story, Father Phillip began speaking slowly and carefully, "James, it would appear that you are at a great crossroad in your life. When a man joins the seminary it is with the hope that he will answer to the Lord's prayer 'that they be one' and that he will develop a deep joy in his own vocation through the grace of the Holy Spirit. It is the time whereby you learn to live in an intimate and unceasing union with the Father through His Son, Jesus Christ in the Holy Spirit. Renouncing marriage for the sake of the

Kingdom of Heaven you would be exercising that perfect charity whereby you can become all things to all men in your priestly ministry. It is not to be taken lightly."

Father Phillip paused. Jim held his breath waiting to hear what guidance he could offer. He had known Father for four years, he trusted him completely, and knew he would help Jim through this troubling time. When Father spoke, his voice was soothing and wise.

"It is a gift from God to be called upon to serve Him through the priesthood. There are many other ways in which one can do His work on earth. It is for you to decide, with the help of the Holy Spirit, which path is right for you. But let me offer some guidance and observations." Jim waited for him to continue.

"If you are asking if you are held to the promise of a dying woman, the answer is no, you are not. Furthermore, if you are having serious doubts about your vocation, then you should not go to Rome. It will cost the diocese a lot of money to have you study there, and if there is a possibility that you may not be ordained into the priesthood, you should decline the honor. Do you understand the implications of your decision?"

"Yes, Father," Jim responded quickly.

"Then I pray that you will make the right one. Remember, a priest once ordained is always a priest according to the order of Melchizedek," Father Phillip said.

Feeling that the conversation was over, Jim stood up to leave. Father Phillip indicated that Jim sit down.

"I have more to say, Jim. There is not a person in this seminary that does not know that you are a man amongst men, and someday, a priest among priests. What you bring to the table is more than any other man that I have ever known."

Father Phillip thought for a moment and continued, "You can relate to the hard working because you have worked hard your whole life; you've dug graves by hand! You can relate to the veterans because unlike most of the men in combat who could not see who they killed, you had face-to-face confrontations when you killed them with your knife. You can relate to the broken-hearted because during WWII, when you were in combat and bullets were flying over your head, you received a 'Dear John' letter from Anna. You can relate to those who have lost loved ones. Your father deserted you; Tom, your best friend during the war, hung himself; and your mother had passed on."

Jim could feel his eyes well with tears as his mind worked through all the memories that Father Phillip was outlining for him.

"Son, the church needs you. You came into the seminary a man who was lost and running away from life. Unlike other war veterans, your experience was truly horrific as you were assigned to kill men, to look them in the eye as you killed them with your knife."

Jim couldn't speak but nodded as Father continued.

"You need the church. You need the solace that only Jesus Christ can provide. As far as the *'promise'* you gave to your mother, only you can withdraw from that as if it did not happen. If you look in the dictionary, the definition of promise is *vow, oath, pledge, word.* You come to me almost weekly to confess the hatred you have for your father because he broke his vow of matrimony, *his promise,* to your mother and he left you without a father. Are you any better than your father? You had only spent two weeks with this young woman yet you feel that she is your soul mate; that you want to throw away your whole life for *two weeks?* God has offered you so much more, James. And you have so much to offer the people of God."

Father Phillip handed Jim a tissue and said, "You are carrying a lot of baggage, but with the grace of God, I know you can change more lives than one hundred priests would be able to do combined! The church needs you and you need the church. Son, go with God."

At these words, Jim broke down in tears, sobbing. He felt unsure; he felt devastated as if he had just been told that Jennie was dead. He knew right then that his choice was no longer his choice. Father Phillip had made it for him. Jim wondered if Father's advice would have been different had he confessed to making love to Jennie?

Jim also knew that because of this choice that he no longer had, he had to go to Jennie, to tell her that he was going to Rome, and that although he would always love her, they could not be together. Only in their distant memories could they exist in each other.

Chapter Seven

It was late, and Jennie hugged her pillow tightly to her breast as she and Martha talked. "All I am saying is, if for whatever reason it doesn't work out with Jim, you should have someplace else to go." Martha spoke firmly, as she had come to do these past few weeks.

She had been a very good friend to her, and Jennie felt tears of gratitude well up in her eyes. "Martha, I just wouldn't feel right imposing on your sister and her three children. Besides, I'm sure everything will work out fine with Jim."

"I am too. But what if he can't leave the seminary right away? Look, I have already talked to my sister. Right now she is looking for a place for you where you can live and work until the baby is born. You probably won't even need to go to her, but just in case, take her address with you." Martha handed her a piece of paper with a name and address scribbled on it.

Jennie took it and she pushed the pillow she was clutching out the way and patted her slight belly. "If he knew the situation I am sure he would come here and marry me now. Since he has no way of knowing, I have to go to him and tell him. He was only waiting until his mother got a little stronger, and she has to be well by now. You'll see, Martha. Everything will be perfect." Jennie smiled broadly, hopeful that everything would work out. She was privately glad Martha had insisted on giving her the address. She didn't tell Martha that she was scared of the possibility that Jim had decided to stay with the church.

No one except Martha knew the real reason she was leaving the convent so suddenly. Her small bag contained her few possessions and was already packed when Jennie told Mother Superior she was leaving. She was surprised and tried to talk Jennie into staying, and was baffled when Jennie wouldn't say why she was abandoning her vocation. There was no way Jennie could tell her the truth; she was too ashamed. When asked to leave an address as to where she could be reached, Jennie simply told the concerned nun that that was not possible at this time.

Shrouded in secrecy, Jennie left that same day. She walked briskly to the bottom of the hill where the train would pick her up and take her to Overbrook's St. Charles Seminary and the love of her life. She imagined Jim sweeping her up into his strong arms. She wanted to drown in the sea of his blue eyes, wanted to tell him over and over how much she loved him. She hoped he would tell her the same.

As she waited silently for the train, she dared not look back at the top of the hill and the convent, which had served as her home for many years. She heard a whistle blow in the distance, and knew the train was just two miles down the tracks, at the main station. The next stop would be here, where the train came only twice a day, to deposit and collect nuns coming and going. Jennie felt odd knowing that for this trip, she would not need a round-trip ticket.

She boarded the train to Overbrook, and collapsed into the first available seat, nervous with anticipation.

Father Robert had given Jim a strange look when he had asked permission to leave the grounds for a day. Jim had told Father Robert that he had something urgent and personal to see to, and the rector had given in. Silently, he rehearsed what he would say to Jennie when he saw her. All he knew was that he *had* to talk things through with her. The train ride seemed to last forever, although it was only a short trip from Overbrook to Fort Washington and the convent. He unconsciously smoothed his black suit with his damp hand again and again. He tried not to entertain notions of what she would say when she saw him.

As the train eased its way to a grinding stop just at the bottom of the hill, Jim glanced up and saw the stately convent in the distance. He took a deep breath, stood and stretched, and stepped down the metal steps onto the platform. Unbeknownst to him, the exact time he was emerging from car one, a young novice who had just forsaken her vows was slipping into a seat in car two. They were both on a mission to find their true loves, missing fate and each other by a matter of precious seconds.

Jim pulled his overcoat tighter around him as a cool blast of air engulfed him and set out for the top of the hill to the Sisters of Good Works convent. It was a windy afternoon, and as he trekked up the hill towards the large brick building his eyes fell upon what he supposed was the convent's chapel, a large cross sitting atop the only turret. He wondered what was in store for him behind the regal doors leading into the holy place.

Not knowing the protocol for visitors, he simply clanged the heavy brass knocker and waited for someone to answer.

The door opened slowly and a portly nun looked Jim up and down inquisitively. "May I help you?" she asked

"Yes, Sister. If I may, could I please see the Mother Superior," Jim asked hopefully, nervously shifting his weight from one foot to the other.

"Do you have an appointment?" she asked suspiciously.

"No, I do not. However, it's very important that I see her regarding one of your novitiates," Jim said as politely as he could.

The nun looked at Jim cautiously once more before letting him in. "You may wait right here while I inquire about the Mother Superior."

Smiling gratefully, Jim said, "Thank you, Sister. I knew I would find hospitality here."

"The Sisters of Good Works are always hospitable."

He surveyed his surroundings as she disappeared around the corner. It was actually quite peaceful inside the large foyer. There were plush chairs on either side, and the walls were covered with framed pictures of the founding nuns and the more recent additions to the convent family. Ahead, he could see a grand spiral stairwell. He figured it must be prayer time, because it was so still in the building. Suddenly, he heard the sound of shoes clamoring against the wood floor. Jim straightened his stance as a very noble yet stern-looking nun made her way across the foyer.

"I understand that you would like to see me regarding one of our girls," she said kindly.

"Yes, Mother Superior. I have just come from the train and am sorry to inconvenience you, but I'm looking for the novitiate Jennifer Whalen." Jim paused and asked, "I was hoping to speak with her?"

Surprised, she exclaimed, "You must have just missed her then! She left here only a little while ago. She would not tell me her reason for leaving the convent, but I know the train took her to wherever she was going." She narrowed her eyes, sensing this man might have had something to do with her leaving and said, "You wouldn't happen to know why she left or where she was going, would you?"

Feeling as if someone had squeezed his heart from the inside out, Jim mumbled, "No, I have no idea."

"Well then, is there anything else I can do for you?" she asked suspiciously, as if she blamed him for her departure.

"No, thank you," Jim muttered and let himself out the front door.

He felt his throat tighten with fear. He had to find her. How could this have happened? Where could she have gone? His mind racing, and he knew he had to find a payphone.

Jim rummaged through his wallet, and whispered, "Please, please, let it be in here." His search was rewarded with a business card that Hank Whalen had handed him before he and his wife had departed for California. Hank had given it to Jim saying, "Look us up in you ever make it to the West Coast." Jim thought he would never have had to use the number on the card. It was Hank's work number at the bank. Jim reached into his pocket and threw every bit of change into the payphone, hoping it would be enough. Once again, he was rewarded when a woman's voice answered kindly, "First Central Bank, Mr. Whalen's office."

Feeling a small bit of victory, Jim asked, "May I speak with Mr. Whalen please?"

"Who's calling?" the receptionist asked.

"Jim Gabriel."

"One minute Mr. Gabriel. I'll see if he's available."

Jim rubbed his temples. This was not what he was expecting to happen. He had to find Jennie.

"Jim!"

"Sir, Mr. Whalen, I'm so sorry to bother you at the office, sir." Jim said.

"It's always wonderful to speak with you Jim. You know, Madge and I were just talking the other day about how grateful we were when you helped us with all that packing. By the way, my back is much bet…"

"Sir, do you know where Jennie is?" Jim interrupted.

"What do you mean? She's at the convent."

"I just found out that she left the convent and I was hoping you would know where she went."

"What do you mean, she left the convent? Madge just spoke with her last week and there was no mention about Jennie leaving! I can't imagine where she would have gone?"

They spoke a few minutes more, discussing the possibilities of where Jennie could be. Each promised to get in touch with the other as soon as they found Jennie. Jim hung up the phone, feeling defeated and depressed. He could not imagine why she had not waited for him like they had planned. His chest ached and he was sure it was because his own heart was breaking.

Jennie stood outside the seminary gates and watched a group of men playing touch football on the green lawn. She squinted to see if one of the men was Jim. She couldn't tell for sure as they were just far enough out of sight. It was getting colder, and she shoved her one free hand into her coat pocket while the other clenched the handle of her suitcase. The football was thrown well out of the set boundaries, and when one of the seminarians went to retrieve it, he saw Jennie peering through the gate and figured she must need something. He threw the ball back to the others and jogged over to where Jennie stood.

"Hello, I was wondering if you knew where I might find James Gabriel?" she asked hopefully.

"Actually, yeah."

Jennie's heart skipped a beat knowing she was on the path to finding her true love.

"He's headed for Rome today. What a lucky guy – one of the chosen few who get to study in Rome!" The seminarian spoke of Jim proudly.

Jennie felt her stomach lurch. She stared blankly at the man and forced out a whisper, "Are you sure?"

Confused by the shocked look on her face, he answered more carefully this time, "Yes, ma'am. I saw him leave earlier this morning. Even wished him luck."

With a momentary burst of hope she asked, "How long will he be gone?" Perhaps he was only going for a short period of time and didn't want to upset her by telling her, she thought.

"Oh, the schooling in Rome is a few years, at least," he stated matter-of-factly.

Jennie turned and ran down the street as fast as she could. She didn't stop until she was far from the seminary. She was blinded by hot tears and gasping for breath as she crumbled onto a nearby street corner bench.

People were staring at her and she covered her wet face with her hands and wept freely. She had never felt so alone as she did at this moment. How could he have broken his promise and abandoned her like this? She felt foolish for believing that he ever loved her as much as he said he did.

She sat on the bench for a very long time, trying to decide what to do now. The thought that he might not be at the seminary had never occurred to her. She had been prepared to hear him say that they would have to wait a few days to be together until he could settle things with his mother and the seminary, but this news of him going to Rome was a blow she had not counted on.

As she sat on the cold bench, she tried hard to understand why he had left her like this. Not a distrusting woman by nature, she now doubted her very being in the wake of his betrayal. She recalled the events of the summer and longed to hear the tenderness in his voice, to see the obvious love he had for her in his eyes. It had been a love she had never felt before, and was certain that he had felt too.

When the next bus pulled up to the corner, she forced herself to get on it. She took a deep, shaky breath, and held her head high as she gave the bus driver her fare. Virtually penniless and homeless, she pulled the crumpled paper out of her pocket that contained the address of Martha's sister.

Jim returned to the seminary long after 'lights out' had been called. He quietly tried to slip past the rector's room to get to his own, but was stopped by Father Robert's voice from inside.

"Jim! I thought you were already in bed. I was gone all day and didn't have a chance to check in on the men," Father Robert chastised as he stood in his doorway wearing a plaid robe.

Jim slowly raised his heavy eyelids to meet the intense gaze of the rector's. He was emotionally exhausted from the day's events.

"I am sorry Father," Jim said without further explanation.

Frustrated, Father Robert began, "Jim, you have put the committee in quite a predicament. You were to have given us an answer regarding Rome *yesterday*. The men from other seminaries are scheduled to fly out tomorrow for Rome. If you don't leave with them, you will have missed this opportunity. Studies have already begun, and the latest you would be accepted into classes is this week, do you understand?"

"Yes, and I regret not giving my answer sooner. I will go to Rome," Jim said joylessly.

Father Robert smiled, clapped him on the shoulder and said, "Smart decision. You better go pack and then get some rest. Your flight is at noon."

At Philadelphia International Airport, Jim tried one last time to find out where Jennie had gone. He found a payphone and dialed Mr. Whalen's office.

The same woman from yesterday answered. "First Central Bank, Mr. Whalen's office."

"Mr. Whalen, please. This is Jim Gabriel calling." Jim was put right through to Hank.

"Mr. Whalen, I was hoping that you had heard from Jennie?" Jim prayed she had contacted her aunt and uncle.

"Oh Jim, nothing, no word. I called the convent yesterday after I spoke with you and Mother Superior is as stunned as we are. I can't imagine where she would have gone," Hank said, genuinely concerned.

Jim was too upset to go into detail about his impending journey to Rome, simply said goodbye and hung up the receiver dejectedly.

He boarded the plane, knowing he had no choice but to go to Rome since he had no way of finding Jennie.

As the plane took off, Jim looked through the window and watched as the Philadelphia skyline faded from his view, knowing that he was leaving Jennie behind somewhere. And when the plane soared through the clouds, ironically, Jim could not help but think that surely now he was closer to God than ever before, whether he wanted to be there or not.

Chapter Eight

Jennie's hair was kept back in a loose bun, and the large red and white checkered apron looped over her neck and knotted in a bow behind her protruding belly. She reached to wipe most of the crumbs off the rectangular booth table.

There was no time to waste. The hungry truckers were steering their rigs off of Route 611 and into the parking lot, beckoned by the brightly painted rest stop sign announcing Frank's Food, Open 24 Hours.

Luckily Jennie's shift didn't last quite that long, although after putting in a ten-hour day she literally crawled up the back staircase which led to her small apartment. She lived in the tiny, dismal room as part of the room and board agreement that Martha's sister, Candice, had negotiated for her some five months ago with Frank, the owner. He was a heavy-set burly man who owned the truck stop and was in need of help during the late shift. It had been very kind of Candice to find this job for her, especially when she had three small children of her own to worry about. Jennie stayed with her a few days before beginning work as a waitress, and during those days Martha's sister had never once asked her about her situation, which she had been extremely grateful for.

Her current situation could have been a lot worse than it was. The only downfall of her job was her boss and landlord, Frank. When she had first started working there, he berated her with questions about where the father of her child was and where had she come from, anyway? He had been drunk, and a nasty drunk at that. His voiced dripped with sarcasm, and it was only after one of the truckers told him to leave her alone that he stopped.

Except for Candice, no one from her new life knew of her past and she intended to keep it that way. As a result, she was very much alone in this small town of Doylestown, and even though she was only about twenty miles from Holmesburg, it might as well have been two hundred miles. She rarely left the confines of the diner, and only did so to attend Sunday Mass in town.

"Jennie!" Frank barked from behind the counter, his voice booming over the others in the noisy room, "Hurry it up, girl. There are hungry men waiting!" He rested one chunky hand on the smooth countertop and ran the other through his wiry mop of jet-black hair.

She made one last swipe at the tabletop with her damp cloth before hurrying to set the place mats.

"Here you go, Frank," Jennie mumbled as she handed him an order for the kitchen. The diner smelled of fried onions and stale cigarettes, and the odor continuously made her nauseous.

As Jennie scrambled toward the next table of customers she could feel Frank's black eyes searing into her back. He was continuously suggesting lewd things, and she continued to ignore him. She needed the job, not to mention the room and free meals. As long as Frank's lewdness did not progress to anything more revolting, she supposed she could handle it.

"Hey, Jennie," Frank called in his gruff voice, "Did I tell you how cute ya look with that big belly and all? Very volumptous, indeed." Not only was he crude, he couldn't even properly say the word voluptuous, Jennie thought, disgusted. Frank began to chuckle at his comment, which made him all the more disgusting. His round face squinted like a prune and his gut jiggled up and down beneath his dingy cotton shirt.

Jennie scanned the room to see who might have heard his outburst, but nobody seemed to be paying her any attention. Even the other waitresses were too busy taking orders or cleaning tables to notice how rude Frank was being to her.

She wished, not for the first time, that she were anywhere but here. She was tired of Frank's crude remarks about her body. What did he expect a pregnant woman to look like at eight months? It was becoming more and more difficult to work as she grew. Her back ached, and at the end of her shift her feet always swelled so much she couldn't wait to get her shoes off and her feet into a warm tub of water.

She glanced at the large round clock that hung above the doorway and was pleased to see that her shift was almost over. The thought of a warm bath to soothe her would get her through the next half-hour.

"Good night, girls," Jennie called to the two waitresses who worked the midnight shift. Three to eleven was bad enough; Jennie couldn't imagine working the eleven to seven a.m. shift.

She peeled off her stained apron and deposited it in the soiled heap of laundry in the back room. Frank was yelling at the chef because he was using too much beef in the hamburgers and was cutting into his profits. Jennie did not want another run-in with Frank so she quietly slipped behind the storage shelves along the back wall of the cluttered room to get upstairs to her room.

She opened the door and walked as fast as she could up the twelve steps that led to her apartment. Frank lived next door in a larger apartment that took up most of the living space on the second floor. Jennie was very grateful that her apartment came with a secure door and a lock of its own, but she figured that Frank had a spare key, as all landlords must. Sometimes she felt that when Frank would slip away from the diner, he had been upstairs rifling through her things. This thought repulsed her and she didn't want to think of such unpleasant things now.

Her apartment was really a studio set-up, with a walk-through kitchen and a pullout couch that served as her bed. The room did have its own bath and toilet in the corner, where a curtain acted as the door. Although it was a small place, Jennie had done her best to make it comfortable.

She moved over to the window to pull down the shade and peered out through the filmy glass onto the highway. She sighed deeply and sorrowfully as she watched the headlights of trucks and cars whiz by. It was these times late at night that she felt the most alone.

The window was partly open, and the calm April breeze did little to comfort her. It had been a long time since she had seen fresh flowers sprouting and butterflies flitting amongst the leafy trees of spring. She thought of Pennypack Park, the honeysuckle and the rippling waterfall. Jennie remembered the last words Jim had said to her. *We will be together soon, but in the meantime, I will think of the waterfall and how the water continues to flow, as our love does. This love shall sustain us until we can be together again.* She sadly wondered if Jim ever thought of the waterfall, and the love for her that had seemed so real at the time.

Jennie yanked down the shade abruptly, as if to close the thoughts of Jim from her mind, and walked over to the old-fashioned ceramic tub. She turned its shiny white handles on full blast and watched as the tub began to fill. She slipped off her dress and allowed the warmth of the water to soothe her aching pregnant body.

Instead of getting upset by thinking of Jim, she turned her thoughts to her baby and gently caressed her belly. In a soft voice she said, "Hello sweet angel. How is my most precious gift?"

The doorknob rattled suddenly and Jennie stiffened with alarm. She sat frozen in the water as the door handle shook. Someone was trying to get in.

To frightened to speak or move, it was not until the door burst open with a force that Jennie was able to break free from the paralyzing panic that gripped her. She jumped out of the tub and grabbed her bathrobe, covering herself as she allowed a panicked shriek to escape from her lips.

Frank loomed in the doorway and looked at her with his beady eyes. He stepped into the room and closed the door, and his malignant presence filled the room.

Before he could say anything, Jennie screamed for him to get out, and wrapped the material of her robe tighter around her body to conceal the nakedness he had surely seen.

As he came toward her, she could smell the stench of him. He reeked of cigarette smoke and alcohol and he wobbled slightly as he moved.

"Jennie, everyone knows you ain't got nobody. What you need is a man who is willing to help out a poor, lonely creature like yourself," Frank crooned in what she supposed was his attempt at seduction.

"Frank, please go *now*."

"Why, I seen the way you look at me with those big eyes of yours. And believe me, I know what you're thinking."

"I don't know what you're talking about, but if you don't leave this instant I am going to start screaming."

"Yeah, right. I've heard that one before, baby doll."

Frank edged closer to her, a lopsided grin on his round face. Jennie backed away from him, and slipped on the wet tile floor. She cried out in pain as she hit the hard floor squarely on her backside.

Frank reached down as if to help her up, but then seemed to change his mind. He came at her with a look of a lunatic and Jennie was sure she knew what his intentions were by the look in his eyes. Terrified, and sensing she needed immediate help, she began screaming loudly and desperately.

At the sound of her screams, Frank grew angry, reached forward and delivered a stinging slap to Jennie's left cheek.

Fear and anger knotted inside her. Momentarily stunned into silence, she looked at him with growing hatred. The sound of footsteps broke the trance and Jennie knew help was on its way. She began to cry, from the humility, the pain and the terror that Frank had brought upon Jennie.

Frank slowly moved to a standing position, placed his hands belligerently on his hips and spat at Jennie's face.

"You pathetic piece of cheap trash!" he slurred the words angrily. "You should be so lucky to have a man like me. I could have taken care of you and that illegitimate baby that you're carrying!"

He was able to say no more. The diner's chef and bus boy had raced upstairs to see what the commotion had been. Disgusted, Frank turned his back on the sobbing Jennie and pushed his employee's aside as he shouldered his way out of the room.

"Jennie, are you okay?" The chef was reaching out to help her up.

"Yes, just go. Go!" Jennie cried, unable to bear the humility of it all.

When the door closed behind them, she slowly rose and locked the door firmly. She felt dizzy with shock. She had no energy left but continuous tears streamed down her face. She felt so ashamed, yet she had done nothing to provoke Frank and his attempted attack on her.

Despite all that had occurred, her head was amazingly clear. Each side of her brain was battling the other. She was hysterical with tears and felt that all she could do was cry and scream at the injustice of her life. Fortunately, the stronger side, the more sensible part of Jennie's brain took control. It was very clear what Jennie must do. At all costs, she had to remain calm and rational, so as not to jeopardize her health or the health of the baby.

Appreciative that there was some unknown inner strength within her to actually surrender to, Jennie simply followed the directions her subconscious gave her.

The directive was quite simple, and ran over and over in her confused brain. She had to leave immediately.

Since she owned very little, she was dressed and ready to leave within a very short time. She surveyed the room to make sure she was not forgetting anything; she did not want to have to come back. Her puffy red eyes scanned past the open closet, bureau, tub, and bed. Her gaze stopped here. She had almost forgotten that she had kept some tip money in an old shoebox on the closet shelf. She pulled the dust-covered box out, and crammed the wrinkled bills into her suitcase.

She swallowed hard, raised her chin, and picked up the bag. It was heavy, but she did not hesitate. Scurrying down the back staircase, she slipped out the rear entrance to the diner and made her way down route 611 on foot, getting further and further away from the flashing neon lights from the diner.

It was the middle of the night, and she was growing chilly. She wasn't sure how far she had actually walked, but she knew she could go no further. The highway was dark, lit only by the occasional headlights of a truck or random car passing by. Exhausted and confused, she gave in to the demands of her body and let the worn handle of her suitcase slip from her fingers. She sat down on top of the case, unsure if it could hold her weight. Once she knew she wasn't going to break the suitcase, she exhaled and tried to quiet her busy mind.

She didn't know what she was going to do, and considered calling Martha's sister, Candice. But it was late in the night, and she didn't want to disturb the family. She didn't have enough cash on hand for a hotel, and didn't know where she would sleep.

The chill black silence surrounded her. She began to shake as terrible things ran through her mind. What was going to happen to her and the baby? How did things turn out so wrong? She closed her eyes, feeling utterly alone and miserable. The pain in her heart became a sick and fiery gnawing until all she could do was yield to the compulsive sobs that shook her.

A sudden light engulfed her, and Jennie turned to see that a police car was making its way down the highway, heading in her direction. She didn't want to bring attention to herself, but also didn't want to get up and run. She stayed there, crying, a deer in headlights. The police car pulled to the side of the road.

The headlights shown right in her face, and she shielded her eyes from the brightness. She could not see the car, just two rings of lights that surrounded the headlights, but she heard the car door open and close quickly. She stood up from her seat on the suitcase, and waited as the policeman approached her.

"Ma'am, is everything all right?" the officer asked.

"Y- Yes sir. I'm fine," Jennie stammered.

Now in plain view, standing not more than five feet away, she could see his silhouette and the starched navy blue uniform. He removed his cap, and he looked powerful and strong. Jennie immediately knew that his dark eyes were trustworthy and that he was a sensitive person. She suddenly felt safe; she felt that the end of the nightmare had arrived.

"Where are you heading all by yourself, so late at night?" he asked.

Taken back by the question, Jennie simply stared at him blankly before responding, "I- I guess I don't know."

A look of pity flashed in his kind eyes. "I'm Officer Richard Falpone. And you are?"

"Jennie."

"Okay, Jennie. Do you have a last name?"

"Whalen. Jennie Whalen."

"Are you in some kind of trouble Ms. ..." he hesitated, noticing her protruding belly, "or is it Mrs. Whalen?"

"No, it's Ms.," she whispered, and thought to herself that her life would be so different if she had been Sister rather than Ms.

He cleared his throat, "Well then, would you be so kind as to tell me why you're out here in the middle of the night with no place to go? It's dangerous, you know."

She didn't know what to say; what would be an appropriate answer, so instead of answering, she lowered her head and began to tremble.

Sensing that something was incredibly wrong, the officer placed a comforting hand on her shoulder.

In a soothing voice he said, "Ms. Whalen, it can't be that bad. Listen, it's cold out here. Let's go sit in the squad car and you can warm up a bit while we figure out what to do."

Jennie liked the way he took it upon himself to make her problem theirs, and followed him into the warmth of his car.

After she felt thawed emotionally and physically, she turned to face him.

"Officer..." she began.

"Please, call me Richard."

"Okay, then you call me Jennie." Jennie moved her head back and forth and said, "You are an awfully nice policeman."

Richard laughed and Jennie smiled shyly, but it still did not erase the look of anguish that was causing a deep line to appear between her eyes. He was drawn to her in a way that made him want to protect her, to make all her troubles disappear. He didn't usually feel this way with the people that were in his police car, but usually those people wore handcuffs and were locked in the back.

He took in her long chestnut hair. Her eyes confused him. The deep brown muddy pools in her eyes appeared to be a paradox. He could see the innocence of a young woman, but knew she had experienced more in her young life that she would have liked to. He shifted in his seat and took a deep breath. She smelled like a wildflower that grew on the side of the road, pure yet intoxicating.

Embarrassed by these unprofessional thoughts, he began to rid his mind of them, a trick he had learned a few years ago while still in training. "Are you running away from something, someone? Has the father of the baby hurt you?" He paused to see her reaction.

"Oh, no. No, no, no," Jennie said adamantly shaking her head. And before she knew what was happening, she told Richard - this kind stranger - everything, leaving nothing out. She was baring her soul, much like she should have done in confession. She realized that she absolutely needed help, and it would do no harm to be honest with Richard. Besides, she didn't think she could bear this most recent humiliation alone.

Richard's back stiffened when Jennie got to the part about the attempted assault by Frank. Jennie watched as his square jaw set and his well-defined features became distorted as he listened, and she knew he was becoming angry at what had happened to Jennie.

"Frank's Diner is in my patrol area. I can have him arrested if you want to press charges," Richard said angrily.

"No Richard." Jennie reached out and grasped his forearm pleadingly, "I am in enough trouble as it is. I just want to forget the whole thing – I don't ever want to go back to that horrible place."

He looked at her uncertainly. Something about her plea must have dissipated some of his anger, because he now looked at her compassionately.

"What do you say we go find ourselves a nice cup of coffee and try to make some sense of all this?"

"Well…" Jennie hesitated.

"Come on, you said yourself you don't know where you're going, and there's no way I'm leaving you out here with no solution to your problem." He nodded his head to show that the decision had been made.

Jennie curled her hands around the steaming cup and brought it to her lips. The scent of fresh coffee relaxed her immediately. She felt warm, and cared for; something she had not felt in such a long time. The tension began to dissipate with each sip of coffee.

She wondered why this state trooper was being so kind to her. As she stole a glance at him over the rim of her cup, she knew for sure that Richard was someone that she could trust completely. He caught her gaze, and his smile caused soft lines to crinkle around his kind, gray eyes.

"Jennie. Is there somewhere you can go? I know you said your parents died when you were young, what about your aunt and uncle who raised you – where did you say they are now?"

"They moved to California," she said blandly.

"And there's nobody else?"

"Well, my friend from the convent put me in touch with her sister. That's how I got the job at Frank's, but Candice has three kids of her own and I wouldn't feel right going to her. I hardly know her."

"What about Jim, the father? Can't you go to him?"

Jennie placed her cup back into its saucer. It was very quiet in the restaurant. They sat along the window in a small booth, able to see the few trucks passing by at this time of night. It was much cleaner than Frank's place was, and the air smelled more like fried eggs and hamburgers than of stale smoke and onions. Although she was probably only about fifteen miles north of Frank's Diner, she felt like she had arrived in a different world and realized that perhaps Richard's presence had something to do with it.

"I can't go to Jim," she said softly, fearing how her voice shook when she said his name. "He was supposed to come for me, but he chose to go to Rome to study instead."

They sat in silence for what seemed like a very long time. Day was on the verge of arriving, and Jennie felt completely exhausted.

Finally, Richard spoke to break the silence. "How long until your baby is due?"

"About five weeks."

"Perhaps this will sound strange, but I am going to offer anyway," Richard said hesitantly. "I have a two-bedroom apartment. I used to share it with my partner, but he just got married. You have nowhere to go. You should come stay with me where you will be safe until your baby arrives. That is, if you'd feel comfortable doing so?" He looked directly into her eyes and smiled showing perfect white teeth.

"Oh, no, I couldn't impose like that," Jennie exclaimed. "Besides, I hardly know you!"

Richard assumed a very diplomatic tone, "That may be, but let's look at your options. You're eight months pregnant, you don't have a job or a place to go. I'm a state trooper who just happens to have a spare room available in my apartment. So, there seems to be no other option." He laughed, realizing how absurd he sounded.

Relaxing in his seat a little more, the lines of his strong face softened. "Jennie, this is not something I come across every day. Correct protocol would be for me to take you to the police station so that we could find some sort of shelter for you. But I don't think you're the type of girl who could handle staying in a homeless shelter, right? And, considering all that you have been through tonight, I think you would feel safer in my home as opposed to some shelter. It's up to you, but either way I am not going to just let you keep wandering down the highway," he stated firmly.

She could tell he meant what he said. Really, what choice *did* she have? She paused before answering.

"Richard, if you seriously don't mind, I really don't have anywhere to go…"

Richard smiled.

"But first thing in the morning I'll leave," Jennie said adamantly.

He agreed, full well knowing she would not have any new options in the morning.

Jennie slept so soundly that when she woke, it took her a few moments to remember where she was. She tugged the soft, white cotton sheet over her belly, and her sleepy eyes adjusted to the hazy morning light. *Richard's,* she thought. *I'm at Richard's home.*

She wondered why she had agreed to go with him, and then thought of his kind eyes and tender voice. But she knew she couldn't impose on him further and lifted herself slowly from the bed. The baby was active, shoving fists into her belly, trying to make more space. *A few more weeks, that's all, and then you'll be out. And then what?* Jennie was scared of what the future held for her and her child.

She carefully made the bed, even tucked the sheet corners securely beneath the mattress. She had slept in the dress she had been wearing last night and now yanked out a clean but wrinkled new one from her suitcase. She dressed hurriedly, as if she was expected somewhere.

Richard was humming loudly as he stood in a long blue bathrobe flipping pancakes at the stove. Jennie watched him from the doorway, captivated by the sight. The cheerful kitchen smelled of sausage,

Nicholas Di Bello

flapjacks and warm syrup. She caught her breath as he flicked his wrist and sent a pancake tumbling through the air above the steaming skillet. It fell back into the pan with a slumping sound. Jennie giggled.

Hearing her laugh, Richard turned around and smiled brightly. "Good morning. Did you sleep well?"

"Yes, very well. I forgot where I was!"

"Well, not to worry. You are in the capable hands of the world's most famous pancake chef! Why don't you sit down and we'll have some breakfast," He motioned to the small rectangular table in a corner of the kitchen.

She followed his instructions and waited to be served.

"My you do look well-rested. You're eyes have a sparkle that I was sure belonged there," he said as he sat down beside her.

Jennie blushed. "Thank you. Thank you for everything, you have been more than kind. I'll get out of your hair right after breakfast."

After Richard swallowed a forkful of pancake, he responded quickly, "No rush, no rush. I think I have things figured out for you." He smiled mischievously.

"Do tell," Jennie was intrigued.

"My old roommate – you know, the one that just got married? Well, his wife runs a beauty salon in town. She's been looking for a receptionist because hers recently left. I made a call this morning mentioning that I know someone who might be able to help out temporarily?" He grinned and stabbed at his pile of pancakes. "You know how to answer phones?"

"Interesting that this all just suddenly popped up," Jennie taunted skeptically.

"I would say so," he grinned again. His smile was so reassuring, Jennie knew what her answer would be but she played along.

"And I suppose I could just stay here during that time, right?" she quipped.

"Sure! That is a *great* idea," he teased.

She studied his face and thought he must be crazy to do all of this for her.

"Listen, Jennie. I know you have your mind set on leaving; that you think you're imposing, but hear me out," Richard leaned across

160

the table and touched her arm carefully and gently. "This might not be the nicest place in the world, but you will be safe here. You can get back on your feet, with no strings attached. Besides, what are your plans once you have the baby? You have to think about the baby now and not just your pride."

She looked at him, feeling the warmth of his touch on her arm. "I know you're right. I'm just so confused right now, but I have to think of my baby. I will take you up on your offer on one condition."

"And what would that condition be?" Richard asked.

"Tomorrow, I make breakfast."

Throughout the next few weeks Jennie came to rely on Richard more and more. He had become a close confidant and an unwavering friend. It was becoming more and more difficult for her to get around as her belly continued to swell, and when Richard was not working, he was always nearby to help her. He knew she was growing restless and was uncomfortable, so he took her places to keep her mind off the pregnancy. They had been out for leisurely walks, dinners, and now, tonight, the movies. As they exited the theater, he held her arm tightly so she would not fall. He was always protecting her, and she relished his attention and care.

"Did you enjoy the movie?" he asked.

"Yes, I did. Thank you for taking me. I don't know why you insist on taking a big, fat pregnant girl out in public. It can't be very much fun for you." Jennie looked up at him curiously. It was not the first time she had thought this, but it was the first time she had voiced it aloud. He looked very handsome in his blue slacks and collared shirt, and she had noticed quite a few women gazing in his direction tonight.

"Oh, sweet Jennie. You could not look any more beautiful than you do right now," he teased.

"Oh, stop!"

"No, seriously," he stopped walking and took her hand in his. "Jennie, I have not been this happy in a very long time. You've really brought joy into my life, and I can't believe I've only known you three weeks. I could not imagine spending my time with anyone more lovely."

Jennie felt confused by his confession and she pulled her hand away from his soft grip, and continued walking down the moonlit street. Yes, they had grown fond of each other, but it was a purely platonic relationship, nothing more in Jennie's mind.

Sensing he had made her uncomfortable, Richard said no more and they walked the rest of the way home in silence.

Back at the apartment, Richard cleared his throat and asked, "Would you like some tea before bed?"

"Yeah, that sounds good. Maybe it will soothe the baby so it won't keep me up twisting about in my belly all night," she chuckled. "Ooh! The baby must have heard me. That was a big kick." She pulled a kitchen chair out from under the table and lowered herself into it.

"Can I feel it?" Richard asked excitedly.

"Hurry up and place your hand right here," Jennie grasped his hand and placed his palm on the spot where the baby was kicking the hardest.

"Good Lord, I feel it! I feel it!" he exclaimed. "How amazing," he said astounded.

Jennie spoke softly and smiled, "It really is, isn't it?"

Entranced in the moment, they sat side by side with Richard's hand on her belly long after the baby had stopped moving. He lifted his hand slowly to her cheek and pushed her hair behind her ear.

"I know you haven't wanted to talk about what is going to happen once you give birth, but don't you think it's time to discuss it?" Richard looked at her intently.

Shifting in her maternity dress, she looked down to avoid his gaze. "I don't know what I'm going to do yet," was all she would offer.

"Jennie, there isn't much time left." He paused, and then tilted her chin upward so she would be looking at him. "Jennie, you know I would do anything for you. I know that we have only know each other for a short time, but …"

Cutting him off, she interjected, "It's late. Let's discuss this some other time." She rose stiffly from the chair and turned to leave the room. "Be ready to leave for Mass by six thirty, all right?" They always went to early Mass on Sunday.

"Okay," he conceded, "but this conversation is not over."

She said goodnight and headed up the stairs for bed. Once comfortably tucked under the covers, she thought about Richard's question. The truth was, she really didn't know what she was going to do. She felt so safe here with him. She didn't want to think about the future. She had never told Richard that she still hoped Jim might leave Rome and return to her. She fell into an uneasy sleep with thoughts of the baby, Jim, and Richard.

Jennie was jerked from a sound sleep with a jolt. Groggy and confused, she tried to sit up in bed just as another sharp pain seared across her belly. She cried out, unable to contain herself, never having felt anything like this in all her life. She realized that the bed linens were soaked through, and with a shock, understood that her water had broken and she was in labor. She was afraid to move. She wasn't due for another two weeks and was not prepared for this to be happening now. She called out to Richard who was in her doorway immediately.

Richard scanned the room as if expecting to see an intruder hovering above Jennie's bed. He clenched and unclenched his fists, trying to determine how serious the situation was.

Sensing his confusion, Jennie calmed him by saying, "It's okay, Richard. I'm okay. I didn't mean to scare you. Can you take me to the hospital?"

His eyes cleared suddenly as he realized she was not being harmed, but was in labor. Frazzled, he asked quickly, "Have you packed a bag? Do we call a doctor?"

Jennie watched as Richard scurried around the room, gathering things that she instructed him to put in her suitcase. The contractions were getting worse, and Jennie tried to pull her wet nightgown off and put on the housedress that Richard had found for her. Richard noticed her struggling and ran over to the bed to help her get dressed. He carefully lifted her from the bed and Jennie leaned against his strong body as he led her to the front seat of his patrol car. It took a few minutes because the contractions were coming faster now, and Jennie had to pause to regain composure after a wave of pain hit.

They raced through town and whenever a car was ahead, Richard would signal the sirens so the driver would move out of the way. Through contractions, Jennie thought how lucky she was to be in such capable hands.

It was a quick but extremely painful delivery, and when it was over, Jennie was handed a tiny bundle wrapped in a blue blanket. She couldn't believe that something so small could cause so much pain. She was sweaty and exhausted, but as she held her baby close to her bosom, she forgot about the agonizing labor and marveled at the little miracle that now lay sleeping in her arms.

She heard the hospital room door open and smiled as Richard appeared at her bedside with a dozen red roses.

"He is beautiful, Jennie, just beautiful," he spoke in a whisper. "And you look absolutely radiant holding him."

"I know I am his mother, but have you ever in all your life seen anything more spectacular?"

"No, no I haven't," he agreed. "I called your friend Martha and told her that you delivered a healthy baby boy. She's going to tell the Mother Superior that she has a family emergency to attend to. She'll be here later today."

"Thank you, Richard. I don't know what I would do without you." Jennie smiled up at him and asked, "Would you like to hold him?"

"Of course!"

Jennie looked at her baby's perfect miniature features: his precious little nose, his rosy lips and his lengthy fingers. His head was covered with light brown fuzz. She felt so blessed and she silently thanked God for this tiny miracle as she passed the baby to Richard.

Jennie laughed as Richard awkwardly moved the baby from one arm to the other, trying his best to cradle him properly. "Don't be afraid, just let him hear your heartbeat," she advised.

Richard finally got the baby into a comfortable position and he and Jennie watched quietly at the wonder of the world that was taking place right there in the room. They remained riveted until a friendly nurse arrived and said it was time to take the baby to the nursery for some standard newborn tests. Richard reluctantly handed him to the nurse and then turned his attention to Jennie as the nurse left with the baby.

Taking Jennie's damp hand in his, Richard leaned over and tenderly wiped away small beads of perspiration on her forehead. "He really is perfect, Jennie. Just like his mother." He looked deeply into her glistening eyes. "I have never seen you look more beautiful than right now. Seeing you holding your son... Well, it's just amazing."

He stopped and gently pushed a moist lock of hair away from her face. He continued slowly, as if he had rehearsed the words, "I care about you very much, you know. This past month has been the happiest of my life. You are a truly an incredible woman, Jennie. You have so much strength and goodness in you, and every time you are near I feel like I am with an angel. I truly felt that you were on that road the night I found you for a reason, and it was no accident that we met. I know you think of me as just a friend, but I was hoping that you would consider a proposition of sorts," he cleared his throat nervously. "I do love you, Jennie. We could get married, and I would adopt your son and raise him as if he were my own." He looked down at his shaking hands as he awaited a response.

Stunned, Jennie stared blankly at his nervous face. He was so handsome, and had so much to offer. His hair was tousled since they had been at the hospital all night, and the stubble on his face made him look tired but rugged. It was very unlike the flawless, smooth texture of Jim's face, she observed. Jim. He would always be with her. Always. Especially now that she had given birth to his son.

She took a deep breath and began, "Richard, I love you too. I love you as my dearest friend, someone I can tell anything to. I know that one day you are going to be a wonderful husband and father. You are very kind to offer me such an incredible and selfless proposal but I can't. I am in love with Jim." She paused to see his reaction.

Richard's head fell from her gaze in despair. Jennie reached out, and with a loving touch, raised his chin so she could look him in the eyes.

"Please, try and understand," she pleaded, "he is the love of my life, and I think he loves me, too. He doesn't even know about the baby. If he decides to leave the church, I have to be ready to go to him."

"What if he never leaves? How are you going to raise a child on your own? If you are so sure he loves you so much, why don't you just write to him and tell him that he has a son?"

Jennie passionately responded, "It would not be fair of me to take away his vocation if he truly has one. That is a decision between him and God. I am sure he had a good reason for going to Rome, and if he comes back to find me I will go to him and we will raise our son together."

He stood from the chair and walked to the window, not wanting her to see his devastation. In a strange voice thick with emotion he said, "What are you and the baby going to do in the meantime? You know that you are welcome to stay with me as long as you like."

"Richard, that is why I love our friendship so much. You are always thinking of me; you always put my needs first. I have been thinking about this a lot lately, and I think I know what I am going to do. But your opinion is very important to me so I would like to run it by you."

He composed himself and returned to her bedside. "You know you can tell me anything."

Jennie closed her eyes, unable to look into his as she spoke, "I have prayed for the wisdom to make the right decision for the baby. I have come to see that it would be very selfish of me to raise my son as an unwed mother with no real education or skills. I have rediscovered my faith in the Lord, and feel that He is still calling me to serve Him through the church," she paused. Opening her eyes wide, she searched Richard's face for understanding before continuing. "What I am trying to say is that I have decided to give the baby up for adoption."

"No!" Richard exclaimed.

"Please, let me finish. It wouldn't actually be a legal adoption. You see, I know this family – the Goddard's. They live in Holmesburg, the town that Jim and I grew up in. The Goddard's desperately wanted a child but were denied the right to adopt because of their age. Perhaps an arrangement could be made such that they would agree to raise the baby without actually adopting him. I think I will then re-enter the convent asking for permission to be placed in a convent near my hometown."

"This doesn't make any sense. If you think that Jim might come back for you, why would you give your baby to someone else and go back to a convent?" He stared at her bewilderedly.

"I know it sounds complicated, but it really isn't. You see, the Goddard's would have to agree that they could keep the baby until his real parents came for him, kind of like foster parents. That way if Jim does come back, we could get our son. In the meantime, the baby would receive proper care and the attention of two loving adults, and I could be near them if I go to a convent in Holmesburg."

"Jennie, I think it's a crazy idea that will never work," Richard said vehemently. "Besides..." he stopped short, as there was a light knock on the door as someone entered the room.

"Jennie!" Martha exclaimed, "I just saw the baby in the nursery. He is adorable!" Martha was dressed in a crisp white shirt, full black skirt and a black and white habit that covered most of her blond curls. She rushed to Jennie's side and kissed her on the cheek.

"It is so good to see you. You look terrific," Jennie gushed as she hugged Martha awkwardly from her bed.

Martha turned her attention to Richard, who was standing to the side of the two women. "You must be Richard. Jennie writes about you all the time in her letters," Martha smiled up at him.

"Well, if she wrote about me even half the amount of time she talked about you, then I am honored," Richard extended his hand to her.

After a few minutes of talk about the birth and how beautiful the baby was, Jennie looked up at Richard.

"Richard," Jennie began, "Can Martha and I have some time to catch up on things?"

"Absolutely. That sounds like a great idea, I'll go down to the cafeteria and grab a little something to eat. It's been a long stretch of excitement these past few hours." He said he'd be back later and told

Martha it was a pleasure to meet her before he turned and left the room.

Once the door was completely shut, Jennie turned to face Martha. "We have a lot to talk about. You don't know how glad I am that you are here."

"I wouldn't have missed it for the world," Martha said as she settled her plump body into the bedside chair. "You are missed at the convent, you know."

"Am I?" she responded absently.

The two women were silent for a moment, and then Jennie turned and leaned to one side of the bed to be closer to Martha. She said, "I have to tell you something very important. When Jim and I were together, he spoke very fondly of a Father Phillip, his confessor-advisor at St. Charles. Jim told me that seminarians were assigned to a particular confessor throughout their years in the seminary. Seminarians told their confessors *everything.*"

Martha waited for Jennie to tell her more. Jennie took a sip of water and continued, "Last week, I called Father Phillip."

Martha's eyes widened at this news.

"I had to. I couldn't go into this blinded. I desperately needed to know why Jim never came for me, and why he chose to go to Rome instead?"

"What did you find out?" Martha asked.

Jennie took a deep breath and continued. "At first, I told Father Phillip I was an old friend and he would not divulge any information. Finally, I asked him if Jim had ever mentioned a girl named Jennie, and the silence on the other end of the phone was deafening."

"Father Phillip knew of you?" Martha asked incredulously.

"Yes, but I don't think he knew everything about us. He told me that Jim's mother had passed away last fall, and that on her deathbed she made Jim promise he would honor her dying wish and become a priest. *It was her dying wish.* However, Father Phillip did tell Jim that he should come to me to tell me of his plans. He said that he knew Jim cared very much for me but Father also knew that Jim had a true vocation to the church and that is why he went to Rome – because of his vocation and his promise to his mother."

"So now what happens?" Martha asked.

"I do not want to raise this baby alone, I love this child too much for that. He deserves both a mother and a father. Do you remember that couple that tried to adopt last fall and couldn't? The Goddard's?" Martha shook her head in recognition at their name and Jennie continued. "I want to find them and see if they would agree to raise my son for an indefinite amount of time. They were so desperate for a baby, and I know they are good people." She stopped to see her friend's reaction.

Surprisingly calm, Martha simply nodded her head and said, "I agree with you that your son should be raised in a loving family with two parents, and I remember the Goddard's as kind-hearted and caring people. But what do you mean when you say they could raise him for an indefinite amount of time? Why couldn't they just adopt him?"

Fidgeting nervously in her hospital gown, Jennie said, "What if Jim comes back for me? What if he leaves the church and comes to find me? If he did, I would want our son so that we could raise him as a family."

Martha looked at Jennie hesitantly while she considered what she would say. "Well, I suppose that might happen but why are you suffering so? Why don't you just find a way to tell him about the baby? I'm sure he would want to be with you and your son."

Annoyed that first Richard and now Martha did not understand her feelings, she said in an agitated tone, "I will under no circumstances deny Jim the right to take his vows as a priest. If he leaves it will be his own decision, without any influence from me."

Eyes wide from Jennie's outburst, Martha reached across the rumpled bed and took her hand, "I understand. Whatever you decide, I will support your decision. This must be heartbreaking for you." Martha squeezed Jennie's trembling hand to show her support.

"Thank you," she whispered softly, "I knew I could count on you. I would like to spend a few weeks with my son. Since you and I worked with adoptions at the convent, I was hoping that you could contact the Goddard's and discuss a temporary adoption with them. I do not want them to know that I am the mother. Do you understand?"

Nicholas Di Bello

"Why? What difference would that make?"

"I am going back into a convent and my plan is to request residency at St. Dominic's in Holmesburg. Remember the Goddard's live there? I plan to go to that convent because those are the nuns that teach at the elementary school at St. Dominic's, the same school that Jim and I attended," Jennie paused.

"Part of the requirement for the Goddard's to have my baby is that they must promise to enroll him in school there, when he is old enough, if Jim and I haven't come for him by then. Just make sure they understand that the birth mother requires he stay in the Catholic schooling system. That way, in case Jim does not leave the church right away, I will be able to serve God in the best way I know how while watching our son go to school."

"Jennie, you certainly have thought all of this through completely. What does Richard say about all of this?"

"He asked me to marry him, but I can't. I am in love with another man; the father of my son, and it would not be fair of me to be with Richard when I only want to be with Jim."

"Jennie, Jennie. I do not envy the position you are in," Martha said sadly, then in a lighter tone, she asked, "Have you decided on a name for the baby?"

Jennie was relieved to be talking of something else and she smiled and said, "I think I am going to name him after my father, so he will be Daniel Whalen. What do you think?"

"It sounds like a perfect name for a perfect little boy."

Just then, the door swung open and Richard and a nurse entered the room. Richard smiled at Jennie and Martha.

"How are you feeling, Ms. Whalen?" The nurse inquired as she checked Jennie's blood pressure.

"Good, thank you nurse." Noticing the nurse was holding an envelope when she came in, Jennie asked, "What have you got there?"

"This is your son's birth certificate. Have you decided on a name?"

Exchanging a glance with Martha, Jennie replied, "As a matter of fact, I have. You have excellent timing."

"Good, then I will leave you with these forms to complete," she handed her the folder. "I'll be back to pick it up in a little while. If you have any questions, just call for me." She turned and left the room, closing the door behind her.

"I didn't know you had decided on a name, Jennie," Richard said as he walked over to stand beside Martha, who was hovering over Jennie and the papers.

Jennie looked at him and said in a concerned tone, "I just decided a few moments ago. I am going to name him Daniel, after my father."

"Isn't that just beautiful?" Martha asked Richard.

"I think that is very nice," he said quietly.

Too distracted to notice, Jennie's smile faded and her brow furrowed. "Richard, Martha and I have just been discussing my plans for the baby." She relayed all the details to Richard.

Richard looked at both Jennie and Martha with obvious skepticism. He ran his fingers through his hair, and spoke slowly, trying to make sense of the bizarre situation.

"So, let's just say that the Goddard's agree to raise Daniel, not knowing who the mother is or how long they will be able to keep him. Do you really think they would agree to those conditions in the first place?"

Jennie nodded vigorously, "I do, I really do. The Goddard's so completely wanted a child. I really think they will do anything, even with the stipulation that I'd require. And I know they are good people. The day I met them, after they left the agency, I glanced at their application and saw that really, the only thing halting the approval for adoption was their age. I feel very comfortable with this decision." Jennie stated. She had never felt more sure of anything, and knew that if she wouldn't be reunited with Jim, at least she could live out her days watching her son grow happily and loved by two people that wanted nothing more than to be parents.

Martha spoke up, "But if they can't officially adopt Daniel, and you don't want them to know that you are his mother, then we can't give them his birth certificate, right?" She motioned to the papers next to Jennie's bed.

"I hadn't thought about that," Jennie admitted, looking hopefully from Martha to Richard for an answer. No one spoke, and she sighed, "We have a few weeks to think about that one. In the meantime, Martha, they'll remember you when they came to the agency. Will you call the Goddard's and tell them their good news?"

Jennie, Martha, and Richard walked heavy-heartedly down the quiet street towards the center of town. Jennie crossed her arms tightly around her waist. She had lost most of the baby weight during the last four weeks since she had delivered, and was wearing a pretty yellow dress that she hadn't worn since before she became pregnant. With one hand she gently touched her shrunken belly wistfully, wishing that her son Daniel – Danny – was still safely tucked inside instead of in the hands of the Goddard's.

Martha and Richard had delivered Danny to them earlier that morning while Jennie had waited back at Richard's apartment. She cried the entire time they were gone. She had truly bonded with Danny the past month and letting him go had taken all the strength she had left. She felt as though her heart had shattered into a thousand pieces, and even if it could be put back together, it would always bear a tremendous scar.

She looked up at Richard with moist and puffy eyes. She had spent the better part of the last week weeping and agonizing over this day. Richard was her cornerstone. He was so supportive and compassionate, and completely wonderful to Danny. She had not even stopped to think how he must have felt. She was sure he had grown to love Danny.

She looped her arm through his, and squeezed his hand compassionately.

"It really went well with them?" Jennie asked again.

"Yes, yes. It couldn't have gone any better," Martha answered sincerely.

Richard said, "They agreed to all of your terms. It didn't even matter to them that they didn't have the original birth certificate."

Jennie held the envelope snuggly under her arm. It contained Danny's original birth certificate. The one Martha and Richard had given to the Goddard's had been a copy that stated the baby's name as Daniel Goddard. Although it was an official birth document, it had never been certified by the town of Harrisburg, as the original had been. The valid birth certificate listed the child's name as Daniel Whalen. Aside from the three of them, no one would know it even existed.

They opened the heavy glass door that led into the Doylestown Bank. Jennie asked to open a security box and the bank manager led them to a small room where a gray metal box sat on the table in front of them. The manager handed Richard three keys and left the room.

"I guess this is it. Daniel's birth certificate will be safe here." He closed the lid tightly and handed each woman a small silver key.

The air outside felt cooler than when they entered the bank. It appeared that all three were a little more at ease now that they had packed away the memory of Daniel's birth for the time being. What Richard and Martha hadn't known was that Jennie had clipped a lock of Daniel's hair and placed it in the envelope along with his hospital bracelet and the one that Jennie had worn at the hospital as well.

Martha was expected back at the convent so Jennie and Richard walked her to the train. As Martha said goodbye, Jennie remembered she had a favor to ask her. "Martha, I forgot to tell you that I found the order that teaches at St. Dominic's. They are the Sisters of Saint Thomas Aquinas. I've contacted them, and in order to accept me as a novice they need a letter of reference from my old convent. Could you please ask the Mother Superior if she could write them a letter on my behalf?"

"Of course I will, and I'm sure she'll be happy to do it for you. Even though you left so suddenly, she still talks very highly of you. She knows you are a good person." Martha said.

After sending Martha off, Richard and Jennie walked home quietly. They were each preoccupied with their own thoughts - each trying to deal with the loss of the tiny miracle that had brought so much joy to their lives in such a short time span.

Two days later Jennie picked up the telephone in the kitchen where she and Richard were just finishing an early dinner.

"Hello?"

"Jennie!" Martha's frantic voice seemed to jump through the mouthpiece, "You are never going to believe the conversation I had with the Mother Superior!"

"Isn't she going to write the letter for me?" Jennie interrupted.

"Yes," she said hurriedly, "but that's not what I have to tell you. After she agreed to write the reference letter for you, she started asking me why you left the convent. I told her that you had a problem with the adoptions that didn't work out and you became despondent and disillusioned. Then I told her that you had found some part-time work while you were trying to figure out your vocation. Listen to what she told me."

"What?" Jennie asked impatiently.

"She told me that on the day you left the convent, a young seminarian came looking for you shortly after you had left. When Mother Superior told him you had left and that she didn't know where he could find you, he became very upset. She got the impression that your relationship with him was not a casual one and she thinks that your leaving had something to do with him. She asked me if I knew who he was and what his visit had been about. She said she would have thought for sure you would have seen him at the train station that day, since you must have been leaving the station just as he was arriving."

Jennie felt the air from her lungs evaporate and her fingers and hands trembled. "So he had come to tell me about his plans to go to Rome just as Father Phillip had told him to do so?" Jennie whispered hoarsely.

"Yes, yes he did," Martha concurred. Before they hung up, Martha told Jennie that the Mother Superior had agreed to give her a letter of reference and that she had said to wish Jennie the best.

Jennie hung up the phone and relayed the unbelievable story to an equally stunned Richard. She began to cry, filled with emotions she couldn't grasp. She was happy that he had come to her as promised, which he really must have loved her. She grieved that they had missed each other that fateful day, and as it seemed, only by seconds. If only she had stayed at the convent a little longer, or left one day later. The implications of Martha's news was too astounding for her, so she fell into Richard's outstretched arms with tragic sobs wracking her body.

Richard, being ever so supportive and loving, held her until her tears subsided. He gently lifted her chin up, looked into her tormented tearful eyes and said, "Jennie, now that you know he came looking for you, why don't you go to him, tell him about Daniel, and get married?"

Jennie pulled away from Richard and a shadow fell over her face.

"The die has been cast. I will do nothing to influence his decision to leave the sacred priesthood. We have committed a grievous mortal sin against God. In His infinite wisdom, God has judged that we carry this cross that we created of our own free will all the days of our lives so that one day we may be with Him in paradise."

Chapter Nine
1959

Jim sighed heavily as he slid into the handsome dark leather chair. Having just finished eating his supper with Cardinal Rissoto, as was customary, he leaned across the broad mahogany desk to turn on the Waterford lamp. Its soft glow illuminated the gracious study that was his as Secretary to the Cardinal. Ignoring the mound of papers that lay in an orderly pile atop the desk, he instead leaned back comfortably in his chair to ponder the days events.

At thirty-six years of age, Jim had acquired a decidedly aristocratic look about him. Always very handsome, the past ten years had done nothing but enhance his comely features. His once fair head of soft waves had given way to a more platinum hue with strands of silvery white accents. He never lost his boyish grin, or the twinkle in his blue eyes. His complexion had remained smooth and the narrow, straight bridge of his nose completed the overall appearance of a man whose looks time could not touch. As he loosened the white collar of his long, black cassock, he smiled at the memory of the cardinal's comment earlier in the evening.

"The very first time I laid my eyes on you some four years ago, I knew that there was something special there. I couldn't quite put my finger on it, but I knew that you were going places, and not just because you graduated from Rome at the top of your class, either. Something in your eyes... a look I haven't seen around here in a long time," Cardinal Rissoto, the archbishop of Philadelphia, proclaimed in his characteristically deep voice that commanded authority. An older man, he had a humorous, kindly mouth and a light olive complexion. He was good to Jim, and they had become friends quickly despite the significant age difference between them.

He still remembered the first time they had met, the air had been electric with the sheer power of the office of the cardinal, and Jim felt so honored to be assisting this holy man who was so important to the archdiocese of Philadelphia. Cardinal Rissoto had looked so regal in his vestments; Jim felt nothing but respect for his position and thanked the Lord that such a great honor had been bestowed upon him.

Even then though, he remembered feeling uneasily unworthy in his presence. Perhaps that was the look in his eyes the cardinal had been referring to. As his mind wandered back to the six lonely years in Rome, he remembered when he walked the crowded streets during the day with a heavy heart and restlessly tossed and turned in his sleep each night from the weight of a secret longing. Never far from his thoughts, he closed his eyes and visualized the sweet form of his torment. How could he love so purely and despise so vehemently this vision that was permanently etched in his mind? There had not been a single day free from Jennie's beautiful apparition.

Sadly, he recalled the frantic days before his ordination into the priesthood when he tried in vain to locate her one last time. Knowing that this was his last chance of finding her, that after ordination all would be lost forever, he looked in phone books, asked around Holmesburg, and even called her aunt and uncle in California in an attempt to locate her. The new residents of the Whalen home told him that Hank and Madge Whalen had passed away a few years ago. They did not know anything else about the situation, having learned that information from the realtor selling the home. Jim decided the situation was hopeless, and conceded that God wanted him for His own so he was ordained in Philadelphia with his original seminarian classmates from St. Charles four years earlier.

When the Bishop proclaimed, "You are a priest forever according to the order of Melchizedek," Jim knew that whatever hopes he had had for himself and Jennie were irrevocably destroyed. He accepted this fact and prayed daily for the grace of God to give him the strength to be a faithful servant and to uphold his duties in a manner worthy of His calling.

In a futile effort to snap out of his reverie, Jim opened his eyes groggily, as if he had been in a deep sleep. He still felt a million miles away as he slowly turned stiff limbs in his chair. It was like he had sunk to the bottom of an abyss and was desperately trying to swim to the top for air. This was not unusual whenever his thoughts turned to

Jennie. Feeling a little more like himself as he took a couple of deep breaths, he stood, pushed back the beautifully carved arms of the chair, and faced the door just as Cardinal Rissoto's tall frame filled the open entrance.

"Father Jim! I thought I might find you here, good man. I was just enjoying an after dinner drink and wondered if you might join me."

"It is good of you to ask, however I was just getting ready to go down to the basement and throw for awhile."

"Very good! May I join you? You know how I love to watch you throw with your back turned. How you always manage to hit those darn balloons is beyond me, the Lord must be with you," joked the cardinal.

During the six years Jim spent in Rome, he had not been allowed to throw knives. One of the first things he had done after having been appointed Secretary to the Cardinal four years ago was to get in touch with his old seminarian friend Mike, who he had been ordained with. Father Mike's brother was a carpenter in Holmesburg and had agreed to come to the chancellery to build him a revolving vertical plywood panel with the outline of a person in nails. He attached balloons to the nails and threw his knives at them while the platform was turning. He had in fact duplicated the very vertical platform that his father had thrown at with his mother as the target all those years ago in the circus.

They chatted idly about the next day's High Mass in which the cardinal was to be the main celebrant as the two men strolled down to the cellar of the grand old high clergy house. They were about the same height, the cardinal slightly taller, and from the rear their black garb looked identical. Their hemlines swishing against the polished oak floorboards as they walked, the only true distinguishing factor between them was the color of their appointments, Jim's a snowy white and the cardinal's a royal purple. Other than their vestments, the two men might have been interchangeable if viewed from behind.

The cellar was dark, damp, and smelled of stale air. Cardinal Rissoto chuckled softly as Jim struggled to find the light switch in the dark room. Long graceful fingers cautiously roamed the cold, hard cinder block wall for the switch. Once found, harsh white light illuminated the dingy basement. He did not even notice. To Jim this was a place of sanctity.

"How can you stand to come down to this dreadful place for two to three hours every day?" Cardinal Rissoto asked, as his squinted eyes jumped around the shadowy room nervously.

"What do you mean?" Jim smiled easily at him, "This place is my sanity, my temple. You have to admit that it is very relaxing down here, don't you?"

Looking skeptically at him, the cardinal said, "Sure, very therapeutic. Whatever you say. I just come to watch you throw. I have never seen anything like it in all my life. Show me the one where you come up from the ground and fling a knife right at the target's balloon head, that one is truly phenomenal." His full face lit up as he spoke, and relaxing a little, he sat down heavily on a box of crates and waited for Jim to begin.

"That particular throw did come in handy in the war," Jim agreed as he blew up ten blue balloons and fastened each to a nail protruding from the large upstanding plywood contraption. Having secured each one, he knelt down and fished out his brown leather satchel from behind the target board. Pacing twenty steps backwards, he pulled out three six-inch blades and handed the leather pouch to the cardinal. Cardinal Rissoto played an active role in the sport, standing up from his seat to give the wheel a mighty tug that sent it spinning.

"Okay," the cardinal called, having done his job and signaling to Jim that he was clear of the target.

Crouching with his back to the moving plywood, Jim deftly maneuvered his black leather clad feet beneath his long cassock. Spinning around like a whirling top, he sprang to his feet while releasing the blades all at once in a controlled combination.

Pop, pop, pop! All three knives burst the balloons representing the target's head.

"You got 'em all right!" Cardinal Rissoto clapped his hands together, enthralled.

"I have to hand it to you Father Jim, I used to think that spending so much time down here would interfere with your work as Secretary, but I was wrong. I am glad that you took up golf like I suggested, though. Although, it really isn't fair for one man to have so much talent. You are a great golfer, too!"

Humbly Jim acknowledged the compliment. "Thank you, I have always been a good athlete, praise the Lord."

"I would say so. By the way, isn't this the weekend that you have to serve in the reserves?"

"No," Jim shook his head, "that's next weekend."

Shortly after being ordained into the priesthood and taking his appointment here, Jim joined the army reserves as a chaplain. He automatically became a first lieutenant due in part to his status as a decorated World War II combat soldier.

"Refresh my memory, what group did you join?"

"The Ranger battalion. Their expertise is similar to my experience with the Demolition Detachment in the war. Next weekend I'm taking the course in sky-diving," Jim spoke animatedly, "they only teach the course a couple times a year."

With unabashed admiration Cardinal Rissoto stated, "You really are one of a kind, Father Jim. One of a kind."

It was Sunday, and the cardinal had just served as the main celebrant in the holy Mass. Jim had assisted him, and when they had changed out of their vestments and into their normal black street clothes, Jim asked the Cardinal Rissoto if he would hear his confession. The cardinal obliged and the two sat face-to-face in one of the pews opposite the confessionals that lined the right side of the beautifully ornate church. The vaulted ceilings displayed a heavenly mural of Jesus Christ in paradise. Jim realized with dismay that it was not any easier to confess his sins as a priest than as a layperson in the community. One sin in particular caused him great suffering. It was the only sin that remained constant since boyhood and challenged him as a priest. Clearing his throat, Jim said, "Bless me, your Eminence for I have sinned against God. I have yet to be able to forgive my father's misdeeds. I confess that I still hold hatred in my heart for him."

This was not the first time Jim had confessed these words to Cardinal Rissoto and he sighed at Jim's confession now. The cardinal leaned forward and said, "Jim, we've discussed this before and I will say it again. It is not a sin for you to not be able to forget and forgive what your father did to you and your mother. Your feelings for your father are not hatred; you feel scorn, contempt for the man, if you will, and that is not a sin." The cardinal paused for a moment and said, "If this is what you need to hear, then I will absolve you from this so-called sin. For your penance, go and kneel at the statue of the Blessed Mother and ask her to give you the grace and wisdom so that you may find it in your heart to love your father in his disgrace, if he is still alive. Remember, Jim, according to John, Christ said, "Love one another as I have loved you." Jim bowed his head in respect and went to kneel by the Blessed Mother statue.

Jim made the sign of the cross and stood up from the kneeler at the base of the statue when he finished his penance. He was surprised to see Cardinal Rissoto walking toward him with the archbishop of New York. They passed the long rows of empty pews and motioned for Jim to join them. The church was completely empty except for the three men.

"Father Gabriel, you remember Archbishop Morgan," Cardinal Rissoto said politely.

"Your Grace," Jim said reverently as he kissed the ring on the hand the archbishop extended. The mere presence of this holy man invoked a sense of awe in Jim.

"Archbishop Morgan, if you recall, Father Gabriel is a decorated soldier. He is a World War II Medal of Honor winner as well as a recipient of the Silver Star, Purple Heart, Croix de Guerre, and the Victoria Cross... Did I leave any out?" He smiled broadly at him.

Embarrassed and flustered by the cardinal's address, he said humbly, "I would rather be thought of as a fine priest than as a celebrated hero, Your Grace."

"Don't be so modest!" Cardinal Risotto quipped amiably.

Archbishop Morgan nodded respectfully. "I commend your spirit, Father Gabriel. I have been hearing impressive talk of your work with Cardinal Risotto from my bishops in New York. I trust we will be seeing each other on a more regular basis shortly," he hinted.

It was no real secret that Jim was being groomed to become Bishop Gabriel. Really, it was an illustrious appointment, but it was not one that he thought he wanted. Why does Cardinal Rissoto always introduce me as if I am some sort of trophy, he wondered. He would much rather be thought of as a priest first, a decorated war veteran second. He said as much to the cardinal time and again, but was routinely dismissed with a chortle and a quip to stop being so darn modest.

He was invited to dinner with the two exalted men, and gladly accepted. They were to dine at the finest restaurant in all of Philadelphia, a treat indeed. Once there they discussed topics such as the papacy of Pope John XXIII. It was a very involved discussion, and his wealth and depth of knowledge on the subjects at hand impressed both the cardinal and the archbishop alike.

After the men had finished with dinner and Archbishop Morgan had departed for New York, Jim and Cardinal Rissoto slouched comfortably in two plush leather chairs in the cardinal's study. It was late, and so there would be no interruptions from the rest of the clergy who resided in the house as they enjoyed an after dinner drink.

"Father Jim, your insights tonight were truly enlightening, my friend," he said with candid respect for the younger priest.

"No more than yours," he said without guise.

Cardinal Rissoto laughed softly as he lifted his glass of Amaretto, "I admit you are wiser than I." In a more serious voice he said, "Someday, with the hard work and dedication I know you possess, and because of your studies in Rome, your knowledge of human behavior, and your military status, I am confident you will become a bishop. You realize the Catholic Church is grooming you for such a prestigious position."

Jim took a long sip out of his own glass, cherishing the taste of the sweet liqueur and thought of how he would broach what was on his mind. He said slowly, "There is something of great importance that has been troubling me. I have been giving this a lot of thought, and would like to discuss this idea with you." He chose his words carefully, "It has been my honor to serve in this position during these past four years. However, I worry that I am losing touch with the lay community..."

"Don't be ridiculous, Jim."

"Please, let me continue," he said calmly, leaning to rest his half-empty glass on a nearby end table. "I understand and am humbly honored that the powers that be within the church wish to have me become a bishop. I have given this a lot of thought, and feel that my calling lies elsewhere."

"What are you saying?"

"I feel that my true ambition lies within parish work. I want to be with my flock, just as Jesus Christ was with His." Relief swept through him. He had been carrying this heavy burden like a harness on his shoulders for a long time now. It felt good to finally free himself of what was expected of him and admit his own desires.

Stunned into silence, Cardinal Rissoto looked at him incredulously. His customary eloquence was gone and he finally stammered, "Why would you relinquish your future in the high clergy to become a simple parish priest?"

"I realize that the church has spent a lot of time and money on me, sending me to Rome, and I know that my being a war hero has helped my disposition within the clergy. I never wanted it to be that way, though. I became a priest so that I could help the less fortunate and bestow the word of God to His people. That is all I ever wanted. As a bishop I would be too far removed from the community to serve the way I feel I am called to. Can you understand?" Raising one eyebrow, he waited for a response.

His tight expression relaxed into an affectionate smile and Cardinal Rissoto said, "Jim, I think you are a man of many hidden and many more apparent talents and passions. I hope that in parish life you find your calling, your heart's desire." He raised his hands in the air, and said, "Heaven help us." Laughing, he downed the remainder of his cordial.

"I fear I lost my heart's desire long ago, but perhaps all is not lost," Jim spoke in a moment of unthinking passion, automatically wishing he had not said the words aloud as he too finished his drink.

If Cardinal Rissoto noticed the connotation of his words, he did not say so. The two men discussed a plan of action late into the evening. The cardinal would look into finding a suitable congregation close to Jim's hometown of Holmesburg, and when the decisions had been made on Jim's future as a parish priest, the gentlemen said goodnight to one another and departed for their bedrooms.

It was a few months before Cardinal Rissoto found a suitable congregation with an opening for a parish priest. His new parish was in Port Richmond, a small, poor section just southeast of Holmesburg, Mayfair and Frankford, right along the Delaware River in Philadelphia. Since Jim had been raised in Holmesburg, he knew the area well, and felt excited about embarking on this new religious adventure. He was expected there by the end of the week.

"We are all going to miss you, Jim," Cardinal Rissoto said affectionately as he finished telling him the details of his new assignment as parish priest at St. Ann's Church in Port Richmond. They stood in his office, beside a stack of papers so immense that it was nearly impossible to tell that there was a desk beneath it. Clearing his throat emotionally he said, "As a token of my love and respect for you both as a fine priest and a good man, I would like you to accept my Hudson as a parting gift. Trust me, you will need it in parish life. They do not have even half of the luxuries that you have become accustomed to here, I'm afraid." He chuckled softly.

Jim stubbornly refused, "I could not possibly accept such a gift. Your own brother gave you that car! Besides, I am fully prepared for the humble lifestyle that I am assuming. In fact, I welcome it."

"I respect your noble intentions, however on this one issue I must insist. You will have a much greater need for the vehicle than I. I have drivers and church limousines at my disposal. Here are the keys; I won't take no for an answer," he reached into the top drawer of his desk, fished out two silver keys and handed them to Jim.

Accepting them reluctantly, he said with emotion, "Thank you, I hope I don't regret the decision to leave such fine company as yours. It has been my privilege to learn from a great man such as yourself."

Chapter Ten
1960

It was Saturday, August seventeenth, two days after his thirty-seventh birthday. Jim was rushing to change out of his khaki shorts and button down shirt into his priestly black suit. It was extremely hot today, and even though it was nearly six o'clock, his small room inside the rectory at St. Ann's was still stiflingly warm. Quickly fastening his white clerical collar to his black button down shirt, he grabbed a comb off of his old bureau to tame his thick wavy hair.

Thank goodness I remembered to shave this morning, he thought as he caught a glimpse of his handsome profile in the mirror hanging over his dresser. There was no time now to tend to such matters anyway. He was running late, he was supposed to already be inside one of the confessionals, ready to hear the sins of the St. Ann parishioners. The pastor, Father Charles Duffy, would be mighty upset if he walked in late. A stout, crabby older man, Father Duffy did not approve much of what Jim did. It had been that way ever since he had joined the congregation, some three months ago. Jim thought it might have something to do with the fact that for one he had held an envied position within the Catholic hierarchy, one that Father Duffy would likely never personally attain. For another, Jim was a war hero whereas he himself had never even fought in the war, having joined the priesthood instead. Despite the pastor's obvious distaste for him though, Jim had not let that interfere with his priesthood. He was actually quite happy here. He felt that here at St. Ann's he could make a difference in people's lives, something that had been lacking in his previous position.

Joining fellow parish priests Father Thomas Murphy and Father Valentine DiMarco, as well as Father Duffy in the confessional booths, Jim noticed that the line outside of his confessional was triple that of the other priests. This was not unusual; it was well known that Father Jim was by far the most lenient priest when it came to penance. In contrast, Father Duffy's line was always the shortest as he was notorious for his harshness. Quietly slipping into the back end of the cubicle, he sat down on the hard wooden bench, cleared his throat loudly to alert the person on the other side of the mesh screen that he was ready to hear their confession, and readied himself to forgive the penitent.

Two hours later, Jim emerged from the confines of the confessional, looked to see if there were any parishioners left that wanted to confess, and seeing that there were none smiled and stretched his aching back.

"Well, well, Father Jim. Once again you have outdone us," Father Valentine DiMarco laughed good-naturedly from the pew he was sharing with Father Duffy and Father Murphy. The two priests had been done for over a half an hour now, Father Duffy had been done for over an hour.

"What are you doing – bribing people to come to your confessional?" Father Murphy joined Father DiMarco with some teasing of his own. The two priests had been at St. Ann's for at least three or four years each. Many a loving reference was made to their Abbott- and Costello-like presence. Not only due to the fact they could usually be found together at any given time, but because of their physical appearance as well. Tall, thin, and intellectual, Father Murphy bore a striking resemblance to the famed comedic actor Abbott, while Father DiMarco's round physique and jolly temperament mirrored Abbott's sidekick Costello almost to a tee.

Jim liked the pair, as did the entire parish, if only for the comic relief they offered. In reality, they gave much more to St. Ann's than mere amusement. Together, they had been with the parish for longer than Father Duffy, who was their superior as well as Jim's. They had helped the community through economic hardships and changing times. While other parishes in the diocese lost the tight-knit religious communities they once had, St. Ann's withstood the test of time and remained a faithful congregation of good Catholics to this day, due in part to the hard work of Father's Murphy and DiMarco.

For his part, Father Duffy credited most, if not all of St. Ann's devoted parishioners to his own workings. As head of the parish, he had the final say in most church activities. Tonight, his heavyset body cloaked by his long clerical dress, he looked at Jim in disdain.

"Father Jim, could I have a word with you?" he said while rubbing one plump hand on the top of his balding head while the other rubbed the stubble on his chin. Without waiting for an answer, he walked away from the other priests towards the back of the large, quiet church.

Jim obediently followed. Looking fairly distraught and shifting strangely from one stubby leg to the other, Father Duffy said, "Father Jim, what do you think this is, some sort of game?"

Surprised at the angry tone of his voice, Jim responded quickly, "What are you talking about?"

"You know darn well what I'm talking about. Every Saturday the line of people waiting to go to your confessional is snaked around the inside of this church. Why do you think that is?"

Jim stared at him blankly.

"I'll tell you why," he snapped. "It's because nobody takes you seriously! When a sinner comes to you and tells you his sin you say, 'Oh! Dear penitent, I am so sorry for you. You poor soul, God loves you. Try really hard to be good and if you say the first part of the Hail Mary, I'll say the second part.' I overheard you!" Father Duffy was furious.

Irritated by the accusation, Jim defended himself. "It is true, I do sympathize with our congregation and their sins. It is my duty as a priest to absolve them of these sins as best I see fit. I love these parishioners as if I were their father."

"If a person comes to you having committed adultery – after confessing to you they want to go out and do it again! You are supposed to supply a hefty penance to a sinner," he reprimanded. "You give the same easy penance to every person, whether they took the Lord's name in vain or robbed a bank!"

"I am just trying to be a good and fair priest, I am sorry to have upset you," Jim apologized. He wondered if part of the reason Father Duffy was so angry was that no one ever wanted to go to his confessional. Jim knew how proud Father Duffy could be.

Jim's apology seemed to infuriate him further. It was as if he wanted Jim to argue with him, rather than be so agreeable. Eyes wide and balding head red with fury, he said no more but simply turned his considerable frame and walked out of the church in a huff, never suspecting that Jim would follow him.

"Father Duffy, I'd like to explain my position on the sacrament of penance."

"Your position?" he flared.

"Yes, Father. In the Bible, Jesus Christ said to the apostles the sins you shall forgive are forgiven and the sins you retain are retained. We, as priests, Father Duffy, forgive sins but only God can judge these people, and He will judge them on their day of reckoning. If I have a penitent on my right who has committed adultery, he may have sorrow in his heart, and I hope that he will not commit the sin again. But the penitent on my left who has committed adultery may know in his heart and mind that he will commit the sin again. He may even intend to commit it after he leaves the confessional. And yet I have no way of knowing in either case what it is in their hearts and minds. We can only go by what is on their lips, not what is in their hearts, because only God can see that. On the final day, God knows those things and He will judge them accordingly, whether I give them half a Hail Mary or a thousand."

"But you take it too far, Father, by saying half of the Hail Mary for them."

"Because we have to make it a joyous experience for them, not something to fear. Let us not drive the parishioners away."

"You're making a mockery of it Father Jim, and I will not have it."

"I don't consider it a mockery, Father. I consider it my sacred duty."

Later that night, Jim awoke soaking wet. Confused and disoriented by a vivid dream, it took him a few minutes to organize his thoughts enough to know that he was actually lying in his own bed at the rectory. Sweat had drenched his bed linens straight through to the old mattress. Pulling himself up to a sitting position, he swung his legs over the bed frame, stood, and changed into a clean nightshirt. It was four o'clock in the morning.

He had dreamt that he was back in high school, eighteen years old and dating Anna Murphy, the girl he was sure he was going to marry. It had seemed so real, the soft curves of her body, her trusting eyes. He remembered touching the silky strands of her blonde curls and thinking she smelled like a flower. Anyone would have agreed that she was the most beautiful girl in Holmesburg. He had loved her very much, and thought that she held the same feelings for him. They had talked of marriage more than once on their long walks. Then he left for the army, and his world shattered. He still felt a little sick when he remembered receiving that awful letter from her telling him she was in love with his best friend, Dante, and they were going to get married. He had gone crazy, and to this day did not know if she was the real reason he had entered the seminary. Well, maybe initially, he thought, but certainly not the reason he took the binding vows of priesthood in the end.

It was funny to be thinking of Anna now, after so many years. Especially since if his thoughts did turn to a woman, that woman was always his precious Jennie. True, he did once love Anna, but nothing in this world mirrored his feelings for Jennie. Why did he think of her then? Suddenly, it came to him. Tomorrow was the beginning of a yearly block collection that the parish held. He and fellow parish priests were to individually go to every parishioner's home and collect monies for the congregation. He knew when he first came to St. Ann's that Anna and her husband Dante lived in town and belonged to his parish. He always looked for them in church, but never saw them there or anywhere else for that matter. From looking at the church records he knew that they had not used their church charity envelopes for the past five years. He decided that it was just as well he not see them after all these years - he still felt betrayed by the two people he had trusted most at the time. But it was his duty to go to their home tomorrow and ask them for a contribution. He knew that Dante would be working, and prayed Anna had a job as well that kept her out of the house during the day. Pushing aside these unwelcome thoughts, he drifted back into an uneasy sleep.

It was a busy morning. He had already stopped at ten homes in the parish. All that he had to show for it was a measly ten dollars, though. It was not that the parishioners were stingy, quite the contrary. Everyone that had the means was very generous. Unfortunately, there were a lot of parish families that were living in virtual poverty. When he came to one these houses and asked for contributions, he inevitably ended up giving the family some of the money he had collected from other homes. He felt it was the right thing to do, he wanted to help them, and his heart went out to them. He recalled the kind charity of others when he and his mother did not have a penny to their names.

He stopped to talk to some neighborhood children who were throwing a baseball around, throwing them a couple of pitches in the middle of the street since there was really not much in the way of yards in any part of Philadelphia, Bridesburg included. It really was a beautiful day, he noticed as he looked up to the sky and felt the warm rays on his face. The sound of the boys laughing, enjoying their game, hung on the air making the day seem even brighter.

He had been putting off going to Anna and Dante's home as long as possible, but now it was one of the last names on his list. Feeling unusually self-conscious in his black suit, he held his breath and hoped no one would answer the bell as he pressed it with one long finger.

The door did not open immediately, and feeling that no one was home, he turned to leave. He turned from the door and just as he did, he heard the knob turn and the creak of wood as it opened. Swiftly pivoting around, the naturally golden tan of his skin faded to a ghastly pallor as he took in the view that stood before him.

"Hello, Jim. I have been waiting for you all day," Anna crooned from just inside the doorway. She stood before him wearing a bright silk kimono that loosely covered her creamy skin, her golden curls piled atop her head, tied casually with a silk ribbon. She smiled at him seductively, her negligee wrapped loosely enough to reveal her full, ivory breasts. Mistaking his obvious examination for approval, she leaned toward him temptingly.

She was breathtaking. Furious, he stepped inside and closed the door behind him. Without speaking, in one quick movement, he spun around so that he was behind her. Grabbing her kimono at the shoulders, he pulled it off letting it slip to the floor. Now stark naked, he deftly moved in front of her and placed one foot on the bright, silky fabric. He gave her sensual curves a raking gaze. His stare was bold and assessed her frankly.

"How dare you put my manhood, and worse, my priesthood to the test," he spat the words, feeling himself tremble with anger.

Anna leaned over in an attempt to retrieve her garment, but Jim's foot kept it pressed firmly to the floor. Speaking in a softer yet still firm tone he said, "Leave it there, this test is not finished. I am not going to ask you why you left me for Dante because it was in your letter. I want to know what happened to your marriage that you would stand before me like this."

Wrapping her slender arms across her exposed body self-consciously, she seemed to think about the question. After a moment of silence she began, "Dante and I were happy in the beginning, pretty happy I guess. Then I realized I never stopped loving you," she searched his eyes and finding no sympathy there, she continued, "One night while we were making love I called out your name. Dante was so upset. Anyway, I became pregnant and things got better for a while. Then one day, against Dante's wishes and orders I went horseback riding - you know how I loved horses, Jim. Well, I guess the horse got spooked, because it ran out of control through the woods. A low tree limb knocked me off the horse and I lost the baby from the fall. Dante was crushed. We tried for four years to have another, but I could not get pregnant. He started to drink, and I had an affair. He found out and moved into the spare bedroom and has been there ever since, about seven years now." Finished, her shoulders drooped, and with a moan of distress turned away as if ashamed.

Jim reached down, picked up her robe, wrapped her trembling body in it and tied the sash securely around her thin waist. She began to sob and he pulled her into his strong embrace. Pressing his lips against the soft skin of her forehead he said, "I never stopped loving you but I am a priest and I will be a priest forever."

He gave her a clean handkerchief from the left breast pocket of his suit and while she wiped her eyes he told her how he had fallen in love with a wonderful girl. Confiding that he had made love to her, he told of how she disappeared and how he has not seen her since and probably never will again. They talked for a long time, both sharing intimate details about themselves.

They had been sitting on the cold hard wood in the foyer for over an hour, and when Jim stood to leave, he asked, "What is Dante's favorite meal?"

Looking at him inquisitively she said, "Meatloaf."

"Set up a table with candles, get a cake pan in the shape of a heart, and make a meatloaf in it. Have dinner ready for him when he comes home from work."

Anna replied doubtfully, "It won't work. He doesn't love me anymore and I don't know if I love him enough to do this."

His voice filled with emotion. He said, "If you love me like you say you do, do it for me. I love both you and Dante because God has willed it." Moving very close to her, he took both of her hands in his and looking deeply into her eyes, he said, "This may be the last chance you will ever have to put your life back into happiness."

Taking a deep breath, she sighed hopefully, "I'll do it, Jim."

"Take everything that belongs to him that is in the spare bedroom and put it in yours. Lock that door and don't ever open it. What time does he get home from work?"

"He doesn't come home 'til late, usually drunk. At five o'clock he goes straight over to the Elbow Room Bar around the corner," she grimaced with distaste, like the words left a bad taste in her mouth.

He promised her that Dante would be home by six o'clock. Asking her to kneel down for his blessing, he blessed her and the house. He turned to leave, but stopped and faced her instead. "I want to see you and Dante at the nine o'clock Mass on Sunday. I will be saying that Mass. My confessional is on the right side in the rear of the church. I promise I will not judge you and Dante, but I will love you and forgive you as God has." Kissing her on the cheek, he said, "Do not deny me this one favor."

Jim made a few more collection visits before heading over to the bar. He gave the last of the money he had collected that day – ten dollars – to the final family he visited. They were in desperate need of food and clothes and the husband had just been laid off from his job as an engineer in a downtown meat packing plant. Jim drove to the Elbow Room without a dime in his pocket, and parked in the nearly empty parking lot and waited for Dante to pull in. He watched as Dante walked inside and after a few minutes, Jim entered the bar. He looked out of place in his black suit and frowned at the dark, dingy room that was filled with smoke. Jim approached Dante just as the bartender was serving him a beer.

"Make it two," Jim motioned to the bartender, holding up two fingers for emphasis.

Startled, Dante looked up and his eyes opened wide at the sight of him. "Father Jim! I didn't think you drank!"

"I don't," he said. Turning to the bartender he asked, "Do you know this man?"

Placing two beers in chilled glasses on the counter he said amiably, "Sure! He's my best customer!"

Putting his palm over the top of Dante's glass so he could not lift it he said emphatically, "He *was* your best customer!" Lifting Dante's beer as well as his own, he carried them down to two men sitting at the other end of the bar. Returning to a surprised Dante, he told him to follow him outside so they could talk.

Once outside in the warm summer air, Jim shook Dante's hand as they exchanged greetings. "I stopped at your house for block collection today and saw Anna. We had a long talk and I blessed her and your house before I left. I forgive you for stealing her away from me while I was at war, old friend. Anna told me how your marriage is in a shambles, and took complete blame for it. It hurts me to see the two of you like this."

Obviously uncomfortable with the discussion, Dante said with forced lightness, "Don't worry about us. I am glad to see you are happy, and to think, a priest! I was impressed to learn about the Medal of Honor you received and all." Middle-aged and having the appearance of a man broken down by hard times, he gazed down at his dirty work boots, his broad shoulders slumping dejectedly.

Looking sympathetically at him, Jim said, "I have a story I want to tell you that a priest friend of mine told me. It's about a soldier who leaves his wife and two children to fight in World War II. Three years later he returns home from the war and there are three children, not two. His heart is broken to find out that while he was fighting the Germans his wife was having an affair and now he must be the father to another man's child.

He went to my friend, his parish priest, and told him the story. The priest informed him that there were only two things he could do. First, he could leave her and the children, two of whom were his, or he could forgive his wife, accept the child as his own and love him as best he could. The priest assured him that God would bless him well. He decided to accept the conditions as they were and my friend tells me that they are the happiest couple he has ever seen. The husband was happy because he forgave his wife and he knew the little boy and his two girls needed him to love them. He also knew that God would reward him in Heaven. For her part, his wife realized what a decent man he was to accept those conditions, forgive her, and love that innocent boy."

Pausing, Jim looked intently at Dante. "It is your decision to make, but as we stand here talking your wife is home cooking you dinner. I believe she still loves you and I know you love her. Put your pride aside and have dinner with her. Take her into your bed so that the two of you can be husband and wife again. Remember one thing that will never change, and that is my love for you and Anna. You are in my prayers always."

Dante agreed to give it another try and as Jim was walking to his car he called over his shoulder, "I'll see you in church on Sunday!"

Satisfied that he had done his best both as a priest and a man, Jim returned to the rectory just in time for supper. As his fellow priests and Father Duffy hungrily ate the beef stew that was served to them in the rectory's dining room, Father Duffy put his fork down and turned his attention to Jim.

"Father Jim, I have already collected the money that Fathers Murphy and DiMarco received today. How much did you collect?" he asked eagerly.

Swallowing a chunk of potato whole, Jim tried to think of what to say. "Well, you see, it is very complicated," Jim started while Father Duffy raised an eyebrow skeptically. "You see, the parishioners where quite generous. The only problem was, some of the other families I went to were in such squalor that I felt it my duty, the church's duty, to help them. So…I gave them what I collected." He squinted his eyes in anticipation of the rage that would surely ensue.

Choking on his dinner, Father Duffy dropped his fork and grabbed for his throat making grotesque gargling noises. China and silverware clattered on the table as they all went to help Father Duffy. They pulled him out of his chair, not an easy task due to his weight. Father Murphy grabbed hold of him and in one swift movement pushed in his rib cage. A piece of steak flew out of Father Duffy's mouth and landed in the middle of the table. All was quiet as they stood in stunned silence. Father Duffy regained his composure, cleared his throat a few times, and began to bellow loudly.

"You have got to be kidding me! Are you trying to kill me, is that it? We need that money for the church, you have no right to go giving it away like that!"

"But I was just trying to help the needy, like Christ would do."

"Don't mock me, Father Jim. That's it; you are officially off the block collection. For the rest of this week you are to visit the sick. Is that clear?"

Irritated and confused by his outburst, but not wanting to further infuriate him, Jim simply replied, "Yes, Father. I understand."

When Sunday came Jim knew that something had to be working right for Anna and Dante when he saw them sitting together in the first pew, as promised. After Mass, as he was greeting all the parishioners, he met both of them, and trying not to be too conspicuous, put his arms around them and drew them to him. He whispered to them that they were in his prayers. Happy that his interceding had helped, he changed out of his Mass vestments and into his familiar black suit and white clerical collar.

He left the rectory and went into town to see the sick in the congregation, as per Father Duffy's orders. The weather was warm, hot in fact. It was August, though, so it was to be expected. He loosened his collar and wished he were wearing shorts instead of his heavy suit. He pulled into the only open spot he could find on the crowded street, and stepped out of his cherished car that the Cardinal had given him. He said a silent thank you to the Lord that he didn't have to use the parish car – there was no air conditioner and it didn't run very well.

It was a beautiful clear day in Philadelphia, and the local children were making the most of it. It looked like the street was blocked off further down from where Jim stood, and he could see a mass of children gathered in a large circle screaming with delight. Looking harder, he noticed that they were wearing bathing suits, and he realized they must have opened one of the fire hydrants to cool themselves down and have some fun. He smiled at them as he made his way up the steep steps of the row home he had come to visit and waited for Mrs. Comb to answer the bell after he rang.

"Father Jim, I am so glad you could come visit us today," the kind woman exclaimed as she invited him into her shabby home. "Alicia is so sick today, we couldn't make it to church," she explained as she pulled off her pink apron. Jim noticed she was wearing a faded blue housedress and she was sweating.

"I'm sorry your daughter isn't doing well, but it's always a pleasure to spend some time with you," Jim said pleasantly. It was very hot in the house. He looked around to see if the air conditioner was running but he didn't see one.

As if sensing his discomfort, Mrs. Comb said, "I'm sorry it's so warm. Our air conditioner broke and we don't have the money to fix it right now. May I get you a cold glass of lemonade?"

Jim took off his suit jacket, placed it on the ratty living room sofa, and said, "No, thank you. Why don't we go upstairs and see how Alicia is doing? I haven't seen her pretty face for a long time." Alicia was five years old and suffered from asthma. Her condition had been worsening, probably due to the hot temperatures.

Mrs. Comb slowly opened the door to her daughter's room. Even though it was one o'clock in the afternoon, the shades were drawn and the room was very dark. The child was lying in bed, breathing heavily, as if every breath was a fight.

"Alicia," her mother spoke softly, "look who has come to visit you."

"Father Jim!" Alicia exclaimed breathily, and then paid the repercussions as she struggled to get air into her hungry lungs. She was a small, thin girl with curly brown hair and wide brown eyes and it pained Jim to see such a precious child in pain.

He read Alicia a few of her favorite stories, said a prayer, and then returned downstairs to talk to her mother. "Mrs. Comb, isn't there a way to fix your air conditioner that wouldn't cost a lot of money? I have a friend who's a doctor and he told me that it's important to have cool air flowing in the house if you are an asthmatic. I think Alicia's condition would be greatly improved."

She sat down heavily in a kitchen chair, holding a damp dishrag in one hand. In a tired voice, she said, "I know. Our doctor has told us that, too. We just don't have the money to fix ours or buy a new one right now."

Jim felt pity for the family's dilemma. He knew her husband worked hard in a factory in Frankford, but times were hard and there was not enough money to make ends meet for too many people. Making up his mind, he said decisively, "Mrs. Comb, I know where I can get you an air conditioner. It's not new, but it is in good working condition. I can go get it now."

Rising to her feet and dropping the dishrag, she hugged him. "Father Jim, you truly are a miracle. Thank you."

He drove back to the rectory quickly, and headed right for the living room. The large, comfortably furnished room was nice and cool in contrast to the heat outside. The only air conditioner on the first floor of the house was hard at work pumping out ice-cold air from its position within the stonewall of the room. He walked over to it, turned the small knob to the off position and pried it out of the wall with great effort. A large gaping hole in the masonry of the wall was all that remained as he lugged the air conditioner out to the car. He placed it safely in the backseat and headed back to the Comb's house.

He had been gone all day, and was tired when he returned to the rectory later that evening. He didn't even feel like eating, and he had already missed the dinner hour anyway. Fathers Murphy and DiMarco were watching a television show in the living room, and it must have been quite humorous because Jim heard their laughter from the hallway as he headed for the stairs to his room.

At the foot of the stairwell, Jim heard a familiar brusque voice calling to him from the kitchen doorway.

"Father Jim, is that you?" Father Duffy called.

Instinctively skeptical by the tone of his voice, Jim said hesitantly, "Yes, Father Duffy, it's me."

Father Duffy walked over to the stairwell and said sternly, "Do you have any idea where our air conditioner is? It seems to be missing, and no one knows why. I had a funny feeling that you might know something about it. Typically when strange things happen around here you have a hand in it." Narrowing his already small eyes, which made them almost disappear into the fleshy mass of his face, he stared at Jim suspiciously.

Smiling easily, Jim said, "Actually, I do know where it is. You remember the Comb family, don't you? Their daughter is very ill with asthma, and the family can't afford to fix their broken air conditioner. I figured they needed one more than we did, so I gave ours to them. You should see how happy they were, Father." Jim looked at him triumphantly, very pleased at his act of kindness.

A red flush crept up Father Duffy's neck, cheeks, and finally made it to the top of his shiny balding head. Jim watched in amazement, half expecting his head to start steaming like a teakettle. Father Duffy opened his quivering lips to speak, but no words came out. Finally regaining enough composure to push out his words, his voice took on the tone that Jim had grown accustomed to.

"Are you kidding me? Who do you think you are pulling such a stunt? I'll tell you what you are. You are a loose cannon! I make the decisions around here, not you. You had no right to do what you did.

You are to go back to that house immediately and bring back our air conditioner. Do I make myself clear?"

"But Father, that family needs it more than we do," Jim pleaded.

"Did you not hear me? I have had enough of you and your crazy antics, Father Jim. We do not have enough money to buy the rectory a new one. We are not a charity, do you understand?"

"I thought it was our duty as priest to act charitably, Father..."

"Don't you mock me! Just do what I say." He turned and walked away from Jim, who stood numb with shock.

The next morning, Jim woke early and went to see his friend, Dr. Angelo DiRenzo, at his Holmesburg office. The waiting room was packed as usual, but after the receptionist told the doctor who was there to see him, he was immediately invited back into his friend's office. While waiting for him, Jim sat down in one of the fine leather chairs and admired the expensive furnishings of the room. He and Angelo were childhood friends, and had kept in touch through the years. A kind and generous man by nature, Angelo always lent Jim a helping hand with whatever he needed. Jim breathed deeply and took in the clean and sterile smell of the place. He noticed a picture of himself and Angelo sitting on the expensive maple desk. He smiled as he remembered the day it was taken, a few years ago when they had gone on a fishing trip together. Just then the door opened and in he walked, a tall, thin handsome man with black hair and a ready smile. He pulled the stethoscope from around his neck, casually tossed it on a nearby chair, walked over to Jim and hugged him affectionately.

"Jim, how good to see you, old friend. To what do I owe this surprise visit?"

"Can't I just stop by to say hello?" Jim teased.

"I know you too well for that. You always phone ahead, and besides, you look concerned. What's up?"

"You do know me well, Angelo. I hate to ask, but I need a favor..."

He interrupted, "Anything, you know that."

"I was wondering if you could lend me some money for an air conditioner," Jim began and told him the entire story of what had happened with Father Duffy.

"That's awful! I know he is a priest and all, but forgive me for saying I never did like that man," Angelo said angrily.

"We all have our faults, Angelo. Father Duffy is not so bad," Jim defended.

"Oh, Jim. You are too good a man. Of course I will give you the money."

"I promise to repay you, I have some money saved up from my pay as a captain and chaplain in the Reserves. In a few weeks I should have enough to pay you back."

"Don't be ridiculous, I don't want your money."

"I insist," Jim said stubbornly.

That same day, he purchased a new air conditioner and brought it to the Combs. Using the excuse that he was able to locate a new air conditioner, he retrieved the old one and replaced it with the one he had just bought. Later that evening the rectory's living room was whole again with the missing appliance back in place. Neither Father Duffy nor himself ever spoke of the incident again, and Jim was able to repay his friend, Dr. Angelo DiRenzo, a few weeks later.

Chapter Eleven
1960

By 1960, riding the rails had become a lifestyle for more than a million men throughout the United States. Beginning with the growth of the railroads in the 1870s, continuing through the Great Depression, and persisting until the 1950s and beyond, hobo jungles were common at American rail yards, and a nasty cat-and-mouse game had developed between the lost souls who hopped freight cars and the railroad police - whom the hoboes referred to as bulls - who tormented them every step of the way. By any means of reckoning, it was a perilous existence for the hoboes. These were men who had taken to the road in order to run from their own mistakes, escape the mess they had made of their lives, avoid the responsibilities of being a husband and a father, or find a kind of freedom in having to fend only for themselves. A man could die a sudden and violent death, for instance, simply by mistiming his leap onto an open boxcar; or he could be pulled forcibly from the boxcar by one of the railroad bulls at the very last instant, just when it seemed he was safe. More often than not, that would result in a severe beating by the bulls, who were paid a meager wage to keep the rail yards free of the vagrants.

If a man succeeded in timing his leap onto the boxcar correctly – and avoiding the bulls altogether – he had a new set of problems to deal with. It was inadvisable to fall asleep, lest he roll out the open door of the boxcar and break several bones, if he were to survive the fall at all. Depending on the season, closing the door of the boxcar in order to eliminate the hazard only succeeded in introducing a new one – succumbing to heat exhaustion in cars that often reached 120 degrees while traveling in the desert or the Deep South. In addition, falling asleep could make the vagrant an easy prey for another hobo who wished to pick his pocket and rob him of the few possessions he had. Still, these restless souls had to keep moving in the hope that they would find odd jobs, earn a little money, and have enough to eat to stay alive for another day. Very often, these men went days without food.

The hobo jungles – or camps – provided something of a refuge for the men, who often banded together on the sunny side of a hill, near a source of water, or a short distance away from a rail yard. Whether they had come together for a sense of protection or for a little companionship in an otherwise lonely existence, the men would build a fire, swap tales of the hobo life, and toss scraps of food into an old pot to create a Mulligan stew; and then, after grabbing a little shut eye, they would hop another freight and do it all again the next day. Although relationships were formed in hobo jungles, it remained a distrustful, restless existence for most, as evidenced by the fact that none of the men used his real name. More often than not, you would meet a man one time and one time only, or you would run into him every year or two at best. In November of 1960, one of these men went by the name of Zeke; and he was just another lost soul in the rail yards of Chicago, shivering in a tattered and filthy shirt and doing his best to get by.

Crouching behind some shrubbery – about fifty feet from the train station – Zeke imagined himself in sunny Florida for the winter. A few other hoboes were hiding from the railroad police along with him, waiting for the right freight train to pull out of the station so that they could hop on board.

"Shut up!" came a voice close by. "I think I hear a bull coming!"

Zeke slumped down even closer to the ground behind the tall bush, his gangly frame pressing against the cold dirt. He hoped the policeman would not see him, and was grateful for the warning from a fellow bum.

He heard the familiar whistle of a train about to begin its run, and slowly lifted himself off the ground, knowing that this was his train. It was heading for Georgia, and that was one step closer to his destination.

He jogged alongside the immense train car as it pulled out of the station, and struggled to swing aboard while trying not to slip under the fast moving wheels. He had seen many men die a gruesome death like that, and hoped he would not be one of them.

"I'm gettin' too old for this," he huffed as he rolled onto the floor of the car. At 61, it wasn't getting any easier to hop the rails like he did in the old days. Looking around him, he saw that he was in some sort of cargo car; there were lots of big boxes covered with tarps. He hoped they were secured well; he didn't want any of them to slide his way and crush him during a bumpy ride. He shared the boxcar with three dingy looking strangers, and they spoke little as they headed for warmer weather and hopefully some odd jobs and food. They all looked far too skinny with their ratty clothes hanging from their limbs.

Zeke was tired, but as always, he dared not fall asleep for fear of rolling out of the boxcar or being robbed by one of the other men. In his exhaustion, it seemed like forever before they neared the station in Georgia. He hopped off the slowing train and landed hard on the ground, rolling over a few times before coming to a stop as the train pulled into the station with the familiar grinding screech of metal against metal. Quickly finding some hedges to hide behind, Zeke waited for a train heading to Florida.

Just as the train heading south began to pull away from the station, an arriving train from Philadelphia pulled up to it on the other side. As the train to Florida neared, he ran beside it until he found a place to grab on. His hand slipped on the slick metal plate extending from the boxcar, and with his long legs swaying in the wind, he tried desperately to regain a strong enough hold to pull himself to safety. Suddenly, he felt two arms grab his waist and he was pushed into the car. Another hobo had been attempting a jump for the same train and Zeke had not seen him earlier. Where had he come from and how strong had he been to secure a spot on the edge of the boxcar and still be able to push Zeke into it, he wondered? Thinking quickly, he then returned the favor and reached down for the man and brought him to safety. They took a moment to regain composure and thanked each other.

"Name's Slick Willy," said the man after making himself comfortable against a towering cargo crate. "Didn't really think I would make this hop, seein' as how my ride from Philly just pulled in."

Zeke immediately guessed that his fellow passenger was a drunken bum. They were pretty easy to pick out, and with dirt and what looked like bits of food caught in his beard and hair along with his unnaturally frail looking body that could not have been more than forty years old, the signs pointed in this direction. But still, he had helped him and he didn't look dangerous.

"They call me Zeke," he offered. Nowadays, only a few people knew him as Gordon Gabriel, his real name, but that had been by accident. When he first adopted this way of life fifteen years ago, he had not known the rules. He had been a drunk then himself, and that made it all the easier to pick out a fellow drinker. But Zeke had given up the liquid heaven long ago and eyed his traveling companion carefully.

Even though he was filthy, his clothes were ill fitting, and his shoes didn't match, it was obvious that Zeke had been handsome earlier in his life. His once shiny dark hair had faded to silver over the years, and although very thin, he had retained some traces of his once athletic build. He ran a calloused hand over his cheek and noticed that he had a lot of stubble. Reaching for his worn knapsack - the only thing he owned - he looked for his razor, and found it beyond his throwing knives, a pack of gum, a comb, a sandwich, and a matchbook. He was particular about being clean-shaven, even if the rest of him would not be clean for some time.

The miles passed in silence before Slick Willy struck up a conversation.

"Where you comin' from?" he asked in a bored tone.

"Chicago," Zeke answered, without further explanation. He planned on saying no more, but noticed something quite curious about Slick Willy. "Hey, where did you get those shoes? They look new."

Willy revealed a mouthful of missing and crooked teeth, and smiled proudly. "There was this priest in Philly who was a soft touch, you know?" He laughed as if picturing the holy man. "Anyways, he came to the hobo camps, always givin' us stuff and tellin' us stories. One day, he saw that my shoes had all kinda holes in them and gave me his very own, right off his feet! He musta drove home in his socks!"

Slick Willy went on to recount other instances of the priest's generosity, gleefully explaining how easy it was to take advantage of him. He told Zeke that the priest would give the drifters all the money he had and anything else they needed, as long as they told him how much they had suffered and listened to him talk about Jesus Christ.

"Yeah, he's a real sucker all right. But you wanna know somethin' crazy? He has these knives that he likes to throw at a piece of wood, like a target. We'd set it up for 'im and he'd entertain us for hours. He was real good, too." Slick Willy nodded his head for emphasis as if Zeke was not going to believe him.

Zeke sat up straight, nearly falling over as the train bounced over the tracks. "What was the name of that priest?" he demanded.

Slick Willy paused, his brow furrowing in concentration. "Father James Gabriel," he said finally. "Yeah, that's it!"

His son! As soon as he heard Jim's name, Zeke knew what he had to do. When they approached the next station, he opened the door to the boxcar and jumped into the wild brush that grew along the tracks, landing hard as he clutched his knapsack. As he gathered himself, he looked up to see Slick Willy leaning his head out of the boxcar and staring at him in amazement, Willy's head getting smaller and smaller as the train pulled away. Zeke realized that he hadn't uttered another word to Willy since he had heard Jim's name. After hiding from the bulls for more than an hour, he hopped a train heading north.

Once he arrived in Philadelphia, he headed straight for the first Catholic Church he could locate. Embarrassed by his unkempt appearance but determined to locate his son, Zeke knocked on the rectory door. When a priest eventually responded, Zeke asked if he knew Father James Gabriel and was directed to St. Ann's parish.

It was getting late, and Zeke was tired, cold and hungry. He wasn't even sure that he was in the right place, but he had followed the directions exactly, and he felt certain that he could find St. Ann's the next day. He knew from experience that he could find the nearest rail yard by walking around until he saw a certain kind of smoke, the kind that would rise from an empty fifty-five gallon steel drum filled with burning trash or a fire built right on the ground; and eventually he saw a plume of smoke rising in the distance. He sniffed the air as he approached, but it was too cold for the smell to carry; and he was left with the simple hope that the men would allow him to share their food and rest until the next morning, when he would complete the journey to his son's parish.

As he made his way toward the smoke that billowed to the sky, he saw two men hovering over a steel drum fire warming their bare hands. The men were talking loudly and laughing as if they were old friends. Zeke approached them cautiously, keenly aware that they might respond aggressively and attempt to drive him off.

"How do you do?" he asked agreeably.

"Who're you?" the tall, lanky one asked evenly, as his breath hung in the cold air.

"Name's Zeke. I heard there's a priest who looks after folks like us. Is that true?"

This time, the younger man answered. "Sure is. Good man, that Father Gabriel. Why, he done give me money to buy this here shirt I'm wearin' just the other day."

"Would you fine men mind if I warmed my hands by your fire?"

"Help yourself," the young one said.

"What about this Father Gabriel?" Zeke continued, eager for information but careful not to tip his hand.

"Some of the fellas just take and take from 'im, and he let's 'em do it. He's always tellin' us stories 'bout Christ, and sometimes I think that maybe he's really Him. May sound crazy and all, but never in my life have I ever seen a man like 'im." The older man confided this in a tone barely above a whisper, as if he did not want his friend to hear.

He talked for a long time, telling Zeke stories about what Father Gabriel – or Father Jim, as they all called him – could do with a knife. The men told Zeke how Father Jim was a Medal of Honor winner for his heroism in World War II, and Zeke was so proud that his son was not only a priest but a hero as well. By the time he fell asleep under the stars, he was warmed by the wonderful life his son had led since he had left him, and an overwhelming sadness engulfed him that he had not been a part of it.

Jim was in a hurry. He slid into the plush leather seat of his trusted blue Hudson wearing a heavy wool coat over his blue jeans, and he revved the engine impatiently. He drove quickly through the busy streets of Philadelphia, weaving in and out of traffic. He had been invited to lunch at one of his parishioner's homes, and he didn't want to be any later than he already was. Because he liked to get to know the people in his parish on a personal level, he looked forward to occasions like this. It made him feel that he was making a difference.

He made his way along the cracked sidewalk, rang the doorbell and frowned, disappointed in himself for arriving fifteen minutes late. No one answered on the first two rings. He debated pushing the button a third time when he heard someone calling his name from behind. He turned and saw a man that he vaguely recognized; but he didn't know his name. The man motioned to him from the sidewalk.

Jim walked over to him. "Hello there! Do you live on this street?"

"Father Jim, my name is Mark Mallory. I'm a member of your parish. I have a big favor to ask you. I have a five-year-old son who is very ill and needs to get to the hospital. I saw you drive up in your car and wondered if my wife and I could borrow it to take him there."

The man shifted from one foot to the other, and didn't look Jim in the eye. Jim made it a point to learn the names of the people in his parish, and he had never heard the name Mark Mallory. Still, it was possible that he had forgotten the name, or that the man simply lived in the parish but never worshipped at the church.

"I'll take you there myself," Jim said. Just then, Mrs. Comb opened her front door.

"I wouldn't want to inconvenience you," the man said a little too quickly.

Jim paused. The man needed to get to the hospital, but he had promised to have lunch with the Comb family and he had been anxious to see how little Alicia was doing with her asthma. He had never lent his car before, but he didn't see any harm in letting the man take his son to the hospital as long as he returned the car at a time they agreed on. Jim told him that he could borrow the car just as long as he brought it back in a few hours, after he had visited with his neighbors. Once he made his decision, Jim handed over the keys without reservation, pleased for handling the situation effectively. This way he could kill two birds with one stone. He entered the house for lunch with a light heart.

Four hours later, his car still had not been returned. He figured that it must be taking longer at the hospital then they had anticipated. Jim borrowed Mrs. Comb's phone to call the hospital in an attempt to find out how much longer they would be, but the woman on the other end told him that no such family had checked in today. Worried that they had been in an accident, Jim called the police, but no accidents had been reported. As he hung up the telephone, he had very few regrets about the decision that he had made. After all, it was the Godly one. And though he enjoyed the Hudson, he wasn't particularly worried about his mode of transportation. But he deeply regretted that this Mark Mallory – or whoever he really was - was such a lost soul. That was the tragedy – that someone would be so lost as to steal from a priest. He didn't care about the loss of his own comfort or how he would explain to Father DiMarco what had happened to his car; Father Jim was worried for the man who was in such obvious and desperate need. He asked Mrs. Comb's for a ride back to the rectory.

A few days later, there was still no sign of his car or the family. He learned from some neighbors of the family that there was talk of them packing up and driving towards California. Jim was heartbroken that one of his beloved parishioners would do such a thing to him, but did not feel he should press charges against the man. He now had to share the broken-down parish car with the other priests of St. Ann's instead of driving his beautiful Hudson, but what really bothered Jim was that he had cherished the car as a gift from the Cardinal. Now that the question about the Mallory family had been answered, he regretted the loss of the cherished gift most of all.

Two days later, as Jim drove through the dark, narrow streets on his way to Anna and Dante's house for dinner, he began to shiver. He wished the heat worked in the parish car, and he wondered why Anna had sounded strange when she had invited him over. He hoped that she and Dante were well. They had been coming to church every Sunday for the past three months, and they always looked happy together. Jim told himself that he was worrying for nothing. He pulled up in front of their modest row home, cut the engine, and hurried to the front door.

Everything seemed normal enough as they ate Jim's favorite meal, spaghetti and meatballs, hot Italian sausage and an old Italian favorite – steak sliced thin and seasoned with plenty of spices and rolled in sausage. He closed his eyes and savored the delicious meal.

"Anna, you have outdone yourself," Jim smiled, toasting her with a glass of Chianti.

"Well, this is a special occasion," Anna smiled and reached for Dante's hand.

"What occasion might that be? You have been mysterious all evening."

"Let's have dessert first. I make a mean cannoli." Anna laughed good-naturedly and rose from her seat, losing her balance. As she teetered back and forth on her heels, Dante hurried to his feet and steadied her. Jim grew concerned as Dante held Anna's arm tightly, and he asked if Anna was all right. Jim noticed that Dante was being very overprotective as he continued to hold on to Anna asking her if she was okay.

They must have noticed the strange look on his face, because they looked at him, then at each other and nodded as if coming to a conclusion about something.

"Well, I guess now is as good a time as ever," Anna giggled softly while pulling away from Dante's hold.

"Jim, we want to show you something." Dante motioned for him to follow as he led the way through the dining room and up the stairs to the bedrooms. "Do you remember how you told Anna to take all of my things out of the spare room that I was sleeping in, lock the door and never open it again?" Jim looked at Dante, confused.

"Well, I think you would have to agree that although we broke that promise, it was for a good reason." Dante swung the door open and flipped on the light.

The room was beautiful. It had been decorated in soft hues – yellow and green pastels, stuffed animals, a rocking chair and a brand new bassinet filled the room. Jim was speechless as he looked at Anna and Dante who were beaming.

"We didn't want to tell you over the phone," Anna gushed. She held her breath and stated what Jim had already figured out. "I'm pregnant!" she said triumphantly.

"But that's not all," Dante smiled. "We both feel that if it hadn't been for you, we never would have gotten back together. It would be our honor if you would allow us to name the baby James Dante Russo if it's a boy."

Jim looked at Anna and Dante in amazement. He swallowed and said, "I am the one who is honored, good friends. I'm glad that I had some part in your happiness. You are truly blessed."

During the short ride back home, a sense of peace came over Jim. Maybe his priesthood was working after all. This realization caused him to change his mind about returning to the rectory, and he decided to check on the hoboes instead. It was a particularly cold night and they might need help finding refuse for burning, or there might be something else he would be able to assist them with.

Zeke picked at the various components of the Mulligan stew – pieces of bologna, potatoes, onions, and cornmeal. All six of his companions had contributed to the stew, mostly by scrounging around in trashcans or waiting for a handout at the back doors of local restaurants. After their search for food, they had returned to the camp – a small clearing behind a few abandoned boxcars – and began to regale one another with tales from the hobo life, some accurate and some embellished, simply to pass the time. But tonight Zeke was preoccupied. It was strange that he kept missing his son, the man they called Father Jim. It seemed that Zeke was never around when the fabled priest stopped by. He was beginning to wonder if he would ever actually see him in the flesh, and his desire to talk to him grew with each passing day. As the other hoboes described Jim's good deeds, Zeke felt a strong sense of pride, but he questioned whether or not he was entitled to it, given the fact that he had abandoned Jim and his mother all of those years ago.

Despite the cold, they were doing their best to keep warm by huddling around their fire. Zeke had already set aside the remainder of his stew when he heard the sound of footsteps crunching the blades of frozen grass and growing louder by the second. One or two of the men were sleeping at that point, but the others immediately became alert, frightened that the railroad bulls were about to chase them. Suddenly, one of the men leaped to his feet.

"Father Jim! You almost gave us a heart attack," Spaghetti Jones yelled as he ran to greet him. So named because of his long, skinny body, it was almost comical to see him moving so quickly.

"Good to see you, son," Father Jim slapped him on the back.

Too stunned to move, Zeke stared at the handsome, sturdily built man who stood before him. It had been more than thirty years since he had laid eyes on Jim, and he fought back tears as he struggled to his feet, pushing away an old tattered blanket.

For a moment, he was terrified by the thought that Jim might recognize him. He quickly put his mind at ease by remembering that his son had been extremely young when he abandoned him, and the years had not been kind to Zeke's appearance. Still, he approached slowly and extended a callused hand in Jim's direction.

"And who do we have here, gentlemen? This must be the priest you've told me about. Nice to finally meet you."

Father Jim smiled as he looked directly into Zeke's eyes. "Where are you from?"

Zeke relaxed a bit and took another moment to look Jim over before he spoke. "Chicago," he said. "I was headin' south with the rest of the snowbirds when I ran into a guy from around here. He was talkin' about a priest who was the greatest knife thrower in the world."

"I don't know about that," Jim replied.

"That's what he said. Anyway, I've been fascinated by knife throwers ever since I saw one in a circus act. That was right before I..." Zeke fell silent.

"Right before you what?" Jim asked.

Zeke took a deep breath. "Right before I left my wife and son." A flash of contempt crossed Jim's features, but he said nothing, and the contempt hung in the air between them. Zeke had been brave to say it, but now he was paying the price. "I took them to see the greatest knife thrower in the world," he said, "Gordon the Great."

Zeke studied Jim intently. His long years on the road had taught him how to read people. It had become a necessity, a means of survival; and he had a knack for it. But Jim's expression was unfathomable. Zeke waited for something to betray Jim's emotion, so that he could get a sense of where he stood with his son, and so that he could determine whether or not Jim hated him. Nothing else mattered at that moment. As Zeke stood silent and waiting, he saw Jim grow pale.

"Gordon the Great was my father."

It was all Zeke could do to keep from bursting into tears.

"No kiddin'?" he said cheerfully. It had a false note to it, but Jim was too preoccupied to notice.

"When did you see him?" Jim asked.

"Christ, it must be thirty years ago." Zeke blurted, covering his mouth when he realized that he had used the Lord's name in vain. "Scuse me, Father. I didn't mean that."

Jim laughed aloud. "Don't worry about it. Did you ever see him again?"

They were pumping each other for information, desperate for every scrap, just as the hoboes were desperate for scraps of food. But only one of them knew of their actual relationship.

"No, I never did," Zeke said, struggling to control his emotions. It was as if Jim had asked if Zeke had ever seen his son again, instead of the innocent question that he had asked about Gordon the Great. For Jim, however, the question was anything but innocent. Despite the contempt he had for his father – the "hatred," as he had put it to Father Philip while confessing at the seminary – he had an overwhelming need to learn of his father's whereabouts precisely as he stood before him.

"I've never met anyone who saw my father throw," Jim said vacantly, his voice trailing off as he thought of the day that Gordon the Great had disappeared with Sheila from the circus, leaving Jim and his mother to fend for themselves. Zeke knew all about fending for himself – the hobo life had pounded it into him – but he only knew about Jim and Kate's struggles externally, he only knew about their struggles in the abstract. He felt a strong sense of guilt – that much could be said for him – but he had no idea of the every day reality that they had experienced without a husband and father. He had run from that reality, and seeing Jim drove it home to him powerfully, until the guilt was accompanied by an overwhelming sense of shame. At the same time, however, the survival instincts that he had developed over the past thirty years prevented him from betraying his position.

Whatever else could be said about the combination of emotions that Zeke was feeling, however, at least he knew who he was talking to, at least he was on solid ground in that respect. Jim didn't have that luxury and was working at a disadvantage. As far as he knew, he was talking to a man who had seen his father perform, and it was nothing more than that. Zeke was just another lost soul like the thousands he had ministered to already, and it was Jim's sacred duty to do what he could for him spiritually.

They talked around the fire for a while, and in a lighter moment, Jim told Zeke about the replica he had made of his father's spinning target from the circus. The target was in the basement of the rectory, and before Jim left the hoboes that night, he promised to show it to Zeke.

Zeke slept well that night, despite the frigid weather, proud to see the man his son had become. At the same time, though, a part of him regretted the fact that Jim had failed to recognize him. He knew that it was for the best, and that Jim would want to have nothing to do with him if he discovered Zeke was his father. In the end, he convinced himself that it was much better this way, and that it would be easier to get close to Jim. But he would have to swim against the current when it came to the strong desire to reveal his actual identity and accept the consequences, however harsh they may be. His son had every right to despise him, but in a very small part of him, Zeke nurtured the wild, fantastic hope that Jim would welcome him with open arms.

"Is your mother still alive?" Zeke asked as he rode with Jim to a downtown soup kitchen. He was still living dangerously when it came to the need to extract as much information from Jim as possible without betraying his own identity. It was Thanksgiving and Zeke was very aware that he had missed many Thanksgivings with his son.

"No," Jim frowned, as he struggled to keep his own emotions in check. He thought of Kate every day, and it was something that he did on his own, without the prompting of others. After all, she had been the one constant in his life, and they had adored one another with all of the purity, devotion, and commitment possible between a mother and child. But now, as an impoverished stranger asked about Kate innocently, Jim missed his mother keenly, particularly since he had spent every Thanksgiving with her except for the ones he had been in Rome. "They say she died of a heart attack, but I know better. She died of a broken heart."

Zeke winced at Jim's words while Jim stared straight ahead, gripping the steering wheel tightly. They had no idea what they were doing to each other with their questions and their responses, and it would be like that for as long as Zeke kept his secret. Because they had their own positions to protect, they were helpless to do anything different.

"Why do you say that?" Zeke asked, torn between wanting to hear it and not wanting to.

"Why?" Jim exclaimed, finally glancing over at him. "Because she loved my father until the day she died."

Choked with emotion now, Zeke looked away. Jim glanced over at him again as he made his way through traffic. He had no suspicions at that point. After all, he had witnessed similar behavior in the hoboes before. Any mention of wives and children – and any association with the lives and families they had left behind – was likely to set them off, whether they were discussing their own families directly or casually discussing someone else's. That was the kind of guilt and shame they were living with – a volatile mixture if ever there was one – and Jim recognized it as their own particular cross to bear. Now, as he learned of Kate's helpless devotion, Zeke's internal conflict was as strong as it had ever been in all of the years since he had abandoned her, and it took his own son to cause it. At the same time that he felt a stupid manly pride at the hold he had over Kate, he was ashamed to realize that she had never gotten over the hurt he caused; and there was a good chance that Jim hadn't gotten over it either. He had an intense need to confess to Jim – not as a parishioner, but as a father – but he had an even stronger need to protect himself and survive. Just as it had done when he had decided to run off with Sheila and leave the circus life behind, self-interest won out in Zeke, and he continued to maintain his silence over his actual identity. All he could do was talk around the subject and make it up to Jim in other ways, just like he was doing in helping him feed the poor on Thanksgiving.

"Is your mother buried around here?" he asked innocently.

"Yes – at Saint Dominic's," Jim said, pulling up in front of a soup kitchen in downtown Philadelphia. "You can get out of the car, Zeke. We're here."

"Aren't you coming in?" Zeke asked, frightened that Jim had changed his mind about their working side-by-side. Suddenly, Jim realized that a stray fragment of hostility had found its way into his tone, and he regretted it immediately. After all, it wasn't Zeke's fault that his mother wasn't there to share the Thanksgiving holiday. And so, after Zeke wolfed down a traditional Thanksgiving meal before the others arrived, they stood side-by-side on the serving line, dishing out the turkey, stuffing, mashed potatoes, and cranberry sauce to vacant-eyed men who wandered in from the cold.

The next day, without mentioning it to Jim, Zeke found his way to St. Dominic's Cemetery and began to wander the grounds, searching desperately for the grave of Katherine Gabriel. He had no idea what he would say or do, but he knew that he had to say something, even if it intensified the conflict he was feeling.

Despite the care that Jim had shown him in the preceding weeks, Zeke had refused to give up the wandering life and turn himself over to the Lord, and as a result, he still had a ragged appearance as he crossed the grounds of the cemetery. Eventually, the supervisor, Neil Shaunessay, noticed Zeke and emerged from the maintenance shed to question him. Neil was Jim's old boss from his grave digging days, and like always, he ran a tight ship when it came to the cemetery.

"Who are you and what are you doing here?" he demanded.

"My name's Zeke and I'm lookin' for a grave."

"Is that right?" Neil responded distrustfully, still not convinced that this ragged looking man had a legitimate reason to be there. "And whose grave would that be?"

"Katherine Gabriel's," Zeke answered defiantly. He was standing his ground, and he wouldn't take no for an answer. At the sound of Katherine's name, Neil's demeanor softened.

"Are you a relation?"

"In a way I am."

"What's that supposed to mean?"

"I'm a distant cousin of hers. Are you gonna show me her grave or not?"

At that point, Neil put whatever personal feelings he had aside. "If you're here to pay your respects to Kate, that's good enough for me. She was a good woman, and she's sorely missed. Follow me."

Not quite ready to face the wife he abandoned – and eager for something to brace him – Zeke looked Neil in the eye. "Say, you don't happen to have a touch of whiskey, do you?"

For a second or two, Neil attempted to regard Zeke sternly, but the possibility of having a swig of whiskey at that hour of the day was a welcome one, and now Zeke had provided an excuse. "I've been known to keep a pint or two in the maintenance shed," he smiled. "Come on, we're walkin' past it anyway."

An hour later, they still had not visited Katherine's grave, but they had made a good deal of progress on the cheap bottle of rye whiskey that Neil had hidden in the drawer of his desk.

"I understand her husband was a circus performer," Zeke said.

Neil stared at him. It was an innocent question, but something about Zeke didn't quite add up. For one thing, he had never heard of a long lost cousin; and for another he couldn't imagine anyone in Katherine's family looking like the ragged man that sat with him. Zeke was obviously a bum, and he made no attempt to hide it. Perhaps Zeke wasn't her cousin at all.

"Yeah – he was in the circus. He went by Gordon the Great."

"He was a knife thrower, wasn't he?"

Neil eyed him suspiciously. "How'd you know that?"

"Father Jim told me."

"You know Father Jim?"

"Yeah, we've been spendin' some time together."

"What do you mean – spending time? He's ministering to you?"

"Yeah – ministering. You know, he's helpin' me out with things, and he's talkin' to me about Jesus Christ."

Zeke tried to toss this off with a look of disdain – the way a hobo would if he didn't have an ulterior motive. But Neil was having none of it.

"I thought you said she was your cousin."

Zeke blushed, although it was difficult to tell with his ruddy, wind-blown complexion. Neil decided to ease up some, realizing that the whiskey might have distorted his thinking.

"Yeah," Neil said, "I saw Gordon the Great a couple times, and he was one of the greatest knife throwers you ever saw."

"One of the greatest?" Zeke flared, the old pride he felt in his knife throwing ability coming back to him with a surge of jealousy. "Here gimme that."

Neil handed him the pint of whiskey. "He was the greatest knife thrower I ever saw in a circus."

"What's that supposed to mean?" Zeke took a swig of whiskey. For a brief second, he considered punching Neil in the nose if he didn't get an answer he liked. But then he realized that Neil's body had been hardened by thirty years of digging graves, the same thirty years that he had spent allowing his own body to fall apart. If a fistfight broke out, Zeke didn't stand a chance. As a matter of pride, though, he told himself that the admirable restraint he was showing had more to do with the fact that Neil had yet to point out Katherine's grave.

"It means that as good as Gordon the Great was, his son's even better."

"Father Jim can throw a knife?" Zeke asked. He realized that Jim had mentioned a knife-throwing target in the basement of the rectory, but they hadn't gotten around to looking at it. They were too busy dancing around the subject of Jim's upbringing and the hardships he'd endured with his mother.

"Gordon must have taught him well, because Jim became a war hero with those knives." And he went on to recount the stories of the German pillbox and radar station, describing Jim's heroism in minute detail. As he did so, Zeke's guise melted away, until it was obvious that he was feeling the kind of pride that you can only feel for your own flesh and blood. "You're him, aren't you?" Neil said suddenly, with a mixture of wonder and contempt. "You're Gordon the Great."

Zeke lowered his eyes. "I won't deny it."

"Why would you? It wouldn't do any good. Any fool could see the way you looked when I told you about Jim."

"Tell me some more," Zeke said. He lifted his face again, and a tear was running down his cheek. He had shaved that day, just like he always did; and Neil realized that it was the only part of him that wasn't embarrassing. After all these years, he still had some of his looks, if you searched for them carefully. "Tell me anything you can."

Their friendship developed, Zeke visiting Katherine's grave every day and pouring out his heart to her, apologizing one moment and justifying his behavior the next, never solving the violent conflict inside of him but expressing it again and again, because really that was all he could do: throw it off, get it out from inside, even though Katherine's silence whipped up the guilt and the shame even more. Maybe he should turn to God like his son the priest had said, and he might have considered it further if it didn't go against his grain the way that it did. He knew that he could please his son with it, but he would have felt foolish and insincere. Besides, what was done was done, and he couldn't undo it, not for Katherine, Jim, or anyone else. He would just have to live with it; that was all.

It was during the month between Thanksgiving and Christmas that Neil Shaunessay befriended him and Zeke learned about the life Jim had lived in Zeke's absence; and he listened hungrily to everything Neil said. For some reason, Zeke was insatiable when it came to these details – far more insatiable than he had been on the many occasions when he hadn't eaten for days. This was a different kind of hunger, although he realized that he would never be able to reclaim any of the lost years or make up for what he had done. Still, this was the only way he had of being a part of Jim's life – and he could only do it retroactively, after Jim and Katherine had experienced all of the suffering that had come to them at his hands.

Within days, he had heard it all, as Neil recounted the way Jim had gone off to war to defend his country, joined an elite demolition unit, earned one medal after another, and received a Dear John letter that broke his spirit. And then Neil told him of Jim's return from combat, the years of grave digging under Neil's supervision, and how the heartbreak of losing Anna to his best friend had combined with the guilt of killing men at close range, until it all became too much for Jim and he ran away from it all by joining the seminary.

As Neil described these events and Jim's responses to them, Zeke could not ignore the fact that both of them had escaped from the torment of their lives, and that both father and son had running away in their blood. But characteristically enough, Zeke had escaped into alcoholism and a refusal to face responsibility, while his son had proved the better man by becoming a priest and taking the sorrows of others upon himself. In his moment of truth, Zeke had refused to take responsibility for two people and two people only – his wife and son – while Jim had taken a vow to watch over an entire parish, spread the word of the Lord, and make a difference with everyone that he met.

"You never showed me that target," Zeke said, as Jim opened the rectory door and led him inside. "What are you waiting for?"

"It didn't seem that important," Jim smiled.

"Are you sure about that? Maybe you're not the knife thrower you say you are."

It was a week before Christmas, and the Port Richmond section of Philadelphia was bustling with holiday cheer. Father Murphy, Father DiMarco, and even Father Duffy had helped Jim decorate the church and rectory. It didn't look half bad, Jim decided as he observed the way the Christmas tree filled the rectory's sitting room and reflected a rainbow of colors from the Christmas ornaments and the tinsel. He led Zeke through the sitting room and down the basement stairs.

After setting up the target, Jim proceeded to display his many skills as a knife thrower, and Zeke watched him with a remarkable combination of pride and competitive envy. His son had clearly surpassed him, as sons are wont to do, and he lacked the decency to be entirely pleased about it. At the same time, though, a part of him was genuinely thrilled, and Jim was very much aware of the fondness that the older man had for him. When he analyzed his own feelings, Jim felt oddly comfortable around the old man, and he couldn't quite put his finger on what it was about him that made him want to get to know him better. At first, it was because he was the only person he had ever met who had seen his father perform, but now it was something else. He looked Zeke up and down and tried not to pity him, as Zeke looked around the brightly decorated room in his ragged clothing. For a moment, Jim felt disgusted that he was dressed as well as he was. As a man of the cloth, he was ordained to help his flock, and he was wearing a nice, clean black suit and lived in a nice house all fancied up for Christmas, unable to help the impoverished man who stood before him.

"The rectory is decorated beautifully. This must be a very special time of year for you," Zeke noted.

Jim threw another knife and decided to confide in him. "You know, my mother used to make this time of year so wonderful, even though we never had much. We were poor, but she always found some extra money to buy me a present, even if it wasn't much more than a second-hand toy some other boy no longer wanted. We would decorate our tree with bits of aluminum foil when we didn't have money for ornaments, and it sparkled brilliantly." Jim stopped throwing, and stood a few feet from the target with a knife in his right hand.

As Zeke stared at the knife, a surprising thought occurred to him. Here was someone who had used a knife just like that one to take another man's life in combat – perhaps it was that very knife. What would Jim do if Zeke confessed to being his father at that very moment? As Zeke considered this dark thought, he freely acknowledged that the idea of a priest like his son attacking him was preposterous, but the guilt and shame he felt sent that particular thought bubbling to the surface. Once again, he briefly considered turning his life around in the way that Jim had suggested – before banishing the thought from his mind.

"She sounds remarkable," Zeke said. "Tell me about your father. Was he a good man?"

Jim sneered with disdain, raised his arm, and threw the knife violently into the target, hitting it at dead center. He proceeded to tell Zeke in a cold voice about the abandonment that he and his mother had suffered, and how they never entirely recovered from it emotionally, although they had managed to make a life for themselves and move on.

Zeke stared at the knife lodged into the center of the target, and then he swallowed hard. "You know, I left my wife and son, too, just like your father did. It's not somethin' that I'm proud of, but I think it was for the best."

"Of course you do!" Jim sneered, suddenly realizing that he didn't sound like a priest at all. Where had the priestly comportment gone, the deep sense of forgiveness, the selfless devotion to others? In this instance, talking to a man that had admitted to the same monstrous behavior as his father, he had to summon it by an act of will.

Still, it was impossible for Zeke to abandon the rationalization that had enabled his survival for years. After all, what was an attempt at living with oneself if not an instinct of survival?

"I drank a lot back then, so much that I'd end up in another woman's bed and not even remember how I got there. It got to be so bad that I just figured the best thing to do would be to leave them. I thought they'd be better off..." His voice trailed off and he looked down at his shoes.

"That's too easy, Zeke. And it's far easier than it was on your wife and child. It's never better to walk out on the people who love you – not for them anyway. It might have been easier for you."

"Maybe you're right," Zeke said sadly. He felt dizzy now, as the rationalization spun away.

Jim experienced another remorseless impulse, but gathered himself and continued in a gentle tone. "I hope that your wife and son had it better than my mother and I did. Times were tough for us. It was a hard life that my mother led, but despite everything that happened, and despite the fact that she never would have admitted it, she loved my father until the day that she died." And then he felt another strange sensation that he never expected to feel. It was a certain bashfulness, as though he were a child again, if only for a moment. "I think I told you that before."

"You did, Father."

The pride that Zeke had felt before had disappeared. It no longer mattered that he had enthralled Katherine and held her in his sway for a lifetime. Now there was only shame at the pain he had caused her. Jim threw another knife at the target, concentrating so fiercely that he only heard the sobs when he lowered his arm to his side. He gasped as he saw Zeke sitting with his head in his hands, crying heavily.

"What's the matter?" Jim asked. "What's wrong?" He was alarmed at the effect that his words had on the man. It wasn't like Jim to say the wrong thing.

Lifting his head, he looked up at Jim in a powerless way, as though his future depended on Jim's charity. "Could you ever forgive such an awful man?"

With the concept of forgiveness, Jim was able to find his way back to a priestly mode, and to overcome the personal feelings that had informed his previous response.

Placing a tender hand on Zeke's arm, he said, "God forgives all who repent. You must forgive my harshness, but I am just a man and I have my own weaknesses. I have never been able to forgive my own father for what he did, but that is not to say that he has not made his peace with the Lord. I can tell that you feel remorse for what you did to your own family, and I truly pity your decision. I suggest you pray for forgiveness, Zeke. I wish I could offer you more, but I'm afraid you have discovered my weakness. It is entirely possible, though, that your own son has made his peace with you."

"He hasn't," Zeke whispered sorrowfully.

Jim felt an unexpected wave of tenderness, and he paused to regard it. "You don't know for sure. A man's heart is full of complexity. You seem like a good man. I'm sure somewhere deep down your son either has or will accept your failings. Have you ever thought about going to him?"

"Many times," Zeke said, nearly breaking down at the thought that he was with his son at that very moment. He felt, but could not express, the complexity that Jim had referred to. "I know that he wouldn't be able to forgive me, and that I would be too embarrassed for him to see what I have become. I would only hope that he somehow knew how much I love him."

On Christmas day, they returned to the soup kitchen downtown. Although he could not bring himself to lead a righteous life, Zeke felt considerable joy being aligned with the righteous if only for a short time; and he took great pride in the fact that he and Jim were standing together feeding the hungry. As they dished out food, Zeke begged Jim to tell him how he had won all his medals in the war, and Jim obliged with some reluctance and humility.

When they were finished at the soup kitchen, Jim drove him back to the hobo jungle, satisfied that he had continued to make slow but steady progress in Zeke's spiritual development. He was extremely concerned, however, by the persistent cough that Zeke had. As Zeke opened the door of the car, Jim mentioned that the cough was getting worse, but Zeke refused Jim's offer to take him to see a doctor. Once again, Jim wished that Father Duffy would allow Zeke to stay at the rectory to get out of the cold for a night or two, but Father Duffy had been adamant in his refusal.

Jim tossed and turned in his warm bed, reliving his argument with Father Duffy. He simply could not understand how the priest would not allow a sick, homeless man to sleep in the rectory on such a night. He had only asked that Zeke be allowed to sleep in the basement, but Father Duffy had refused even that. Jim could still hear the cold indifference in Father Duffy's voice. "Jim, I simply will not allow it. If I let one man stay, before you know it all the other men will be lined up on our doorstep."

Jim had argued to no avail, and now found it very difficult to drift into sleep, feeling guilty that he had shelter and a warm place to rest his head while Zeke did not. At least he has a warm coat, he thought. The previous week, Jim had given his thinly lined winter coat to one of the women in Zeke's jungle, and had given Father Duffy's expensive, plush coat to Zeke without thinking of the repercussions. Oh, had Father Duffy laid into him for that.

"That's it!" Father Duffy cried. "I can't take it anymore. I want you out of here! Tomorrow we are going to the chancellery to see the Cardinal."

They had made the trip early the next morning, waiting in the grand hallway for his eminence, the Cardinal, to call them into his office. Father Duffy was still not speaking to him, and Jim silently watched the portly man pace back and forth on the expensive Persian rug. Jim noticed the magnificent artwork that graced the cathedral walls.

The double doors swung open and the secretary beckoned them into the room. Because he was closer to the doors, Jim started but was immediately stopped by the secretary.

"Father Duffy will be seen first."

With a vindictive smile, Father Duffy brushed past him and the heavy doors closed with a thud.

After exchanging greetings, the Cardinal asked Father Duffy to tell him what the problem was with Father Jim, mentioning that he had heard of Jim's good deeds. After Father Duffy described all of the things that Jim had done and all of the reasons why he wanted him removed from his parish, the Cardinal sat silently for a few moments before addressing him.

"I will transfer him, but let me tell you something, Father Duffy. This man may not be the holiest, but he is the best. He is more Christ-like than any other priest I know, and in fact, I am embarrassed and ashamed because of the way I live. I have a limousine with a driver; I live in grandeur... Do you realize that Christ rode around on a jackass? You want me to chastise a man who is more Christ-like than anyone I've ever met? I find that hard to do. But you won't have to worry about him anymore."

The doors opened and Father Duffy emerged, red in the face. After Father Duffy pushed past him, Jim followed the secretary into the room and stood before the Cardinal.

"Before I start, I want you to know that I am embarrassed and ashamed of what I have to tell you," the Cardinal said slowly from behind his enormous walnut desk. "I want you to know that I am proud of you as a priest. But you must remember that if every priest gave away everything in the parish like you do, the Catholic Church would not be able to exist. What you are doing is noble but impractical."

Jim shifted uncomfortably in his chair and interjected, "I'm sorry, your Eminence. I know the church expected great things from me. I don't want to be a bishop. I don't want to be a Cardinal. I just want to be a priest. I want to be out there with my flock. I can save you a lot of trouble. You know that I am a Major in the Army Reserves, and that I'm a decorated combat soldier, which I'm proud of. I'm not proud that I killed so many men in war, but I'm proud to have served my country. Let me go back into the military, to be a Chaplain. I can relate to those men."

"I have no problem with that, Father Gabriel, but right now we need a chaplain for the prison. I will assign you to St. Dominic's. You will have to say daily Mass and perform your functions over at the prison. You will not have to participate in any parish activities, no block collection, etc. But when you get over there, you have to promise me that you will not give away the place," he smiled. "You will devote all your time to the men in prison. You can relate to them because of your experience in the war, and they will respect your achievements because of what you've done. You are a man amongst men, and a priest amongst priests. Will you go to St. Dominic's?"

Flattered by his remarks, Jim said, "Thank you for your kindness. I will gladly accept that assignment. St. Dominic's is dear to my heart, and it will be nice to go home."

Late into the night two days later, the hallway telephone rang while Jim was asleep. He jumped out of bed, and answered it on the third ring.

"This is Northeastern Hospital calling. I'm looking for Father James Gabriel," a woman said.

"This is he."

"Your father has been brought into the emergency room, and you should come down at once."

"There must be some mistake," Jim stammered. "I don't have a father."

The woman paused in exasperation." You *are* Father James Gabriel?"

"Yes."

"You know a man named Gordon Gabriel?"

"Yes."

"Then there's no mistake."

Jim hurried into the emergency room, nearly tripping over a chair in his rush to get to the receptionist's desk. He was confused, and eager to get some answers, and he practically pounced on the young woman seated in the receptionist's area.

"I'm looking for Gordon Gabriel. I received a call from someone on your staff."

Jim took a seat while the woman found someone to help him. He shivered in the chair and wished he had a coat to keep him warm, but in his rush, he had forgotten to grab one. Jim struggled to make sense of the possibility that he was about to see his father. After a few minutes, he felt a gentle touch on his shoulder.

"Father Gabriel," the nurse said, "please come with me."

Jim followed her down a long hallway until he was introduced to one of the physicians. The doctor glanced up at him and closed the folder he was holding.

"I'm afraid I have some bad news for you. Your father came in with severe pneumonia, and I doubt that we'll be able to save him. We're doing everything we can."

"Doctor, I don't mean to sound impertinent, but I haven't seen my father in more than thirty years. I can't imagine that he would know who I was now, let alone know where to find me. I think there might have been some sort of mistake."

"I see." The physician looked baffled. A nurse joined the men, handed the doctor a bulky garment and whispered in his ear. Nodding in agreement, the physician turned to Jim and said, "The man who came in tonight was wearing this coat. In fact, he refused to take it off and we couldn't adequately treat him. When we tried to remove the coat forcibly, he became violently agitated, and we realized that his agitation was threatening him as well. Later, he nearly became delirious and demanded that we call his son. He swore to us that his son had given him the coat. That's when we called you."

Jim's eyes slowly fell to Father Duffy's coat. "Wait a minute, " he said, still not understanding. "I gave that coat to Zeke..."

When it finally hit him, he swayed for an instant and thought that he might fall to the ground. As the physician steadied him and led him to a chair, he replayed the last few weeks with Zeke until it all fell into place. The vaguely familiar glint in Zeke's eye, the story about abandoning his family, his interest in knife throwing... these and other images flashed before him in quick succession. Clutching the coat in his hands, he asked to be taken to Zeke's bedside.

Zeke was sleeping, and in his confusion, Jim wondered what he should do. If it had been anyone else, he might have allowed the man to die peaceably without attempting to wake him, and he might have administered the Last Rites. But as father and son, they were moving ever closer to a final confrontation. If Zeke survived long enough to awake, Jim realized that there was no way to avoid it, and he wondered about his own demeanor. Would his best self emerge, enabling him to comfort the man as he lay dying? Or would he experience the "hatred" that he had claimed to Father Philip? If the "hatred" emerged, would he torture the dying man with bitter recriminations? Jim simply could not answer these questions, and he began to struggle in similar ways he had when he had to make the decision of whether or not to leave Jenny behind and go to Rome. While Zeke slept, he decided to return briefly to the parish car and retrieve the Bible and deathbed kit that held the oil of Chrism. Perhaps he would administer the Last Rites.

When Zeke woke up, Jim looked at him as he had never looked at him before, and without a word passing between them, Zeke realized that Jim now knew of his true identity. For the first time since Jim had been a child, Jim was about to speak with him with a full knowledge of who he was. To the bottom of his soul, however, Zeke knew that he was too weak to protest any recriminations that Jim decided to confront him with, just as he was too weak to refuse to accept the

Lord. But something else was at work as well. Not only did he know that he could please Jim by accepting the Lord, he was a little more ready for it now, and it didn't feel nearly as foolish or insincere. He almost felt that he would welcome it if Jim urged their conversation in that direction.

Zeke looked up at him, struggling to speak. His voice was hoarse and afflicted. "You've been so kind to me these past few weeks."

"I was your priest," Jim replied. "I'm kind to everyone."

Zeke winced at this, and at that moment, the guilt was transferred to Jim. He felt himself weakening at that point, and suddenly he remembered the day so many years ago in which he had felt himself weakening with Jenny. That was another kind weakening, of course, but it was another instance of straying from the path. Despite the personal animosity that he felt toward his father, he was determined to treat him humanely. Before, when he had insisted to Father Philip that he felt "hatred" toward his father, he had been clear-headed about it; but now he was keenly aware of his own emotion. When he heard the resentment in his own voice, a sense of revulsion came over him. Perhaps hatred was too strong a word, but he resented his father in every fiber of his being. At the same time, however, he was too selfless – and too devoted to the concept of forgiveness – to succumb to his weaker impulses now. He would have to dig deep down and overcome the resentment if he were truly the man and the priest that he hoped to be. All at once, he realized that he couldn't deny his father much longer.

Now, as he formulated his reply, he felt himself inclining toward his father emotionally, precisely as he held himself erect in the chair. Despite all of his training – and all of his experience at the bedsides of the sick – he had never experienced anything like it.

"You asked me once if I could forgive you," Jim proceeded, "but at the time it was a hypothetical question. And I gave you the best answer I could. Now I will give you another one."

Zeke cringed again, and seemed to shrink even smaller in the bed. If Zeke had held Katherine in his power all the days of Katherine's life, Zeke was in his son's hands now.

"If you repent for your sins, I will forgive you. If you embrace Jesus Christ as your Lord and Savior, I will embrace you as my father."

"I will," Zeke said eagerly, a deep cough interrupting him. "I will repent for my sins."

Suddenly, Jim recalled the remarks he had made to Father Duffy about the impossibility of seeing into a man's heart. Only God could do that, and it was up to the priest to have faith. Only God could know if Zeke was being sincere, but Jim had no choice but to forgive him. Once he realized that, however, another emotion entered into it: the joy that he felt at being able to forgive his father at that moment. Despite the sharp recollection he had of the bitter existence that his father had condemned them to – and the struggles that he and Katherine had overcome together – Jim felt God's love as he made the decision to forgive his father for what he had done. Jim reached into the kit that priests carry at such occasions, and he pulled out the oil of Chrism and the other objects necessary to administer the Last Rites.

Zeke looked up at him from the bed, frightened in something of a childlike manner, but as trusting as a child as well. Slowly, and with great care, Jim initiated the Last Rites, making the Sign of the Cross with the Oil of Chrism and whispering to Zeke quietly, explaining that this was a reminder of the baptismal promise to die with Christ in order to rise to new life with Him. Then he opened the Bible to James 5.14 and began to read from the text. He wasn't sure when Zeke began to weep – or when he himself felt the hot tears on his own cheeks – but he knew that they were weeping together.

Then Jim imposed his hands on Zeke's head, prayed over the oil, and anointed Zeke's forehead. As he did so, he began to recite the Lord's Prayer. "Are you ready to embrace Jesus Christ as your Lord and Savior now?" he whispered, and Zeke looked up at him in the same childlike way as before.

"Am I worthy of it?"

"You are," Jim said softly, realizing that Zeke was weakening by the moment.

Jim blessed him once more. "I not only forgive you but I love you," he said, and together they experienced the radiance of absolute love.

Jim stayed with him all night, and he was there holding his hand when Gordon the Great closed his eyes for the final time.

As Jim entered the rectory, Father Duffy was waiting for him with a self-righteous sneer.

"The hospital called after you left. Now they're insisting that he's your father! I told you they were taking advantage of you."

Jim responded coldly, looking Father Duffy in the eye. "He *was* my father, and now he's dead."

Father Duffy gasped and stammered a reply, but Jim was halfway up the stairs.

The next morning, Jim made arrangements for his father's burial, telling the undertaker that he wasn't worried about burying Zeke in a suit, but that he insisted on burying him in the overcoat that he had given him. The undertaker nodded his head. He had known Jim for many years; the two men had developed a friendship, and there was nothing that he wouldn't do for Jim. As Jim walked out of the undertaker's office, he knew that his wishes would be respected.

"Your father never missed a day," Neil Shaunessay said, holding Jim's hand in his own.

"What do you mean?" Jim stammered.

"He came to your mother's grave every day for the past three weeks, until he got sick with the pneumonia. Sometimes he sat on the ground, and sometimes he stood at her graveside. But he was always there."

"What did he say to her, Neil?"

"I can't answer that, Jim. I kept my distance and respected his privacy." Neil paused and looked in Jim's eyes. "He must have loved her in his own way."

"Thank you," Jim said vacantly, and he started to walk away. Suddenly, he stopped in his tracks. "Why didn't you tell me he was my father?"

Neil winced. "He made me swear that I wouldn't. Can you forgive me?"

It seemed to Jim that there was no end to the forgiveness that he was called upon to bestow, even at great cost to himself.

"Of course I can," he said, and he turned to walk away.

Zeke was buried a few days later in the coat that Jim had given him. Even Father Duffy complied with this request, celebrating the Mass with Jim with more than fifty priests in attendance. All of the spiritual leaders of Jim's life paid their respects that day, including Father Philip, who had been so instrumental in Jim's decision to continue his preparations for the priesthood in Rome; and in an honor that Jim would never forget, the Cardinal attended as well, gracing them all with his presence. As the cemetery workers lowered Zeke's casket into the ground – bringing him to rest a few feet from Katherine's grave - Jim thanked the Lord for giving him the chance to spend the last few weeks with his father. He now realized that his father had loved him and his mother in his own way, and when it all was said and done, he was at peace with the forgiveness that he had bestowed. Zeke was, after all, just a man who had given in to his weaknesses. How could Jim withhold his forgiveness after his own failings had surfaced all of those years ago with Jennie? And so, in the end, he saw his father for what he truly was - a man. Not good, not bad, just a man, not so unlike himself.

The next two weeks were a little odd. Father Duffy seemed to have turned over a new leaf; he was uncharacteristically kind to everyone, including Jim. He thought it must be because Father Duffy had gotten his way and that Jim was leaving the parish, but that was not the case. On the morning of his departure, Father Duffy had surprised him by taking him aside, apologizing for all of his misdeeds, and giving him a glimpse into Father Duffy's character, explaining that some of his bitterness arose from the fact that as a young seminarian he should have been selected to study in Rome, an honor that typically went to the two brightest and most promising seminarians. Instead, the son of a wealthy contractor who had made significant contributions to his parish and to the seminary itself had been selected, depriving Father Duffy of an honor that he had earned. Eventually, the young man who had gone in Father Duffy's place left the seminary with less than two years remaining in his course of study, costing the church all of the money that it had invested in his training and rubbing salt in Father Duffy's wound. After explaining himself in that way – and expressing regret over the bitterness that threatened to consume him – Father Duffy asked Jim to stay. Contenting himself with the fact that he had helped Father Duffy become a better priest, Jim declined the offer, stating that it was time to move on.

When tears of happiness flow together, they create an ocean of everlasting love. – S.E. Elliot

Chapter Twelve
1962

Jennie was tired. She had not slept well for the fifth night in a row. She glanced at the clock on her nightstand, wearily pushed away the cozy blanket that had kept her warm all night and stepped onto the cold wooden floor. As she went through her morning routine she contemplated why she had not slept in days. At first, she tried to blame her insomnia on the holidays, as she never felt quite right during the season. But she knew it was more than that, and part of her depression was that she wanted to be closer to her son, Danny.

She knew this year had truly been a blessing for her. She was teaching the seventh grade at St. Dominic's, and while it was a challenging position, it was where she belonged. She had spent the past twelve years focused on watching Danny grow, and she found a certain peace knowing that her son was nearby, well-cared for and loved very much by the Goddard's. She knew that the Goddard's had never told Danny that he had been adopted, and she was just as sure they never would. Danny was finally in the seventh grade – her grade – and he was with her in the classroom every day, learning and thriving, and bringing such joy into her life. Surely she didn't deserve more. Jennie wondered if the Goddard's ever questioned her overt attachment to Danny, if they could somehow *see* that her fondness for him want way above teacher-student relations. Sometimes she wished they *would* see, so they would know the truth.

And of course, Jim was never far from her mind, and she had to admit that part of her restlessness was because of him.

Last week, Jennie had been reading *The Catholic Standard & Times,* which was the official newspaper of the Archdiocese of Philadelphia. As she did every week, she skimmed the pages and read about local church celebrations, the Bishop's latest projects, and sometimes, there was even a story on the elementary students at St. Dominic's. She had relied on the paper for important information, but when she opened the paper that January morning, she never expected to read about Father James Gabriel.

Jennie took in the words as if she were reliving a dream. The headline read *Celebrated Priest and War Hero Comes Home to St. Dominic's*. Jennie's hands began to tremble and she could feel sweat forming on her brow as she read the article.

Father James Gabriel, celebrated war hero and priest, has accepted a position as Chaplain at Holmesburg Prison. The prison is a maximum-security facility located in Philadelphia. Formerly at St. Anne's in Port Richmond, he will take up residency at St. Dominic's Church. Father Gabriel said, "It will be good to get back to my roots. I attended St. Dominic's Elementary School, and played in Pennypack Park as a child. My mother raised me in Holmesburg."

Father Gabriel attended St. Charles Seminary and went on to higher studies in Rome. He was a decorated war hero, having served with the elite 408th Demolition Detachment during World War II where he earned many medals including the Medal of Honor.

Jennie brushed her short, cropped hair and readied herself for Monday's Mass. Today would be the day; today, Jim would know that she was a nun and teacher at St. Dominic's. Jennie had heard that he had arrived late Friday evening and that today would be his first day serving Mass. Today would be the greatest day of her life since the last day she had spent with Jim what seemed like a thousand years ago. Jennie went downstairs and joined the other nuns for morning prayers. She said a silent prayer that she herself didn't even understand. Over and over in her mind, she kept saying, "Please Lord, please Lord. Let thy will be done." Her hands trembled as she followed Mother Superior Mary Magdalen and the others to Mass.

As Jennie entered the pew to the right of the altar, she willed her hands to stop shaking. Sister Anna Maria glanced her way but said nothing. The Mass began and Jim walked down the center aisle with two altar boys flanking him. Jennie knew he would not be able to tell who she was from this distance, and could not wait for Communion, where it would be God who would reunite them after all these years.

Jennie was mesmerized during Jim's homily, where he spoke of giving more of yourself than you have to offer. She thought of how handsome he looked, even after all the years that had passed. He was certainly a man of the cloth, and Jennie could tell immediately that the congregation would fall in love with his teachings and mannerisms. She had always known he would make a wonderful priest and she was thankful that he had succeeded in his vocation.

Jennie was jolted out of her daydreaming when she heard "...this is the body of Christ which has been given up for you..." Jim raised the Holy Eucharist above him. He continued with the blessing of the wine and soon it was time for the nuns to file out of the pews to receive the body of Christ.

One by one, the nuns knelt along the railing that separated the altar from the congregation and lowered their veils in an act of piety. As was customary, the nuns would receive Holy Communion first and then return to their pews. Only then, would the congregation follow suit.

Jennie watched as Jim started distributing Holy Communion to the nuns at the left of the altar. Her hands trembled as he slowly made his way across the altar toward her. As he approached Sister Anna Maria, who was to Jennie's immediate left, she inhaled deeply. This would be the moment of truth. How would he react to seeing her, she wondered. Jim offered the Host to Sister Anna Maria, and as she made the sign of the cross, Jim moved to his left, positioning himself directly in front of Jennie. She lifted her veil to accept the Eucharist, and her eyes locked with Jim's. It was a look that would be etched into their minds for the rest of their lives and all through eternity.

"Jennie?" He whispered her name in stunned disbelief as the chalice dropped from his hand and round wafers fell to the marble floor. Every nun turned toward Jennie and Jim, who were still staring at each other in shock.

Trying to regain composure, Jim bent down to retrieve the chalice and as he did, his arm brushed against Jennie's folded hands. He took the now empty chalice back to the tabernacle, retrieved another chalice of Hosts and a cloth and returned to where Jennie was kneeling. Jim bent down to cover the fallen Hosts with the cloth. It was sacrilegious to pick them up and serve them – the only holy way to discard fallen Host was for the priest to eat them after Mass.

Jennie knew the congregation would surely be staring and wondering what had just occurred between the two of them. Jennie glanced at Mother Superior Magdalen and noticed she too, had an inquisitive look on her face.

Jim lifted another Host from the chalice and, with shaking hands he placed the wafer on Jennie's tongue while saying, "The body of Christ." As Jennie said amen, their eyes locked once again, and the intensity of his eyes on her face was unbearable. Jennie lowered her veil, made the sign of the cross, folded her hands and looked down. Jim stepped over to offer Communion to Sister Elena, who was next to Jennie and certainly wondering what had just transpired between the two.

Neither of them knew how they got through the rest of the Mass, and Jim seemed obviously uneasy at the altar. He had hoped the congregation would assume that he was just nervous about saying Mass at St. Dominic's for the first time.

After Mass, Jim rushed back to the rectory. He couldn't believe that Jennie was here! His Jennie! He recognized her immediately. She still had beautiful smooth skin and perfect rosy lips. Her big, brown eyes still sparkled but now also had shown a wisdom that had come with the years that had passed between them.

Jim climbed the stone steps of the rectory two at a time and raced to the phone to call Mother Magdalen, but he stopped before he began to dial, thinking that he had better wait. He needed to calm down a bit before he made this important phone call.

An hour later, he dialed Mother Magdalen's phone number and cleared his throat when she answered, "Mother Magdalen, here, who's calling please?"

"Mother Superior, this is Father Gabriel, Father Jim Gabriel."

"Father Jim! What a pleasant surprise! How are you finding things here at St. Dominic's? Are you settling in?" she inquired.

"Yes, very nicely, thank you," Jim replied, and then continued. "I'm actually calling about Sister Jennie. Certainly, you must have noticed the oddity that occurred today during Mass?"

"Yes, I was a bit curious."

"Well, before Jennie... uh... Sister Jennie and I went into the religious life... well, we would see each other. We were sweethearts, Jennie and I." Jim paused and expected Mother Magdalen to speak, but when she didn't, he continued. "I am asking your permission to go see Jennie, if I may?"

"I don't have a problem with you visiting with Sister Jennie." Her kind voice put Jim immediately at ease. "I sense it is quite important that you speak with her, and I suppose you may go see her in her classroom."

"Her classroom?" Jim asked.

"Why, yes, Sister Jennie teaches the seventh grade. Room one-o-two at the school," Mother Magdalen replied.

Jennie sat at her wide oak desk and looked over the week's plans. She couldn't concentrate knowing that Jim was home, and fulfilling his priestly duties here at St. Dominic's, of all places! She busied herself with lesson plans and when the classroom door swung open and Jim filled the empty space in the doorway, Jennie's breath held still. She felt that if she breathed, she might wake from what had to be a dream. As he walked toward her, she stood up and walked to the front of her desk, not knowing what to say, not wanting to say anything. They were both wearing black and they studied each other like they were meeting for the first time. As she made her way over to him, she realized she had been dreaming of this moment for such a long time! She had spent so many years thinking about Jim and wondering what could have been.

She glanced up at him and smoothed her skirt and straightened her habit. They stood before one another, neither speaking. She truly did not think she could, it was as if her breath had been stolen by the intensity of his clear, blue eyes. Amazing, she thought, how he had not changed all that much throughout the years.

"You are still just as beautiful as I remember," he whispered hoarsely. "After all these years! To think that you've been here! I looked for you *everywhere*."

"You found me," she spoke softly; afraid that if she spoke any louder he would disappear from what had to be a dream.

"There has not been one single day when I have not thought about you, Jennie. When I was in Rome I would wander the streets at dusk and dream of you. All these years, not knowing what had happened to you, if you were happy, what could have been if only I had been able to find you…" his voice drifted off.

"You were not the only one yearning for what might have been. I thought of you just as much – if not more – but over the years I pushed those feelings deep into my heart, believing you had chosen priesthood over me. But now, I don't know what I'm feeling," she looked at him hoping for an explanation, or maybe just a sense of understanding.

"I know, I know," he murmured and raised a hand to stroke her cheek.

Jennie pulled back slightly, feeling as if lightning had struck, his touch on her skin was so powerful. Then she slowly moved closer to him and she could smell his cologne, could see the stubble on his chin; could see her own reflection in his eyes. Her eyes locked on his face, and he lifted her veil away from her head, placing it carefully on the desk nearby. He stroked her short, cropped auburn hair, amazed at how beautiful she still was. His strong arms circled around her and in an instant, their lips met. They melted into one another, cherishing this moment they knew should not be happening. They held onto the kiss for what seemed an eternity, each knowing this kiss would have to sustain them for the rest of their lives. Memories of the time they spent together many years ago flooded their minds – a dam breaking, an old movie being rewound and played again, over and over.

Jennie found herself buried deep into his chest and could feel their hearts pounding, could feel the heat of his body against hers. Neither knew how the kiss began, or when it had ended.

"No matter what we are both feeling, we must have control. You are a nun and I am a priest. I love you; I have always loved you. But we can never be together, for it would be a sin against our God."

His warm breath next to her ear was almost more than she could stand, so she gently pulled herself out of his tight grip. "Yes, of course." She could say the words, and know they were true, but could not look in his eyes. That would be asking too much. She had given up hope of him coming back to her long ago, but even so, with him so near like this… She had almost forgotten how much she really loved him.

"I think we should pray for strength and forgiveness. We need God to help us through this," Jim said.

Jennie agreed, and they decided to meet in the church after school, when Jim would be done with his duties at Holmesburg prison.

Jennie was kneeling at the foot of the cross when Jim entered the church and knelt beside her. There were no words spoken, just a comfortable silence that only two people completely in love, and completely lost in each other, could share.

Their gazes fell on the crucified Christ. Tears streamed down Jennie's face, as she mourned the love that was never to be. Jim spoke quietly. "Dear Jesus, forgive us for we know not what we do. Give us the strength to continue to serve you the way we have chosen to do so, forsaking all others." They each made the sign of the cross and Jennie followed Jim outside into the afternoon sun.

"Jennie, you are my heart's desire; and you've always been right here," he touched his chest. "It is a blessing that we have found each other. I am thankful that I will see you every day that God allows me to live on his great Earth. That is enough, that is all that we both deserve and we should be so thankful for even this small gift."

Jennie, still numb from the whole day's experience, hugged Jim tightly, turned abruptly and walked back to the convent. It was not the first time Jennie had walked away from him like this, but Jim was relieved to know that she would never be far again.

As Jim headed back to the rectory, he realized he had left his Bible and notes from the morning's Mass back at the church office. He took a detour and as he was heading up the stairs to the office, Mother Magdalen was coming out.

"Father Jim, you're just the man I'm looking for. Would you mind joining me in my office?" Mother Magdalen asked. "I have something I need to speak with you about privately."

Jim followed Mother Magdalen down a long hall, entered her office and settled into a comfortable armchair. She closed the door and sat down behind her desk.

"First off, it's so wonderful that you are here at St. Dominic's. You are going to be a positive light for so many people in our congregation," she looked at him intently.

Shifting nervously in his seat he said, "Thank you, Mother Magdalen. I am so glad to be back where I truly belong."

She nodded and leaned closer to Jim, "However, this is not why I asked you here. There is something of a personal nature that I would like to discuss with you."

Jim wondered if there had been any chance she had seen the kiss Jennie and he had shared earlier that day.

"I was looking through some old photos last night, when I came across an old army picture given to me many years ago."

Realizing that this had nothing to do with Jennie, Jim relaxed against the soft cushions of the chair and listened.

She opened up a small drawer in the coffee table that separated them and handed it to him. The picture was black and white and appeared to be very old, although it was obviously a very cherished photo of Mother Magdalen's. She handed it delicately over to Jim. In it, eleven men were standing side by side in army fatigues. Some were smiling but most were not. Boys, really, with their faces painted green and brown as if that would be enough to disguise them from the Germans.

"Where did you get this?" He asked incredulously.

"Then it *is* you!" Mother Magdalen exclaimed with excitement.

"Yes. This was the Demolition Detachment I was a part of," Jim said, pointing to himself in the photo. Young and muscular, he looked handsome, even in his fatigues and camouflage paint.

"I knew it had to be you after I read that article in *The Catholic Standard & Times*," she said. "How many 408th Demolition Detachments could there have been?" Then she leaned over and put one finger on a fellow soldier and said, "This boy was my fiancé, a long time ago." A wistful look clouded her eyes.

"Thomas Young?" Jim said in astonishment.

"Yes, yes. Like I said, it was a long time ago; I was very young. We were in love, and had met at the USO in Philadelphia. We were planning our wedding when he got orders to leave Fort Dix and go to Fort Benning in Georgia. He told me he had to take airborne training so he would be able to join an elite group called the 408th Demolition Detachment. He never told me what he did in the service though; it seemed as if it was very top secret, and I know whatever the group did, it was very dangerous. When he was called to duty, it nearly broke my heart. We wrote each other practically every day," she closed her eyes remembering the words from her fiancé. "So sweet, his letters, they were. One day, the letters just stopped coming. I couldn't understand why. It was so unlike Tom and I was sick with worry. I would have called his parents to see if they knew anything, but he was an orphan. So I called the army to find out what had happened to Tom, because I knew in my heart that for the letters to stop coming, it could only mean one thing... and they told me that yes, he was dead." She paused and looked at her folded hands for a moment.

Jim could see tears forming in her eyes as she continued, "You see, we were not married yet, so I was not family. I tried to tell them that he didn't have any family, but they wouldn't listen. I was so heartbroken over losing Tom that I just knew I would never love a man that way again. I entered the convent a short time later, but always wondered what had happened to my Tom." She looked hopefully towards Jim, "I was hoping you could tell me something."

Jim felt Mother Magdalen was a good person and had experienced tremendous heartbreak, not unlike what he had himself experienced. How could he tell her the truth about her beloved fiancé? He couldn't break her heart further and tell her that the man she loved had died in shame. That he had hung himself after causing a debacle of enormous proportions, made better only by the fact that Jim himself had been able to save eight of the men in the Detachment team, including Tom. How could he tell her that it was due to Tom's failure that Jim had shown his own bravery and in so doing won numerous decorations including the Medal of Honor?

"He was a very brave man, Thomas Young. You should be proud. In fact, if it hadn't been for him, many men would have died on that cold night in France. He made the mission a success, and was shot trying to save another man. I held him in my arms, and he was at peace."

Mother Magdalen wept openly, and Jim handed her a clean handkerchief from his shirt pocket, as he too shed tears as he remembered the real way Tom had died.

"I have not told you everything yet," he said and she lifted her tear-stained face to listen, "Tom was my best friend, he was a good man. I was told to clear out his personals, and when I did I came across a bunch of letters that he had received. Now I know they were from you. There was one letter that he never had a chance to mail. The address was a USO address, and it must have been for you. When I was discharged I tried to find you, but the USO was gone and I had no other address. The only thing I knew about you was that you were to be Tom's wife and that he was very much in love with you."

Mother Magdalen gasped and raised a shaking hand to her temple. "You mean there was a letter for me? Do you have it still?"

"I am sure I do. I have never thrown anything that important away, ever. I will find it for you."

"Where is he buried? Do you know?" she asked

"I will try and find out, I promise."

Jim went back to the rectory and took out a box that was labeled WAR RECORDS - PERSONAL. He was desperate to find the letter from Tom to his sweetheart. In a way, it made him feel better about his own situation with Jennie, knowing that such a great nun as Mother Magdalen had once had a love so strong. He found the letter in the box, just where he thought it would have been. It was addressed to Lorraine Harding, and Jim realized that was the Mother Superior's name before she had chosen her religious name of Mary Magdalen. It was late, and he wondered if he should wait until morning to deliver the letter to her. Jim knew if he were waiting to read the last words from his love, he would want it immediately. He ran to the convent and handed Mother Magdalen her long-awaited letter. Her hands were trembling as she took it from him. She thanked him profusely, and before Jim left, he promised Mother Magdalen that he would find out where Thomas Young had been buried.

Chapter Thirteen

It was yet another blustery January day, but worse because of the freezing rain that pelted the classroom windows and roof. All morning long the rain came, the sound of it on the rooftop like a million ping-pong balls being dropped from the sky. It was hard to concentrate but the children were behaving very well, Jennie noted. Usually any excuse to not participate in their lessons would do.

The lunch bell rang, and the seventh graders leapt from their seats, scrambling to be the first in line to the lunchroom. They were rushing for their coats, mittens and scarves when Jennie called, "I'm sorry boys and girls, other than those children that go home for lunch, you are absolutely not going out in the schoolyard today. You will have to stay in the lunchroom and play for the hour."

They moaned all the way down the long corridor, stuffed lunch pails in hand. Why was it that children loved to be outside in inclement weather, Jennie wondered?

Jennie closed the door to her now quiet classroom and was thankful to have some time alone. She looked at the neat desks that made up her classroom, and thought about how much she loved to teach and how content she had been during this extra special year. A wide smile graced her fair features as her thoughts turned to Danny. She couldn't believe that this year, *both* of the people who she truly loved – her son and his father – were near, and she truly did feel blessed. And ever since Jim had come to St. Dominic's she had an overwhelming desire to scoop her son up into her arms and hold him close. Jennie knew it was foolish for her to be thinking this way, but all the same... her eyes roamed to the back of the classroom and settled on the children's coats hanging in the back. If only there was a reason to comfort Danny, she thought.

Making up her mind, she went to the back of the room and pulled Danny's jacket off its metal hook and quickly stuffed it into the only empty desk in the room. She felt guilty, but at the same time, she was desperate to have some contact with Danny where she would be needed to offer comfort. Her decision made, she went back to her desk to await the children's return from lunch.

When the final bell of the day sounded at three o'clock, the classroom emptied quickly, children rushing out as if it had been a fire alarm and not a school bell. Only one stayed behind. Danny Goddard stood among the empty coat hooks, looking upset.

"Sister Jennie, I can't find my coat!" He cried in a cracked voice.

She could see his beautiful sharp blue eyes well with tears as he searched the empty coatroom once more.

She placed her hand on his shoulder she said, "It's okay, Danny. I'll help you find it. It's got to be here somewhere."

Hand in hand they searched the room, Jennie filled with the same maternal joy she had felt when he was a newborn. She relished the mere touch of his small hand in hers. He started to really cry, but tried to hold back the sobs so she would not see. She felt a powerful urge to hold Danny in her arms, to cradle and comfort the sobbing boy, her only son.

She took a deep breath and pulled him close to her, clinging to him tightly. He seemed comforted by her touch, and this made Jennie extremely happy. She breathed the fresh scent of his golden locks deeply, cherishing the moment, committing every smell, every touch, to memory.

She whispered softly in his ear, "I love you, Danny. You are a good boy and a good student."

She turned him so she could look at his face. How beautiful he was! The tears had dampened his rosy cheeks, and they glistened. Like an angel, she thought. Her angel.

He smiled a big, toothy grin that made her laugh. "You're the nicest teacher I've ever had."

Her heart soared, and she squeezed him close one final time wishing the feelings she had would never end. Reluctantly, Jennie let Danny go and they searched a while longer until Jennie retrieved the coat from the empty desk.

"Here it is! I knew we'd find it together. We make a good team."

Danny was so happy to have found his jacket, he cried, "You're the best, Sister Jennie!"

And Jennie would treasure those words for all eternity.

The prison was designed as a maximum-security institution, surrounded by eight-foot thick walls of reddish undressed Trenton Sandstone, thirty-five feet tall. The layout followed the popular wheel and spoke plan, with access to ten corridors of cellblocks that radiated out like spokes from a hub. Each of the thirteen hundred inmates that called the prison their home lived in a cell that measured eight by eighteen feet, with a small skylight, and was furnished with an iron bedstead, a husk mattress, a blanket, table and chair. There was a modest chapel on the grounds, where Jim served as chaplain to the condemned men.

Jim's mornings were very scheduled, with him saying Mass at St. Dominic's every morning at six, and then returning to the prison to say Mass at eight. He would then be available to hear confession. Most days he would attend to the spiritual and psychological needs of the prisoners. The men began to depend on Jim and trust him, and because of their trust, Jim worked hard to allow them privileges most inmates would not receive. Throughout the months, Jim rallied to get the prison's recreational facilities improved. He noted they needed more time outdoors, should have more physical activities. At best, the inmates got exercise by making license plates and working in the boiler room. Other inmates' duties included kitchen work, tending to the laundry, or working in the library. Jim felt the prisoners needed to relieve stress and anxiety in more positive ways and eventually, Jim was able to organize a baseball team, and regular softball and soccer games. A billiard table and a ping-pong table were donated to the prisoners as well. The prisoners were happy to be treated with respect and the productivity at the prison was at its best. Fewer and fewer fights were breaking out, and the living conditions were improving just as the prisoners' spirits were.

Jim would tell stories of his war days and how he was a decorated combat soldier. The prisoners would listen as Jim talked of how brave the Americans and the Germans were. Each had fought so hard to

247

defend their respective countries, Jim would tell the men. Jim felt that he was doing good, creating a content community within the prison walls and proclaiming the Word of God.

But what the prisoners loved most were the times that Jim would perform his knife throwing stunts for them. These shows were not easily permitted and it took time before Jim received approval from the prison authorities to perform. But after seeing how much of an impact Jim had made upon the prisoners, he was granted permission to demonstrate his abilities with the knife.

On the day of the first knife throwing demonstration, a large metal screen was constructed and Jim stood behind it while the prisoners watched from their seats, heavily guarded by prison security. But Jim had great faith in these men and knew that they would do no harm to him. They had grown to love and respect him, even through all of their misdeeds. Jim knew that most of the men, when released from jail, would be model citizens and a credit to their community.

The prison auditorium was filled to capacity as Jim took center stage. A wooden spinning wheel had been constructed and balloons surrounded the outline of an imaginary body. With a quickness Jim still could not believe he possessed, the knives flew from his hands in perfect unison and blasted into the balloons, creating an echo that sounded much like a gun going off. Once the balloons were replaced, Jim threw three knives consecutively, slashing the wooden wheel while it spun around. Had there been a human attached, much like his mother had been during the circus, she would be unharmed. After doing some of his signature tricks – the overhand throw, the side-arm spin and the buggy whip, where Jim would raise up from a crouched position on the floor and hit the target head on – Jim would spend the next part of his show talking about the need to trust, respect others, and be true to God. His shows always ended in thunderous applause and as Jim bowed graciously, he promised the inmates that if they kept up their part of the bargain – to remain respectable and hard-working prisoners – Jim would continue to make the prison a better place for the men.

Jim was also hard at work forging new relationships with all of the nuns. Throughout the months after Jim's arrival, he would often stop by the convent and chat with the nuns, and they welcomed his visits, especially the older nuns. He always greeted them the same endearing way.

"Good morning, Sister Anna Maria," Jim would reach for her hand and kiss her cheek. "And there's a kiss from God for you." All the nuns appreciated Jim's gracious and entertaining mannerisms and looked forward to his surprise visits. And in turn, his visits helped the nuns to work together more harmoniously. He softened them up and the atmosphere in the convent and the elementary school eased into a calm productive routine. Children were learning more and misbehaving less; the nuns were becoming more patient and there was less need for harsh discipline. If anyone were to ask what the sudden change had been, all the nuns would have to agree that having Father Jim in their parish had done amazing things for their spirits. He truly had become a light for them, and they cherished his friendship. Religious life had become not only more spiritual because of Jim's arrival; it had also become pleasurable and fun.

When Easter arrived, Jim wanted to plan something special for the nuns. After all, they worked hard, prayed hard, and taught hard, and he recognized their dedication to the church and their Lord and he wanted to reward them for their gifts to others.

Some of the nuns were planning on going home to visit family during Easter and Jim knew those who were not going anywhere would be disheartened. Father Jim led the Easter Mass and later joined the nuns for a wonderful celebratory meal. The sun shone brightly the next morning when Jim arrived at the convent. He had requested the presence of any of the nuns who would be staying at St. Dominic's for Easter for a special day trip. Since Jim had worked at the prison as chaplain, he was paid a bit more money than other priests because others in the parish received a stipend for performing weddings, christenings and funerals; the things that Jim could not do as he was busy at the prison. He had taken his extra income and rented the bus and planned a whole day in New York City. The sisters had been told to be ready for departure at nine o'clock in the morning.

They ventured into the city where they did some sightseeing and enjoyed a wonderful lunch.

"Father Jim, this has been an incredible day!" Sister Beatrice gushed.

"It's not quite over ladies," Father Jim winked as he took another bite of his salad. The sisters glanced at each other in confusion. What else could be planned? Hadn't Father Jim done enough already, Sister Jennie wondered?

"Ladies, finish up lunch. We don't want to be late for our next stop, now do we?" Jim urged them to finish eating, and the bunch chatted excitedly about where they would be going next.

There were oohs and ahs from all over the bus when the nuns realized their next stop was Radio City Music Hall where they saw the world-famous Rockettes perform and then enjoyed a stage show. Afterward, they stopped at Rockefeller Center and watched the skaters. On the bus ride home, the nuns chatted excitedly about the wonderful day and thanked Father Jim over and over for treating them to such a fun time.

Jennie was nervous. Although it was a warm June day, she felt chilled as she made the short walk over to Mother Magdalen's office. She felt like there were about a hundred butterflies swishing about her stomach. She was about to make an unorthodox request at the elementary school. Even so, her resolve was strong as she knocked firmly on Mother Magdalen's door.

"Good morning, Sister Jennie. I didn't realize we had an appointment scheduled for today." She looked at her quizzically; it was not often that Jennie would stop by unannounced.

Jennie nervously pressed her sweaty palms into her skirt and said, "No, no. We don't have a meeting planned. I just wondered if you had a few moments to talk to me about something?"

"Of course, my dear," Mother Magdalen said and told her to make herself at home in the spacious office.

"Mother Superior," Jennie started, "You know how much I love teaching the seventh grade, don't you?"

"Why, yes. Of course."

"I have grown very attached to this particular class," she paused.

"Oh?" Mother Magdalen raised her eyebrows.

"Yes, very. I know it is highly unorthodox, but would it be possible to continue on with them next year? I mean, could I teach eighth grade?" She held her breath and waited, knowing her request was ridiculous. Each nun had their own grade that they taught and that was that. But the thought of not being near Danny every day was too much for her to bear, and she knew that teaching eighth grade would guarantee her more time with her son.

"You know that Sister Anna Maria teaches the eighth grade. I'm surprised at you."

Jennie responded quickly, "I know, I know. Of course I would ask Sister Anna Maria if it would be okay to switch grades. If she minds at all I won't think of it again. It's just that... this particular class is very dear to my heart. I can't explain further." She looked up with pleading eyes, hoping Mother Magdalen would not probe further.

Fortunately, she didn't. Instead she stated simply, "I suppose that if Sister Anna Maria doesn't have a problem with it, then I'll allow it. Although I must say it is highly unusual, Sister Jennie. But I have noticed your attachment to the students this year and how fond they all are of you. Yes, I suppose you may change classes." She seemed to convince herself.

Jennie reached out and hugged Mother Magdalen tightly, thanking her profusely.

"Sister Jennie! You'd have thought the Lord himself had just paid you a visit!" She laughed and returned the hug.

"I think He just did," Jennie stated quietly.

Jennie rushed from Mother Magdalen's office and went to find Sister Anna Maria in her room. Although it was obvious that Sister Anna Maria thought Jennie's request was a little odd, she agreed to take over the following year's seventh grade so that Jennie could stay with her class and see them through their lessons and graduation of eighth grade. Jennie was filled with immense happiness knowing that she would have another year with her son Danny.

As Jim neared the rectory, he wondered if he should pay Jennie a surprise visit over at the school. This was the last week of classes before summer break. He decided to change out of his black suit into layman's clothes before heading over. After all, it was a hot day and the dark suit made it feel even hotter.

By the time he walked into the schoolyard, he could tell that school had let out for the day. All was quiet and as he entered the corridors his steps echoed loudly, reverberating off the cinderblock walls that were covered with posters, flyers, and children's handiwork. Knowing Jennie would still be there, probably grading tests, he smiled with anticipation and opened the door to her classroom.

As expected, Jennie sat behind her desk, red pen in hand over a stack of neatly piled papers. She was not alone, though. A student was busy erasing a blackboard, while chalk dust hung above his head. Jim thought it made him look like an angel and chuckled at the image. He had seen this boy here before, erasing the board after school, but could not remember his name.

"What a pleasant surprise, Father Jim." Jennie said, standing up from the desk.

"I just thought I'd stop by to see how your classes were going," Jim replied. They were speaking more formally than they would if they were alone.

"You remember Danny Goddard, don't you?" she asked.

Danny turned toward Jim.

"Of course," Jim said. "Good to see you, son."

Danny said hello and resumed his work at the blackboard. Handsome, Jim thought before turning his attention back to Jennie.

"I thought you might like to take a walk."

"I would love to. Pennypack Park is so beautiful this time of year and it *is* a nice day."

It was not unusual for them to take a stroll through the park, although they never discussed what had happened there so many years ago, and *never* ventured near their waterfall or stream. It was an unspoken pact, a silent secret. He sort of liked it that way; it made him feel closer to her. As close as he dared, anyway.

They walked for a while, talking about everything and nothing, enjoying each other's company.

"Oh! Look at the roses!" Jennie exclaimed like a little girl, pointing with delight at the red, white, and yellow roses nearby.

"My, they've really bloomed since last week," he said, stepping in for a closer look.

They really were spectacular, each petal bright and full of life, soaking up the sunshine and flaunting each perfect head like a proud peacock displaying its feathers. Searching for the perfect one, he plucked a red one as rich in color as fine Bordeaux, and gently removing Jennie's veil, tucked it behind her ear.

"It pales in comparison to your beauty," he said, and placed a tender kiss on her cheek.

Her cheeks turned a deep crimson, as if radiating outwards from the precise spot his lips had touched. "Thank you," she stammered.

"You seem to grow more beautiful with each passing day, Jennie," he whispered. A strange but familiar feeling coursed through his body, making him a little dizzy. Her eyes captivated him. He wanted to grab her, pull her close, and kiss her passionately. She jerked her head suddenly to the left, and the spell was broken.

"Let's sit over there." Jennie said, motioning to a wooden bench.

Afraid to speak for fear of what he might say, he kept silent, content to sit by her side.

She was quiet too, and after some time had passed, Jim asked, "How are you feeling?"

"Just a little tired," she said. "Maybe I'll go back and take a nap."

They walked back to the convent together, crossing through the cemetery. Turning to Jenny, he said, "This is where Tom Young's going to be buried."

"Tom Young? Mother Magdalen's sweetheart?"

"The very one."

Without thinking, Jennie grabbed his arm. "Oh, Jim that's wonderful! How in the world can you do it?"

"It's practically done."

In the past week, Jim had questioned Neil Shaunessay about the availability of a lot in a specific section of St. Dominic's Cemetery.

His idea was to contact the United States Army about exhuming Tom Young's body from his grave in France, transporting it back to the United States, and placing it in a lot that was visible from Mother Magdalen's window. The first obstacle turned out to be that all of the lots in that section of the cemetery were already owned. When Jim questioned Neil further, however, he learned that one of the lots was owned by a family that had moved to California, and that there was a very real possibility that the family would never use the lot at all. Jim contacted them by telephone, and offered to buy the lot from them, explaining that he wanted it for a fallen soldier who had formerly been the fiancé of the Mother Superior. As soon as Jim offered this explanation, the family responded by offering the lot as a gift. It was a two-grave lot, and Jim immediately realized that Mother Magdalen would be able to rest near Tom in death.

Next, Jim contacted the Department of the Army to determine if Tom's grave had ever been moved from the St. Francis of Assisi cemetery in rural France. Typically, soldiers who had been killed in France were moved to an American military burial ground in Normandy; but as it turned out, the Army had refrained from doing this because Jim had already given Tom a proper burial. The Army had placed the appropriate military cross on Tom's grave and paid for perpetual care. Eventually, Jim gained permission to exhume the body and transport it to the United States at his own expense, and was planning to do it very soon.

"That's wonderful, Jim," Jennie exclaimed. "But how did you get the money?"

"My friend, Dr. Angelo DiRenzo, came through for me again."

"Mother Magdalen will be thrilled," Jennie followed Jim as he walked her to the front step of the convent.

"I want to dig this grave myself," Jim said, "and I don't want to use a machine."

"Why not?" Neil asked. "We have back-hoes for that."

"I don't want his grave to be dug by a machine, and that's final," Jim answered.

"You're in no shape to dig a grave by hand."

"You don't understand. Tom was my best friend. He was a better man than I."

"I find that hard to believe," Neil said.

"On one of our missions, we had to eliminate a German sentry, and when he turned to us we realized that he was very young. 'He's just a kid, Tom said. How can you kill a kid?' But apparently, I didn't share his reluctance."

Neil could tell that Jim was growing emotional, so he did his best to reassure him.

"It was war, Father Jim. You had a job to do."

"Be that as it may, it has bothered me ever since."

"If you dig that grave by hand, it'll take at least two days."

"I realize that. I'll dig it by the end of the week, and then I'm flying to France."

True to his word, Jim dug the grave himself, and over the course of the two days, Jennie brought sandwiches and lemonade, just as she had when Jim was a seminarian so many years before. Once the grave was prepared, Jim flew to France, purchased a new coffin, and accompanied Tom's body back to the United States. A week later, Jim conducted a Requiem Mass attended by all of the nuns and Tom was buried in his final resting place. His grave lay in full view of Mother Magdalen's window, adorned with the military cross that the Army had placed on Tom's grave in France. Later, Jim replaced the cross with an impressive headstone.

Summer flew by quickly, and Jennie and Jim were able to spend some quiet moments together. They often prayed after Mass, and sometimes, they would join the other nuns for walks through Pennypack Park, where they would inevitably see families picnicking and children flying kites or playing catch. Jim told the nuns how he spent his days at the prison; that he could see great changes in the inmates, and how he truly felt he was doing God's work there.

When they were alone one afternoon, Jennie confided in Jim that she had never been happier. She adored teaching students and couldn't wait for the new school year to begin, where she was privately thrilled to know she would be with Danny every day. She hadn't seen much of Danny during the summer but had heard that he and the Goddards vacationed at the New Jersey shore. Jennie knew he was happy and content, and it gave her great peace to know he was so loved by the Goddards.

In late July, the nuns vacationed at the New Jersey shore as well, traveling to their retreat at Cape May Point for a two-week holiday. In order to minimize the amount of time that Jim was away from Jennie, he fulfilled his two-week obligation to the Army Reserves during the same time period.

It was a beautiful summer day in late August when Jim knocked on the convent door to ask Sister Jennie to accompany him on a walk. Mother Magdalen opened the door, greeted Father Jim with a smile, and invited him in. Jim asked her if she would like to join them on their walk, but she declined, saying that she wanted to water the flowers on Tom's grave.

After Jennie changed into more comfortable clothing, she and Jim walked for close to an hour. While they were walking, it began to rain unexpectedly and Jim led them to a nearby railroad trestle. Because there were gaps in the railroad tracks above them, Jim did his best to shield Jennie from the rain. As he pulled her close, Jennie looked up at him, and Jim was once again aware of the strong attraction that existed between them. As they declared their love to one another, he pressed his lips to hers and they kissed passionately. Just as they had at the back of Jennie's classroom when they were first reunited, they kissed for a long time; but they knew that they could go no further.

As they walked back to the convent together, Jennie asked Jim if they had committed a sin.

"It is not a sin for me to love you and for you to love me," he replied. "Jesus Christ loved Mary Magdalen and she loved Him. She was at the foot of the cross when He was crucified."

"I guess you're right," Jennie frowned, still not entirely convinced.

When they arrived at the driveway that ran between the convent and the rectory, Mother Magdalen came out of the convent to meet them. She seemed to look at Jennie for a long time, and then she looked at Jim.

"I was worried about you when it started to rain. Is everything all right?"

"We're fine," Jim answered, as Mother Magdalen looked at him dubiously.

After Jennie excused herself in order to put on dry clothes, Jim turned toward the rectory, but Mother Magdalen stopped him.

"Father Jim, I need to speak with you. I noticed that Jennie's face was flushed. What happened in the park?"

Jim hesitated as he observed her stern expression. "I kissed her... passionately,' he said, "and that's all."

"That's all?" she asked somewhat mockingly. "Isn't that enough?" She frowned. "I know how you feel about each other, Father. After all, I remember perfectly well how I felt about Tom. And I'm truly grateful for what you've done for me. Having Tom's grave right under my window comforts me every day of my life. And your impact on the nuns, the prisoners, and the parishioners has been remarkable. The happiness you've brought isn't the most important gift you've given us – although it's substantial. But more than anything else, we are grateful for the love that you've created. Two of the nuns that constantly bickered before your arrival are now conversing with one another pleasantly, and two others who never spoke at all are now doing the same."

"I've been fortunate, Mother Magdalen. We all have."

"Please, Father, don't interrupt me. According to John 15:12, Christ said to the apostles, 'I command you to love one another as I have loved you.' That is what you have done for us. But I cannot condone what happened between you and Jennie today, and I would ask that you not let it happen again. God has brought you together to test your resolve, and together you must show him that Jesus Christ is your true love."

"Mother Magdalen, I give you my solemn promise that it won't happen again. "

"Very well, then. There's no need to speak of it further."

Jim leaned forward and embraced her tightly, and Mother Magdalen took on a puzzled expression.

"What was that for?"

"That was the embrace that Tom would have given you if he had come home from the war."

Summer gave way to fall and the rush of the school year kept Jennie content yet busy. She would see Jim occasionally during religious functions but spent most of her time on class lessons. She hadn't realized that teaching eighth grade would be so challenging, but she knew all the hard work was worth it, especially when she saw how well Danny was doing in class.

The holidays were an especially exciting time at St. Dominic's parish as children prepared for Christmas and the New Year, and as the nuns organized school events. There were pageants, holiday bazaars, caroling, gift exchanges, and beautiful candlelight services on Christmas Eve. Jennie was thrilled to receive a homemade card from Danny that year, expressing his gratitude and love for his teacher. In it, he had written, *"To Sister Jennie, You've taught me so much more than you can ever know. I am so lucky to have had the BEST teacher in the world two years in a row. Love, Danny."* That card was the most priceless gift Jennie would ever receive and she cherished it with all of her heart.

After the rush of the holidays, a slow-paced boredom settled over the convent. The nuns had been so busy preparing for the anniversary of Jesus' birth that when it was all over, there was a definite lack of enthusiasm felt throughout. Father Jim took it upon himself to liven things up.

One Saturday afternoon, he entered the convent with two burlap bags thrown over his shoulders and announced loudly from the foyer, "Ladies, I have a message here from God."

Of course, his playfulness got the attention of even the eldest women and soon the foyer was filled with curious nuns.

"Father Jim, what have you got there?" Jennie asked.

"Well, it has come to my attention that you all are burned out from the Christmas events, that some of you are feeling low, and I've come to bring some good cheer."

There was a rustle of comments throughout the group as Jim threw open one of the bags to reveal shiny new skates in assorted sizes.

"What on God's good earth do you have there?" one of the nuns asked.

He announced loudly that he was taking all who were interested to Pennypack Park to ice skate.

"It's a glorious day in God's country and we should be out enjoying this day! Who's with me?"

Some of the nuns begged off having never skated before, but Sister Jennie and a half-dozen others all agreed it would be a fun outing. Twenty minutes later, the nuns were suited up with new skates and their warm overcoats and wobbling onto the ice at Pennypack Park.

"I can't believe I'm ice skating again!" Jennie yelled excitedly as she tested her skills carefully.

"You're doing terrific Jennie! How long has it been since you ice skated?" Jim asked as he spun around to face her.

"Since my mother died. You remember I told you she was a wonderful skater and that we would come out here when I was a little girl, don't you?" Jennie asked.

Jim winked at Jennie and smiled brightly. "Of course I remember, why do you think we're here?"

Jennie beamed right back at Jim and said, "You truly are a gift from God, Father James Gabriel."

Sister Anna Maria came buzzing by on her skates and screamed with delight before collapsing onto a nearby bench. The others passed Sister Anna Maria and chided her for giving up so quickly. Throughout the afternoon, Jim would take each of the eager nuns by hand and lead them onto the ice; telling them to stay focused and soon all the nuns were skating around as if they had been doing it for years.

Over hot cocoa at the convent later that night, Sister Nadine, who had just learned to skate that day, said, "Father Jim, this has been a fabulous day. Thank you so much for taking all of us skating!" The others agreed and it was suggested they do it again soon. They all laughed through the evening and relayed the days' events to the nuns that hadn't gone with them. Soon everyone was telling stories of their childhood and remembering good old days. The laughter filled the hallways and echoed through the foyer. It had been a long time since such genuine happiness sounded out through the convent and Sister Jennie was grateful for the love Jim had shown toward all of them.

The nuns began to look forward to unexpected surprises from Father Jim. He had silently made it his vow to bring the nuns together and to reward them for all of their goodness. As winter thawed into spring, Jim would often bring treats to the convent, and a favorite was when Jim would throw a hoagie party at the convent. He would bring in foot-long sandwiches and announce, "Dinner's here!" This would alert the nuns to his arrival and soon the convent's dining room would be bustling with laughter and camaraderie as the women ate and joked. It wasn't unusual for Jim to bring special snacks on his surprise visits as well – water ice, soft pretzels, cannolis from Termini's Bakery, tomato pies from DiPalma's in Holmesburg, and imported prosciutto and provolone cheese from the Italian Market in South Philadelphia. Sister Nadine had joked heartily to Jim as he entered with a bagful of treats, "What are you trying to do Father Jim, fatten us up?"

Jennie was amazed at Jim's good-heartedness and generosity toward not only her, but to all of the other nuns as well. March brought about more surprises from Jim as he arrived at the convent with an invitation to the movies. The nuns and Father Jim took a bus to the Fox Theatre in downtown Philadelphia to catch the matinee of *Lawrence of Arabia*. This was a spectacular treat since it was not often the nuns would have a chance to see a film. Father Jim was opening new doors for the nuns and his continued pampering gave way to a happier environment at the convent and at school. As far as Jim was concerned, the nuns had far less freedom than the priests to come and go as they pleased, and it meant a great deal to him that they were taking kindly to the attention he was showing them.

Despite all of the attention that he was showing the nuns, however, Jim still had time to visit the hoboes on a regular basis, and on one of his visits to the rail yards he was shocked to see that Father Duffy was sitting among them. But what was even more surprising, Father Duffy was wearing a pair of sneakers that he had dyed black, having given away his own shoes to one of the hoboes. Jim recognized the trick immediately, since he had used it on a number of occasions himself. "Father Duffy," he said, "I see you have a new pair of Florsheims."

Father Duffy smiled at Jim sheepishly. "The Lord works in mysterious ways, Father. Have a seat." And together, they shared the Mulligan stew with the hoboes.

Chapter Fourteen

Feeling more tired than usual, which was a feat in and of itself since she could not even remember feeling well rested, Jennie laid her head in her hands atop her desk. Maybe I am getting the flu, she thought. Her temple did feel warm, even to her own palm. She had been feeling this way for days, and she was beginning to think she should consult a doctor. The flu was never anticipated and this was definitely the wrong time of year to be sick, Jennie thought to herself. With Easter a few short weeks away, there was so much to do. The Easter pageant, special projects for the children, and an Easter party were all on her list of things to plan for.

And Jim was nagging at her, asking her to see his friend, the doctor. He kept telling her that she looked pale and was getting too thin; she kept telling him not to worry. It was nice having someone worry about her, though. And maybe he was right; it was time to see a doctor. But not his doctor. She would find one herself.

She walked into the stuffy waiting room, and told the receptionist that she had a twelve o'clock appointment. Settling into one of the chairs, she looked around. It smelled funny, she noticed. All doctors' offices did. It was hard to pinpoint what the smell actually *was*. Sickness, yes, the room smelled like sick people. She was not alone. Two other patients sat near her, reading magazines. One, an older man, kept sneezing loudly and grabbing his handkerchief. Great, she thought, I'll probably leave here in worse shape than when I came in.

After a long while, a stout nurse called her back into one of the examination rooms.

"Sister Jennie, what a surprise!" Dr. Craven smiled upon seeing who his next patient was.

A member of St. Dominic's, he and his wife were generous contributors to the church.

"Are you not feeling well?" he inquired, beginning to take notes. This was her first time here.

"I think I'm coming down with the flu."

262

"Well, then. Let's have a look."

He took her temperature, examined her throat, and felt her glands.

"Is something wrong?" Jennie asked.

"No, no. You do have a fever, and your lymph nodes are a bit enlarged. You look a little pale. Are you experiencing any other symptoms?"

"Like what?" She looked at him, confused.

"Are you tired, weak?"

"Yes."

He continued to make notes. "Is your throat sore?"

"Yes, a little, I suppose."

He lifted her blouse and pressed on her abdomen. "Does this hurt?"

"It feels a little tender. My stomach has been bothering me lately."

"Is anything else bothering you?"

"Well... I've had a persistent cough. Oh, yes." She lowered her eyes and felt herself blush. "I've been bleeding a little."

He looked concerned. "I'm going to take some blood samples."

She was surprised. "Why? Can't you just give me penicillin?"

"Based on your symptoms, and the fact that you've been feeling this way for several days, I think we should be on the safe side. Just to rule out some things. Don't worry, it's just routine," he added, seeing the distressed look on her face. "I'm sure it will be nothing."

She left his office thinking Dr. Craven was being overly cautious. She was sure it was just the flu and no need to overreact. Dr. Craven told her that the results would not be in for a day or two. She told him that she would be busy at the school, tidying up her classroom, getting next semester's lessons in order. He asked how he could get in touch with her about the test results, and she told him that if she were not at the convent, it would be fine to relay the message to Mother Magdalen. He said he did not like to do that, and preferred to talk to his patients directly, for confidentiality purposes. He finally conceded after Jennie persisted. She didn't want Dr. Craven to have to track her down when he could easily tell Mother Magdalen the results of the blood test, as she was sure it was nothing anyway. He had never treated a nun before, and agreed that the Mother Superior was her legal guardian.

She had been so busy this past week she had not had time to catch her breath. She still was not feeling well, but between cleaning up her classroom and getting ready for Easter, she refused to slow down for a slight fever. Besides, she had not heard from Dr. Craven, so she assumed that her tests had come back fine, as she had known they would. Mother Magdalen had left a note tacked to her door this morning asking her to stop by her office after breakfast. This was not that unusual as every month or so she would meet with each nun in the convent to discuss various topics.

The door was half-open, but Jennie knocked anyway.

"Come on in," Mother Magdalen called.

She entered to find her sitting in her large leather chair, facing her bay window. Jennie looked at Mother Magdalen and thought how peaceful she looked. She followed her gaze out the window and saw a handsome headstone.

Jim had kept his promise. Jennie had known about Mother Magdalen's lost love. She knew he had had to pull a lot of strings and use his war hero status to find the body of Thomas Young. Once he found out where he had been laid to rest, he had gone to great lengths to get permission to bring the body to St. Dominic's. Jennie knew Jim had asked his friend, Dr. Angelo DiRenzo for the money to pay for the headstone. Seeing the way Mother Magdalen was gazing at it so contentedly made it seem worth the trouble. She told herself to remember to tell Jim about this later.

Mother Magdalen turned slowly towards Jennie, and the serene look of calm that had graced her face just seconds before became clouded.

"Please, sit." She motioned to a chair. "I'm afraid I have some bad news, Sister Jennie."

Something about her tone of voice made Jennie hold her breath and wait. Thoughts of Jim flashed through her mind like lightning, only interrupted by an image of Danny. She had never seen Mother Magdalen like this before.

"I received a call from Dr. Craven…"

Jennie relaxed. Thank God that is all this is about, she thought, relieved.

"Jennie." She walked over and placed a hand on her shoulder. "The results from your tests came back."

Jennie tensed. Mother Magdalen had never called her Jennie before, and the look in her eyes… could it be sympathy?

Before she could wonder any more, Mother Magdalen continued. "My dear, the Lord works in mysterious ways, and it is not our place to judge that which he has deemed." She shifted and gazed through her window at the headstone. "Dr. Craven has informed me that you have leukemia."

Jennie didn't speak, just stared at Mother Magdalen as the word leukemia swam around her brain sounding illogical to her. Finally, Jennie cleared her throat and whispered, "There must be some mistake. I have the flu. The doctor must have made a mistake."

The unmistakable look of pity in Mother Magdalen's eyes told Jennie that there was no mistake. Jennie leapt from the chair and pushed away Mother Magdalen's hand. She felt as if she were on fire; her knees buckled and she slid to the ground, sobbing.

Mother Magdalen ran to her, held her in her arms and consoled her. Jennie didn't know how long they remained like that, but finally feeling as if she could stand without Mother Magdalen's support, she backed away and sank into a chair.

"Tell me what the doctor told you. I want to know everything."

"Maybe we should discuss this later. You should go lie down dear. You look tired."

Jennie refused and Mother Magdalen began to explain.

"I took a lot of notes, so I wouldn't forget anything." She retrieved a notepad from her desk.

"Please, start from the beginning. How serious is it, and how long until I get better?"

Again, pity and sadness appeared on Mother Magdalen's face. She began to read from her notes.

"Dr. Craven says your leukocyte count is very high. You also have anemia, which is probably why you felt bad enough to see him in the first place. You have something called, let's see... thrombocytopenia, which is why you've been experiencing prolonged bleeding." She paused and looked up at Jennie.

"That doesn't tell me what I want to know. How bad is it and what are we going to do about it?"

"The doctor said you have acute leukemia, which is the most severe type."

Fighting back the tears, Jennie resolved to find the positive.

"Okay, so I have a bad case of it. When will I get better?"

Consulting her notes once more, Mother continued. "He said the next step would be to suppress the leukemia cells in the blood, bone marrow and tissues; control your bleeding; relieve the anemia; and try to prevent infections."

Reassured and with renewed hope, Jennie exclaimed, "Fine. If I take this course of action, I'll be just fine."

Mother Magdalen put her hand on Jennie's arm. "Jennie, do you hear what I'm saying, this is a severe case." She paused and Jennie stared at her. "I have given this a lot of thought and think it would be best for you to go to our retirement home, where you can be tended to properly."

"But why would I want to go there? I can be cured right here, you just told me what Dr. Craven wants to do..."

"I'm afraid you don't understand, Jennie. There is no cure."

Again, Jennie stared at her. "What do you mean, no cure?"

"The disease is fatal."

These were words Jennie could not bear to hear and suddenly felt faint and nauseous. She simply stared in disbelief now, tears streaming down her cheeks. "How long do I have?" she asked.

"No one knows for sure," Mother Magdalen said gently. "Three months, four months, maybe as long as six or seven."

"Why does He hate me so much?" Jennie said suddenly.

"Who do you mean?"

"Who else? God!" She was practically screaming.

The look of shock on Mother's face quieted Jennie, and she sat numbly once more.

"My dear, sweet child. It is not our place to question why. He has a plan and we must have faith. It is our place to accept whatever he deems appropriate with grace and dignity."

They sat for a long time in silence as Jennie considered her fate. The concept of her own mortality was too huge for her to grasp. It was like an enormous iceberg that was impossible to swim around or to ignore. But she was strong. She would not just wither away and die. She would fight with every breath.

Clinging to her determination, she said firmly, "I appreciate your concern for my well-being as I know you only want what's best for me. Your love, support, and religious guidance through the years have prepared me for this battle. You know I respect your opinion greatly, but in this case I feel you are mistaken. I do not wish to go to the retirement home. I want to stay here and teach my class, like always."

"Sister Jennie, I'm afraid I must insist. Now is not the time for you to be teaching. You should save your energy. And besides, we do not have the facilities here to provide you with the care you are going to need."

"Please, Mother Magdalen. It is of vital importance that I finish out the year with my students and see them graduate."

"Jennie, this is not right for your health. You need to be where you can receive proper care. I cannot let you continue at the school."

Unable to think of a reason as compelling as the truth, Jennie felt she had no choice but to tell her about Danny. She started at the beginning and told Mother Magdalen everything. She had already known that Jim and Jennie had been sweethearts, but now she was learning for the first time that Jim was the father of Jennie's child. The thought of Jennie's life-long love of Father Jim – and of her own life-long love of Tom Young - caused her to lose her composure. Staring out at Tom's headstone vacantly, and then looking back at Jennie, she struggled to formulate a reply. All the while, Jennie wondered if she had made a terrible mistake.

"I should have seen it all along," Mother Magdalen began. "That boy does look remarkably like Father Jim. And to think that Father Jim doesn't even know! It's not my place to judge, but don't you think you should tell him?"

"No," Jennie said firmly. "I made my decision long ago. It would not be fair of me to tell him now."

Mother Magdalen nodded in understanding. "Still, that is a heavy burden for you to have to bear alone."

"I have borne it this long. Now you see why it is so important that I remain with my class. I want to spend as much time with Danny as I can." She paused and looked Mother Magdalen in the eye. "Particularly if I only have a short amount of time left."

"Very well, you may teach as long as you feel up to it."

"There is one more thing. I don't want anyone to know about my illness. Please don't tell Father Jim or the other nuns."

"That I cannot do, Sister Jennie. We are a family. Your problems are our problems. You won't be able to hide your illness forever, and you're going to need their support. As a practical matter, there will undoubtedly be days in which you won't feel up to teaching."

"No, I don't want them to know."

"Those are my terms," Mother Magdalen stated flatly.

"All right, but don't tell Father Jim."

"Jennie, he has to know. He'll see your condition just as the other nuns will. And you're the one that should tell him."

"Oh, Mother, please don't make me do that. I couldn't bear it."

"Very well, then, I'll tell him."

That night, after the nuns prayed together in the convent chapel, Mother Magdalen stood before them. "Girls, I have something very important to discuss." As she began, Sister Jennie slipped quietly from the back of the room. Several of the nuns noticed this and wondered about it, while others kept their eyes on Mother Magdalen. When Mother Magdalen continued, however, their questions were quickly answered. "Before I begin, every one of you must make a solemn promise to me and to one another that what you are about to hear will remain with us, and that you will share it with no one. If any of you are unprepared or unwilling to make that promise, you must leave the chapel immediately."

The sisters listened carefully, but not one of them moved. They didn't even glance at the door. "As you know, Sister Jennie has been feeling poorly lately. Her doctor has informed me that she has a serious condition and every one of you must be strong as I explain it to you, because Sister Jennie will need your strength. She has an acute form of leukemia and is not expected to live for more than a few months." Several of the nuns gasped as they heard this; others began to cry. "The normal course of action would be for Jennie to be sent to the mother house for treatment; however, there is more. Long before we knew Jennie as a nun, she conceived a child, and that child is one of our students."

If there had been a dry eye before this news, there were no more, as everyone was obviously struck by this news.

"Years ago, before she entered our order, Sister Jennie gave Danny Goddard up for adoption, and now he is one of our eighth graders." All at once, Sister Anna Maria understood why Jennie had asked for permission to teach the eighth grade instead of the seventh, and one at a time each of the other nuns began to realize why she had done this. For a split second, they took their eyes off of Mother Magdalen and glanced at Sister Anna Maria, who nodded in recognition.

"What you don't know is that Father Jim is Danny's father. He and Jennie were sweethearts years and years ago, and they made a mistake that they have been paying for ever since."

It was all becoming clear to them now; why Father Jim had dropped the chalice during his first Mass at St. Dominic's. All of the nuns began to sob openly and console one another in their grief for the love between Sister Jennie and Father Jim, and for the son that was unaware of his real parents. Every one of them loved Sister Jennie and Father Jim, and to hear all of this at once was nearly too much for them to bear.

"Please listen to me carefully, girls. Father Jim is unaware that Danny is his son. The circumstances are highly unusual and they're extremely complicated, but Sister Jennie was determined that he should continue to do God's work without the additional burden of fatherhood. I must ask you to respect her wishes."

Something was bothering Jim. Jennie was acting strangely lately. Maybe it had something to do with the flu bug she had caught.

Several times he had asked Mother Magdalen what was wrong with Jennie, if it was something more serious than the flu, but she always seemed to avoid answering him directly. It was starting to worry him. She was well enough to teach, though, and he noticed that she had not missed a single day of school. Even so, he was suspicious. Something was not right. He decided he would find a way to talk to her doctor and feel things out.

Dr. Craven was a member of St. Dominic's, and Jim had mentioned one Sunday after Mass that it would be nice to have dinner with him. Dr. Craven immediately invited him to the Vesper Club in downtown Philadelphia, where Dr. Craven was a member. At first, they made small talk, and Jim made a concentrated effort not to blurt out the one question that had been occupying him for days. He was doing very well, he thought. It was already time for dessert and he had controlled himself to that point. He was sure the doctor had no idea why he was really here.

"Speaking of the elementary school," Jim said, "it's a shame about Sister Jennie."

Dr. Craven looked at him closely, wondering why Jennie would have discussed her illness with Father Jim at this early stage.

"Yes, it is a shame. I would be surprised if she finished out the year. Her condition is deteriorating faster than I would have hoped."

Jim dropped his fork. "Because of the flu? What's going on with Jennie, doctor?"

Dr. Craven stared at him, his face reddening with anger. "Father Jim, you didn't know? You tricked me into getting confidential information from me! I expected more from a man of the cloth."

"I'm sorry, doctor, I had no other choice. I knew that you were bound by confidentiality requirements, but Jennie is important to me." Jim avoided Dr. Craven's eyes, so that he would refrain from revealing more than he intended.

Realizing he did not have much of a choice, the doctor told him everything, including Jennie's life expectancy.

"There is always hope, Father Jim."

Dr. Craven tried to soften the blow for him, but Jim was inconsolable for the rest of the evening and he asked the doctor to drop him off at St. Dominic's Church. His head would not clear and he could not accept what the doctor had told him. The air was cold as he left Dr. Craven's car, and Jim made his way into the church.

Falling before the cross, Jim unburdened his heart. "My Lord, why have you forsaken me? I have been through *enough!*" He wept openly, holding his head in his hands.

Hearing a noise behind him, he turned around quickly, startled. He had thought he was alone. There, kneeling in front of the statue of the Blessed Mother, was Jennie. Overcome, he simply stared at her.

"Jim!" she cried, running over to him. "What's wrong?"

"Oh, Jennie!" He embraced her and held her tightly. "I know, I know." He sobbed into her shoulder. "Why didn't you tell me?"

"Because I love you too much to cause you this amount of pain," she said, "and I didn't want you to treat me any differently. I am exactly who I have always been, and I don't want to be babied or treated like an invalid. I am going to see my students graduate in June."

Taken back by her strength and her resolve, he saw how incredibly strong she was. This realization made her even more beautiful and endearing, and he wanted nothing more than to tell her she would be all right. Her tranquil composure was comforting, and together they talked well into the night, each praying their own prayers – her for strength, he a miracle.

Several days later, he asked Mother Magdalen if he could take the nuns to the Rockefeller Center as he had last year around Easter time, and Mother Magdalen agreed. Jennie was having a tough time coming to terms with her illness and Jim remembered how she had loved Rockefeller Center at Easter last year. He wanted to take her skating, and knew that it might possibly be the last time Jennie would ever be healthy enough to do so.

Just like the year before, Jim rented a bus and gathered any nuns who were interested in going to Rockefeller Plaza. Ever since he had purchased the skates for the nuns and took them to Pennypack Park, many had taken skating up as a hobby, so quite a few sisters joined them.

"You look like a pro," Jim said when Jennie arrived at the bus. She wore a black skating leotard and a calf-length skirt.

"Oh," she sighed, "I feel like I did when I was a little girl skating with my mother."

"Well then," Jim teased, "let's get you out on the ice and you can skate the way I know you can."

Round and round they went, gliding hand in hand on the silver ice. He was not paying attention to the other nuns; his focus was on making the day special for Jennie. All of the other nuns were too busy tripping and falling over the ice, laughing and skating, to notice them anyway. Jim realized that Jennie's cheeks had taken on a healthy glow and he smiled up at the sky, thankful. He remembered feeling this way when they had skated at Pennypack Park, and he was so thankful they had this time together, this time to make some memories. Jennie clutched his arm as they skated together and Jim knew she was happy. After a while they stopped for hot cocoa and drank it on a bench.

"It is a perfect day. Thank you, Jim." Jennie smiled up at him.

"Any day I spend with you is perfect, Jennie. Today is a wonderful day and you still know how to skate beautifully. Wouldn't you rather ditch me and swirl around the ice by yourself for a bit?"

"No," she said emphatically. "I would rather hold your arm than skate around the world."

"Even so, why don't you give it a try? I'll sit right here and cheer you on."

It took some additional prodding, but she finally agreed. She looked so elegant, dancing on he ice like a swan. Suddenly, she bent her legs, spun her arms, and began to twirl like a top. Jim watched in amazement at her beauty and grace. He watched her spin faster as he held his breath. All at once, she spun out of control, arms and legs becoming entangled. She crashed on the ice, arms flailing.

"Jennie!" he cried, hurrying over to her. Reaching down and pulling her to her feet, he held her in his arms. The fall had shaken her and the color drained from her face. Her skin looked sallow, and her lips were blue from the cold. For a moment he thought she might cry, but instead she pulled herself from his arms and brushed herself off.

"I'm okay," she said. "Let's go around once more."

It was beginning to get dark, and the other sisters were unlacing their skates and sipping hot cocoa, obviously done for the day and anxious to get home.

"Are you sure you feel up to it?" he asked.

"Yes," she said defiantly.

And so they did. He knew her knees must have been bruised in the fall, and she was already so weak. She didn't protest even once, though, and he knew better than to ask if she wanted to quit.

On the bus ride home, Jennie sat next to Jim and took his hand into hers. She looked into his eyes, and recalled the eyes of a younger Jim many years ago. They didn't speak for a while. Finally, Jennie said quietly, "I will remember this day all of my life. Thank you."

"As will I Jennie, as will I." Jim replied.

Chapter Fifteen

It was late June, school was finished, and as Jennie had promised, she was front and center for her student's graduation the week earlier. The sun was shining brightly but Jim thought it would be more appropriate for the clouds to darken and a tremendous storm to hit.

Jennie was sick, really sick this time. He entered the lobby of Nazareth Hospital, made his way to the gift shop and bought a dozen red roses.

Jennie had been there all week and he had come every single day. He pushed the door of her room open, and saw that Jennie was sleeping. He quietly slid into a chair beside her bed and suppressed tears that were on the verge of spilling. Each day her condition had worsened. The doctors didn't give them much hope, but he held tightly to the notion that she would feel well enough to leave. As he gazed at her, he felt his reserve dwindle.

She had lost so much weight recently that her frame was emaciated, visible beneath the thin sheet that covered her. He put the flowers into a pitcher and sat again, listening to her labored breathing.

Her eyes fluttered open, and he was relieved to see a spark of life in them. Jennie was fighting this thing with everything she had. She was so much stronger then he was, he thought.

She must have sensed his despair, however, because she reached out and grasped his hand. "I got to see my students graduate, didn't I?" As if telling him, "Look, I've come this far."

He tried to smile but was unable to force it. There was so much he wanted to tell her, so much left unspoken. Not knowing where to begin, he remained silent, watching her chest heave up and down.

"My dear, sweet Jim," she whispered. "There is something I have to tell you."

"Please, Jennie, you need your rest. You can tell me later."

"I don't have much time left, let me finish. I know now that I should have told you long ago… " She paused and lowered her gaze from his own for an instant.

"Tell me what?"

"I thank God that you came back into my life, you have been my dearest friend. I don't know how to tell you what I have to tell you, and I am very tired, so I'm just going to say it. Do you remember that beautiful night we shared all those years ago?"

"Of course I do, Jennie," he said softly.

"A child was made that night."

Jim gasped and began to say something, but Jennie raised her hand to silence him. "I named him Daniel. You know him, Jim. The Goddards adopted him; he was in my eighth grade class. Danny Goddard is our son."

He looked at her in disbelief. She went on to tell him the entire story. He was speechless as one emotion after another came and left his mind. Anger, despair, joy, shock – his mind was racing. He realized that he had seen Danny in his cap and gown at graduation. And to think that Danny was his son!

"He looks a lot like you," Jennie said, touching his arm lightly. "Please don't hate me. I did what I thought was best."

He reached up and stroked her matted hair. "How could I ever hate you, Jennie? You are my life, my love. It has always been you and always will be."

"I love you, too," she whispered.

A tear rolled down her cheek and he lowered his head to kiss it away. He kissed her lips as well, gently and sweetly. He didn't care what was right and what was wrong; he just knew that he loved her.

"Promise me that you'll watch over Danny," she pleaded.

"I promise."

It was as if history was repeating itself. He had made a promise to his mother on her deathbed years ago – to honor her wish to become a priest, and now he was promising Jennie to watch over their son. She had heard the promise that she had been hoping for years, and Jennie was able to succumb to the battle of her own life. Later that night, Mother Magdalen told Jim that Jennie had passed away.

With Danny assisting him as an altar boy, Jim conducted the most difficult Mass he had ever performed - the funeral Mass for Jennie. Not only was he laying to rest the woman who had become so precious to him, he was also keenly aware of Danny's presence and of the fact that Danny had no idea of his own parentage. As far as Danny knew, the Goddards were his parents, Jim was the parish priest, and Sister Jennie had simply been his teacher. Even the Goddards were unaware that Jim was Danny's father. To him, he was simply the priest that was conducting this beautiful funeral Mass and leading their son through the service.

"Kyrie Eleison, Christi Eleison, Kyrie Eleison," Jim intoned in Latin, before coming to a sudden halt. When he finally faltered, overcome with emotion, it was Danny that gave him strength. Tugging on Jim's stole and looking up at him, he said, "Father Jim, Sister Jennie would want us to be very brave." Jim stared down at his son in wonder and an unmistakable feeling of love passed between them very briefly. It was the last assistance Jim would need in conducting the service.

God alone can finish. –John Ruskin

Chapter Sixteen
1964

Not only did Jim honor Jennie's wishes about watching over Danny, he also gained the Cardinal's approval to serve an additional year as Chaplain at Holmesburg Prison. During that year – as he continued to make life better for the nuns – Jim began to interact with Danny and a group of his friends. At about the same time, Jim purchased a Chevrolet station wagon, and several times a week Danny and the other boys would pile into the car and Jim would drive them to baseball games at Connie Mack Stadium, basketball games at the Convention Center, and football games at Franklin Field. Longer outings included Yankee games in New York and Notre Dame football in South Bend, Indiana. Jim had always loved sports, and it was a great joy for him to watch these games with the boys, and play pickup basketball with them in the schoolyard at St. Dominic's.

At the conclusion of the additional year at the prison, Jim met with the Cardinal again and asked if the Cardinal had someone in mind who could replace Jim as Chaplain at Holmesburg Prison. At the time, Jim intended to carry out his original plan of going back on active duty as an Army Chaplain.

"I appreciate your concern," the Cardinal replied, "and I also appreciate the fact that you've given me the time you promised. So, yes, I do have someone in mind, and if you have your heart set on going back on active duty, you have my blessing. I don't know how we'll get along without you, Father – particularly the nuns of St. Dominic's and the hundreds of people you've touched – but I won't stand in your way. I do have one request though."

"Anything, your Eminence."

"I want to see you throw your knives one more time."

Jim smiled broadly and promised to comply.

As his days in St. Dominic's parish drew to a close, Jim was surprised by the deep well of emotion he felt for his life and times. He

278

was saying goodbye to people he had known for years, people who had touched him and who he himself had touched through good times and bad. On the day before his departure for Germany – where he would take on the role of Army Chaplain – Jim placed roses on the graves of his mother and Jennie, and before he left the cemetery he made his way to the maintenance shed to have a few words with Neil Shaunessay. As the minutes passed, the two men reminisced about the old days, when Jim had dug graves as a seminarian, and they spoke softly about the final days of Jim's father. When it was time for Jim to go, they embraced solemnly and turned their heads away from one another to hide their tears.

After making his way back to the station wagon, Jim drove to Angelo DiRenzo's medical office and asked one of the nurses if he could have a word with the doctor. The waiting room was full of men, women, and children that Jim knew – people among whom Jim was universally admired – and all but the youngest among them took a moment to wish Father Jim good luck. When Dr. DiRenzo was finally between patients, Jim joined him in his office and attempted to express the gratitude he felt.

"It was only money," Angelo frowned, "and I've got more than I need."

"But you're wrong, old friend. The money you lent enabled me to touch many more people than I would have touched without you. You may not realize it now, but you made a major contribution to the spiritual development of the people you affected, and together with what you have done for them physically" – and here Jim waved his arm to indicate the medical office – "you have a great deal to be proud of."

Immediately moved by what Jim had said, Dr. DiRenzo dabbed at his eye with a handkerchief.

"I don't know if I've ever seen you cry," Jim smiled.

"Then you weren't watching me at your mother's funeral."

The two men held each other in a long embrace, until Angelo broke the silence.

"All right, I've had about as much emotion as I can stand in one day, Father, and I have patients to see."

"Are you kicking me out?" Jim smiled.

"Yes, I am," Angelo said, and they shook hands as Jim started for the door of his office.

As night fell, Jim realized that the most difficult goodbyes lay ahead. He still had to speak with the nuns. As gratifying as his relationship with them had been, he had never expressed himself adequately on the relationship he had with Jennie, and he felt strongly that he owed them an explanation. Because they had made a solemn promise, Jim knew that his "secret" was safe, and that the nuns would never reveal Danny's origins; but he had never expressed regret for what he had gotten Jennie into.

Late that night, after Jim had said all of his other goodbyes and the nuns had prepared their lesson plans for the next day, they gathered in the living room at the convent.

"There is something that I've been meaning to speak with you about, sisters. It's been on my mind for a long time, and it is only through human weakness that I have failed to express it to you."

"We've seen no weakness in you," Sister Anna Maria interrupted. "We've only seen God's absolute love."

"Thank you, Sister. That's kind of you to say. But I was weak with Jennie and we all know it. I was a war hero when we first met, and not so ugly as I am now." He smiled at them, and the nuns burst out laughing. "At the time, Jennie was in a vulnerable state. She had lost her parents and was living with her aunt and uncle. I should have suppressed the attraction I felt for her, but I didn't. No matter how you look at it, it was one of the greatest failures of my life. None of it was Jennie's fault. I should have known better. I should have protected her from my impure thoughts, but I was weak and what's done is done. I take full blame for it and I'm ashamed."

Again, Sister Anna Maria spoke up. "It's ancient history now, Father. Jennie forgave you and she forgave herself. You devoted yourselves to the Lord and in his infinite wisdom He knows that. You certainly don't have to explain yourself to us."

"I want your respect, sisters – I won't try to hide that – but I'm far more concerned with the way you feel about Jennie."

"Jennie was one of our own," Sister Anna Maria followed. "She was courageous to the end and faithful to her calling. You worry too much if you think we harbor any ill will toward her, or any disrespect."

"Do all of you feel that way?" Jim asked suddenly, gazing around the room and seeking out each of them with his eyes; and in a resounding chorus, they assured him that they did.

"I also want you to know how much I cherish each and every one of you. Priests say Mass, hear confessions, and tend to the sick; but nuns are the backbone of the Catholic Church." Once again, Jim paused, and it was obvious that he had filled them with pride. "All of you have known what it means to possess physical beauty, but as physical beauty fades, inner beauty increases, and it is by your inner beauty that God will judge you. As religious instructors to the very young, you not only instill a sense of reverence for Catholicism but you are mothers to all of the children you teach. You mold them, you shape them, and you spend more time with them than their parents do. And for that you should be very proud. But your greatest distinction is that you are the brides of Christ. I know that each of you feels it keenly, as Jennie did. You are wonderful women and I love every one of you."

In unison, several of them called out, "We love you, Father," while the others who were too overcome with emotion to speak sniffled and dabbed at their eyes. Now, however, Jim singled one of them out, turning directly to Mother Magdalen. "Christ said to the apostles, 'I go to prepare a place for you. There are many mansions in my Father's house.' I have always believed, Mother, that there are degrees of Heaven, and that all good people do not end up in the same mansion. I believe that the best among us find their way to the highest and finest of these mansions. You may not be canonized on this earth, but you will have a special place in Heaven. Of that I am sure."

"Thank you Father Jim," she whispered, obviously touched by the words he had lauded her to the others.

"One of my fondest memories is the way you helped the children off the school bus when it snowed," Jim continued. "You were out there in the wet and cold making sure those children didn't fall.

Because of your dedication, they had never slipped and fell on the ice and snow, and you made sure they never fell spiritually as well."

One by one now, Jim made his way around the room, kissing the nuns chastely on the lips. "Before, I told you that the kiss was from God. But the kiss I'm giving you now is from me."

The next day, Jim pulled the station wagon into the driveway of the convent, unloaded his bags onto the sidewalk, and asked for Mother Magdalen. When she joined him outside, he handed the keys and the title to the station wagon to her, and she read the title out loud. "St. Dominic's Convent. You're giving it to us, Father?"

"When I was a much younger priest than I am now, the Cardinal gave me an automobile. It was my precious Hudson sedan. I only hope that you and the sisters get as much pleasure out of this car as I did." Jim kissed her goodbye and turned toward the street, where a limousine was waiting for him to take him to the airport.

After tending to the spiritual needs of the soldiers in Germany for approximately two years, Jim was called to Washington, where he was offered an advancement to the rank of Brigadier General. The assignment for Army involved the direct supervision of Army Chaplains all over the world. The main requirement was that he would reside in Washington, operate a headquarters at the Pentagon, and give up direct contact with soldiers in the field. The man who made the offer was the Army Chief of Staff and Jim had no desire to offend him, just as he had wanted to spare the feelings of the Cardinal all of those years before when Jim was being groomed to someday become a bishop.

"General Sullivan, I'm deeply grateful for your offer, truly I am. But I'm a combat soldier at heart, and my desire has always been to be close to the soldiers in the field. With all due respect, sir, may I decline the offer? I would rather maintain the rank of Colonel and continue to minister to the troops. That is where I have always done my best work."

"Reverend Colonel, I'm making this offer precisely because you were a combat soldier, and a highly decorated one at that."

"I appreciate that, sir."

General Sullivan smiled. "But?"

"I would rather decline the offer. In fact, I have a request."

"Oh, you do, do you?"

Jim paused, fearful that he had gone too far. But the General was still smiling.

"I would like to go to Vietnam, where the troops need me the most. I think about it every day."

"I can't change your mind?"

"No, sir, not if you give me a choice."

Prior to his departure for Vietnam, Jim took a 30-day furlough, residing at St.Dominic's Rectory. He had the opportunity to meet his successor at Holmesburg Prison, and he was able to spend time with the people he cared about, first and foremost, his son, Danny. As his month-long leave came to an end, he found it extremely difficult to say goodbye to Danny, who was still unaware that Jim was his father. Still, they cared for each other very much and it was extremely hard for Jim to leave Danny this time.

"Danny, I'm really going to miss you. We've had some great times together, huh?" Jim asked on the day of his departure.

"Yep, we sure did. I'll never forget that Notre Dame game you took us to. What a day!" Then Danny paused and asked, "You'll write, won't you Father Jim?"

"Of course, Danny. And I'll call too. I'll always keep in touch. You know I love you."

"I love you too, Father Jim," Danny said as he hugged Jim tightly, tears in his eyes.

It was easier to say goodbye to the nuns this time than it had been two years earlier, and they sent him to Vietnam with good wishes and promises of prayer.

"We'll pray for you, Father."

"Don't pray for me – pray for the young men that are fighting in Vietnam. Every one of them is a hero."

Jim arrived in Saigon in March 1967 and was met at the airport by General Bill Bennett who had been in Jim's detachment during World War II. Although Bennett was delighted to see him, he deeply regretted Jim's presence.

"Jim, I heard through the grapevine that you turned down an opportunity to supervise Army Chaplains all over the world. Is that true?"

"Yes, it is, Bill. Believe me, I had my reasons."

"Do you realize how prestigious that assignment is? You would have been working at the Pentagon. Many of us would kill for an assignment like that, so watch your back."

They shared a laugh, but then Bennett took on a serious expression. "It's no joke over here, Jim. In all of the other wars that the United States has fought, there was always a front line, a clear line of demarcation between the enemy and us. Here there is no front line. There are just as many enemy troops behind us as there are in front of us, and they're under us as well."

"They're under us? What do you mean?"

"There are tunnels all over the place, and unlike the other wars we've fought, we're engaged in underground combat as well." He pursed his lips grimly. "These soldiers are doing things that no other American fighting men have ever had to do. They're the bravest soldiers we've ever had. Be careful, Jim. It's more dangerous than you think."

If you take up the sword, you shall perish with the sword.
Matthew, Chapter 26:52

Chapter Seventeen
1969

It had been a while since he had called the Goddards. Too long in fact, but the war was growing unspeakably worse every minute and his free time was severely limited. In addition, it was difficult to secure a phone to call the States, but he had pulled rank to do so tonight. He had a feeling that something was wrong and wanted to hear Danny's voice - it always comforted him.

Throughout the years, Jim had kept his promise to Jennie as best he could, spending as much time with the boy as possible without being too obvious about it. He was a good kid, too, and did not seem to mind being with him, whether they were going to see a ballgame or just having dinner with Danny's family. The Goddards were good people, and welcomed him into their lives warmly. He wondered how they would react if they knew the truth, but didn't want to spend time wondering about the "what ifs." He had learned long ago to accept the precious moments he had with Danny and never push too far. But it was lonely in Vietnam, and he ached to hear his son's voice.

Nancy Goddard had picked up the phone on the first ring, as if she were expecting a call, and when Jim identified himself he thought she sounded a little disappointed, like she was hoping it was someone else. He soon found out why. She sounded awful, sick with worry as she told Jim what had been going on since the last time they had spoken.

She told him how on Danny's eighteenth birthday he had gone to sign up for the draft. Not knowing he was adopted, he had been shocked when the Selective Service Board told him that there was no record of his birth. He confronted his parents, and they told him the truth. Danny became enraged, wanting to know his true identity. Nancy got in touch with the state trooper that had been there the night they were given Danny and got a hold of his original birth certificate that stated his name as Daniel Whalen, mother Jennifer Whalen, father unknown.

For a moment, Jim held his breath and waited to see if Mrs. Goddard had put two and two together, connecting Sister Jennie with the mother's name. He exhaled with relief as she continued the story without hesitation. How could she know, really? The nuns only went by one name, and most of the time that name was different from their birth name. Still, he was glad they had not found out that Jennie was Danny's birth mother.

Nancy recounted Danny's grief; how he said they were not his parents and that he hated them for not telling him all these years. She began to cry, but continued telling Jim that he had joined the army the next day, informing them that he hoped he was killed in the war so he would never have to see them again.

"He's here in Vietnam?" Jim asked, hoping he had misunderstood her.

The devastation in her voice was clearly evident. "Yes, Father Jim. We haven't heard from him since he left. Is there any way you could find out if he is okay?"

"I'll do my best," he answered.

Jim hung up the phone, and immediately called General Bill Bennett to ask for help in finding Danny. Jim told Bill he had no idea which unit Danny belonged to or where he was stationed. Bill said it would take some time, but he would do anything for the man who saved his life and the lives of many others. Jim was grateful and waited eagerly for the call that came a few days later.

"Jim, I found him. This line is not secure, so I need you to contact your G-3 and he can call me on the operations line. My code name is 6 Charlie Zulu. He'll brief you from there."

Within hours, Jim spoke with his G-3, General Jack Walsh, who had already spoken with Bill Bennett. It turned out that Danny's unit, The Lost Company B, had gotten lost in a demilitarized zone and had been cut off from the rest of their battalion. Now, they were stranded on a ridge in a highly volatile area. Out of 120 men in Danny's original unit, only 19 were alive. A labyrinthine tunnel complex supported the Viet Cong in that area and enabled them to systematically eliminate the majority of Danny's unit in a savage battle on their first night on the ridge. The remaining 19 men were able to seal off the tunnels with hand grenades, but now they were pinned down. Generals Walsh and Bennett agreed that Jim's unit would supply transportation in the form of a Chinook helicopter and six highly trained soldiers known as "tunnel rats." The tunnel rats were essential because entire companies of Viet Cong soldiers were able to survive and fight for long periods of time using the tunnels as a base of operations. These tunnels contained escape holes, underground food and medical supplies, storage areas, kitchens, planning rooms for Viet Cong commanders, and other components. Based on their location on the ridge, it was impossible for the 101st Airborne Rangers and the 3rd Marine Battalion 26th Division to rescue them. Any helicopters flying in the area were highly vulnerable because of the anti-aircraft capabilities of the enemy.

In addition to the six tunnel rats, Jim had two former members of the Viet Cong Army that were highly loyal to him since he had interceded on their behalf when the ARVIN – the Army of the Republic of South Vietnam – was about to execute them. Because Jim had persuaded the ARVIN to spare their lives, they had begun to assist the Americans and South Vietnamese ever since. Not only had these two men been born and raised in the Quang Tri area, they were willing to put their lives on the line for Jim and had become an invaluable resource.

The plan was for the Chinook helicopter to land approximately five miles from the ridge where Danny's unit was pinned down. After landing, Jim and the others were transported to the battle zone, where Jim, the six tunnel rats, and the two former Viet Cong met with General Bill Bennett and devised a strategy to rescue the men from the ridge. As soon as Jim and the others arrived at Bennett's command post, Trong, one of the Viet Cong, alerted Bennett to the fact that he recognized one of the men that was with Bennett. This man had formerly served in the North Vietnamese Army with Trong and was widely regarded as a born killer and an expert knife thrower in his own right. The second he laid eyes on him, Trong drew his weapon and advised Bennett to take the man into custody, which he immediately did. Bennett confided to Jim that he had been using this man to lead his soldiers into the tunnels to determine the enemy's location. "Now I know why he always came back alone. He was killing them down there."

"How do you know Danny's alright?" Jim asked, afraid of the answer.

"Right now he is," Bennett replied. "I know because he's the radio operator and we've been in direct contact with him."

Trong turned to General Bennett. "Sir, this is where I was born and raised. I know these tunnels like the back of my hand. The reason your men can't get in there and do what they have to do is that the tunnels were built two stories high under the ground. In a tunnel at the base of that ridge, there is a command post that controls the entire area. Adjoining the command post is a barracks with 120 men, and every night they come up through the tunnel to kill your troops. While you and your men are walking around, the Viet Cong are under you."

"I need to destroy that command post," Bennett said. "There's a 175 millimeter artillery piece camouflaged on the face of the other ridge and we haven't been able to destroy it. That artillery piece has been harassing our positions every night, and neither our troops nor the marines in the area have been able to get to it. We can't get planes in there, so we need to blast away at the camouflage and destroy that weapon."

"Father Jim is the only one who can help you. In that tunnel, there is a steel door that protects the command post and an armed guard that stands watch over the door. In addition to the guard, there is a photoelectric eye that is placed in such a way that you can't go over it or under it on foot. I was one of them and I know it."

"What are you suggesting?" Bennett answered impatiently.

"The tunnels are built in a series of angles, so it is impossible to shoot in a straight line. That is why Father Jim is the only man capable of eliminating the guard. He will have to throw his knife."

Jim had been silent during this exchange, but now, as he realized that he would be asked to take a human life, he shifted uneasily. At exactly that moment, General Bennett realized the implications of Trong's suggestion, and he glanced quickly at Jim. But Jim was not betraying his emotion.

"Because of the placement of the photoelectric eye, Father Jim will have to throw from a sitting position," Trong continued. "And he will not be able to throw overhand, which would trip the device and alert the men in the barracks. Instead, he will have to throw in a sidearm or underhand motion."

Jim turned to General Bennett. "Bill, I'm a priest. I'm not a combat soldier anymore. You know that."

"Jim, we need you."

"I can't do it. We'll have to find another way."

Bennett looked at him long and hard. He had a hole card, but he hesitated to play it. "Your son's up there. If we don't get him out, he's going to die like all of the others."

"As a priest, I am forbidden from bearing arms." Sensing the inevitability of what was about to happen, he continued. "However, tonight I will put aside my priesthood and become a combat soldier once again." Without another word to Bennett, Jim looked up to Heaven. Bennett and Trong stared at him, rapt with attention. They had never heard a holy man directly address Jesus Christ in such personal terms. "Father, my heart is heavy and my body weary because of a grievous sin I committed against you when I was a foolish young seminarian. That sin became my cross to bear. I stand at the base of this ridge where my son is trapped. He is the product of that sin, but he is an innocent boy. If you find it in your heart and you feel that my cause is just, then let me be victorious over my enemy. Father, do not judge me on that sin alone, but judge me on my priesthood where every day I accepted you as my Lord and Savior, at the same time lifting your cross up high so that people could understand the pain and suffering you went through on the cross to die for our sins. Those people whose lives I touched accepted you as their Lord and Savior. Tonight, Father, I lay down your cross and take up mine. The night before you died when you were in the garden of Gethsemane you looked up to Heaven and asked your Father 'If it be your will, let this cup pass me by.' I say to you tonight, 'Not your will but mine. Do not let this cup pass me by. Before the cock crows, may I be with you in paradise.'"

Bennett grabbed Jim's arm. "What are you talking about? You're not going to die. You're going to get your son and walk off of that ridge with him."

Jim ignored this, and continued to address the Lord. "Father, when you were dying on the cross, you looked up to Heaven and said, 'Father, forgive them for they know not what they do. But Father, I do know what I'm doing and I ask for your forgiveness.'"

Jim removed a small metal container from his pocket, exhibiting the infantry insignia and the crossed rifles that he wore so proudly when he was a combat solider. Turning to Bennett, he said, "Bill, remove the crosses from my lapel and put my rifles in their place. Tonight, I am a combat soldier again." Bennett reached out and removed the chaplain insignia from Jim's lapel, replacing them with the crossed rifles.

Once again, Jim looked up to Heaven. "Father, because of my son, and only because of him, I must lay down your cross and pick up my sword."

Jim and Bennett embraced, and then Bennett looked at him. "Good luck. I'll see you when you get back."

"I will bring my son back," Jim said evasively, and an hour later he entered the tunnel with the six tunnel rats, the two Viet Cong, and the weapons they needed to complete the mission. Crawling on their hands and knees for approximately thirty feet, they arrived at a fork in the tunnel. The path to the right led to a series of airshafts that were situated above the barracks and the command post. Four of the tunnel rats proceeded down that path, armed with a satchel of hand grenades. Along with the final two tunnel rats and the two Viet Cong, Jim crawled along the path to the left. As he made his way through the dust and sweltering heat, Jim was fully aware that he was about to take another life, and he began to struggle internally. Suddenly, however, an image of Danny in happier times crossed Jim's mind, and he realized all over again that the sin he had committed had put Danny in harm's way. Determined now to see the mission through, he reached a spot where the tunnel again was constructed at an angle. By then, he had approached to within twenty feet of the armed guard. He could see the guard, but the guard could not see him. In extremely close quarters, Jim maneuvered his body so that he could continue to crawl feet first and position himself to throw the knife. Inching forward, he reached the optimal point. If he crawled another foot along the path, the guard would detect him; but it was still a difficult throw. Only one man in all of Vietnam could make that throw, and now that very man removed his knife from the leather case that held it.

At the precise instant that he was ready to throw, Jim gave a low whistle in order to gain the guard's attention. In one swift sidearm motion as the guard turned to face him, Jim threw the knife, catching him directly in the throat and killing him instantly. As the guard fell to the ground, Jim realized exactly what Tom Young must have felt when he was unable to kill the young German soldier at the radar station years before; but unlike Tom, Jim had succeeded in carrying out the first part of their plan.

Now that the guard had been eliminated, he immediately made radio contact with the four tunnel rats, directing them to drop their grenades down the airshafts. These explosions killed a score of Viet Cong in the barracks and the command post. Simultaneously, Jim placed timed explosives around the steel door and took cover while the explosives detonated.

After the steel door disintegrated from the impact, Jim's companions poured through the open doorway, blasted away with their M-16s, and killed the remaining Viet Cong. With Trong leading the way, Jim and the others rushed to the end of the tunnel and emerged into a clearing at the base of the ridge. At that point, Jim established radio communication with General Bennett and in turn, Bennett alerted Danny that help was on the way.

Running up the ridge unimpeded by enemy fire, they reached Danny and the others, and it was then that Jim realized that Danny had been wounded in the shoulder just as Jim had been in World War II.

"Father Jim!" Danny exclaimed. "Is that you?"

"Yes, Danny. Let's get you out of here."

Now that the tunnel had been eliminated, General Bennett was able to send a group of men up to the ridge with stretchers for the wounded. As they reached safety, Jim spoke with Danny quietly and broke the news to him that Jim and Sister Jennie were his real parents.

"You deserve to know all of it, Danny, and I've put it in a letter for you. General Bill has the letter." Still dazed by the events of the past few minutes, Danny struggled with the news that the priest he loved was actually his father and that the nun that who had taught him in the seventh and eighth grades had been his mother. He loved both of these people, but now he didn't know how to feel about the Goddards.

"Whatever you do," Jim said firmly, "remember that those two people raised you as though you were their son. They loved you all those years; they were there for you. Sister Jennie and I loved you, but we weren't there. We couldn't be because of the vows we had taken."

While Jim and Danny spoke, General Bennett ordered the 101st Airborne Rangers to deploy into the area, and within minutes they brought in heavy artillery and began to pound away at the opposite ridge, thereby destroying the foliage that camouflaged the 175 millimeter artillery piece that had been plaguing them. Although this phase of the operation was completely successful, General Bennett's men committed a tragic oversight and inadvertently allowed their murderous Viet Cong prisoner to escape. Now, the man that Trong had warned them about snuck over to the low branch where Jim had hung his satchel.

Quickly removing a knife while Jim and Danny walked in the opposite direction, the prisoner broke the silence. "Father Jim!" The minute Jim turned in the direction of the sound, the prisoner hurled his knife and struck Jim in the middle of the chest. As Jim collapsed to the ground, General Bennett shot the prisoner with his sidearm, killing him instantly.

Danny cradled Jim's head in his arms and sobbed openly as Jim looked up at his son calmly. "Dad, please don't die," Danny pleaded.

Tears fell from Jim's eyes as he heard his son call him dad. As a priest, he never thought that he would hear it.

"Reach into my pocket," Jim gasped. "Do you see the box?"

"I've got it," Danny said.

"Remove my crossed rifles and keep them so that you will always remember that I was a man amongst men. Return my crosses to my lapel because I am a priest and I will be a priest forever."

Danny continued to cry as he carried out his father's last request.

Jim looked up to Heaven. "Father, it is finished. Into thy hands I commend my spirit."

As Jim's life on earth ended, you could hear a cock crow from a distant farming village.

General Bennett distinctly remembered the extreme respect Jim had shown for the dead soldiers during World War II. He watched as his men retrieved all of the bodies from the top of the ridge where Danny and the others had been pinned down. The process was slow and solemn as the men placed each soldier's body into a bag and loaded them onto a waiting helicopter.

Danny, through his tears, would not allow any of the other soldiers to remove Jim's body and insisted on doing it by himself. As Danny carried his father's body to the helicopter, General Bennett looked on and whispered, "Your father would have been proud."

Epilogue

Daniel Goddard placed a dozen red roses on his mother's grave at St. Dominic's Cemetery and a dozen white roses on his father's. He addressed his birth parents as they rested side by side.

"I graduated from medical school today," he said, "and I wanted to share my achievement with you. I hope I've made you both proud." He rested a hand on each of their headstones, and continued, "We are a family, now and forever. I love you and I always will."

On a clear summer night, when the stars are at their highest and brightest, you look beyond them into the Heavens. There, you will see Sister Jennie and Father Jim walking hand in hand in one of the gardens of the many mansions of our Father's house, for theirs is the Kingdom of Heaven.

About The Author

Nicholas Mario Di Bello, Jr. was born on March 29, 1930 in Philadelphia and is the middle child of five siblings. In 1956, Nick married Catherine Joan and they raised seven children and are the proud grandparents to 13 grandchildren (with more on the way). Nick spent 15 years in the military and a short time in the seminary, which becomes the fictional backdrop of *Consummatum Est (It Is Finished)*. Nick has been successful in many of life's endeavors and is pleased to add published author to his list of accomplishments.